The Covenant

Also by Naomi Ragen

NOVELS

The Sacrifice of Tamar

The Ghost of Hannah Mendes

Jephte's Daughter

Sotah

Chains Around the Grass

PLAY

Women's Minyan

Naomi Ragen

THE COVENANT

The Toby Press

The Toby Press *LLC*, 2006

POB 8531, New Milford, CT 06776-8531, USA
& POB 2455, London WIA 5WY, England
www.tobypress.com

Second Edition

Grateful acknowledge is made for permission to reprint the following:

Excerpt from *The Consolation of Philosophy* by Boethius,
translated with an introduction by V.E. Watts (Penguin,
1969). Copyright © 1969 by V.E. Watts. Reproduced
by permission of Penguin Books, Ltd.

Excerpt from *The Masterpiece*, translated by J.K. Ringold.
Copyright 1999 by Uitgeverij de Arbeiderspers. Reproduced
by permission of *The* Toby Press *LLC*.

ISBN 1 59264 163 6, *paperback*

A CIP catalogue record for this title is
available from the British Library

Typeset in Garamond by Jerusalem Typesetting

Printed and bound in the United States by
Thomson-Shore Inc., Michigan

For all victims of terror, and those who loved them.
May God comfort all mourners and
wipe the tears from all faces.

Acknowledgments

When I first conceived of this book, what concerned me most was conveying with accuracy the lives of women who had survived the Nazi concentration camps. It was a daunting responsibility for someone born in America after the war. I tried my very best. I would like to thank all those who helped me to conceive the inconceivable.

First and foremost, I thank my dear mother-in-law, Shirley Ragen, who spent three of her teenage years with her two sisters as prisoners of Auschwitz. Her descriptions, so painfully and vividly recalled, shared over many years, formed the basis for my understanding. I would like to thank Sara Pecanic, and the other dedicated librarians at Yad Vashem in Jerusalem, for helping me to find dozens of rare memoirs written by survivors. I thank the many authors for their courage, honesty, and skill. I thank Lisa A. Goodgame, coordinator, onsite and scholarly access, of the Survivors of the Shoah Visual History Foundation, for facilitating my access to remarkable taped interviews of women survivors of Auschwitz. And I thank Mr. Steven Spielberg, whose vision and generosity created the foundation, and makes its archives an invaluable resource for writers and scholars.

I would like to thank Ruthie Gillis, wife of the late Dr. Shmuel Gillis, for agreeing to share her story with me. Dr. Gillis, a beloved and respected senior physician in the Hematology Department in Hadassah Ein Karem, was killed by terrorist snipers on the Jerusalem–Hebron highway on February 1, 2001. My meeting Mrs. Gillis, mother of five and a woman of exceptional faith and love, will never be forgotten.

The story of Dov Kalmanovitch, the first victim of the Intifada, is true. I thank him for sharing it with me.

I thank Yehuda and Esther Waxsman for many years of friendship and inspiration. It was the heartbreaking kidnap and murder of their nineteen-year-old son Nachshon—an off-duty IDF soldier—by terrorists in October 1994 that triggered the creative process which resulted in the birth of this book.

For the information on the world of Islamic terrorism, I relied on many books and personal interviews. I particularly thank retired Israeli Secret Service Agent X, who cleared up many questions I had and helped me to make this book as close to reality as possible.

I thank Asher Ragen for his many valuable insights. I thank Dr. Michael Widlanski, lecturer at The Hebrew University's Rothberg School, for sharing his extensive expertise in Arabic language and culture. I thank Rachel Atlan for sharing her knowledge of Paris and the French language.

Little did I know when I began writing about a terrorist incident that I would not have to rely solely on research; that my family and I were fated to be present at one of the worst terrorist incidents in Israel's modern history: the Passover Massacre in the Park Hotel in Netanya in 2002 in which twenty-nine people were murdered by a suicide bomber, and hundreds injured.

I thank Jennifer Weis, my talented editor at St. Martin's Press, (publisher of the first American edition) and my agent, Lisa Bankoff, of ICM, for believing in this book, and supporting me through the terrible year in which I struggled to recover from the reality of a terrorist attack in order to write a book about a terrorist attack.

As always, my heartfelt thanks to my husband, Alex, for thirty-three years of loving friendship, pioneering a new home in an ancient homeland.

Naomi Ragen
Jerusalem, October 1, 2003

How do people do it, live? And especially;
how do they ward off the blow, how do they
scramble to their feet after the final blow,
how do they find the escape route out of a
locked house?

—Anna Enquist, *The Masterpiece*

Chapter one

Maaleh Sara, Judea
Monday, May 6, 2002 · 5:30 A.M.

It was the sound of the birds in the morning he loved most, Dr. Jonathan Margulies thought as he lay in the cool early morning darkness. So different from the sounds of his own childhood in Baltimore, where hearing a bird sing amidst the traffic, the trucks rolling down the superhighways, could not happen. He closed his eyes, listening to the sweet noises. They were goldcrests, or sylvia warblers, he thought, having once looked them up in a book.

He breathed in the tangy odor of the slightly damp fig leaves that rested on his windowsill. My own fig tree, he thought with wonder. To own such a thing. To have land in which to plant it, a tree that could grow for a hundred years, a tree that bore fruit that belonged to you. Not the stingy little bags purchased at great price in supermarkets, but bushels, more than anyone could ever eat. Fruit to share with friends and neighbors, to store, to bake, to eat carelessly, greedily. Fruit from God's own generous, open hand.

Trees were the thing that connected a person to his space on this earth, he thought. They were like your family. Your rootedness began with theirs. They weren't movable. They held on to the land,

I

soaking up its goodness, turning it into nourishment whose sweetness dribbled down your chin. Once you experienced that, he thought, you were part of that place.

What a joy.

He threw off his light blanket, enjoying the cool breeze that drifted over his thin pajamas. It was only early May, but already the days were growing hot the moment the sun climbed over the horizon, its fierce, abundant light drenching the land, the people, nothing like the thin, tepid rays he remembered back in North America.

He looked over at his very pregnant wife, listened for the breathing of his young daughter, basking in the peace of his small, pretty house. My own house, my own land. My own family. And a fig tree, he thought, feeling suddenly overwhelmed by the abundance and goodness of his life.

On such a morning, he thought, it was almost possible to forget the war hanging over everything he loved, everything he'd built.

He threw his legs to the floor, willing his body to follow: "The throwing off of sleep is the beginning of all salvation," he whispered to himself, using the same proverb his mother had used in his high school days to pry him out of bed for early morning Talmud classes.

He was tired. He'd stayed up late the night before poring over case files and consulting with medical colleagues in Boston, New York and London. He glanced at Elise, watching the gentle rise and fall of her chest, the tendrils of honey-colored hair that fell around her rosy face on the white pillow. She looked so young—like a child—he thought, pulling the light summer blanket tenderly over her bare shoulders. But even that feathery touch was enough to wake her.

"Jon?"

"Shh. Go back to sleep."

She heaved her swollen body up on her elbows. "We left all the supper dishes, the pots.... Not to mention the floor, which is a swamp." She started moving her feet toward the edge of the bed. "And this afternoon Ilana has that ballet recital at the community center. And—oh—it's my *Bubbee* Leah's birthday next week! I've got to buy her a present..."

He sat down on the edge of the bed, blocking her. "Here's the rag. Where's the dirt?" He offered himself up.

She poked him in the stomach. "What would your distinguished colleagues and admiring patients say if they knew the learned professor of oncology arrived after a morning of wringing out dirty floor rags?"

"They'd agree that any treatment that successfully keeps the fetus in the womb until its heart and lungs are fully developed was good medicine, Elise. Especially," his voice grew kinder and more gentle, "if the mother had a history."

She studied her fingers gathering and twisting the material of her nightgown. "You're bullying me."

He smiled. "Is it working?"

"Yes! But don't let it go to your head. It's all those diplomas...It has nothing to do with your macho pushiness, believe me." She folded her arms across her chest, sinking back into the mattress.

"I believe you. So? Do I have your word? It's only six weeks, honey. Then we'll all be home free."

"Listen, Jon, I'll be honest with you. I don't care if you are a doctor. I just can't promise to lay here all day long and do nothing. It's stressing me out."

"You can, darling. And you will," he said firmly.

End of story, she thought glumly. "Yes, Doctor."

"Why don't you work on your jewelry?"

It had started as just a hobby, stringing little colored beads when she was pregnant with Ilana. But encouraged by her success in selling her pieces to boutiques and by word of mouth, she'd taken a course at Bezalel in gold and silversmithing. And she'd never gone back to being a teacher of English to rambunctious fifth graders—who hated the language—again.

"I can't really use my tools laying here in bed."

"But you were doing such beautiful work with the bead necklaces and earrings..."

"I'm sick and tired of stringing beads...I'm sick and tired of everything. I want my body back. I want my life back..."

"Elise, Elise. Be smart. Here you have a man with floor-scrubbing credentials, child care experience and a long, positive relationship with credit cards for purchasing takeout food. All this, he's laying at your feet—a once in a lifetime opportunity! Take advantage."

"Don't think I won't," she warned him. "Just not Chinese or Hamburger Ranch. I'm sick of all that grease. If I could just make some vegetarian risotto, with some pumpkin soup…" She sighed. "Okay, I suppose not. And don't forget, *Bubbee* Leah…"

"In this I'll need some advice and guidance. Presents for septuagenarians, especially incredibly fussy ones like *Bubbee* Leah, are out of my realm."

"Why do you say that? My grandmother isn't fussy at all!"

"Every single time we send her a present she complains nonstop that we shouldn't have spent the money…that she doesn't need anything…"

"Oh, do you have a lot to learn! That doesn't mean anything! That's just being European. That's what they *have* to say. It's like some ritual. They have this rule book, but no one else is allowed to read it, you know? In the book, it says if you get a present, you have to make the giver feel like an idiot, like he's wasted his money and you are angry at him for even thinking you might need a gift. But if you don't get anything, then you should be hurt and miserable and offended for life."

"Oh, is that the rule?"

"Absolutely. Trust me." She nodded emphatically. "I was thinking, maybe a cookbook?"

"With her cholesterol and heart problems? Don't you think she'd find that depressing?"

"Not at all. She doesn't do much cooking. But she likes to read and talk about food. That's what she did in Auschwitz. She'd 'prepare' meals, describing the ingredients, the step-by-step preparation. I don't think she gets to bookstores very often in Boro Park."

"You know what? I'll call you on my cell phone as I browse the shelves in Steimatzky's, so you can browse with me. You know I love *Bubbee* Leah. It's just…she's just such a mystery."

"I know. All women are." She reached out for him. He took

her hand, kneeling down beside her, putting his other hand over the unborn child they had both prayed so hard for after two miscarriages. "There are so many dangers out there we have no control over, Elise. This, at least, we can do something about."

She twined her fingers through his, their hands tent-like and sheltering over the baby. What a crazy time to bring a child into the world, she thought, a world which overnight seemed to have gone insane. The World Trade Center had been attacked for no reason anyone could figure out, collapsing in rubble, killing thousands before the eyes of an incredulous world. Palestinian terrorists killed children at Bar Mitzvahs and Passover seders; Indonesian terrorists killed Christians attending church services; Basque separatists blew up beach parties on the Costa Del Sol; and Pakistani Muslims opened fire on nurses in a Christian hospital. People didn't seem outraged or even surprised anymore, just kind of weary and dumbfounded. And even journalists pretended to no longer be able to distinguish right from wrong, bending over backward to see the murderer's point of view. Homicide seemed almost a lifestyle choice these days. Like being gay or vegetarian, it had earned a certain respect, even glamour, at least among media types who seemed eager to adopt the terrorists' own incredibly self-serving and immoral self-image as martyrs and heroes.

It wasn't supposed to be this way.

She looked around at the whitewashed walls, the geraniums spilling over the window boxes. Like every young couple, they'd dreamed of building their own little house with a red-tiled roof and a big garden full of fruit trees and herbs. And so, when they saw the ad in the paper announcing that the Israel Lands Authority was accepting bids for plots of land zoned for one-family homes in Maaleh Sara, they'd jumped at the chance.

They already had friends living there and had heard good things about the neighborhood. It was only a short ride from Hadassah Hospital. They had wonderful schools, a great number of professional, English-speaking immigrants, great climate and a warm, religious atmosphere. It was also fairly inexpensive. "We can build a great three-bedroom home with a garden for the same price as some cramped two-bedroom walk-up in some crowded Jerusalem apartment building. Besides, smell the air. It's country air, healthy for kids," Jon had argued, convincingly.

She'd needed a little convincing. While Jon had waxed dreamily about how Abraham and Isaac had passed this way on their journey from Hebron to Mount Moriah, how Ruth had kneeled to gather sheaves from Boaz's fields and how King David had shepherded his father's flocks through the hillsides, she'd peered nervously at the nearby Arab villages, counting how many they'd have to drive through in their daily commute.

"Look, I know some of the people in these villages. They come into Hadassah all the time. Some are even my own patients," Jon said when she expressed her fears. "People are people. It'll be like moving into any other neighborhood. Some people won't like us, and some will. We'll do everything we can to be good neighbors."

It was so simple to think of it that way. And in many ways, it had been. Their workmen—plumbers, electricians, gardeners—all lived in nearby villages. Often they'd drive them home to get supplies, meeting their wives and kids. They'd buy cement and plumbing supplies at huge discounts from Arab stores their workmen knew about. In those early days, everyone was so young and hopeful. There were young families everywhere—Arab and Jew—and everyone seemed to be planting trees and adding on rooms to hold new babies. In the deepest sense, they really were neighbors, and sometimes even friends. Looking around at the sparsely populated area of rolling hills and trees, they'd think: there is so much land, enough for everyone to share.

A few short years later, in the eye of the storm, when people started calling their neighborhood an "illegal settlement" or "occupied territories," they couldn't believe how naïve they'd been. It was like that Kafka story about the cockroach, Elise told Jon. You went to sleep a person, and woke up a bug. And before you could even understand what was happening, peaceful roads had turned overnight into shooting galleries, terrorists lying in wait around every bend, under cover of ancient olive trees. And innocent people—kindergarten teachers, handymen, students—people she knew—had been gunned down in cold blood. Palestinians too: gunmen from the new Palestinian regime could pick anyone they chose off the streets, accuse them of "collaborating," and put them in front of a firing squad. There was no trial, no jury, no appeal. It was sickening.

How can we live this way? she often wondered. Why put ourselves through this? After each attack, they'd sit around the kitchen table fingering warm mugs of soup, talking and arguing deep into the night, bringing up every option.

"Maybe we should just move," she'd suggested once.

Jon had looked at her, surprised, his face pale, the dark shock of hair hanging boyishly over his eyes as he wordlessly took her hand in his. He didn't have to say it. She understood. When all was said and done, it wasn't ideology that kept them here: this was their home. They'd pored over the architect's plans, picked out the floor tiles, agonized over the style of faucets, fixed the leaks and planted the young trees. It was theirs and they loved it.

Besides, they had a mortgage. And no one was going to buy their house, not now. That was the reality. Where, exactly, were they supposed to live? Almost every place in Israel had suffered some kind of terrorist attack. And then there was the element of simple shame: how could they cut and run when neighbors and friends who had suffered tragedies—lost husbands, wives, children—bravely stayed put?

If they could only hold on, they told each other, things had to get better. This craziness couldn't last much longer. The politicians would have to gather the arms, arrest the terrorists, get rid of the inciters...They'd have no choice. Right wing or left wing, that's simply what governments and armies did: protected the lives of their citizens, no?

She told herself these things bravely each day, several times a day. But each time Jon took the car out, each time he or her daughter entered that open road, her heart ached in fear, and her body grew taut and weary waiting for their return.

She remembered the words of a Hamas terrorist at the beginning of the Intifada explaining why Hamas would win and the Jews would lose. It was because the Jews "loved life more than any other people," he'd said with utter contempt.

Nothing could be truer. Jews loved life. Their own and other peoples'. And Jewish doctors loved it best of all. Jon's war against cancer was relentless, and he never gave up.

He still looked like the twenty-three-year-old army medic that had come knocking on her door one Saturday night, a blind date arranged by her roommate Rachel. "My brother knows this great guy," Rachel had told her. "He's American like you. And smart and funny and kind…and very religious. And he's studying to be a doctor!"

"So why don't you go out with him yourself?" she'd shot back, wary.

"He's a new immigrant, from Baltimore, who's in the same unit with my brother. You are so lucky you grew up in America! And I'm such an idiot for not studying harder for my matriculation exam in English…"

"I bet he's conceited. Medical students always think they are the catch of the century and any girl lucky enough to go out with them ought to kiss their feet. They walk around like God's gift to women. And most of them are short and pushy. Little Napoleons."

At five feet two and with a young girl's wispy frame, Elise was constantly on guard against being pushed around and treated like a child. In self-defense, she'd honed a sharp tongue that had been known to pierce many an inflated ego. Men seldom appreciated this. Even the chauvinistic group leaders of her high school youth group, B'nei Akiva, strapping young fellows charged with turning them into land tillers and pioneers, had retreated one by one, intimidated. And thus, despite her long honey-colored hair and striking blue eyes, Elise had spent many a Saturday night decorating the walls of the local Zionist clubhouse with blue and white ribbons, instead of going out on dates.

Rachel hadn't given up. "You don't fool me, Elise. All that hostility is just masking shyness. You are *going* to go out with this guy. You know the saying: if you make two matches, your place in heaven is reserved for you. I've already fixed up my cousin. So, you are my ticket to the Afterlife. Are you going to cooperate or not?"

How could you deny someone her ticket to the Afterlife?

She'd picked out a pretty dress the color of lilacs. At the last minute, she'd pulled off the velvet tie-back, letting her hair fall loose and soft around her face. When Rachel ushered him in, Elise thought it must be some kind of mistake. This bashful, tall boy with the kind brown eyes, the dark unruly hair—studying medicine? He hardly seemed out of high school.

He'd suggested they go to the theater. She'd suggested a stroll along the Promenade. He'd agreed immediately. They'd proceeded to battle the sharp, cold Jerusalem winds that whip up such a storm at night along that long stone walkway which is Jerusalem's boardwalk, except that instead of the sea, there is a heartstopping view of the city. She'd waited for him to complain, to point out, rightly, that the sheltered walls of the Jerusalem Theater would have been a much wiser choice. He never did. Their cheeks stinging, their hands frigid, they talked and walked deep into the night. And as they spoke, the wind magically disappeared, and their hands grew warm.

They had so much in common. Both had come from America to Israel as young adults, leaving their families behind. Both had lost their parents early in life, and felt independent, and free to choose. As post-Holocaust Jews, the idea haunted them that at the crucial moment, so many of their extended European families had had no place to run to, no country willing to take them in. And although both had been grateful to have been born within the sheltering arms of the greatest democracy on earth, neither felt it belonged to them the way these rocky little hillsides did: a place where "when you had to go there, it had to take you in."

Of course, their families had been against it. Their friends—brought up in the same Zionist youth groups and singing the same pioneer songs in Hebrew around campfires, educated in the same yeshiva high schools where the Hebrew Bible and the books of Prophets sat side by side with texts on college-placement calculus and Shakespeare's plays—thought they were nuts. And their parents had blamed the Hebrew day schools, which had taught them English and Hebrew simultaneously, and made them sing "The Star-Spangled Banner" and "Hatikvah" one after another at assemblies.

Their parents had paid the enormous yearly tuition for these private schools to ensure that their kids turned out faithful, traditional Jews who loved Israel, not radicals and dreamers bent on abandoning the safety of their American birthplace with its economic promise, to actually live in that little Middle Eastern plot of land surrounded by hostile Ishmaelites. They were horrified at the thought of their children in khaki IDF uniforms, learning how to shoot an Uzi. What they had wanted was for them to finish college, get married and live in a nice rent-controlled apartment in Flatbush while they saved money for a down payment on a two-family house in a nice Jewish neighborhood in Queens, not too far from their parents and survivor grandparents—who had suffered so much.

Why couldn't they be like everybody else: attend a local Young Israel, buy strictly kosher food, and give generously to the UJA? Neither of them could explain the reason they had taken such drastic and life-changing steps, journeyed so far into the unknown. It wasn't something you could really explain to someone whose heart didn't skip a beat at the Tomb of Abraham, who didn't choke and tear at the words of "Hatikvah" (*Still in my heart, deep inside, a Jewish soul is yearning. We have not lost our hope, our hope is two thousand years old...*).

Alone, they had made *aliyah* (meaning "journey upward," a term used by all Jews to designate immigration to Israel) immediately after college. It had been hard and lonely, but also exhilarating. Meeting each other and falling in love had filled in the empty spaces left by the ravages of the sudden uprooting from their birthplace, the loss of their families. Their wedding day had been the ultimate "ingathering of the exiles," Jon had joked, bringing in family members from around the world. And neither had ever been lonely again.

In the way of all new immigrants making a new beginning, they had wanted a family right away. But it had taken them four years and untold fertility treatments to conceive their first child, Ilana, now five. There had been two difficult pregnancies that had ended badly. This pregnancy too had not gone easily. In her sixth month, Elise had begun showing signs that her cervix was beginning to thin, the marker of oncoming labor. She had been confined to bed rest ever since.

"You've got to stay in bed, Elise. And then the heir will be born with a lusty cry, and grab the breast, and shake out the milk," he said in his finest Herr Professor manner, stroking his nonexistent beard. Then he suddenly got up and looked out the window at the gentle, rolling hills and the houses beyond.

"Nouara," she said, matter-of-factly.

"Nouara," he admitted, smiling at her mind reading.

He looked toward the mosque and minaret over the hill where Nouara's husband, Shawan, was probably just finishing his morning prayers. He too would be washing floors, dressing the kids, then heading for Hadassah Hospital in that beat-up Peugeot of his. He would be there today, as he was every day, feeding his small, pale wife sweet fleshy dates brought especially from Jericho, bottles of Seven-Up and plastic containers of his mother's matchless humous. Five times a day, he fell to his knees and prayed toward Mecca, just as three times a day his wife's doctor prayed toward Jerusalem.

Nouara ali Abad had had leukemia off and on since she was a teenager. For the last year, she had been in Dr. Jonathan Margulies' care. As an intern and then a resident, Jon had known Nouara long before she became his patient. He had seen her beat the illness, grow back her long dark hair, marry and bear three healthy children. And now she was back, worse than ever. She had not yet turned twenty-two. Now she was his patient.

Elise heaved herself heavily over the bed and walked up behind him, reaching up and touching his cheek. "You'll think of something, my love. You always do. May God help her…"

"Or Allah," he said, tucking her arms around his waist.

"Or Allah," she acknowledged.

He turned around slowly. "And may God help you if you overexert yourself, Elise, please." His dark brown eyes pleaded with the helplessness of husbands facing pregnant wives.

"I give you my solemn word of honor to make you proud of me, my love," she said, stretching up as he bent down to catch her kiss in the practiced way of tall men with tiny wives. "I'm going straight from bed to bathroom and back again. Remember: Ilana's ballet recital is at four at Beit Ha Am. So you have to come get her from day care no later than three-thirty…and please don't forget *Bubbee* Leah's cookbook," she murmured into his cheek, enjoying the warmth of his arms, wishing he would never leave.

"I can't promise I'll get to the bookstore today…"

"Then tomorrow…" she wheedled.

"She'll never be as good a cook as her granddaughter." He kissed her again.

"If I'm ever allowed back in the kitchen…I've forgotten what it looks like…"

"Tomorrow. I promise. Now, back into bed," he demanded.

"In a minute."

He waited patiently for her to pad in and out of the bathroom, then helped her navigate her way back under the covers. "You know how much I love you, right?"

"From here to the moon." She smiled.

"And back again." He nodded.

Then he went into the kitchen, rolled up his sleeves and took out the mop and pail. As he plunged his hands into the hot, soapy water, he thought how fortunate it was he'd decided against becoming a surgeon.

Chapter two

Right after she heard the final fade-out of Jon's car wheels from the driveway, Elise heard the door open and her neighbor Ruth's cheerful "*Ahalan*! What's up pussycat?" followed by Ilana's squeal of joy. The child adored Ruth, who brought her home-baked cookies and never tired of chasing after her, Elise thought with a prick of jealousy.

"Hi, Lanoosh!" Ruth called to the child. "What do you have on? Your dancing shoes? Does Mommy know?"

Ilana twirled into the bedroom. Her long, dark hair was a mass of tangled curls, her big brown eyes sparkled. She was wearing her leotard, backward, and her pink ballet tights sagged at the knees because they hadn't been pulled up properly. She pirouetted around the room.

"Ilana! What did you do?" Jon always dressed and fed her before leaving for work, so the volunteer wouldn't have to. How she'd managed to take off all her clothes and put on her ballet gear...

"But *Ima*, I'm practicing!"

"I know you are. But there's no time, Ilana. Ruth has to go

home and take care of her own children, Sammy and Daphna…Now she'll have to dress you all over again…"

"It's all right, Elise. I'll manage. Come my little dancer, let's dance over to your closet and get some clothes, okay?"

"*Ima*, do I *have* to?" She seemed genuinely forlorn, Elise worried. It wasn't like her.

"Yes, you do, Ilana," Elise said more sternly than she would have if her own feelings about turning her child over to another woman's care weren't so mixed. Ruth was just one of an army of neighborhood volunteers who, unasked, had worked out an elaborate schedule to make sure that every single day, someone would be there to help Elise.

In a place like Maaleh Sara, such kindnesses were taken for granted. Through the years, Elise had done similar things for her neighbors.

A small *yishuv* was more than a housing development. In many ways, it was like one house divided into many rooms, and all the people one large, extended family. If you saw someone's child in need of a Band-Aid, or a sandwich, or just a hug, you provided it, no questions asked. People did the same for yours. The Biblical injunction of "love your neighbor as yourself" wasn't a saying; it was a lifestyle.

Like a little group of space pioneers who had landed on the moon, each family understood that its well-being was dependent upon their neighbors'. In extraordinary circumstances like births and deaths, neighbors watched your children, cooked your meals, washed your clothes and filled your freezer. And on ordinary days, when you needed a cup of sugar, or a doctor's referral, or the name of a plumber, they made sure you got it. You were never alone to fend for yourself.

"Are you coming to see me dance, *Ima*?"

"Not this time, *motek*."

"Because you can't wake up the baby?"

Good explanation, Elise thought. "Right! The baby needs to keep real quiet until it's ready to come out."

"Maybe it won't want to come out?" she said hopefully.

Elise studied her, surprised. "Don't you want it to? So you can play together?"

"Noooh. I have no time to play. I have to practice..." She twirled around the room, then stopped. "Do *you* need a new baby to play with, *Ima*?"

"Come here, baby." Elise motioned to her. Cradling Ilana's warm little face between her hands, Elise kissed every feature separately: the fluttering eyelids, thick little nose, attentive little ears and the rosebud mouth that didn't stop talking for a second. "You'll always be our special girl. Our first girl," she whispered to her as she nuzzled her hair, breathing in the fragrance of baby shampoo, rosemary oil and that special scent that rose from her young, fresh skin. She was so delicious, Elise thought, tightening her grip.

"*Ima!*" Ilana finally squirmed.

Reluctantly, Elise released her. It was going to be such a long day for her; even longer than usual. She hated having Ilana in day care. She missed her terribly, and knew the child was confused and upset by her exile from home and from her mother. But there was nothing to be done. "I'm sorry I won't be at the recital, Ilana. But *Aba* will tell me all about it..."

"But *you* won't see me, *Ima*! I can do it for you now!" She started dancing, hands on hips. Then all at once, she leaped across the room, landing smack in the middle of the bed.

"Ilana! What are you doing!?" Elise shouted, cradling herself protectively, her voice shaking. She pushed Ilana off the bed.

The child stared, her eyes widening, her mouth trembling in a doomed attempt to hold back the sobs, which finally culminated in a terrible wail of insult and injustice.

"Uh-oh, everything all right in here?" Ruth enquired, sticking her head into the room.

"Fine—go on, Ilana. Can't you see Ruth's waiting?" Elise said, mortified and miserable. Ilana went limp as Ruth bent down to pick her up. The child laid her head on the neighbor's shoulder, sucking her thumb as she stared at her mother in wordless disappointment.

Elise stared back, helplessly. "I don't know what's gotten into that child…It's all my fault. I'm so totally useless. Jon won't let me do anything…"

"Don't blame yourself! Just enjoy it while you can, Elise. When the baby comes, you can forget about lying in bed at all hours… Remember what I say." She grinned.

"Don't I know it? Is it seven-thirty yet?"

Ruth checked her watch. "You've got thirty seconds."

"Put on the radio, will you?"

"Do you really want to start your day with the bad news?"

"Why bad?"

"What other kind is there these days?" Ruth murmured, fiddling with the dials until the familiar beep-beep-beep that heralded the news suddenly went on and both women fell into a tense silence.

For the last two years, news broadcasts had brought horrors into their lives that neither could have ever imagined. Suicide bombers detonating themselves in children's playgrounds, sending baby carriages flying, killing grandchildren and their grandmothers. Sniper fire into the foreheads of ten-month-old babies in their carriages. The bloody murder of two fourteen-year-old boys, playing hooky to gather firewood for the Lag B'Omer bonfires, their beautiful young faces found crushed beyond recognition in a nearby cave. Crimes that belied the humanity of those who had committed them. Today the news opened with the funerals of two sixteen-year-old yeshiva students killed by a terrorist who walked into their dorms and opened fire; and the Israeli army attack on the car of a wanted terrorist, in which a nine-year-old girl was killed as well.

"Why are your eyes wet, *Ima*?" Ilana asked.

"Are they?" Elise smiled, wiping her eyes and reaching out to tickle Ilana's tummy. Ruth had dressed her in the red T-shirt that said: "I'm pretty enough to eat," and a pair of blue shorts and brown sandals. She looked adorable.

Ilana giggled, twisting away, trying to tickle Elise back.

Ruth caught the child's hand: "Say shalom to *Ima*, Ilana."

"Don't want to. Want to stay home," she whimpered, squeezing her mother's elbow with her small fingers.

Elise studied the child's bright eyes, her solid, perfect little body with its protruding tummy still covered with tender baby fat. She thought of the road into Jerusalem, the long, winding road past Arab villages and dark-leafed olive trees that camouflaged roadside dangers. That's what terror does, Elise thought. Unlike the healthy sense of mortality most people came to terms with—the idea that you would have your eighty years or so and then die—here you were being asked to accept a minute-by-minute uncertainty, so that even kissing a child good-bye and sending her off to school seemed like a tragic, final scene.

It was unbearable. Yet, they kept bearing it.

But what else could they do? Stay locked up in their homes and never go out? Life had to go on. At least, this is what they kept telling themselves, and each other, pretending to feel a courage and certainty they didn't have.

Slowly, she pried her child's small fingers loose. She felt her vision blur.

"I brought you sugar cookies for your lunch bag," Ruth wheedled, picking Ilana up.

The child's face remained impassive. She was impossible to bribe, and she didn't particularly like sweets. But Ruth's sugar cookies were an exception. Slowly, she relented. "With sprinkles?"

"With sprinkles."

And then the two of them were gone.

The house filled with the lonely sound of the front door clicking shut. Elise turned off the radio, her forehead glistening. Oh, this was no good for her, she knew, no good, she thought, cradling her swollen belly. I'll keep you safe, baby. I'll keep you safe, she thought, rocking. Until the world becomes a sane and decent place again, until the bad guys are vanquished, the murderers imprisoned, the demagogues hung by their ankles in the town square. Until the world is safe, familiar, predictable, and good again.

She reached over and took out her box of beads. Not a bribe, she told herself. Just a sorry-I-couldn't-be-there gift. Something sparkly and pretty with lots of pink—Ilana's latest love. As she began to string the beads she thought about how wonderful it would be if the world was like a beaded necklace. When it didn't come out right, you could just take the whole thing apart and start all over again, learning from your mistakes...

Chapter three

Dr. Jonathan Margulies opened his office door. She was there, as usual, pretending to be busy dusting off something which had long since surrendered every particle to her whacking ministrations.

"Fatima. What a surprise."

"*As salaam aleikum*, Doctor Jon," the woman said with the greatest respect, her weathered face breaking into a huge smile of strong white teeth. "I'm just finishing. I'm in your way?"

Jon smiled and shook his head. "Never. I'm lucky to have you."

He'd known her through medical school and residency. She was almost a fixture in the department. A few times a month, she even came to the house to help Elise with the cleaning. Ilana adored her.

Before the Intifada forced the army to put up roadblocks, she used to travel in to work each morning from one of the little villages just outside of Hebron. Now she stayed with relatives in East Jerusalem. Weighing two hundred pounds, she had raised eleven children, and could lift up his desk with one hand. He had no idea how old she was. The shapeless traditional caftan that covered her ample frame from neck to ankle and the voluminous scarf that hid the color of her hair gave him few clues. Her face showed great character and an abundance of living. She could have been forty—or sixty—he often thought with admiration.

Life for her had not been easy. Her husband was a construction worker who off and on had spent time working in Saudi Arabia along with several of her sons. For long stretches, he knew, she was in charge of a household that she ran single-handedly. He sat down at his desk and turned on his computer.

She waited.

"Is there something you need, Fatima?"

"Doctor Jon, I don't like to trouble you, but perhaps I could ask you a question?" she said in broken Hebrew.

From long experience, Jonathan knew that whatever response he might make, she would ask her question, and she wouldn't leave without an answer.

He shut off the computer. He didn't mind, except that giving medical advice without actually examining any of the various relatives and friends Fatima was determined to cure wasn't particularly good medicine. "Of course. But you know, whoever it is, they really need to see a doctor and get a good examination."

"Yes, Doctor Jon. But this time, this time it is about myself."

He looked at her, surprised, concerned. She never asked about herself. "Are you sick?"

She took a deep breath. "Doctor Jon, the water. It comes out red."

"Water? Do you mean urine? The water you make when you go to the bathroom?"

"Yes. That water."

"And do you have any pain, or tenderness anywhere?"

She shook her head. "No. But I know it is very bad. My sister had this. Very, very bad."

He thought for a moment. "How long have you had this, Fatima?"

"Just now it started. This morning."

"Fatima, what did you eat last night for dinner?"

"Humous, and cousbara salad, and beet salad…"

"Beet salad! That's it. Fatima, you are probably fine. Beets will do that, make the water red. It's harmless."

He could see the relief flood her face. "You really should get used to going to your own doctor, Fatima. You need a good examination at least once or twice a year…"

"No. I don't like doctors. I mean, I don't like to go to doctors, to take off my clothes."

"Fatima…"

"Thank you, Doctor, I'll go now…"

"Fatima. Don't eat any beets for the rest of the week. If it comes back, you tell me right away, okay? And then I'll get Dr. Rosen to examine you."

"*Shukran.*"

"*Bevakasha,*" he replied. She didn't move.

"Doctor Jon…"

"Fatima. It isn't necessary…" he implored without a shred of hope. She ignored him, as usual, heaving the enormous straw basket she often carried on her head onto his desk. It was filled with fresh red grapes from her own vines. They smelled of sweetness and musky undergrowth and the hot, Mediterranean sun. She must have gone back to her village for the weekend, he thought, feeling sorry for what must have been endless waits to get through security checks, endless walks down long dusty roads to avoid roadblocks…He thought of his fig tree, understanding why she'd made the effort.

"Give some to Ilana." She smiled, gesturing toward the smiling, framed picture of the child he kept on his desk as she emptied the basket into a large plastic bag. "She loves my grapes."

"This is true." (That had been his fatal error, years before, revealing to Fatima how much his daughter loved her grapes, thereby ensuring himself what was turning out to be a lifetime supply.) "But Fatima, why so many? You could sell them and make a nice little profit."

She shook her head stubbornly. "I work for money. Grapes are a gift from Allah. They are for family, for friends."

He broke off a bunch, popping them into his mouth, letting the tangy, red juice bathe his tongue. It was delicious. "*Shukran,* Fatima."

She balanced the empty basket carefully on her head, her posture beautiful, her face acknowledging his thanks with quiet pleasure. She closed the door silently behind her.

He put on his white coat and began his morning rounds.

The beautiful Moroccan grandmother was reacting badly to the increase in her chemotherapy dosage. She never complained, but he could see it in the white pallor on her olive complexion, her lack of appetite, her silence. What to do? he wondered. The drug was working at this dosage, the tests showed that. Perhaps an antiemetic to help control the nausea? That too might have side effects. He would have to check her more often, he made a note to himself, try out some other drugs to help with the side effects. And if that didn't work…Maybe a different drug?

In contrast, his twelve-year-old hell-raiser was in fine spirits. A little too fine. He smiled, listening to the complaints of the nurses on the boy's latest practical joke—something involving a syringe and a bedpan—he didn't want details. "If you don't behave, you'll just have to get well and go home!" He shook his finger at the boy, who took off his baseball cap and grinned.

"Want to check your face in the mirror?" the boy asked, bending his shiny bald head forward.

Jon rubbed it with his knuckles, laughing.

Next was the kindly eighty-year-old. Jon carefully checked the condition of the small wound on the bottom of his foot. Because of his diabetes, it had to be carefully monitored, he reminded his interns and the nurse. It was healing, he saw, relieved. A good sign.

Before he could get to the next room, he was accosted by the hell-raiser's anxious mother, who never seemed to sleep.

"Excuse me, but the doctor is on rounds. This will just have to wait for office hours," the nurse told the woman curtly, trying to run interference.

Jon saw the mother's face fall. The boy was her youngest. Her baby.

"It's all right, nurse. I'll just be a moment. Thanks."

The nurse shook her head and shrugged.

Jon knew the nurses thought he was too soft, that he let everyone take advantage of him. And the truth was, he had nothing new to say to the boy's mother. But he also knew that she wasn't really asking a question. All she wanted was her daily dose of reassurance that her son was healing, the medicine working. She, of course, wouldn't let him go, would want to ask the same question, again and again: When will he be well, doctor? When will he come home? And he'd put his hand on her arm in a way he hoped was comforting and say: "Soon, God-willing, Mrs. Gottleib. Soon."

His interns and nurses had learned to wait patiently.

Nouara's room was near the end of the long hall. By the time he got to it, he had heard fifty stories, some of them tragic and unbearably heartbreaking, and some wonderfully uplifting. Cancer wasn't a death sentence anymore. At least, it didn't need to be. It was a clever adversary, though, biding its time, regrouping and waiting—sometimes for years—to break through the defenses. Often he felt as if he was playing a game of chess with the Angel of Death, where he could never achieve a checkmate, only prolong the game. But that, too, was important.

Everyone is going to die, he reminded himself when the sadness of his defeats tore through him. But each battle he won meant that life could go on one more day, month, year. It was a battle worth fighting, worth winning, no matter the eventual outcome.

What would a man give for an hour of life, ten minutes? What price?

He could understand many things about his Palestinian neighbors: their anger and disappointment and sense of injustice. All these things were human and, seen from their point of view, perhaps justifiable. What he could not accept or even begin to fathom was their joyous connection to death. The pride of sending a child to destroy life, their own and others'. How he wished he could take them into this ward and see how people fought for the privilege of one more day of life. *Death has no glory!* he wanted to shout at them through the television screens when they interviewed the beaming mothers and uncles and friends as they fired off guns to celebrate the creation of one more *shahid. Death has no glory.*

Shawan was sitting, as usual, by his wife's bedside. He was a tall, thin man with a giant Saddam Hussein mustache. His thick hair was neatly combed and his shirt was a faded blue badly in need of ironing. His gray pants showed the flecks of paint and concrete that were the marks of his profession. His face was pale under the olive skin, his dark eyes sagging with fatigue. Jon could only imagine how awful it must be for him, caring for the children, spending so much time with his wife, trying to find some kind of work to keep gas in the car and food on the table.

"Good morning, Shawan."

"Doctor. How is she?"

He touched the man's shoulder. "Let me look at her chart, and I'll get back to you."

Nouara lay back on the white sheets, her face pale and drawn, her dark hair covered with a modest scarf, not unlike the ultra-Orthodox Jewish woman that was in the next room with advanced breast cancer. He drew the curtain around her bed, sat down and smiled. "How are you feeling this morning?"

"Ravishing," she said with a trace of a wicked grin. She was a lover of novels, especially the ones with the bodice-ripping titles, and they were the source of most of her English vocabulary.

He lifted his eyebrows and nodded appreciatively. "Good word! And what else can you tell me?"

He listened as she gave him a list of her symptoms and reactions to the drug regimen, all the while flipping through her charts to read the latest lab work. The truth was, the numbers were better. Not the best. Not perfect, but an improvement. He examined her head to toe.

It was good, he thought. Nothing but the usual body weariness fighting the invasive chemicals that were flooding her system, fighting the cancer. She needed very, very careful supervision at this point, someone to keep track exactly of every dosage and every side effect. He made a note to change certain medications, and told the nurse that he was to be paged immediately if there was any change for the worse. He didn't want some outsider clomping into this delicate woman's fragile body chemistry with combat boots. He wanted, literally, to keep his finger on her pulse. This was his war, and he was determined to win it for her, for Shawan, for their children. It was personal.

"I'm happy today, Nouara. The numbers look good. Keep it up!" His hand reached into his back pocket and he took out another Harlequin. "For you. This one is called *Burning Desire*," he read.

She took it from him quickly, glancing with pleasure at the big-bosomed blonde in the arms of the dark horseman before hiding it quickly inside her pillow. She tucked a few wisps of hair underneath her scarf. "*Shukran*, Doctor Jon."

"Anytime."

He was about to leave, when her hand caught his arm. "Doctor, can you tell my husband not to come? At least, not every day?"

He was surprised. "Why?"

She shook her head. "He won't listen to me. But I know it is very hard for him. He isn't able to find work, because he takes off so much time…

And because since the Intifada, Israelis were just too scared to hire Palestinians…. Jon finished the thought for her.

"He's so tired. If something happens to me, he has to be strong. To take care of our children. This is more important. But he won't listen…"

"Nouara, if my wife told me not to come and see her every day, I wouldn't listen to her or her doctor. I'd come. But you know what, I'll try to find some work for Shawan. There are people building houses in Maaleh Sara who could use a hand, and their hours are flexible. He could do both."

Her teeth were white and pretty against her dark face. She took his hand and kissed it.

"You make me feel like the pope, Nouara."

"You are holier," she said solemnly.

"I don't know. My wife is pretty mad at me right now. She says I'm bullying her."

"How is this pregnancy going? Still so hard?"

"No, she's fine. But we don't want to take any chances, and she hates lying in bed all day. She's so tired of doing her beadwork, of reading and watching TV…"

"I know." Nouara picked at the bedcovers listlessly. "Maybe you should buy her watercolors and paper. Let her draw. You wouldn't believe how the time passes when you mix colors." She pulled open the drawer of her night table. It was full of her artwork, fresh and delicate landscapes. What was she drawing, he wondered, glancing up at the window. But only the blank white wall of the maternity wing stared back at him. He studied the paintings: the brown rolling hills, the gnarled trunks of olive trees, the pointy bright green pomegranate leaves. It was the same view he saw from his own window every morning, he realized, the same things he would miss if confined to this sterile white room. She'd drawn the landscape of her heart. And in a way, his own.

"It's so good, Nouara. So familiar. I even think I know what tree that is."

He tried to return the picture. She pushed it back at him. "For you."

"Well, I'm honored. But you have to at least sign it."

She dimpled with pleasure, dipping her brush into a plastic cup of water and moistening the dried blue paint. "From Nouara to Doctor Jon," she wrote in English, and then continued in flowing Arabic script.

"What does it mean?"

"One day, I'll tell you," she blushed.

As he walked down the hall to talk to Shawan, he folded the picture carefully, putting it into his pocket.

Chapter four

The recital hall in Beit Ha Am was in the center of downtown Jerusalem. It had a real theater, a real stage. Once a year, all the community center ballet classes took the place over, filling it with doting parents and giggling little girls with flowers in their hair. The children, dressed in colorful costumes, mingled like a field of wildflowers quivering in the wind, their sweet voices a chorus of excited expectations.

Jon ushered Ilana through the throng, finding her classmates and her teacher. Then he sat back in the darkened theater, losing himself in the music and movement of little children delightedly soaking up the spotlight. First the older kids came out, trying their hand at being future stars, stretching, posing self-consciously, keeping laborious track of the music, delighting in the applause. And then came the little ones: their eyes wide, a little scared, their feet fumbling, searching the stage and the crowd for encouragement, dimpling when they found it. Like little kittens, they brushed up against each other, stepping on each others' toes, their soft beauty almost heartbreakingly fragile under the bright lights.

And then he saw Ilana. Her curls had been pulled up and back into a severe chignon on the top of her head, making her face look heartbreakingly older. Tiny and graceful, full of movement and joy, he felt his heart leap up with pleasure at the reality that such a beautiful creature existed and she was his.

Then all the groups made concentric circles, their colorful pink, fuchsia and magenta costumes interweaving, exploding into a kaleidoscope of color. Jon stared in wonderment and appreciation, seeing only Ilana, delighted at every practiced movement of her knees and elbows as she went through her simple routine.

When he took her into his arms afterward, he felt her body exude the dew of happiness and exertion.

"Was I good? Was I, *Aba*?!"

He hugged her. "The best. I took pictures, so *Ima* can see too."

At the mention of her mother, Jon felt her hands hold him a little tighter. "*Ima* will like what I did?"

"Of course! She'll be so happy!"

It was already getting dark as she skipped beside him to the car for the trip back home, chattering nonstop. As the car door clicked shut, Jon turned to face his daughter in the backseat, double-checking if her seat belt was fastened. As his eyes met hers, he saw the dimples in her cheeks deepen and her face light up.

His little girl. He'd left the clinic at the last possible moment, annoyed and irritated at having to cut his workday short, begrudging the time. He'd found her sitting dejected and miserable in day care. This pregnancy was taking a real toll on her, he realized, leaning over to pat her hand and touch her cheeks, which blushed the same pretty color as her tights. It took so little to make her happy, he thought, ashamed, vowing silently to spend more time with her until things got back to normal.

He turned around, automatically reaching for his own seat belt, then stopped, thinking of Dov Kalmanovitch—the first victim of the Intifada—who had been forced to open his seat belt with a broken arm as a Molotov cocktail turned him into a flaming torch. By the time he'd freed himself, three-quarters of his body had been left with third-degree burns, and his face—it had simply been erased.

Jon remembered meeting the man in Hadassah's burn unit. He and his pretty, young wife, who had stood by her husband with an iron will throughout his miraculous and incredibly painful recovery, had gone on to live their lives, to have more children. The power of human resilience as well as the depths of human frailty were so unpredictable. You could never tell how a person pushed to extremes would behave.

What would Elise do, he wondered, if—God forbid—something should happen to me? And what, he thought, his arm quivering with a sudden strange cold as he fit the key into the ignition, would either of us do if something should happen to Ilana? He felt his eyes sting.

It was unthinkable. Slowly, he released the seat belt.

There were two ways to get home. The first was the shortest and easiest: a twenty-minute ride through the new tunnel that would leave them practically on their doorstep. Or the tortuous, ninety-minute detour that would take them almost into Tel Aviv. The tunnel had been built to avoid conflicts with Palestinian townships as well as the miserable shantytowns still called refugee camps, although most of their inhabitants had never known any other home.

He switched on the news. All the roads were open, things were quiet. He made the left turn toward the tunnel, passing the shopping center in Kiryat Yovel and those new high-rise monsters. He drove uphill past the Egged bus terminal and the Arab grocery stores of Beit Tsafafa until the white expanse of the buildings of Gilo came into view, the red-tiled roofs of the little houses lining the entrance to the *wadi*. There was the Mishav building and the telephone company building with its colorful tiles, and the strange building without windows, which conventional wisdom held was the headquarters of the Israeli Secret Service. The *trampiada*, or hitchhiking station, was coming up. He looked to see if there was anyone waiting, but a bus must have just come by, because it was surprisingly empty. He passed the army roadblock checking cars coming in from the opposite direction from Gush Etzion and Hebron that wished to enter Jerusalem. Ilana waved at the young soldiers, and they smiled and waved back.

After the last house in Gilo, a new fence had gone up, about a kilometer before the first tunnel. As he followed the road upward, he saw the troops encamped on the shoulders of the road, almost unseen. From that vantage point, they had a good strategic view of the entire area, he thought, exhaling, revealing to himself just how tense he really was.

There was the first tunnel. It was only seven hundred meters long, short enough not to interfere with radio signals, so that the music he was playing continued. He emerged onto a bridge—the place where the first shootings had taken place. Terrorist snipers equipped with long-range rifles had taken up positions in the peaceful homes of Bethlehem's Christian neighborhood of Beit Jala, firing at passing cars as one would at ducks in a shooting gallery. Now a new barrier was going up to protect motorists, thick white polyester sheets that reminded him of venetian blinds. They seemed flimsy compared to the enormous stone barriers ahead on the second part of the bridge. Apparently, the bridge couldn't handle such weight all the way across.

There was the second tunnel coming up. He entered, and the car radio went dead. It was very long, almost two kilometers. He looked at the familiar graffiti on the wall. LOVE YOU KEREN, someone had written, and again he wondered, as he did each time he passed it, did that mean "I love you, signed Keren"? or "I love you, Keren, girl of my dreams"? Was our Keren the graffiti expert, or the object of the foolhardy and industrious artist's affections?

He would probably never know. But, then again, you could never tell. Someone in the War of Independence had written his name on a wall on the way to the besieged Jerusalem and years later a songwriter had written a popular song about him. People had looked him up and he'd become quite famous for a time. Maybe immortality was also waiting just around the corner for our Keren, or the one who loved her, he thought, grinning.

He emerged into the cool night air and fluorescent lights. Up ahead was the Efrat junction, where one took a right to Gush Etzion and a left to the Dehaishe shantytown and Bethlehem.

He turned right, his heart skipping a beat. Just ahead, past the large Jewish townships of Efrat and Elazar, was the most dangerous stretch of all. It was there the road grew narrow and dark, and traffic thinned. On either side of the road thick, beautiful olive trees—trees he had always loved—had become sinister terrorist camouflage. Just months before, terrorists had used them as cover, attacking a young family on their way home from a wedding. Three people had been killed. Afterward, the army had begun to bulldoze them, but do-gooder rabbis from America had organized protests with the local orchard owners, blocking the bulldozers and helping to replant them.

He glanced back nervously at Ilana, who was half asleep. Then, as was his custom, he took out his cell phone and dialed Elise.

She picked up immediately. "Jon?"

"Yes."

"How was it?"

"Oh, Elise, if you just could have seen her...She was so beyond thrilled. I can't swear to it, but I don't think her feet touched the floor at all!"

She laughed. "So where are you?"

"I'm just before the turnoff to Maaleh Sara. I'll be home in less than ten minutes. Ilana's practically asleep," he whispered, wanting to keep it that way.

"All right. See you soon. Love you to the moon," she added cheerfully.

But he might not have heard her, she thought, because he didn't answer "and back again."

Chapter five

And this is what Elise will remember: the phone a lifeless, plastic corpse in her hand; and her hand suddenly old, shaking, as if with Parkinson's. She will remember too the infinite slowness of the second hand as it struggles like a fly through honey from five to six, and from six to seven...She will remember thinking: ten minutes, that's all the ride should take, if everything was all right.

And why shouldn't it be, after all? She will not remember getting painfully out of bed, standing by the window, her eyes peering into the distance, her ears straining to pick up the crunch of car wheels over pebbles, the gentle suck of rubber meeting tar.

But she will remember the moment she knew that the ten minutes had passed, the moment that the innocent, quiet driveway was transformed into something dangerous and sinister. And she'll recall the frantic redialing of Jon's cell phone, the heartstopping dénouement of each hopeful ring, ring, ring as it fell into an impersonal silence that settled in her suddenly hollow chest.

The act of calling her neighbor Joshua, the *yishuv*'s security officer, with his access to special beepers, and unlisted army intelligence phone numbers and a bulletproof four-by-four, she will not recall. It was, after all, what needed to be done; it was the part in the scenario that seemed already written and acted, almost will-less, along with the knowledge that he'd take his car and drive out to where Jon had last called, and in minutes, a mere breathing interval, she'd know.

She will not want to remember that some part of her already knew and that the knowing felt like a strange, hot wind, the kind that made one's face shine, sunburnt, kissed by acid fear. The time it actually took Joshua to get back to her will not be remembered as it was, a mere fifteen minutes. It will feel like four seasons: spring-summer, the idea that soon there would be two cars in the driveway, Joshua's and Jon's, and both would be waving and smiling. And Jon would get out and walk around the side of the car to take Ilana out of her seat belt and help her out of the car. And she would see her baby in the pink leotard run to her as she held out her arms. And they would talk and laugh, and provide explanations of harmless mishaps—flat tires, broken carburetor valves—and the great fear in her heart would rise like smoke and dissipate as she held her husband and child in her arms.

She will look back longingly at that season, and remember how quickly it passed, like any joyous summer, and how the autumn engulfed and transformed it.

She will barely remember that transition, or how her knees grew soft and pliable, unable to hold the suddenly unbearable burden of her own motionless weight and how she sank like a parachute divested of its human cargo, a heap upon the floor while the world, her life, swirled around her like a debris-filled cosmic ring aimlessly circling some distant planet.

And she will never forget when winter came, full-blown, knocking at her door. She'll recall in minute detail the moment of hesitation before answering that knock, a moment felt by every Israeli who sees army uniforms outside their door; a moment when the idea of not opening it seems to hold a solution, a way of keeping the horror at bay. With strange, almost frightening clarity, she'll remember the sudden confidence that flooded her at that moment, coming out of nowhere, in the simple idea that everything, despite appearances, was going to be all right; that it would be something difficult, but not catastrophic; something needing treatment, yes, but benign and curable. An injury. A slight blood loss. A fright. A near-miss. A mistake, soon to be corrected. This was the idea that propelled her to the door. And even as she opened it, she will remember not being convinced she wouldn't find Jon with Ilana in his arms on the other side, smiling, Ilana in her tutu, with flowers in her hair...

The notion that disaster does not—cannot—come so close to home; that it stops at the doorsteps of TV strangers, next-door neighbors, the glossy pages of international news magazines; that it is held back by the breakwaters of unseen, benevolent walls that jut up from interstices that have—all one's life—succeeded in keeping one distinct and separate from disaster and unbearable pain, is what keeps us sane. It is the idea that we know such things can happen in the world, but that they will never happen to us. Not to us. And even though we watch the interviews with prying newsmen probing private grief, stare like voyeurs at the tear-stained faces of unknown victims, hear their cracking voices, choked with phlegm and misery...still, don't we all secretly tell ourselves: But what has it to do with me?

It is this idea, this comfort, that shatters forever when Elise finally turns the handle and pulls back the door from its frame.

The security officer Joshua, flanked by two army men and the *yishuv*'s rabbi—whose kind face seemed kinder, whose gray beard seemed grayer—stands there looking at her. There is no Jon. No Ilana. That knowledge washes over the scene like a reality-remover, all colors fading, her own presence suddenly suspect.

She has no business in this scene, is not here, does not wish to be part of it. The rejection is so strong it turns to fury. Everything seems a little darker, the bodies indistinct, their voices lost in some strange vacuum, like one of those strange silent films in which everything takes place in soundless slow motion. She reaches out for the doorpost simply to feel its solid mass, and suddenly can't find it, the oak slithering out of her hand, smooth as snakeskin, as her hand slides down, down. And then, her eyes are closed, and she knows that in a minute her feet will give way.

It isn't unpleasant, this sudden oblivion, the sense of holding on to a friend, her body held firmly and kindly against other human beings. She lets the darkness enter, and feels herself stilled, comforted. Small sounds enter the quiet, unexpected night. Words, with an upward lilt, a murmur of concern, instructions, conflicting suggestions that gnaw at her. Someone hands her water, or tea—a glass, at any rate—and she is sitting now, a chair surprisingly beneath her. She feels light flood back in as she opens her eyes. She feels embarrassed and responsible for the anxious looks on the faces that peer into hers, and this finds its way into an inappropriate smile. She smiles sheepishly as she faces these good men, wanting to be strong. She presses her hand over her stomach. Needing to be strong.

An ambulance siren wails.

Alive! she thinks. If there is an ambulance…. But then the medics crowd through the doorway, and the security officer and the rabbi move aside for them, and they take out a stretcher, and needles. But she will acquiesce no longer, be passive no longer.

"No!" she shouts, and for a moment all activity ceases, and they turn to her, questioningly. She sees that they do not understand what this means, this "no" of hers. No, don't touch me? No, don't tell me the terrible truth? No, rewrite reality? What is this then, this "no" of hers, dredged up from the bottom of a dark place, the first word she speaks into the light?

But she gets no answer, neither from them nor from herself. Doesn't expect any. And besides, it wasn't really the question she wanted to ask, she thinks. She is completely fine now. She is rational, sane, not hysterical. She sets her face into sensible lines, removing the smile. She leans forward, elbows on the chair arms, her back straight. She speaks in low, sensible tones, just loud enough to make herself heard, just loud enough for them to wait a moment with the needle that will send her back to forgetful oblivion. It is not that she is averse to going there, mind you. She looks forward to it. But not just yet, she thinks. She has questions to ask, needs information.

"I feel all right now. I have some questions, please…"

She sees them exchange doubtful glances, but also that their bodies relax for a moment, the weight shifting from both feet to one, the arms dropping, the fingers outspread, flexed.

"Can you tell me what happened?"

The security officer comes forward first. "Elise, I called the army outpost near the junction. They confirmed that there had been an ambush. That Jon's car was hit…"

A small moan escapes her throat and all reason flees. Now she is not living in her head, but in her stomach, in her bowels, a primitive life that does not want to know any details, any facts, greedy and desperate to feed on images: bodies, in any condition. Some instinct makes her understand that she cannot scream out this demand; that it would stop the flow of information, and this she does not want.

With supreme effort, she asks: "Can I see them?"

The army men, two young officers, handsome and lean in clean uniforms, their smooth, shaven faces momentarily wrinkled by extreme concern, step forward.

"Mrs. Margulies, when we got to the car, there were no bodies. The car was riddled with bullets, it had some dark red stains, but there were no bodies. We think, perhaps, they might have escaped. That the car was already empty when it was shot up…. We don't know. Our men are out there now, looking for them."

Her body flooded with relief. No bodies! If they ran from the car, they were all right! They were out there. Alive.

"They couldn't have gotten very far. Ilana would have to be carried…"

Then she remembered. "Dark red stains? Blood? How much blood?"

"We're not sure it was blood. There was a bag of grapes. Deep-red grapes…. It's hard to tell…"

Grapes? she thinks. Or blood? And whose? Her husband's? Her baby's? Blood, draining out of one of them, or both, enough to stain the upholstery of their car. But stain it how much? A scratch, wiped pink over the gray covers? A puddle? Or nothing, juice from grapes in a bag?

"—we don't know yet, Mrs. Margulies…"

She felt her body lift up. "When will you know?!" she shouts. A sudden, searing pain pierces her womb, and she feels the child inside her shift, and something else crush. Someone is screaming, she thinks, as she lies back willingly on the stretcher. A terrible sound, she thinks, as she watches her sleeve folded back and her arm grow naked as the needle is pushed into her throbbing vein.

As the light fades and her head grows heavy, she thinks of distances. How far could they have gone? she will murmur as her mind fills with images of forest groves and highways, and small paths along riverbeds, oceans and high mountains, and then the sky itself in all its cloudy glory.

And beyond that to the moon.

And back again.

Chapter six

Leah Rabinowitz Helfgott closed the living room windows and pulled the curtains against prying eyes. True, things were quiet this time of day, but you never knew what *yenta* might be passing through the streets of Boro Park looking up at windows. She pulled her robe around her and turned on the forbidden television set so frowned upon by the rabbis of the neighborhood. It was a fairly new addition to her household. Five years before, at the age of sixty-eight, she'd decided she needed a little entertainment. "At my age, what harm can it do? Will I go running to bars, start affairs with men?" she'd scolded her pious, scandalized husband, Yossi.

He was gone now—a good man—and she was left with the television and Mendel (he called himself Marco, her son) who lived Out West in *yenimssvelt* with the cowboys and was raising his children to be Yankee Doodles. He called twice a year. Came to visit once in a blue moon. Once, he brought her pictures of his blond wife, the cowgirl, who he claimed was a Jew from Montana (such a place had Jews?!) and his daughter Kristy (God should watch over us, such a name for a Jewish girl!) and his son Aryeh (they called him Liam—but she

39

couldn't remember that, so she remembered lion, and translated it into Hebrew) the skateboarder, rolling around on the streets, he should live and be well. She hardly knew them. He wasn't a bank robber, her son, and he didn't beat his wife. But he was a stranger to her, as strange as if he'd died, this Mendel-Marco person that had been born to her and her Yossi and brought up in the strictest tenets of their faith.

But as the Torah teaches, each man has the freedom to choose his way, and her son had chosen his own. She didn't understand it, but she couldn't say she was angry—at least not anymore. The anger and grief had passed. There were worse things that could happen to a child.

She sat down on the couch from which the plastic slipcovers had only recently been removed. For years she'd let her thighs stick to that gluey, transparent material in the hope of keeping the impractical white upholstery clean enough to impress her guests. But a few months ago she'd realized that she didn't have any guests. You know what the world says: when you laugh, the world laughs with you, but when you cry, you cry alone. Becoming a widow had chased most of her casual acquaintances away—the women in *shul* who invited them to kiddush, and expected to be feted in return; the women from Emunah who wanted her to help them fundraise…. And now, year after year, her close friends wound up in funeral homes, until so few were left it wasn't worth keeping up appearances.

She took her daughter Miriam's wedding picture off the table and dusted it a little, as she did every day. Elise looked just like her, the beautiful mother she had barely known. Such things a person has to live through. Such things in the world…A young mother goes to buy a coat at a factory outlet in Brooklyn one afternoon, a woman eight months pregnant with her second child, and not even late, not even dark yet! And on the way down the elevator, some animal…a teenager yet. He was sitting rotting in jail, a lot of good it did anyone. With her tax money, food they bought him.

She dusted off the picture, sighed and wiped a tear from the corner of her eye. Elise had been a year old. Her young son-in-law Moishe had sunk into a deep grief. But she had not let that happen to her.

Perhaps, she thought, her son-in-law had been horrified at her cool acceptance. Perhaps he'd thought her cold, unfeeling, that she was able to prepare chickens and stuff peppers and check the rice kernels one by one for hidden bugs. That she had been able to wash Elise's hair and teach her to sing Yiddish folk songs.

He had never begun to understand her, she knew. And how could she explain it to him, her nice, religious, American-born, yeshiva-boy son-in-law, so bookish and kind? There was no point, she thought, in talking, explaining, telling the old horror stories of Auschwitz. Instead, she'd let him think whatever he wanted of her. The important thing was that he raised his daughter in happiness. Because this was the only answer she'd ever found to evil: to go on living and to help others live in happiness. This was her only weapon—the one she'd used to fight all her wars. So, she'd helped to find a *shidduch*, a new wife, for her son-in-law—a rabbi's unwed daughter past her prime, willing to take on a young widower and his child. And at the wedding, which she arranged and paid for, she'd danced with the rest of them. No one had seen her tears.

Elise, Elise. My pride and joy, she thought, picking up the picture album that lay next to her prayer book.

When Elise had decided to move to Israel, her father and stepmother had been horrified, but she, Leah, had been prouder than anyone had a right to be. She'd made sure Elise had money. And when Elise found her young man and invited her to the wedding in Israel, for the first time in her life she'd found the courage to get on a plane, even though for her it was the same as being strapped into the space shuttle and hurtled toward the moon. She'd been back a second time for Ilana's birth, and when the new baby was born, she planned to fly in again. For the *bris*.

Of course it was going to be a boy. Elise already had a girl.

She turned the pages of the album. There was her son-in-law and his second wife—such a sweet girl. So nice. They'd been very happy together until Moishe's gentle heart, finally damaged beyond repair, had given out, not long ago. If he'd only survived, he would have gotten to know his granddaughter better, perhaps even held a boy child in his arms, a grandson. She shook her head.

She had no sympathy for weakness, physical or mental—convinced that health was a decision you made, not something that happened to you. It was too easy to give up. To lie back and be a victim. So much better to choose not to be one. So much better to fight, to live and to hope.

Ever since her granddaughter had settled in Israel, she had been glued to the news reports. NBC, ABC, CNN—all those blondes with the white teeth, all those *goyim* in the gray suits—she had no choice but to depend on them for the latest news. Not that she believed a word they said.

It was Waldo and Emily this afternoon, and that ugly, beefy, red-faced *shlub* (this you put on television? Someone a little handsomer you couldn't find?) reporting from Jerusalem. This morning they were showing aggravated Palestinians complaining about the long lines to get into Israel from the West Bank.

"Try to go on a ride in Disneyland, you'll see long lines," she informed the flickering images. They taught their children to be animals and murderers and blow themselves up, then were offended when people weren't so happy to see them, wanted them to please, pick up their shirts and take off their pants to check they didn't have ten tons of nails and a bomb in their underwear. Was that Israel's fault? Who told them to wear explosive underwear? "You don't want long lines? You want to walk into a country of decent people and no one should check you? Then go teach your children a little respect for human life. Why don't you tell them that, Waldo? Shame on you!" She wagged her finger at the assorted talking heads.

She put her hand over her heavily beating heart. Dr. Rosenbloom was right. These television shows were not for her. She shouldn't watch. She glanced malevolently at the dark screen of the Sony. Comes into my living room to kill an old Jew. Just like Hitler, she thought, walking heavily toward the china closet. She reached back past the silver candlesticks and the seven-branched menorah, taking out a silver *etrog* box in the shape of an ark. It was meant to hold a citron for the holiday of Succoth. So you used it maybe one week a year. The rest of the time, why should it go to waste?

She'd explained this to Joyce, the nice volunteer from Meals on Wheels who wanted to buy her one of those plastic boxes with the days of the week and times of the day on it to keep her pills. She didn't need it. She opened the silver cover, taking out the two green pills, and the big pink one—her heart medication. She knew exactly what day of the week it was, and the time: 2:00 P.M. in Boro Park and 9:00 P.M. in Jerusalem.

They'd be getting ready for bed just as she sat down to lunch. She wondered how Elise was feeling. But it wasn't her day to call. She called on Thursdays to wish her a good *Shabbes*. She glanced at the clock, trying to calculate if Elise would maybe call her. Once a week she called, bless her, although never at a regular time, so Leah could make sure she'd be home. But it was all right. She was home most of the time. Where did she have to go since the queen of England stopped inviting her?

God should just watch over her Elise, so dangerous it was now. So dangerous. The world was full of maniacs. You had wars, millions died, and fifty, sixty years later, again you were back with the same maniacs who found joy not in winning, but in killing. Winning was only the second prize.

She headed toward the kitchen and took a glass of tap water, swallowing the pills. From the corner of her eye, she saw a roach scurry behind the stove. I have to remember to tell the cleaning girl, she thought, shaking her head. She knew where the spray was, but the truth was, she hated to kill any living thing. A fly, a bug, even a mosquito. To take away a living spirit, to crush it…just the idea sickened her.

Life was such a precious thing, so fragile. And to give life, the most wonderful of miracles. Such a hard time she was having with her babies, Elise, but still she remembered to call. She remembered birthdays and holidays. God bless her, God bless her. She is the light in my life, Leah thought, she and Jon and Ilana. Her religious grandchildren and great-grandchild in Israel. Pioneers, building a Jewish country where no one could ever knock on the door and round up Jews and ship them off to the gas. A place where Jews could defend themselves. Only lately, they weren't doing a very good job…

Just thinking about her granddaughter and her husband made

her heart slow into a healthy, peaceful repose. Such a good person, he was. A *tzadik*. The way he gave out free medical advice, not like those puffed-up American doctors in *shul* a person could never stop and ask a question during kiddush after *Shabbes* prayers; who rolled their eyes and told a person to make an appointment.... Make an appointment! This was the only advice they gave out free.... And they called themselves Orthodox Jews.... Whether sugar-coated or marinated, an ignoramus is an ignoramus.

Jon was nothing like that. Such *naches*, her grandson-in-law, the doctor, she sighed, heading back to the now immensely comfortable couch in front of the television, her slippers shushing along the linoleum. I sound like an old lady, she thought. An old *kvetch*, that's what she'd become. Could you believe it? After all the incredible horrors and miracles she'd experienced, something as banal as old age would finally do her in, sapping her life, her strength, making her—ordinary.

She smiled. Except for another member of the Covenant (closer than family, than flesh and blood), no one would ever know the terrible irony of such an end to Leah Rabinowitz of Uzhorod: a boring, peaceful old age.

Not so fast, not so fast, that was all she asked of the kindly reaper who came in the form of placid sunrises and sunsets that nipped gently away at the precious remnants of her life, spiriting away pieces no larger than grains of hourglass sand, until her life would not be drained away, as much as transported, molecule by molecule, to another form of existence.

Not that she was—God forbid!—complaining. It was a blessing to go this way, she thought. And she should know. She was a connoisseur of death, a critic, having witnessed its endless faces and forms.

The worst were those that made you suffer while you waited, helplessly, for it to be over. This was why in the camps some people considered cyanide capsules such a treasure. Better than diamonds. They gave you the power to choose, to say when the suffering would end. The worst were those that came to people who weren't ready, who still felt life flowing through them like clear streams that could flip over boulders. To die unwillingly, with that feeling that you still had so much you wanted to do, so much that was still precious left behind—that was the worst.

Most had been spared that. They knew they had no one left to go back to. You could see it in their eyes, the light suddenly dimming, already reconciled, willing it to be over. In the camps, she could always tell just by looking at the eyes who was about to die. It had nothing to do with their weight, or disease—she had weighed forty pounds, suffered typhus and dysentery—it had to do with will; the desire to live on.

She wanted to live. She wanted to go to Israel to visit Elise and Jonathan. To bring Ilana bags of Hershey's candy kisses. (They will ruin her little teeth, and stain her clothes. She shrugged. Teeth you brushed. Clothes you washed. A child needed candy.) To be at the bris for the new baby or (in the unlikely event it was a girl) to attend the party the Israelis invented, the *Mesibat Bat*—the Girl Party.

She already had the trip all planned. She would pray at the Kotel, and stay in a nice room in the Sheraton Plaza and overeat glatt kosher food at their Saturday buffet. Such delicious food! And so much! She would talk to her great-granddaughter, her little *sabra*, in Hebrew, and teach her how to say a blessing over the rain and over thunder and lightning. For everything, she thought, there is a blessing. But no one bothered to teach children that.

She felt her stomach rumble. It was always the same. The green pills you needed to take an hour before eating, but she never remembered them until she was hungry for lunch. She flipped the channels. *Oprah* wouldn't be on for at least another hour.

She always spent her afternoons with Oprah. Such a good person. Not skinny, not white. She tried to help people. Overweight women, children caught in the middle of their trashy, divorced parents. Wild teenagers who gave their parents heartaches. Depressed housewives. Husbands who liked to watch dirty pictures on the computer. She always gave them good ideas, and she never made fun, although she often laughed with them, not at them (not like Jerry Springer—that disgrace to the Jewish people, such a show, such freaks). No, Oprah was sincere. You could hear that in a person's voice. And if there was one thing Leah Rabinowitz Helfgott had imbedded in her genetic makeup like a microchip, it was a phoniness detector. Most people set it off like a five-alarm fire.

Often she felt Oprah was speaking directly to her when she told women to cheer up, to write about what was happening in their lives, about their past, in order to help them—how did she say it: "Rekindle their spirit"?

Lately, she had often felt her spirit, her *neshamah*, sputtering like a day-long *yahrzeit* candle at the end of its twenty-third hour. The dark ghosts of her past often swept through the room, poking her with their annoying, inconsiderate fingers, prying loose the tears she had held back all these years; tears for her murdered parents and sister and nephew and brothers and daughter and for the grandchildren that had never been born; for the Jews of Israel, people she didn't know, black Ethiopians and blond Russians. They were all part of her blood, and they were being murdered and harassed and frightened....

Most of Oprah's solutions didn't really work for her. She'd tried jogging, but her feet began to hurt even before she crossed the street. She had tried using Oprah's "Favorite Things," but all those butter cookies and rich cocoa drinks clogged her plumbing. As for keeping a journal, she wasn't much of a writer, and her eyesight wasn't what it used to be. But she'd kept it all in her head.

That's why making the videotape for the Shoah Foundation, that movie director, that Spielberg, was such a good idea. That nice girl had asked the questions and a man had filmed everything, making a movie. After Leah had gotten over her disappointment that Spielberg himself wasn't going to be directing, it had all worked out fine. Often, early in the morning, she would watch the tape. She looked old and overweight, she thought, her face bloated and angry, not like herself at all. But sometimes she was surprised and secretly pleased at the things she heard herself say, things that brought back such memories. She slipped it in now. She had an hour to kill until she could eat or watch *Oprah*. She pressed play, staring at the screen, listening to herself describe the house in Uzhorod surrounded by woods and fields; the visit of the *tzadik* of Munkatsch who had come with his whole yeshiva and raised his hands above her head in blessing; her father baking Passover matzohs for the village, his beard dusted with flour;

baby Shmilu's blue sun hat left in her hands when Mengele sent him and her sister left, and her right.... And Esther, Maria, and Ariana, who had been with her in Auschwitz, saving her life countless times. Her three *block shvesters*, closer than sisters of flesh and blood, united forever by their experiences and their Covenant vows...

Never liked to talk about it. What was the point? Like opening a sewer cover, allowing all the filth, the degradation to send up its stench to pollute her life and the lives of those she loved. But now the world had gone mad again, denying the past, claiming the facts were not facts but a deliberate lie or an exaggeration. And people were such ignoramuses that they actually listened. If we don't open our mouths now, before we die, then we let the liars win, she'd told the others.

Esther was making her tape now, already planning the big party they'd have when all four tapes were done. She shook her head fondly. Esther and her big cosmetics company and her big parties, her Hollywood parties. Like Zsa Zsa, with all that fancy makeup and the fancy clothes. But maybe it would be fun. She hadn't seen Ariana or Maria for years. A reunion, to see what it had all come to, all their struggles for life; where they'd all ended up, close to the end of their incredible journey.

She didn't add: and if it had all been been worth it.

She heard the phone ringing. For no reason, a small dart of fear pierced her calm and she thought, without hesitation: Elise.

Chapter seven

Hadassah Hospital, Jerusalem
May 6, 2002 · 11:40 P.M.

B*ubbee?*" Elise whispered. "I need to talk to you."

The effect of the sedatives still coursing through her veins gave her a sense of floating on water. She looked at her watch. It was almost midnight. *Why did I do this?* she thought, listening to her grandmother's urgent stream of exclamations and questions. She was filled with sudden panic. So many people had offered to make this call for her: her neighbors from Maaleh Sara, Jon's friends from the hospital, the sweet young social worker from the army, a very nice English-speaking policeman...So many people were out there wanting to help, her doctors told her. There was a news blackout, but of course everyone knew anyhow.

Israel was like one big family, she thought. There was one, maybe two degrees of separation. All it took was for the ambulance driver to mention it to his girlfriend, one soldier to tell his mother, a nurse to call her sister...News about the attack had spread like a brush fire all over the country. Hundreds surrounded the hospital, waiting for news.

Why, then, she wondered, did she feel so alone?

"*Bubbee*, something terrible has happened," she repeated tonelessly. She heard her grandmother's sharp intake of breath. "No…not a miscarriage. The baby is fine. I'm fine…" Her throat contracted painfully. "*Bubbee*—"

How am I going to tell her this? She, of all people? How do you break this news to anyone, especially a survivor with a heart condition? But it couldn't be helped. She'd hear it on CNN soon enough.

Elise felt her breath stick in her lungs, refusing to leave her body, giving her the sensation of choking. She had never had asthma, and it frightened her. It was the beginning of something new, she realized, some bodily reaction that was now going to be part of her life, something she would learn to live with. A friend in college had once described similar symptoms. She'd called it a panic attack.

I can't do this, she understood. I can't finish this call.

"Wait," she wheezed into the phone, putting her palm over the receiver. "Please, Nurse, call Ruth, Ruth Silver…outside…"

Why had she chosen Ruth, she wondered, regretting it immediately. The truth was, she didn't really want Ruth, not really. She didn't want someone she knew and liked to see and remember her at this moment in her life, committing it to memory. She didn't want any witnesses. She was in the process of a metamorphosis, evolving moment by moment. Like some B-movie about an ordinary person injected with the serum of a mad scientist, she might, at any moment, turn into a homicidal maniac, or a wolf man, or simply, she thought, disappear altogether. She couldn't bear the face of pity, confirmation that she was pitiable, from a friend, a neighbor.

"Ruth, it's my *Bubbee*. Please…I…please, Ruth…"

Ruth took the phone, her dark eyes wet. Elise turned her face to the wall.

"Mrs. Helfgott? *Bubbee* Leah? This is Ruth Silver, I'm a friend of your granddaughter…Oh yes, that's right. Daphna's mother, from Maaleh Sara. I'm fine, fine…*Bubbee* Leah…First, let me tell you that Elise is fine. She's under a doctor's care. But Jon and Ilana…"

It isn't fair, Elise thought. It isn't right for me to ask this of her. Of anyone.

"…were riding home from her ballet recital, and their car…"

Elise listened as if hearing this for the first time. So it was all true then. Not a nightmare. Others could not have had the same bad dream…or could they? Unless this too was just part of a dream…

"—No, *Bubbee* Leah, please, just let me finish…"

Elise took a sudden deep breath and grabbed the phone. "*Bubbee*, they are not dead! We don't know what happened to them. The car was hit with bullets, but they weren't in the car. They've just disappeared. I don't know any more, *Bubbee*…*Bubbee*, I'm going to put a policeman on the phone, someone who knows English. He's going to explain what he can, the details—"

She stopped, listening intently to what her grandmother was saying. "A person can live through anything, Elise. Remember that," her grandmother told her.

Elise felt a sharp stab of sudden anger. What was that supposed to mean? That no matter what happened to Jon and Ilana, that she, Elise, would be all right!? she thought, furious. No, that's not it. That's not what she meant, Elise understood with a sudden flash of insight.

Years in Auschwitz surrounded by corpses, medical experiments, starvation, torture; living when millions around her had died. A fourteen-year-old girl with no one to help her…Her *Bubbee*'s own survival was living proof that a person could never predict with absolute certainty what was going to happen to them. No matter how horrible your situation seemed, there was always the chance that you would be the one to somehow, miraculously, come through it, living to see great-grandchildren and die peacefully in your bed. Like people who overcome a list of terrible medical complications, or people who walk to safety out of plane wrecks in snow-covered mountains. Or like her *Bubbee*'s three friends who went on from Auschwitz to found a cosmetics fortune, run a famous nightclub and overthrow a Communist regime…. Living proof, she thought, listening to her grandmother's soft voice whispering comfort and prayers, that no matter what Jon and Ilana were faced with, there was still hope. No matter how bad it looked, they could be the ones…the ones who survive.

"Thank you, *Bubbee*," she whispered.

She didn't feel alone anymore.

Chapter eight

Th
he videographer is just changing to a new tape," the interviewer from the Shoah Foundation explained.

"No hurry, darling. Take your time," Esther Gold said graciously, dreading it. Tiny and imperious, she sat stiffly upright in her uncomfortable antique Louis XIV chair, queen of a vast estate whose circular driveway, manicured lawns, and beautiful, generous rooms framed her with the exquisite simplicity and beauty of a diamond circle pin.

Nervously, she fidgeted with the stunning string of perfectly matched black pearls around her neck and straightened the skirt of her chic gray suit. As she moved her arms, the interviewer's eyes couldn't help being drawn to the shocking tattoo of blue numbers that flashed out through the row of fashionable gold bangles that laddered up her arm.

As the head of a huge cosmetics firm, Esther Gold was used to interviews. In fact, she loved to talk about her rags-to-riches story as a new immigrant, never tiring of the tale of how she had gotten a cousin with the run-down hair pomade lab in the Bronx to make up a batch of her mother's face cream recipe; and how she had sold it customer to customer in beauty parlors, and then at Hadassah conventions, until finally convincing the big department stores to take it on. How she'd met her husband, Solly, a Dachau survivor, who was supposed to cater her wedding, and married him instead of the American groom…. She'd told these stories a million times, and loved every minute. Even the first tape for the foundation had been all right, all the good times, before the war. Now the real torture would begin; opening the coffins, dragging out all the decayed corpses of those obscene memories she had spent all these years trying to put behind her; telling all those things she had never shared with anyone, especially not her family.

Think about the party afterward, she told herself, the celebration, when all four tapes are finally done. How lovely it will be to see everyone, to meet all the children, grandchildren, and great-grandchildren, gathered together for the first time from the four corners of the earth. To see what it all came to, this will to live through the worst of times. And this was the time to do it. Before heart conditions, diabetes, or breast cancer snuffed out the possibility. They were all going in one direction, and it was irreversible.

What about making it in the Beverly Wilshire? she mused. Or why not here, in the backyard, in the tropical garden? There was plenty of room in the house to accommodate everyone for a few days…weeks…even months! Maria's grandson, who'd recently graduated film school and was making documentaries, would have a great time in L.A. She could introduce him around. And Leah's granddaughter Elise with her nice doctor husband and their little *sabra* and the new baby due in a month or two, had never seen California. How lovely it would be to have little kids running around again, making noise, tracking up the Aubusson, putting sticky little fingers on the polished antiques, giving this museum a little life…she thought, looking at her pristine living room.

Only last night she'd dreamed about her own granddaughter. The dream had started with a knock on the door. When she'd looked through the peephole, Elizabeth had been standing there, angry and impatient, wheeling a baby carriage while two little ones clutched her side. And when Esther had opened to let her in, Elizabeth had shouted angry accusations and explanations at her. Instead of defending herself, she'd just gathered her granddaughter into her arms and cried and cried and cried.

It had felt so incredibly real.

She dabbed her eyes with a handkerchief, getting black mascara on the Belgian lace. Her daughter Marietta, Elizabeth's mother, had dealt with the situation much better than she had. Marietta and Elizabeth were not only in touch, but mother and daughter saw each other every few months—although Marietta couldn't actually travel to visit Elizabeth; they didn't let Jews into Saudi Arabia.

From the pictures Marietta had brought over, the children were beautiful, with Elizabeth's blue-green eyes, and her husband's black hair and swarthy complexion. Beautiful Elizabeth. How she longed to see her!

But even if she could bring herself to invite her granddaughter, would Elizabeth agree to come? And if she did, would she insist on bringing the Arab with her? She felt her blood pressure rise and her face flush at the thought of one of her offspring, a convert to Islam....

The interviewer coughed politely, leaning forward. "Ready?"

"No! Wait. Give me a mirror, Morrie," she called out.

"Gran...really!"

Whatever they said about Morrie not being the brightest star, he was her favorite; her choice to take over the company when she died. She kept him by her side.

"I just want to check if my mascara streaked."

"Gran, don't worry about it. This is not going to be broadcast on the Fashion Channel. It's for history."

"Everything you do when you are seventy-five and the head of Elizabeth Estay Cosmetics is for history, Morrie."

"Seventy-eight, Gran," he murmured, handing her a mirror.

She eyed herself, taking in her still remarkably unlined complexion, the lovely blue eyes, the beautifully cut silver hair.

"He never lets me get away with anything, do you Morrie?" she said with a sidelong glance and the barest of smiles. "All right, all right.

Seventy-eight. But even when I'm one hundred and twenty, lying in that expensive, silk-lined oak box, I still want people to look at me and say: 'That Esther Gold! I should only look as good alive as she does dead. Maybe I should buy her creams and potions...' When the time comes, I could be a great advertisement, Morrie. Don't forget."

She handed him back the mirror.

He looked pained. "Really, Gran..."

A small, wicked smile curled the ends of her perfectly made-up lips. "What do you think of this color?" she asked, turning to the interviewer, pouting. "Just in from the laboratory. They don't even have a name for it yet," she said, taking in the young woman's pale lips and colorless cheeks, her ringless fingers with their chewed-off nails. Hearing these horror stories day after day would take the curl out of anyone's lashes. Still..."You are a lovely young lady. You should pardon me, but you should take time from your important work to be nice to yourself. Put on a little moisturizer, some mascara, blush..."

"Really, Gran..." Morrie protested.

"I know what you think. Frivolous. Vain. But sometimes a woman's looks can be a matter of life and death. In Auschwitz, I taught the other members of the Covenant to use machine grease to darken our lashes, and blood to rouge our cheeks to make us look healthier. To avoid selections. With good cosmetics, you can even flirt with the Angel of Death..." She sighed.

"The Covenant?" The interviewer asked, intrigued.

"Have you ever read the Bible, my dear?"

"For my Bat Mitzvah."

"Do you remember the covenant God made with Abraham? It was more than a promise. It was an everlasting bond, an agreement that couldn't be broken: 'Unto thy seed have I given this land...' Believe me, some of the Jews are sorry they ever agreed. They wish God would pick another people to be the Chosen Ones for the next few thousand years...But that's just too bad. You agree, and that's it. That's what the four of us called it, the agreement we made in Auschwitz between ourselves: a Covenant. You can't get out of it—not

like what my lawyers put in my contracts—there's no 'escape clause.'"
She chuckled. "Believe me, it hasn't been easy."

"What did you four agree to do?"

"Ah. I'll get to it. I'll get to it."

They had managed to keep it a secret for almost sixty years.

"Would it be all right if we got going again, Mrs. Gold? I know
your time is very valuable and we appreciate your being involved in
this import—"

She held up her hand. "Just ask." She clasped her hands
together, the knuckles turning white from the grip. "And I'll try to
remember."

"All right then." The woman nodded to the cameraman, who
started the camera rolling. "Let's continue. You had just finished telling us about your childhood, before the war."

*Did I tell it right? Did I explain the golden summer days swim-
ming in bright green lakes as clear as crystal? The falls and winters up in
the mountains, skiing? The evenings sitting beside Father on the garden
swing, with him singing Hungarian folk songs in his rich baritone? Wak-
ing up in a room filled with feather beds, and handmade dolls imported
from Germany and France? The feeling of being loved and privileged and
happy and safe, part of a world that was infinitely generous? Infinitely
compassionate and fair?*

"What is your first memory of when things began to change?"

*In the blink of an eye, Adam and Eve banished from Eden. Had
they also wondered if they'd dreamt it?*

"That was in 1940. In our Hungarian village, Jewish men were
called up for forced labor. Until then, we didn't even realize we were
Jews. Father was spared because he was a war hero, but my brothers
were taken. And then, in 1942, Admiral Hrothy's gendarmes came
to the store. They wrote down everything we had. Soon after, they
boarded it up and took my father away." Her voice grew husky. "I
never saw him again."

"Would you like to stop for a minute?" the interviewer asked
gently.

Esther looked at the young face suffused with understanding

and sympathy: no makeup in the world can make a face so beautiful, she thought gratefully. "No, thank you darling. Let's just keep going..." She waved away the glass of water Morrie held out to her, touching his face. "It's all right. All right."

She took a deep breath. "It was just me and Mother. My brothers were already in labor camps. I remember the day they forced us out of our house. Our own foreman did it. The one my father had trusted most."

The streets, lined with friends and neighbors, people who had worked for her good father, people who had asked for his help, asked for food, clothing, loans, and had never been turned away. Their smug, satisfied faces. Couldn't they have at least shed a few tears?

"The train took us to the central ghetto. They took us into an interrogation room and..." She mopped her forehead. "I'll need that drink now, Morrie..." She waved the water away impatiently. "Double vodka, and don't be cute." The liquid burned down her throat.

"They took me into an interrogation room," she repeated hoarsely.

The fat gendarme with the filthy fingers and the leering mouth. Her skirt lifted, his fingers inside, searching for jewels. A young girl...But you don't die of shame. Only one thing kills you, only one: death. Everything else, you can survive.

"And then, they took my mother."

Mother, whose white hands painted watercolors, who sat at the head of a gracious table speaking of French cinema and Russian literature...

She balled her fingers into a fist. "They molested me. And I knew what my mother was in for. I wanted to grab the guards. To stick my fingers in their eyes, to scratch their faces bloody! But I knew if I did, they would torture and kill us both. I was helpless."

Can she, can any American, conceive of that? Even begin to understand?

Totally helpless.

"I just sat there and waited. When she came out of that room—*how can I explain it?*—it was as if she was already in another world. I knew then that the horrors I was about to face would be unimaginable. But at least, I thought, I wouldn't be alone. I still had my mother.

"We were shoved into boxcars. Each moment, she seemed to grow smaller and paler, almost translucent. She was fading in front of my eyes. I begged her to hold on, but I could see she didn't hear me. And then, suddenly, on the third day without food or water, she turned to me with this otherworldly light in her eyes: 'Live,' she said. 'Teach my grandchildren that...that...human beings are capable of infinite glory.'"

She sat silently, her head bowed, staring at her lap. Her chin trembled as she took deep breaths of the sweet, clean air of her own perfumed home.

Mother.

"I'm sorry, but I have to interrupt. Gran..."

"Not now, Morrie!"

"Gran. It's your friend Leah from Brooklyn."

"Leah? Rabinowitz?" She looked at her watch. "Listen, tell her I'm finally doing the tape. Tell her I'll call her right back. She'll understand."

"Will you excuse us a moment?" he said to the interviewer and cameraman.

"Morrie, this is the reason that people complain about you. You don't listen..."

"Gran!"

She stared at him, her annoyance giving way to alarm.

He took her arm and tucked it through his, helping her out of the chair and over to the phone. "It's Leah's granddaughter, Elise. There's been a terrorist attack. Elise's husband, her child..."

Esther felt a sudden vulnerable space open inside her body, a place that she had kept closed so tight, made so hard over the years. A soft, fleshy spot began to throb, naked and exposed.

This couldn't happen. This was a new world. A world all her work had made safe and comfortable for those she loved. She wouldn't permit it to happen.

"Give me that phone...Leah? My God, my God!" Esther put her

hand over the phone and hissed to Morrie: "Get me Dr. Shavaunpaul at Sloan-Kettering in Manhattan on your cell phone. Use his private pager number and tell him it's me and it's an emergency—

"Leah. This is not like you..." I thought you had no tears left, Leah, my Leah.

Morrie motioned to her urgently. "The doctor's on the phone."

She reached out for it. "Leah, go lay down. My doctor's coming over. Go lay down. Go! What use will you be to Elise otherwise? Take your medicine and lay down. Of course you'll go to Israel, to be with her. Of course, we all will. But now go lay down, so you'll have the strength. Good-bye. I'm hanging up, Leah. Good-bye. Yes. Go, go."

She grabbed the cell phone out of Morrie's hand: "Doctor? Esther Gold, of Estay Cosmetics. Yes, of course.... I've been giving that cardiac intensive care unit you wrote me about a lot of thought.... But I'm actually calling for another reason. I have a friend in New York, not far from you, with a heart condition..."

Her grandson listened, amazed and appalled as his grandmother wheedled and bullied the world-famous heart specialist into making a house call.

"Morrie. Send a car to pick up the doctor and take him to Leah's. And isn't there some kind of private agency that negotiates the release of kidnap victims? Find out, Morrie. And get them on the phone...maybe send the plane to pick them up..."

"Now, Gran..."

"And we need to tell Maria...and Ariana..." She suddenly remembered the interview.

"Oh, the Shoah Foundation people..."

"I've already spoken to them. They understood. They'll reschedule."

"Did you give her a box of samples?"

"I gave them both a box of samples."

She sighed. "You're a big help to me, Morrie."

"Thank you. Now I want you to sit back and listen to me," he said with authority.

"I don't have time…" She stood up.

He pushed her gently back into her chair. "Gran, be realistic. First of all, there's no evidence they've actually been kidnapped…"

"Don't go there, Morrie. Just don't."

"All right, calm down. Okay. Let's say they are alive and well and ransom demands suddenly do surface. These Islamic terrorists aren't going to ask for money, like the South American kidnappers. They've got money, and plenty of it. They'll make political demands, or try to get their terrorist friends out of jail…. In either case, you won't be able to satisfy them. In the end, the army will have to deal with it. Don't you trust the Israeli army?"

"Yes. But I don't trust Israeli politicians."

"Why not?" he said, surprised.

"Because they're like all politicians. Jon and Ilana's lives won't be their only consideration in sending in the army to rescue them. They'll have to decide what the UN will say, or what CNN will broadcast, and what headlines will be in *The L.A. Times*…. I want my own army, which takes orders from me. And I can afford it."

He allowed himself a small smile, then became completely serious. He knelt down beside her, holding her trembling hands and looking into her flashing eyes. "Gran. With all the goodwill and all the money in the world, you aren't going to be able to do anything. You're helpless."

She flung off his hands, bolting upright, all five feet of her shaking with fury. He stepped back, alarmed.

"What do you know about helpless? You want helpless? What about being fifteen years old and weighing forty pounds and waiting outside at a train station in subzero weather all tarted up in a summer dress stolen from some murdered woman? And all around you are beastly armed guards, and their vicious barking dogs, and you know that when the train comes in, you are going to get a one-way ticket to the most horrible death imaginable to any woman? You talk to me, to *me*, about *helpless situations?*"

"Gran…I just…meant…" He stuttered.

"Listen to me, Morrie: those days are over, the days of *helpless*. You see this house? The furniture? You think I worked so hard for this?

Got rich for this? This could burn down tomorrow, it wouldn't mean a thing to me. No. Everything I ever did in my life was to make sure those days were over. Do you understand me, Morrie?!" Her body trembled. "Do you have any idea who Leah Rabinowitz is? What she did for me?" She took a deep breath, fingering her pearls. Her eyes narrowed. "We are going to find Jonathan Margulies. We are going to find Ilana. And we are going to do everything humanly possible to bring them back to Elise and Leah. Is that clear?"

He nodded, taking the phone from her white shaking hands. He dialed.

Chapter nine

Ben Gurion Airport, Lod
Tuesday, May 7, 2002 · 6:30 A.M.

J ulia Greenberg struggled to pull her suitcase off the conveyer belt.

"Need some help?" Sean Morrison offered, his one neat valise already draped competently over his shoulder.

"Thanks, but I can manage," she murmured without gratitude, giving the case a yank and sending it to the floor. Men were always looking for some signs of weakness when a blonde showed up as a foreign correspondent in a war zone. Let them look, she thought, tossing her carefully straightened light-blond mane over her shoulder. What they'd see were her tracks in the dust as they struggled to keep up with her.

Her last war assignment had been in Sarajevo. What those poor Muslims had suffered. She looked around at the crowd of natives, her eyes sympathetically drawn to the women in traditional head scarves, the men in *kaffiyehs*. She had an automatic respect for Third World religions and customs, which she felt had a certain ethnic purity and simplicity simply by virtue of their foreignness. Most liberal westerners did. Minorities were naturally to be defended and championed, the poorer the better, the less powerful the more sympathetic.

This "Jews-as-underdog" thing was really old. More important, it was boring. Here you had one of the most powerful armies in the Middle East, people who had the A-bomb, and they were still trying to cash in on the worn David and Goliath myth with markers they felt they had left over from the Holocaust. It was such a cliché. Besides, she had personally heard enough whining about the Holocaust to last her. Hitler killed twenty million Russians. Did you ever hear a Russian whine about it, build museums, make a fuss, give out guilt trips?

Lifting her eyelash between her fingers, she removed a piece of caked mascara. What I must look like, she thought, wishing the last suitcase would show up already so she could get to a bathroom mirror. Ah, there it was, her enormous pullman chugging down the conveyer belt, its worn tan leather covered with stickers from all over the world. She braced her shapely, weight-resistance-trained arms, grabbed the thick black handles and tugged.

It was not impressed.

Tightening her grip, she gnawed on her lips with determination as she ran alongside the case, yanking with all her might. "Sorry, excuse me," she repeated, bumping into people, stepping on toes, knocking shoulder to shoulder, her tone more put upon than apologetic. What, after all, did she have to be sorry about? Trying to do her job?

This was the way Julia Greenberg had been doing things all her life. Her way, or no way. She continued halfway around the carousel, until finally, a shwarma and pita-fed Israeli with beefy arms and a handlebar mustache simply pushed her aside, taking the suitcase off the belt with one hand and heaving it down beside her.

She could almost feel Sean's cynical, amused eyes burning through her back.

"Thanks," she murmured through stretched lips.

The Israeli smiled expansively. "*Bevakasha, motek.*"

She looked him over, taking in the uncouth tufts of black chest hair peeking through an unbuttoned shirt collar, open-toed sandals and scruffy toenails. She cringed. *Motek* meant sweetie. That much she knew. He was exactly what she'd been led to expect. Despite her name, this was Julia Greenberg's first visit to Israel. The ancestral wave of feeling that had briefly washed over her parents, sending them to the Holy Land as part of some Reform Temple group tour, had not even moistened her. Her mother had returned with dreadful stories about pushy, dishonest cabdrivers, and cheating souvenir dealers in desert roadstops, her only kind words for the ancient Bedouin camel driver who'd given her a ride. Her father, of course, had been just the opposite, waxing with typical enthusiasm over Israel's wonderful agricultural miracles, water desalinization plants, and the marvelous antiquities—hardly stuff teenage girls find sexy.

Her understanding of the country was based on a general knowledge of history of the region, colored by a long conversation over drinks with a BCN on-air correspondent who had done a stint in Jerusalem. Israelis, he'd told her, were unbelievably arrogant and unfriendly. The men were all chauvinists and the women classless loudmouths, especially the fawning Peace Now types, who thought they and Europe were now going to be one big, happy family after they'd embraced Oslo and thrown the Palestinians a few crumbs. The idiots.

The last correspondent, the one she was replacing, was a florid Liverpudlian who loved to use expressions like "Hebrews," and "Jewess," had insisted all Jews really wanted were the Arabs shot or transferred. He'd ignored the turmoil of unrest between different Israeli factions over the Oslo Accords, broadcasting piece after piece showing Arab women struggling down dusty roads lugging small children and baskets of whatever, with Israeli soldiers in tanks in the background; shots of Muslims at prayer, contrasted to Israeli settlers turning over tomato stands in Hebron. More than once, he'd had himself filmed taking off his shoes and bowing respectfully toward Mecca.

The network executives, eager to sell Saudi Arabia, Bahrain, and Abu Dhabi their new BCN-Arabic language subsidiary, had loved it. But eventually, a flood of angry letters and e-mails accusing them of pro-Arab bias, and worse, anti-Semitism, combined with an alarming drop in advertising revenues from American companies who, post–September 11, didn't appreciate the gung-ho tone of the pro-Islamic rhetoric, had convinced them to pull him.

Julia understood that they weren't so much sending her as much as they were sending a *Greenberg*. But she was savvy enough to take her opportunities when and where she found them. If Greenberg gave her a leg up, why in heaven's name should that be a problem, after all the times it had done just the opposite? Whatever anyone thought, she was here on her own terms, to tell the truth as she saw, understood, and experienced it, without prejudice. One of her favorite reporters was Suzanne Goldenberg of the *Guardian*, who had done an outstanding job of changing people's view of British Jewish journalists reporting on the Middle East. Her pieces on the poor, brave mothers of suicide bombers, and on West Bank Jihad museums paying homage to martyrs, had won her an award, which she richly deserved. She had proven wrong all the naysayers who thought she couldn't overcome her racial and cultural bias. She had more than overcome it; she had defeated it completely.

She too felt herself liberated from any bias in favor of the Jewish State, which had been pushed down her throat since childhood at endless, boring holiday dinners full of tiresome relatives and at Hebrew school classes whose primary accomplishment had been to permanently douse any desire or interest on her part to explore her heritage and religion.

What she had tried to do her entire life was distance herself from family bugaboos, the smarmy heartstring tug of imagined ties to groups she had no interest in and felt no connection to. She'd always chosen her friends from those most outside her own family circle. It was her way of reaching out to the world, of fighting prejudice and racial stereotyping, which had dogged her steps ever since she could remember. Her friends were from India and the Caribbean Islands; from Azerbaijan and Pakistan. She was familiar with the rites for Vishnu and for Russian Orthodox Christmas mass. Words like "Yom Kippur" and "Chanukah," however, made her gag, although she couldn't tell why. Something to do with being forced to undergo the strange initiation trials to enter a club in which she had no interest in becoming a member.

Who was she? She was a journalist. An objective journalist. Neither the network's unsubtle hints to continue the "good work" of her predecessor nor her family's synagogue membership was going to influence her in the least.

She loaded the pullman onto a cart and wheeled it toward the bathroom, checking her face in the mirror and doing the necessary repairs. Then she headed for the exit, ignoring the customs inspectors, until one tapped her lightly on the shoulder and politely requested she pull over and open her bag.

They took out the video camera, the tape recorder. "I'm a journalist," she said calmly. "It's for my personal use."

"Journalist?" the customs man said thoughtfully. "Can I see your passport? Your press identification?" She watched him examine the documents. "Julia Greenberg? Is that you?"

"Yes," she answered.

"Write good things about us," he smiled, waving her through.

Sean, who had also been pulled over, and who was still in the middle of having every nook and cranny of his luggage minutely explored by the customs men, gave her a knowing look filled with accusation, as well as envy. She blushed, wheeling her cart out through the sliding doors.

The presumption of brotherhood killed her. She looked forward anxiously to clearing her name. Her eyes panned the crowd of milling foreign strangers. To her relief, she saw someone holding up a cardboard sign with her name on it.

She went quickly in that direction. "Hi. I'm Julia."

"How are you?" the man said with extreme courtesy. "I'm your driver, Ismael. Mr. Duggan, the bureau chief, is outside waiting in the car. Is Sean with you?"

"Yes. He's still going through customs."

He nodded, taking her cart. He had a gentle face, she thought, with a fine black mustache and a swarthy complexion. Sort of an Omar Sharif type.

"You are thirsty, perhaps?"

She was, actually. "A bit."

"Coke?"

"Diet, please." She nodded gratefully. He went off to get it. By the time he returned, Sean had shown up.

"They went through every sock, sniffed my aftershave, opened up my tin of biscuits." He shook his head. He smiled at her with irony. "I suppose being a Greenberg sometimes has its advantages."

She saw Ismael shoot her a curious, sideways glance and blink as he handed her the cold drink. It's just a name, an accident of birth, she wanted to explain, almost apologize. I am your friend, a friend to your people, please believe me. Perhaps one of your best. But for now, she realized, there was nothing she could do. When her reports were aired, they would speak for themselves. Everyone would see who Julia Greenberg was and where her loyalties lay. People would have to admit they'd misjudged her and thought unfairly of her, based simply on ethnic stereotyping.

She followed Ismael and her luggage out to the parking lot.

"Julia." A tall, jowly, rather boozy-looking middle-aged man emerged from a tan Honda Accord parked illegally near the curb. He advanced toward her, hand extended.

"Mr. Duggan. Jack." She smiled, grasping her boss' hand firmly and looking into his eyes with conviction, just as she'd learned in her "Dress for Success" seminars.

He took her hand into both of his and patted it. "Jesus, it's hot in this godforsaken shithole. Let's get into the air-conditioning, shall we? How are you doing, Sean?" he said over her shoulder. "All restocked on the duty-free booze?"

"You know I am." The two men laughed, a secret, male-bonding laugh, Julia thought, paranoid.

"How have things been, Jack?"

"Oh, a settler's brat got herself shot," the bureau chief answered. "And then the IDF went in and demolished someone's house. You know. The usual."

"How old was she, and how did she get herself shot?" Julia asked.

"Well, she was two months old and her parents are Jews who insist on living in Hebron…"

"Two months old? You mean they shot a baby in a carriage?!" she said in horror. She saw Ismael's eyes focus on her curiously, as if waiting to come to some decision. She blinked, uncomfortable.

"Well, if her carriage hadn't been there—" Jack began. His cellular phone rang. "Hello? Okay. Where? Okay. No, I think I'll cover this one myself."

"What's up?" Sean pressed.

The bureau chief shrugged, putting his hand over the mouthpiece. "A settler's car. Father's a doctor, his five-year-old daughter…"

"Who could have done it?" Julia cocked her head, already forgetting her shock about the "got herself shot" when it concerned a two-month-old; already willing to accommodate the phrase. She was nothing if not adaptable.

Being a Jew and a woman in genteelly anti-Semitic male chauvinist British journalism, it was a necessity. Her ideas, beliefs, convictions were…flexible. She had no choice, at this stage in her career, but to keep her nose to the wind to see which way it was blowing, whatever the smell…. With every conversation, she'd sock away more information that would be useful to her advancement. It was not a question of ideology. She believed in telling the truth. It was simply office politics, she told herself, being sensible, paying your dues. Once she became famous and indispensable, she would use her stature to champion the underdog, pierce the balloons of self-righteous crap that went for news these days. But right now, she had no choice but to play along. Because there was only one thing Julia Greenberg could not accommodate at this stage in her budding career: failure.

The two men exchanged expressionless glances.

"Who do you think could have done it, Jack? Should we venture a wild guess? It wasn't the IRA…" Sean guffawed.

"Take your pick, Julia: Tanzim, Hamas, Islamic Jihad…" Jack continued.

"Are they dead?" she asked calmly, taking out a cigarette and lighting it.

"Not exactly…"

Her eyes widened. "Injured?"

"Well, not exactly. It's sort of a mystery."

How many ways could this story go? She shrugged, thinking maybe he had started drinking a little too early. She took out her notebook and began to write. "What are the Israelis saying? Not that

I believe them, of course." She exhaled, taking in with delight the look of surprise on the faces of the men at her toughness.

"Hamas terrorists. Izzedine al-Qassam Brigade," Jack murmured.

"I've really wanted to do an extensive interview with those people. You know, find out what makes them tick; get the rage and frustration from their angle. Talk to their mothers and sisters and wives. See their homes in the refugee camps, what the Israelis have done to them…Do you have any contacts I could use?" she asked.

The men stared. "Well, right now the story is about the attack."

"But if no one was killed…?"

"I didn't say that. I said it was a bit of a mystery. They found the car riddled with bullets last night, but they didn't find any bodies."

She sat back. How awful, she thought. The poor mother…She chewed on her pencil nub. "Can we go straight to the scene?"

"Don't you want to 'freshen up' first, dear?" Sean grinned.

"No, but if you're tired, perhaps we can drop you off and continue on without you, isn't that right, Jack?"

"What did you say your name was, luv?" Jack asked.

Chapter ten

W here are we going now?" Julia asked as the car careened down back roads thickly lined with olive and carob trees, dotted with an occasional ramshackle stone house. The tan Honda Accord bumped along like a drunk on roller skates, and she found herself pressed uncomfortably close to the beefy thighs that pressed in on either side of her.

"Where do you think, dearie?" Sean Morrison said charmlessly.

"I haven't a clue, *dearie*," she retorted, holding down her car sickness. "I assume to where they found the car…"

"What would be the point of that?" Jack shrugged. "The information has just been released, but it happened last night."

"Last night? So, that means the Israelis have probably cleared away anything newsworthy by now…"

"We've got our own sources of information, Julia." Jack nodded with a cryptic smile.

She was stunned. "Do you mean…you know more than the Israelis? You've gotten inside information? How?"

"Well, let's just say that we have a good working relationship with all the concerned parties in the area." Jack grinned, patting Ismael on the shoulder. The driver looked into the rearview mirror and smiled tensely.

"Isn't this dangerous? I mean, you *are* coordinating with the Israeli security forces, aren't you?" Julia demanded. She watched all three men exchange amused glances.

"Right. The IDF, our old pals. Think we should call and let them know we're coming, Ismael?"

The driver shook his head, and the two men roared.

Jack Duggan caught himself. "Sorry. But you'll get the hang of the way things work here, dear. We get exclusive information exactly because we aren't pals with the IDF."

"But your sources, are they Fatah, Hamas, Islamic Revolution, Al Aksa Martyr's Brigade...? Who are we dealing with? And how do you know that once we get there we won't be ambushed and shot?"

Sean made a serious face. "Gee, Jack. It's such a good thing Julia here was transferred, just in the nick of time to save us from ourselves."

She felt her face redden. "It's so kind of you, Sean, to establish the ground rules so quickly and succinctly for me. Now, let me get this straight. You, are an asshole. Have I got that right? And any intelligent question I ask is going to be met with your charming male excess of testosterone? So far so good?" She turned to the bureau chief. "Help me out here, Mr. Duggan."

The older man shifted uncomfortably. "Jack," he corrected her.

"Jack," she repeated stonily.

"No need to get your feathers ruffled, Ms. Goldberg," he murmured, looking out the window. "Keep your sense of humor."

"*Greenberg.* I know all Orientals with the slanty eyes look exactly the same, and all black people, and all kikes, but there are differences."

"What...!?" Duggan gasped.

"Greenberg. Not Goldberg."

"Oh. Sorry. But as far as helping you out, dear, it doesn't look to me as if you need any." He tried a tentative smile.

"Look, Jack." Her tongue pressed the inside of her cheek for control. "I was in Sarajevo. I went through those Croatian roadblocks, and those Bosnian-Serb roadblocks.... All I want is some kind of understanding of where we are headed right now, okay?"

"Look, Julia. This isn't Sarajevo. I know it looks like Israelis against Palestinians, but it's not that simple. We're here to understand the Palestinian side, and that is complicated. Our informants are a mixture of all those groups. Of course, that means we take chances, but so far we have been able to get to the scene of every important demonstration, flashpoint, and attack way ahead of the competition," he said haughtily.

The words sunk in slowly. "Do you mean to say that you have advance notice of terrorist activity from the terrorists groups themselves?"

Jack Duggan didn't smile. "If you ever intimate such a thing, Ms. Greenberg or Blackberg or Redberg, you'll be on the next plane back to the UK," Jack said curtly. "Are we clear on that? Good." He nodded. "Now, to answer your question: our network has no such advance notice," he said, suddenly extremely formal. "We simply have an excellent news team that is on extremely good terms with the local Palestinian population. Whenever an incident begins, chances are excellent that someone will be on the scene and call it in to us immediately. It is not our fault or our responsibility if our competition, or the Israeli government, has a less friendly relationship and less reliable sources."

"So these informants are stringers? Reporters? Fixers? What?"

He turned to her, his eyes cool. "Your point being...?"

"Well, if I have no idea who they are, how can I judge the reliability of the information they are passing on to us? Do they or don't they work for us?"

"Look, Julia, I don't mean to be rude. And I know you've had a long trip, but why don't you just tag along this time and watch? Perhaps you'll see that some of your questions get answered in the field. And if not, I think we can save this discussion for a more congenial and discreet location back at the office, don't you?"

Checkmate, she thought, nodding deferentially. "I appreciate what you are saying, Jack. But if you will just indulge my ignorance for another moment or two. Where in hell, exactly, are we? And are these windows bulletproof?"

"We are in Palestinian Authority territory, controlled by Arafat's security forces, about four kilometers from Kalkilyah and a few kilometers from Israel's coastal cities, Herzliya and Netanya…"

"I had no idea the distances were so small between Israel and the West Bank. It's tiny…"

"Yes…well." He paused, bored. "That's what the Oslo Accords were all about. The Israelis taking a chance on living in peace, not worrying about the closeness to Palestinian townships. To answer your questions, the windows on the car are shatterproof, but not bulletproof, but I'm wearing a chest protector, so I'm all right. You've got one too, Sean, don't you?"

"Oh, never go into this part of the world without one." He nodded soberly.

Her heart began to drum, and she felt her cheeks flush with heat. Then she saw the two men slap their knees and howl.

"All right, all right." Jack patted her knee. "We are just teasing. Everyone knows who we are in these parts, and they are always happy to see us. Believe me, you are perfectly safe."

"And what happens if we broadcast something that our good friends here don't like? Will we still be perfectly safe the next time we come back?" she whispered, suddenly aware of Ismael's steady, expressionless eyes watching her through the rearview mirror.

"I don't think you really want us to answer that, do you, Julia?"

She tore her eyes away from the driver's, gripping her hands tightly in her lap and staring out the window. "No," she said.

The scattered olive trees turned suddenly into a grove of tall evergreens that blocked out the harsh Middle Eastern sun. She could just see the headlines now: BCN REPORTER AMBUSHED ON WEST BANK. AWARD-WINNING JOURNALIST FINDS DEATH ON FIRST DAY OF NEW ASSIGNMENT. COLLEAGUES MOURN. THE BRITISH JOURNALISTS ASSOCIATION CREATES SCHOLARSHIP IN HER NAME…

The car came to a halt, the doors flinging open. Jack and Sean jumped out. Dark shadows lined the road, their faces half covered in *kaffiyehs*, automatic weapons slung over their shoulders.

"It's all right, Ms. Greenberg. You can go out. You are in no danger, I assure you," a voice said politely in charmingly accented English. She looked up, realizing it was simply Ismael who stood at her right, his head made strange and unfamiliar by a red-and-white *kaffiyeh*. "Here. Just cover your hair, and don't tell anyone your name."

She took the scarf from his outstretched hand. Neither piece of advice required an explanation. She didn't ask for one. Sean and Jack were already way ahead of her on the road, surrounded by a group of armed men. Her heart beat wildly as she reached for her pen, notebook, and tape recorder, hurrying to catch up.

"No recorder," Ismael snapped, keeping pace with her. She raised her eyebrows, but slipped the recorder back into her bag. Neither he, she, Jack nor Sean were in control of this situation, she realized. Or of the quality or quantity of information they would be allowed to glean.

The thought rankled her. If they had any illusions she was going to do PR work for the PALS (as the Palestinian Authority was called), they were highly mistaken. It was true that she had come with the intention of showing the Palestinian side, but she wasn't going to allow herself to be manipulated by anyone.

With Ismael's help, she pushed her way through the tight little group that had formed around the bureau chief and Sean.

"What are they saying, Ismael?" Jack shouted to him above the high-pitched and rancorous discussion.

"They are asking if you brought money."

"Tell them no money yet. Tell them to give me what they've got first."

"Money?" Julia repeated, staring at Jack Duggan.

"Just shut up, will you, dear? Let me handle this."

She felt her face grow hot, as if she had just been slapped.

"Tell them that unless they can tell us something about the doctor, the little girl, we're out of here."

Ismael spoke to the group in rapid low tones to the backdrop of bullets falling into empty chambers, as automatic weapons clicked into readiness. Julia realized her feet had gone suddenly weak. She put one heel back to brace herself, hoping no one would notice.

Ismael finally looked up. He turned to Jack. "They say they have a videotape. They want it broadcast."

"Video? Of what? The doctor? The child?"

Ismael interrogated the men again and nodded. "They say they want ten thousand dollars."

Jack shrugged. "Tell them we want to speak to their leader and see the tape, otherwise we are getting back into the car and leaving."

"Jack…" Sean implored. "Take it easy."

"No, we don't pay for news. Never."

Julia exhaled, partially in relief, and partially in preparation for being unable to exhale again until she understood what was going to happen next.

More rapid exchanges took place. Voices were suddenly raised. A weapon discharged.

"That's it. We are leaving," Jack said furiously.

"No, don't go yet," Ismael cautioned. "They are prepared to negotiate. They say we should wait here."

"Here? In this back alley, surrounded by a bunch of loonies with submachine guns?" she murmured incredulously. "Not bloody likely."

"Why don't you wait in the car, Julia dear?" Sean whispered. "We'll tell you when it's time to go."

She looked at him, her lips stretching tight and thin over her teeth. "Tell them I'll go with them, Ismael," she said impulsively. "Tell them, I'll go alone, unarmed. That I'll explain this to their leader. I can guarantee that their tape will be aired on prime time. That the whole world will see and hear what their video has to say. Millions of people. Tell them that."

"I can't allow that." Jack waved dismissively.

"Stupid bitch, you'll get us all killed," Sean spit out.

"Tell them, Ismael," she insisted.

She saw the men confer, and then beckon to her. Her heart in her mouth, her ears ringing with fear, she moved forward, falling into rank behind the men. She pulled the scarf close around her head, tucking in all the stray hairs.

"Wait here in the car for me," she called back to Jack and Sean. "I'll be back."

The group piled into two black cars, late-model Mercedes with cream leather upholstery. She looked at the cars in surprise. She had expected the kind of trucks the Che Guevarra guerillas had used in South America, smelling of straw and pig droppings. This was certainly a revolution deluxe. Someone, she thought, has money.

A small stirring of fear and excitement curdled her stomach juices. She felt the adrenaline pumping through her veins as the cars raced forward over bumpy, unpaved country roads through small villages. Outside, it was almost deserted, she thought, watching the long stretches of dusty road with no sign of human habitation. The landscape was all scrub and rocky earth with a scattering of trees. And it looked as if there was plenty of it to go around.

What about this unremarkable place stirred such remarkable passions? she wondered, as she had traveling over the ice-slick dirt trail through the Dabarsko Polje mountains toward the borders that separated Bosnian-Serbs from Croats. There too, the anemic soil produced nothing but poverty and heartbreak. Yet men were willing to commit any atrocity not to share it, to claim it for themselves.

What a moronic species human beings were, she thought, depressed.

Inside the car, no one spoke. Once again, she felt pressed on all sides by insistent male muscles. She tried, unsuccessfully, to contract. But the more she tried to shrink, the more their flesh expanded to fill the void. Inside her pocket, she fingered a small pocketknife and a can of pepper spray. In her imagination, she could already see herself bloody and undressed in compromising positions.

Whatever was going to happen was going to happen. She shrugged, feeling her excitement mount. As her parents had always warned her, this was not a job for a nice Jewish girl. Which is why she loved it so much.

The cars stopped, and the men jumped out, screaming. Someone pulled at her sleeve, but Ismael slapped away his hand and shouted at him. After that, she was allowed to make her own way out of the car. She had no clue in the world where she was. Amman or Damascus or a suburb of Jerusalem, all were equally plausible. The house in front of her was a mansion built in the Arab style with glowing pink stone and multicolored marble floor tiles surrounded by an intricate pattern of hand-painted tiles. Formal gardens with charming fountains sprayed cooling water into the air, and the smell of jasmine and honeysuckle mingled in the vine-covered portico leading to the front doors.

Terrorism was obviously quite an upscale career choice in this part of the world, she thought, looking around with a mixture of grudging respect and utter contempt. She was led inside and asked to wait. The living room was tiled with black, white-veined marble; low, built-in couches covered with red Persian carpeting and large, hand-embroidered pillows lined the walls. Enormous bronze trays held pistachio nuts, dates, figs, and almonds. A woman covered from neck to ankle in the traditional dark outer coat, her hair completely swallowed by a tightly wound head scarf, brought out a tray with a bronze tea kettle, porcelain cups, and gluey semolina flour cakes, thick with honey. The woman poured with silent graciousness, indicating a chair and table. Julia nodded her thanks, sitting down and taking a polite bite and sip. Her role completed, the woman withdrew as silently as she had appeared, but not before favoring Julia with a lovely smile.

Charming, Julia thought, charmed, as she smiled back. Yet somehow, unbidden, the name Tony Soprano popped into her head. She tried to get rid of it. After all, it wasn't right to make up her mind yet. She still didn't know anything about these people, except that they lived well, had uneven taste, and a good sense of hospitality. Well, and the fact that they had some connection to armed men and the kidnapping (or worse) of doctors and their small daughters. And one could probably take a wild guess that they didn't feel much affection for the Chosen People.

She hadn't changed her name. She wasn't ashamed of who she was. But she also didn't feel like she had to take responsibility for the actions and thoughts of every other Goldberg, Greenberg, Levy, and Cohen in the world either. I am who I am, and they are who they are. As for being a "people," part of a clan…it meant nothing to her. She was born in Britain; that was her people, her clan. That her grandparents had emigrated from Eastern Europe was neither here nor there. Theirs was an accident of birth, as was hers. She rejected its claim on her, refusing to kow-tow to the middle-class idea that one's distant ancestry deserved any special loyalty.

She was a human being, part of mankind. That connection had her loyalty, her fealty. Her country of birth and education too deserved some sentimental connection that she fostered without too much difficulty. She was proud of being British; the achievement of that fair, small, green isle in culture and history and literature was worth being proud of, feeling connectedness to.

But anything in the mystical reaches of some quasicultural/religious backwater ruled by paternalistic old farts who oppressed women and interpreted musty old texts to make life easier—and more profitable—for themselves was quite outside her line of vision. The whole "Israel" thing just didn't interest her. And it had absolutely no hold over her. Quite the contrary. The idea of Jews having their own state was quite repellant. The only thing Jews had in common was their silly, male chauvinistic religion (no sillier or more male chauvinistic than Christianity or Islam, mind you). There was no reason to mark off borders fanatically to preserve it. Just as there were Christians and Muslims all over the world, citizens of every country, so too the Jews should be everywhere. Anti-Semitism was outdated and discredited. It was the Israeli occupation that had people hating Jews all over again. It was something new. And the Israelis had only themselves to blame.

She heard voices drift down the stairs with new urgency. Suddenly, Ismael was standing in front of her. His face was pale. "Come," he beckoned.

She walked up after him, not exchanging a single word. In the hall, she brushed past men holding AK-47 assault rifles. One of them opened a door and jerked his head toward her. She dutifully went inside.

On the walls hung pictures of a frail old man sitting in a wheelchair dressed completely in white. His scraggly beard dripped down his face and onto his robe like spittle. His eyes, like two black stones, lightless and without humor, looked down on her intently. Yes, she thought. A physically challenged, anorexic Santa. A poster child for the Jihad Muscular Dystrophy Foundation. A basketball player for special Olympics against ageism. Good old Sheik Yassin himself.

They led her into a room almost bare except for two chairs and a table. On one of the chairs sat a heavy man with a turban and a thick black beard. He almost looked like a yeshiva student. He said something to one of the men standing next to him, who in turn barked something belligerently to Ismael.

"What?" she turned to Ismael, who shook his head curtly and seemed alarmed.

"Hair. Your hair," he hissed.

She pushed the flyaway blond wisps back underneath the head covering and tied it back as tightly as she could.

The fearless leader barked something else in a high-pitched voice that made him sound like a character straight out of *The Simpsons*—comical, almost ludicrous—a stark contrast to the decidedly uncomical gun-wielding goons spread out all over the place ready to obey his every word.

They were beginning to annoy her.

"Tell them I don't have all day," she suddenly said in a loud, clear voice.

Ismael turned a bright red and mopped his brow. He began to explain, when Mr. Turban held up his hand for silence and beckoned her to take a seat across from him. She took her time. Then she took out her notebook and pen, crossed her long legs, instantly grateful to be wearing slacks and not a skirt. (If a strand of her blond hair offended their sensibilities, then what would an ocean of white thighs do?)

"Now, Ismael, please ask my host who, exactly, is he?"

In response, Ismael leaned over her, his lips almost touching her ear. "You are not in Piccadilly, Princess Diana. And you are going to get us both killed. The man you are looking at is Sheik Mansour, the right-hand man of Sheik Yassin, head of Hamas in Palestine."

She felt her hand tremble as she wrote down the words.

Hamas. One of the deadliest and most merciless groups of terrorists in the world. She felt herself shiver as though she had been playing with a snake that she only now realized was not of the harmless garden variety, but the kind whose poison could kill a man in ten seconds.

The sheik suddenly went berserk—screaming at the top of his lungs and waving his hands.

She jumped up. "What's he saying? What's he saying?" she demanded.

"He says that you are about to receive a videotape of the latest glorious exploit of the holy Izzedine al-Qassam Brigade against the murderous occupiers of holy Muslim land in Palestine. We want you to broadcast this to the Zionists. We ask that your network donate ten thousand dollars to our Muslim Benevolent Fund or this is the last time you will be allowed to enter our homes."

She watched the sheik slam his fist into his hand.

"Get up, the interview is over," Ismael hissed at her.

"But..." She waved her empty pad helplessly. "My questions?"

Two men rose and approached her threateningly. She put her pen away, took one last look at the evil turban-wearer and headed down the steps, Ismael holding her elbow and ushering her out.

"But he hasn't given me a tape...?!"

"Just keep moving," Ismael hissed.

She did what she was told, not that she had much choice: a dozen armed men were dogging her heels and there was no direction to go but out.

They hustled her into their cars and sped down the roads. Aware that at some point someone was going to ask her to describe where she'd been and how she'd gotten there, she looked outside the tinted windows, searching for some landmark. But there was nothing to hold on to. The ramshackle buildings. The donkeys. The small boys with sticks. The old men in dirty pants. The women with enormous baskets on their heads walking through the fields. It was like looking out a porthole at sea.

She felt her stomach begin to churn, the nausea sweeping over her in great waves with every bump in the road.

"Tell them to stop, Ismael."

"I can't do that! It's dangerous..."

"Tell them to stop or in one minute they are going to have digested British Airways food all over their cream leather upholstery!"

She heard him speak. A moment of silence followed, interrupted by sudden snorts of laughter. The car halted abruptly. Crawling over her companions, the cold metal of their guns touching her arms and pressing into her legs, she stuck her head out the door and drained her digestive tract of any lingering traces of nourishment.

She wiped her stinging mouth across her sleeve, then sat back down.

All the way, the men laughed and joked with each other, throwing her amused glances. Thankfully, Ismael didn't translate.

The cars finally rolled to a halt. She followed Ismael out into the open road, looking around for signs of Sean and Jack. And then all of a sudden, she saw one of the terrorists (freedom fighters, she reminded herself; activists; militants) walking slowly and deliberately toward her.

He was an ugly giant, built like those old-fashioned British phone booths: square, with a gut that hung over his pants like ice cream bulging out of an overstuffed cone. The black metal of his gun gleamed like a deadly sea predator in the foggy cool of the shaded road.

She stepped back. If he was going to demand a last-minute rape, this was the perfect place for it, she thought, looking at Ismael's slender frame tensely watching from a distance.

My savior, she thought dryly.

Whatever was going to happen was going to happen. Her hand went to her pocket. She fingered her weapons.

Wordlessly, he pushed a bag into her hand, then turned and walked away.

The other men followed. She could hear the revving of the engines in the preternaturally silent place, where even a leaf scraping along the ground entered into the conversation.

Ismael was suddenly at her side. "There they are."

She gazed up the road, and sure enough, they were: the beer-guzzling, white-man's burden, woman-baiting old British boys' club in the flesh, waiting with rather morose expressions on their faces, to welcome her home.

"What, no brass band?" she murmured. "Aren't you happy to see me?"

"Damn insane, that's what you are!" Jack fumed. "Could have gotten yourself killed with that big mouth of yours, and not knowing anything. And the brass would have been all over me. Blamed me..."

"What have you got there, Julia, old girl?" Sean said, eyeing the bag enviously.

"A video, I think."

Sean turned to Ismael. "Who picked you up?"

"Izzedine al-Qassam."

"My God! You are lucky to be alive. Those guys have lovely ways of getting to know people. Like sticking explosives into human orifices, or pouring glue down throats.... Most talented and inventive, in their own way." He shrugged, lighting up. He took a long drag. "Tell me, dear, how nuts do you have to be to confront a fanatic who is just itching for the opportunity to live it up with his virgins in paradise?"

For the first time in a long time, Julia Greenberg found herself speechless.

To her greater surprise, she found that she actually did have something left in her digestive system. She bent over and felt part of her stomach lining come with it.

"A video," Jack said, taking the cassette out of its cartridge and turning it over. "And who did you say it was from?"

"Sheik Mansour himself," Ismael told them.

"You met the sheik, in person?" Sean said, his eyes wide with astonishment and not a little envy.

"Quite a scoop, Julia, and right off the plane. London will be delighted. And I'll bet this is an exclusive. Congratulations, girl. And welcome." The bureau chief smiled. Julia crawled into the seat beside the driver and closed her eyes, all her courage and bravado suddenly disappearing like helium from a balloon that has flown too high and finally met the pointy, unforgiving spires of skyscrapers not meant to be touched.

They made copies, and then they sat down to watch.

"Okay, press play," Sean told Ismael.

Only the four of them were in the room, which had been cleared of secretaries, stringers, messenger boys, and of course, all "locals," as they called Israeli Jews.

The blank screen went on for four minutes, and then suddenly, when they'd all but given up, the voice-over began, followed by one of the most chilling images they had ever seen.

"Good God!" Julia whispered, a lump in her throat. "It's a child. She can't be more than five or six."

Duggan got on the phone. "Get me the prime minister's office."

He put his hand over the receiver and turned to Julia. "Call headquarters in Oxford and tell them to hold the evening news prime spot, we are going to be broadcasting."

"Hello, this is Jack Duggan of BCN. A videotape has been delivered to our offices anonymously, and it contains an ultimatum showing Dr. Jonathan Margulies and what appears to be his child... Yes, we are here. We'll be expecting you." He hung up. "The Israeli military, probably the *Shabak*—secret service, that is—will be here any minute to pick it up."

"I think we need to contact the mother. She shouldn't hear about this on television," Julia insisted.

"Look, the Israelis are going to do that. We don't want to be involved with hysterical Jewish mothers..." Sean waved her off.

"Actually, that would be a great angle, Julia. Get her to let you film while she's watching the tape for the first time. Do it before the

Israelis take over. Get an exclusive. Let's tell her she gets to see it if we get an exclusive."

"And if she says no?"

"Then she can watch it with the rest of the world."

Julia leaned back. She felt sick and confused, her stomach filled with a desperate discomfort. It was just being tired, being hungry, she thought. "Does anyone have some chocolate?" she asked faintly.

Right now, she needed something to sweeten the terrible taste in her mouth.

Chapter eleven

Nine years earlier · Berkeley, California
September 3, 1993 · 8:30 A.M.

Elizabeth stood on tiptoes, scanning the library shelves hopefully: Boa, Bob, Bod...ah...there it was, Boethius, Ancius, *The Consolation of Philosophy*. She took it down eagerly from the shelf. It was the first reading for the semester. The bookstores had copies on back order, and she had rushed to the library hoping she hadn't been beaten to it by her fellow freshmen. Ah! One copy still sat on the shelf, she exulted, clutching it almost fearfully.

"Oh, you found it!" The voice, a deep male baritone laced with disappointment, startled her.

"I beg your pardon? Are you speaking to me?"

"You found the Boethius. It's the last copy, and the assignment is due next week. I was hoping..."

She looked him over. Six foot two with the build of a linebacker. "You are in Von Nagel's class?"

He seemed amused at her skepticism. "Why not?"

"I don't know. You just don't seem the type. The only people I remember seeing were freshman girls in plaid shorts and very short, pale debating-club men."

"I wasn't aware that there was a body-type requirement. At least, it's not listed in the catalogue," he said with a completely straight face. "Anyhow"—his eyes lingered over her long, lithe body wearing a teeny-tiny miniskirt and a low-cut red T-shirt proclaiming: IF YOU CAN READ THIS, YOU ARE STANDING WAY TOO CLOSE—"you aren't wearing plaid."

"Oh, I'm not the type at all. I'm sure this whole philosophy thing is going to turn out to be a huge waste of time."

"Why would you say that?"

"Well, as my grandmother would point out: 'Who hires philosophers?'"

"My grandfather would agree. A waste of time."

"I wonder if Boethius would agree."

"I'm sure he would. He was very practical."

"How do you know? I thought you were desperately searching for the only copy, the one I just got."

"Actually, I've read Boethius before. During summer vacations in Switzerland at some horse camp I hated. You see, Boethius has been imprisoned, and he knows they are going to kill him any day, and so he's writing all about the meaning of life. What man should be looking for. Those summers, I could really identify with that." He finally grinned.

"You must have been one strange kid." She grinned back.

"You have no idea, so…?"

"So…what?"

"So here we are, both needing the same book, and only one of us having it."

"I thought you read it already."

"But I haven't memorized it. And the assignment is very word-specific, very page fifteen, paragraph two…"

"True. And therefore?"

"I await a generous philosophical response to an existential dilemma."

She laughed. "Well, I suppose we could do the assignment together. The question is when, and where?"

"Your place or mine?"

"Neither. Someplace neutral would be better."

"Library?"

"Can't talk."

"Under the trees?"

"No back support."

"Rome Café on College Avenue?"

"Much too noisy."

He cracked his knuckles and smoothed back his dark hair impatiently. "Are you always so choosy?"

"Philosopher's prerogative."

"Perhaps you would like to suggest something?"

"Look, I was actually heading toward the Botanical Gardens. I can meet you at the entrance at three."

"If it doesn't rain."

"It won't."

The Botanical Gardens of UC Berkeley were green and lush, with rare species of Mojave Desert plants, and birds that rioted overhead like little old ladies gossiping on park benches. That was the setting, where it all began.

His name was Whally. That was all she knew at the beginning. And it was enough. Boethius took care of the rest:

Alas how men by blindness led
Go from the path astray,
Who looks on spreading boughs for gold
On vines for jewels gay?...
But in their blindness men know not where lies the good they
*   seek.*
That which is higher than the sky, on earth below they seek
What can I wish you foolish men?
Wealth and fame pursue,
And when your toil false good has won,
Then may you see the true!

There, in the fading sunlight, two strangers explored life with a man condemned to death hundreds of years before, a man who discarded as false happiness all roads to power, fame, riches, pleasures, or honors. True happiness, according to Boethius, was being self-sufficient. Needing nothing outside. And there is nothing, he concludes, greater or more self-sufficient than the supreme good. Men who seek evil, seek something which has no power; in fact, which doesn't exist at all. Evil men have ceased to exist, pronounced the philosopher, holed up in his cell, waiting for death, surrounded by evil.

They were both students. She, barely eighteen, the first time away from home, in the first bloom of a beauty that turned heads and made ordinary people stop whatever they were doing. She flaunted it, the sleek, tall, young body of the dancer she was before her height cut short any hopes of ballet. But she kept that dancer's graceful carriage. Her hair, a sun-kissed, California blond, had every delicate shade from platinum to golden brown. She wore it carelessly, uncut, letting it fall down her back and across her shoulders. The clothes were careless too. Salvation Army castoffs. Secondhand Chanel jackets purchased from genteel shops that paid parsimonious society matrons for their discards. She loved pairing Chanel with torn jeans or flowing Indian cotton pants and beaded sandals. Somehow, despite her mother's pronouncements to the contrary, she never looked ridiculous, the way fashion models on the runway never look ridiculous in the outlandish and laughable creations of talentless and pretentious designers: see-through blouses and metallic underwear, pointed skullcaps, fur bikinis. There was something in the arrogant, insouciant carriage of those fabulous beauties that made onlookers believe in their self-congratulatory saunter through flashing lightbulbs and applause.

Like the models, Elizabeth was so tall, so truly, remarkably beautiful, there was nothing she could do to dim that glow. Not that she hadn't tried: short haircuts. Big glasses. Baggy pants. Shirts like unfitted sheets. Orthopedic shoes. Purple tights. Gray suits. She tried, but nothing worked. And so she stopped trying, embracing instead the freedom of being the center of attention. She gloried in it, and learned that it wasn't necessary to protect oneself from come-ons and whistles and rude remarks. She was philosophical about it. It was like the rain. It existed in the world and could not be altered. It was often not to one's liking, and even mildly injurious. But it didn't kill you, and in the end, one could find shelter and wait for it to pass.

She liked men, boys, but found few interesting enough to spend time with. The truth was, she picked up men as she did books, exploring them, understanding them, and then, when she had gotten the essential point, she itched to put them back on the shelf to make room for a shiny new one whose binding had not yet been creased.

The longest any relationship had lasted was four weeks, and the only reason it took that long was because she was fifteen and he was twenty. It had taken her time to understand the lag of experience between them. But when, scarcely a month later (quite a bit of it spent in bed, catching up) she found herself on par, she knew he was soon to be history.

What she needed, she realized early on, was a man of endless variety and mystery; part of a whole world that would take many years to explore. That is what every woman with a low boredom threshold needs. And Elizabeth Gold Miller had a very, very low boredom threshold. And such a man was not, by any means, easy to find. Sometimes such women never marry. Or they become the kind that marry so often it becomes a rather tacky joke. It isn't fickleness. They have simply, and sincerely, got the story straight, and realize that there will never be any surprises, any improvements, any fundamental changes. It's the boredom that sends them out on their next quest.

Elizabeth feared that because of her looks, she was doomed to meet men with unreasonably high self-images and no depth, the kind that dogged movie actresses and models. Men who were superficial to begin with, and existentially boring in that which they sought, and thus ultimately unsatisfying and unworthy of respect or interest.

Boethius had it right, she thought. Self-sufficiency.

She had come to Berkeley to become self-sufficient. To understand herself and the world and to explore the limits of human culture and history; the "why" of why are we alive on this earth. Is there a God? What do we need to do to find happiness? What is freedom? And then, Whally had come along.

He really was a mystery. He didn't offer any information about himself, nor did he get involved in questioning her about her family and background. She found him enormously attractive and exotic: the dark hair, the olive skin, the powerful build. And she could see he was smitten with her.

But somehow, the physical part of their relationship was held back in a tense abeyance while they explored each other's minds.

Each conversation ended with a suggestion that they meet again.

And so it was, that year, her freshman year at the University of California at Berkeley. How is it that people who come from two different worlds, two radically different worldviews and backgrounds, learn to love each other? Is there not some automatic mechanism that turns on to thwart the drawing together of opposites? Or do human relationships mimic nature in that the magnetic forces most opposed are in an unstoppable journey toward union?

She was a Jew, the grandchild of a woman arrested, tortured, and marked for death by those who hated Jews. She was an American woman, taught that freedom to dress, feel, learn, work, think, was her birthright, and the right of every human being. She took her unlimited freedom for granted, like the bathroom tiles, or the solid earth beneath her feet.

His name was Whalid Ibn Saud. His family lived in Riyadh. He was from the Saudi Arabian royal family, who subscribed to the Wahabi sect of Islam, a sect that rejected the notion of freedom of religion, who had built a country in which being in possession of an Old or New Testament was a jailable crime. It was a country that denied entry to Jews, and outlawed the presence of Christian churches, Jewish synagogues, and Shi'a Muslims. He came from a patriarchy in which women were still veiled, forbidden to go out into the street alone without male permission, or drive or work. A place where women belonged to men and had no separate existence.

How is it, then, that they fell in love? Because that is what happened. They didn't mean to. But they haunted each other's dreams, and each morning when they awoke, the desire to see each other, to hear the other's voice, was almost unbearable. And so being together became almost as routine as showering, or going to classes. They simply couldn't help themselves.

They didn't put a label on what they were doing, because had they described their relationship as a courtship, it would have been unthinkable to them both. So they didn't think, they acted. On Sundays they drank coffee and ate delicious cakes from Just Desserts on College Avenue. On Saturdays they strolled down Hopkins Avenue, pausing to sit in open-air cafes. Friday nights were spent at Iceland, with the lights dimmed and the music playing, floating around the rink, the sound of scraping ice, the chill delicious against the warmth of their bodies in each other's arms.

She was eighteen and he was twenty. She was a freshman majoring in philosophy, and he a junior, majoring in Middle Eastern studies. They didn't involve friends or family with what they had between them. Their friends wouldn't have understood, gotten along. And getting their families together was impossible to even imagine, and so they avoided imagining it.

Like balloons suddenly let loose from the hands of their creators, all the strings holding them down began to float, dangling in the open air. They rose together, looking down at the familiar earth, watching as everything they'd grown up with, everything they'd always understood and believed, grew small and disappeared.

The view they shared now came from a different height, a perspective that was impossible to explain to those still down below. There, above the clouds, they made perfect sense as a couple. In fact, they were inevitable. The beauty of their bodies, their youth, their love of ideas, their sense of fun, their endless delight in the other.... Why shouldn't they be together? How could the rules of the world be right, if it denied them that simple, logical right?

And then came the moment when they both realized that they were helpless to stop the rush of events, that gale force that had blown them both so far from familiar, safe shores. They never discussed their future. Instead, they escaped into long discussions about abstract ideas.

What about beauty, she'd ask him. Is that too a worthless thing?

"Boethius would say that three days' fever can make it disappear. And if you look deeply enough at any beautiful body, you will see beneath the surface, the guts and liver and kidneys—all very necessary, but very unbeautiful. To love human beauty is to love something whose very existence is doomed. Love should be based on permanence. On solid, secure things."

"Such as?"

"Love of God. Love of good deeds. Love of country and family. Love of ideas."

"And physical love?"

"To make physical love to the person with whom you share a permanent love of all these nontransient things would be the highest form of pleasure," he would intone solemnly.

"So, you are against getting into bed with a pretty girl and having a good time?"

"It would be an inferior form of pleasure, one that sullies and makes more difficult the attainment of the deepest pleasure."

They did not sleep together.

She wanted to. But he held back. She never knew why. Perhaps it was religious conviction. Perhaps fear, a sense that the act of intimacy would force them both into making decisions that were impossible to make, decisions that would burst the fragile fabric that enclosed the hot, moist gas that kept them aloft in their own stratosphere, unbuffeted by the weather and complications down on earth.

But of course, after months of suspended reality, the moment of truth inevitably arrived. It was a Sunday afternoon. They'd gone to Tilden Regional Park, taken the steam train, ridden on the carousel. There were families with children all around them. A young couple sat on a park bench. A three-year-old girl in pink shorts with long dark hair snuggled in her young mother's arms, while the handsome young father held a small baby against his shoulder, rocking it. As they watched, the two parents exchanged a smile as they looked at their children.

That smile.

Everything was in it. Pride, contentment, happiness, connection. Permanence. It was the perfect circle, completely self-sufficient. It was the meaning of life. Nothing could take its place. They both suddenly understood that that was the only future worth having.

There was nothing left to say, no more fantasies to shield them from the inevitable.

"What is going to happen to us?" she asked him. "What is the future?"

"I am going back to Riyadh. I'm going to work at some job. Practice my religion as best I can. Be a loyal son to my parents and family. I love my family and won't shirk my obligations."

"Isn't that terrible, that you have your whole life mapped out, filled with obligations?"

"Don't you feel any family obligations? Any ties of culture and religion and history?"

The truth was, she didn't really understand what he meant by obligations. She felt, and had always been made to feel, that freedom was her right, that anything that held her back or disturbed that right was wrong.

She was an American, and she was guaranteed life, liberty, and the pursuit of happiness. She had had a bat mitzvah, an almost ludicrously elaborate affair on a cruise ship, in which each deck had had its own band and theme. On deck A, there had been a swing band and a forties theme; on deck B, a Hawaiian theme and hula dancers; and on deck C, waiters dressed as Egyptian slaves had borne her (dressed like a prepubescent Cleopatra) on a litter into a room filled with over a thousand guests, mostly her mother's and grandmother's business associates. She'd received an absolute roomful of gifts. Obligations? The weekly Sunday school sessions in her local Reform synagogue that had preceded the shindig. But they hadn't been burdensome. They'd been a pleasure. She had loved the teacher, a kindly young rabbinical student, who in his gentle way persuaded her that there was a God and that He was accessible—indeed quite an understanding and compassionate deity. The beauty of the prayers, the colorful stories of the Bible were like hearing a special kind of music for the first time. Not classic, not rock, something in between that made her soul hum along, even though she wasn't sure she would ever learn the words right or how to play the instrument herself.

But somehow, after the party was over, the presents unwrapped, other things had vied for her attention: junior proms, cheerleaders, debating clubs, school newspaper. Religion was like the good china that the family brought out and dusted off on special occasions: weddings, funerals, *Rosh Hashanah* and Passover. She had learned from her family to leave it respectfully on the shelf.

When she met Whally, she made an effort to learn about Islam. She'd found its tenets, at least on the books, amazingly similar to Judaism's. Both religions had one and only one God. He had no father, no son. And He was the father of all human beings. He was supreme and high, close to the pious who pray to Him, loving to those who love Him, and forgiving to those who asked forgiveness. He gave people peace, happiness, success, knowledge. Unlike the Jews, though, Muslims believed that all prophets were sent by God, and all religious texts were true: they believed in Jesus, Moses, Abraham, and Mohammed, the Old Testament, the New Testament, and the Koran. All are from the same source, and all ask the same thing: that men and women worship the one, true God, which Muslims call Allah. The point was that the individual submit his will to the will of God. To do good, not for God's sake, because God was not in need of anything—the ultimate self-sufficient being—but for man's sake. The purpose of life, therefore, was to worship God, not just by praying, but by living the kind of life God wants for the good of all mankind and for the good of the individual.

The more she learned, the more Elizabeth wondered at the essential similarities between their two religions, except that Islam—on paper—seemed the more tolerant one, encompassing all prophets and all texts.

But then she took out a book on Saudi Arabia. The Wahabi form of Islam practiced by the Saudi royal family was intolerant to a fantastical degree. But that didn't stop the Saudis from building mosques in London, Rome, New York, and Washington. And even though Wahabism forbade the consumption of alcohol and promiscuity, quite a few Saudi leaders were known as drunks and womanizers. As for pursuing peace, the family had initiated countless tribal wars and killed innumerable fellow Muslims.

She confronted him with this.

"Every religion teaches peace and love. Yet, the church has

killed millions in religious wars. And Jews are involved in endless wars against the Muslims."

"Which the Muslims start," she replied furiously.

"Palestine was Muslim until the Zionists came along."

"And Boston was full of Indians. And the British fought the French. Land is fought over and won and lost. It's not a reason to kill people. Besides, my people were in Palestine thousands of years before yours. I thought Muslims accepted Moses as a prophet, and the Torah as true?"

They glared at each other.

This was the future. And it was impossible.

They stopped going out together, crossing the street when they saw each other coming. And the day after their final exams, he left the country and she went home to Los Angeles. They didn't call, or write. And with every day that passed, she felt she was experiencing those symptoms described by drug addicts suddenly going cold turkey: everything hurt, everything felt empty and gray. There was sometimes physical pain, like a stomach flu. There was a deep sense of loss, and confusion. A sense of mourning. All her old friends kept calling, and she kept avoiding them. Young men would come up to her at the country club, introduced by her mother or father as the successful sons of their doctors and lawyers and business partners. She was always polite, even allowing herself a momentary curiosity and attraction. But as they sat down next to her on the beach chair and pattered on about their plans to sail to Bermuda, or volunteer for Greenpeace, or begin a summer internship, she'd examine them. So tall and slender and smiling and reasonable and American, she'd think, finally admitting to herself that she'd lost her taste for white bread.

She played sad songs and lay on her bed in a darkened room, staring at the ceiling, wondering when the ache in her heart was going to heal.

And then, at the end of July, there was a knock on her door, and her mother came in and sat by her bedside. "There is someone to see you. He says he is a friend of yours from college."

"*He* says?"

"Yes, a he. And he doesn't look Jewish, Elizabeth," her mother accused. "In fact, he doesn't even look American."

She forgot to put on shoes, pulling her robe around her and threading her fingers through her bed-disheveled hair. She ran down the stairs. His back was toward her and then he slowly turned, his dark eyes brightening, his whole body straining toward her.

She stopped halfway down the staircase, watching him, unable to get any closer.

"Whally."

"Elizabeth."

He was thinner and paler, with a new mustache that emphasized his foreignness. He was so very different, so exotic, so very un-American, she realized now, and the idea struck her with full force as it never had before.

"What is going to happen to us? What are you going to do with your life?" she asked him, oblivious to the staring servants, her mother watching the scene in horrified silence behind her back at the head of the stairs.

"I won't lie to you. I have family obligations, and I'm going to do exactly what is expected of me. Go back home to Riyadh. Work at some job. Be close to my family, and obedient in all things but one: I'm never going to marry anyone else but you." He shrugged helplessly.

"Don't say that to me!" she shouted. "Don't put that burden on me!"

"Is that what it is, Elizabeth? A burden? Don't you…can't you…love me?"

The question felt like an electric shock. She walked slowly down the steps, stopping only when one step more would have brought their bodies into contact. "Why did you leave me?"

"For the same reason you let me go."

"And why have you come back? Nothing has changed."

"Everything has changed." He reached out and smoothed a curl off her forehead. "I was dead, all the time I was away from you. All the color had drained from the world. I saw nothing in the world worth living for. We have to make it work."

"But how?" She placed her hand on his chest. He enfolded it in his.

"By living half in your world, and half in mine. Six months in Riyadh. Six months in California. When you are there, you will be a Muslim woman, and when I am here, I will do what I can to respect your family's customs. I can't be a Wahabi Muslim. But I can be a Muslim. And our religion tells us to accept Jesus and Mohammed and Moses and Abraham. I can do this, and be a good Muslim. My family will have to understand. And yours?"

"Absolutely not! Are you crazy?" Elizabeth's mother shouted. "Elizabeth—Saudi Arabia?! They are primitive! They chop off the heads of wives who don't behave! They cut people's arms off for stealing! They don't even let Jews in to visit!"

"Mom…" she began, troubled. She felt the insistent warm pressure of his hand on hers, and she turned to face him. She couldn't hear anymore. Slowly, she entrusted him with her other hand as well. They looked into each other's eyes and smiled. Like Boethius, they were totally self-sufficient.

Chapter twelve

Gynecology Ward · Hadassah Hospital, Jerusalem
Tuesday, May 7, 2002 · 1:00 P.M.

Listen, everyone in the country is hysterical. We are like one big family. We are worried about Mrs. Margulies, that's all. Think of me as her brother, her cousin," a reporter from *Yediot Aharonot*, the biggest Israeli daily, wheedled the skeptical young nurse. "All we want is some information. Just let me in to speak to her for a few minutes. Have a heart!"

The nurse, who had worked with Dr. Margulies and who was barely five feet tall in her thick-soled orthopedic shoes, reached up and took the reporter by the scruff of his neck and led him to the hall. "And if he comes back," she told the massive security guard—a Moroccan Jew who had come from Marrakech in 1948, had fought in five wars, and didn't like little Ashkenazim or smart-ass reporters to begin with—nodded.

In the conference room, Dr. Eliahu Gabbay, Hadassah Hospital's director, held a news conference. He was blinded by the lights of television cameras. Everyone was there: NBC, CBS, Sky, CNN, BBC, BCN, *Newsweek, The New York Times*...Reporters from all the Israeli papers—*Maariv, Yediot Aharonot, Haaretz,* and *The Jerusalem Post*—

jockeyed for position in front of the foreign reporters, and were not above physically disciplining those who mistakenly perceived that their American or European network credentials somehow earned them a superior status among the locals.

It was a zoo.

Even before the director opened his mouth, questions began flying in all languages and all directions.

"Can you tell us if the rumors about a Hamas videotape showing Dr. Margulies and the child are true, and if Mrs. Margulies has seen it?" someone shouted.

A reporter with a thick British accent raised his voice over the others, exclaiming: "Can you tell us how this has affected her medical condition? Do you expect her to lose the baby? And what about the Israeli government? Will they negotiate with the militants? Are they planning to release jailed freedom fighters...?"

A shout rose up among the Israelis. "Freedom fighters? People who target two-month-old babies in carriages? Blow up six-year-olds on buses? What freedom are they fighting for anyway? Freedom to murder?"

Dr. Gabbay held up his hands, looking like a put-upon substitute forced at short notice to teach the worst eighth-grade class in the school. "Ladies and gentlemen, please. Can I have your attention?"

The noise level went down a notch.

"Look, if I can't make myself heard, I'll just leave, and you can all go find something else to write about..."

An uneasy silence ensued.

"Thanks." He took a deep breath. "First, I'd like to read a statement."

The reporters groaned, taking out cigarettes, until the guards pointed out the NO SMOKING signs.

"Elise Margulies, wife of Dr. Jonathan Margulies," Dr. Gabbay began, "is under careful medical surveillance to monitor the health of mother and child. We have no knowledge of any videotape. But if such a tape exists, she and her doctors would have to discuss whether it would be in her best interests psychologically, or physically, to view it at the present time. Otherwise, her health is as good as can be expected given the traumatic situation of the last twenty-four hours. Everything that can be done for her and her unborn child is being done."

He put away his papers, took off his reading glasses and looked up. "Now, I'm prepared to answer any questions in my area of expertise."

Shouts rose up all over the room.

"Please. One at a time." He pointed to a well-known Israeli reporter and nodded.

"Can you tell us, Dr. Gabbay, why you are keeping Mrs. Margulies in intensive care?"

"All information concerning Mrs. Margulies's medical condition is strictly confidential. Next."

"Is it true Mrs. Margulies has already given birth and the baby is in critical condition?" another reporter shouted.

"No. This is an unfounded rumor."

"Is it true that the prime minister and the army chief of staff came to see her an hour ago?"

"No. It's not."

"Are the rumors true that Mrs. Margulies is furious at the Israeli government, particularly the army, for not coming to see her?" someone from CNN asked loudly.

"This is not my area of expertise. Next."

"Well, maybe you could get us someone whose area of expertise it is?" the CNN reporter shot back, exasperated. Scattered clapping broke out, and a few guffaws of laughter.

"And when are you going to let us talk to Mrs. Margulies herself? I'm sure I'm not alone when I say, with all due respect to you and the medical staff, Dr. Gabbay, that we are beginning to doubt whether our requests for interviews have been forwarded to the lady," a British reporter accused, straightening his tie.

The director's jaw tightened. "I'm sorry. I'm not a newsman, I'm a doctor. Mrs. Margulies's health and the well-being of her unborn child have to take precedence over every other consideration. Interviews with her are out of the question. Now if you have nothing else you want to ask me, I'll go back to my job, administering this hospital."

"What, that's it?" some slickly dressed American network star roared.

Julia Greenberg raised her hand. "Doctor, Julia Greenberg, BCN. Can you tell us if the tensions caused by the cycle of violence have affected your care of Palestinian patients?"

He colored. "I resent the implication, Ms. Greenberg. Hadassah Hospital serves thousands of Arab patients. Every one of our patients gets the same respect and care. But to answer your question, yes, the care of Arab patients has been affected by the kidnapping of Dr. Margulies."

The room fell suddenly silent. Julia Greenberg felt a prick of satisfaction as all eyes turned in her direction.

"Dr. Margulies was treating dozens of Palestinians for cancer, saving their lives," Dr. Gabbay continued emotionally. "They are weeping for him and for themselves. I hope that answers your question, Ms. Greenberg. And now, if you'll excuse me, I have a hospital to run."

Julia felt her face grow hot.

"Well, this was a waste of time," Sean Morrison said peevishly. "I guess we might as well head back. Coming?" He turned to Julia.

"I don't think so. I think I'm going to talk to Elise Margulies."

"What? Weren't you listening? Don't be insane. These Israelis look serious," he said, eyeing the automatic weapons hanging from the shoulders of the young, tight-lipped security men.

"Eat my dust, Sean," she said with an angelic smile, tossing back her hair.

As she headed out of the conference room and into the halls of the hospital, she felt a hand on her shoulder. When she turned around she found herself facing a good-looking young stranger with a heavy camera hoisted to his shoulder.

"Your question, it was good, if I might be so forward to address you," he said with a tiny formal nod.

Very Eastern European, the accent, she noted, examining his boyish, angular body in the worn jeans that were torn beneath his knee, and frayed to white along the pockets. The T-shirt clung comfortably to his strong, handsome chest and brown arms.

She smiled.

He smiled back, the downward slanting eyes in his long, lean face lighting up, the hawklike nose wrinkling with humor. Very Slavic, very Third World, she thought approvingly. "Why, thanks."

"And I thought his—that director's—response was unnecessary. It was a legitimate question you had, so I thought. He didn't have to be so...difficult about it. But these Israelis, they are difficult."

She laughed, self-consciously smoothing back her hair. "Well, that's a good word for it. Difficult." She put her hand out. "Julia Greenberg, BCN."

He took it warmly. "Milos Jankowski." He smiled disarmingly, clicking his heels together, mocking himself.

"Who do you work for?"

"Polish television; and stills for *Zycie, Gazeta Wyborcza...*"

"That's a mouthful."

"But mostly, freelancer. Documentaries."

"First trip to the Middle East?"

"I was in Egypt. And Saudi Arabia. I prefer Egypt."

"Everyone prefers Egypt," she agreed. "Jeddah is unbearable. Especially for women."

"So, you've been?"

She shook her head. "They don't let Greenbergs into Saudi Arabia. But I feel that's their right. Every country has its own cultural norms."

"Wow. That's very...professional of you."

"But I plan to try again. After I finish here. When they become more familiar with my work."

"So, you think your work here will soften the Saudis' hard line against Jewish journalists?"

"I'm convinced of it."

"And what is your take on all this?"

"If this is a kidnapping," she said cautiously, "and—mind you—I'm not saying it is, then the Israelis won't deal. They don't care about individual lives here. It's an oppressive regime."

He looked puzzled. "But I understand that a few years ago they let out hundreds of Muslim prisoners just to get a few of their soldiers back."

"Really? Uhmm. I hadn't heard. Well, I don't think that's what will happen here. And Izzedine al-Qassam martyrs aren't about to trade over a pound of flesh with Shylock..."

He blinked at the metaphor. "So, you think Izzedine al-Qassam did it? Sheik Yassin, Sheik Mansour?"

"The tape was pretty clear..."

"Tape?"

He looked so boyishly confused, she thought, relenting. "Listen, I can't say too much about it. But the men responsible released a videotape of the doctor. I was the one they gave it to. We're planning to air it tonight. It's an exclusive, so you have to swear not to say a word to anyone. There are rumors, of course. You heard the questions.... Even Mrs. Margulies doesn't know yet. I was trying to arrange a deal to show it to her privately, but the doctors and the army weren't having any of it."

"So it's not a rumor then? It's really true! That must have been frightening. Being with the terrorists. Getting the tape."

She wrinkled her nose. "I dislike the word 'terrorists.' It's so judgmental. And no one will get hurt if the Israelis release their friends from jail."

"So he looks as if he's being well treated, he and the child? That no violence has been used on them?"

She shifted uncomfortably. "Well, that's going a bit far. These are not nice people. Revolutionaries seldom are."

"So, this is a revolution? From what to what?"

"For freedom!"

"Well, if that's true it will be amazing. Palestine will be the first country in the world run by Muslim fundamentalists that embraces freedom as a value..."

"Are you being ironic?" she said, pursing her lips. She was intrigued. Eastern Europeans were usually much further to the left than she was. Where was he going with all this?

He smiled. "Listen, Julia, could I interview you about what that was like, getting the tape?"

"Interview me?" she said, surprised and flattered.

"Yes! Our Polish viewers are very interested in this case. You know, a doctor. A young child."

"Look, Milos, thanks but I'm not really all that important..."

He stopped and reached out to her, squeezing her shoulder. "But you are. You are incredibly important, Julia. It's the first break in the case, and you got it."

His hand was warm and promising. And what he said was absolutely true. She was important. And in a few hours, everyone would know it.

"Well, if you swear it will only be broadcast in Poland, and not before the nine o'clock news..."

He hoisted the camera to his shoulder, aiming the lights in her direction.

"Really, Milos." She patted down her hair and straightened her blouse. "Do you think they'd be interested? In Poland?"

He smiled. "You have no idea."

"Milos?"

"*Babcia?*"

"Where are you?"

"In Jerusalem. I arrived safely. Call your friend Mrs. Gold and tell her. I just finished a news conference."

"So, you had the luck?"

"Why are you talking to me in English?" He laughed.

"I talk English? It is habit. When I dial long distance..." she said, switching to Polish.

"So, what did you find out?"

"I've only been here two hours, Grandmother...! But, you know what, maybe. I found a reporter who got the videotape of Leah's family. It looks like a kidnapping."

"Jesus watch over us.... What did she tell you, the girl?"

"How'd you know the reporter was a girl?"

"Who else would want to give you information, *wnuk?*"

He laughed. "She's a girl, all right. British. And, actually, she didn't give me much."

"You have to find out who gave her the tape. And who arranged it. And where she got it, the place…"

"You mean her sources? She's a reporter. She'll never tell me that. Anyhow, I just met her. And there's a limit to what I can do. I'm not exactly Brad Pitt…"

"Pit?"

"Not a fruit pit. An American movie star."

"You're better. You're a European moviemaker. Much sexier. A British girl isn't used to such a virile man. British men are like old socks."

"I'll take your word for it." He grinned. "I'll do what I can. Please don't drive me crazy."

"Just remember what I did to save lives during the war."

He was suddenly serious. "Who could ever forget that, *Babcia*?"

Chapter thirteen

Hadassah Hospital, Jerusalem
Wednesday, May 8, 2002 · 10:00 A.M.

P lease, I'm an old woman, and I've been on a horrible ten-hour flight. I'm tired, and my Hebrew isn't good…"

Leah explained to the Hadassah Hospital security guard.

The man shook his head impatiently. "No, English," he said in English. "No visiting hour." He waved his hand.

"Look, mister, I'm not moving until you get me someone to help me. My granddaughter, Elise Margulies, is in the intensive care. She's having a baby. You understand? Dr. Jonathan Margulies' wife, Elise…!"

The busy nurse passing by caught the end of the sentence. She stopped and stared. "You are Elise's—"

"*Bubbee*, her *Savta*, as you Israelis say…"

"Can I help you, *Savta*?"

"Oh, honey. God bless you. Yes, please, my feet are killing me…these guards don't understand English. I took a taxi from the airport. I *shlepped* my luggage. They are probably going to blow it up if I leave it here, right? I'm so tired."

"Please, *Savta*, sit down. I'll get someone to help you." The nurse took her over to a chair, then hurried off, filled with excitement, worry, and good intentions.

Leah leaned back, exhausted, listening to the discussion in rapid-fire Hebrew that was taking place all around her. She tried to catch a few words, but it was as bad as Puerto Rican Spanish, and as unintelligible to the non-native speaker. What a *tzimmis*! Here she was, in only a few hours. Go in one door in New York and come out another in Tel Aviv. Life is like a dream. But, as my mother used to say, a good dream is still better than a nightmare.

"Excuse me, Mrs.—?" The kind nurse was back, smiling at her.

"Helfgott. Leah Rabinowitz Helfgott." She smiled back gratefully.

"Mrs. Helfgott. This is our hospital administrator. He will help you."

Leah reached up and caressed the pretty, soft face of the Israeli nurse: a Jewish nurse in a Jewish hospital in a Jewish country. She felt tears well. "Thank you, darling. God bless you."

The young woman took her hand and squeezed it gently. "God bless your family," she whispered, her eyes brimming.

"Mrs. Helfgott...Leah, I'm Doctor Gabbay. How can I help you?"

"I'm here to see Elise."

"Of course. But she's resting right now, and you look as if you could use a rest too."

"Look, Doctor, I don't want to fight. I know you Israelis—you are all soldiers. They let you out after three years, but you go back every year, and when there's a war, you all go in and fight until it's over...I'm right?"

Doctor Gabbay smiled. "You're right."

"So, I don't start up with Israeli soldiers. But I must tell you I have a heart condition, and if you don't let me see my Elise, even just to peek in if she's sleeping, you might have two intensive-care patients on your hands."

She folded her arms across her chest and waited.

"Shoshana," he told the nurse. "Would you be kind enough to take Mrs. Helfgott to see Elise? But please, only for a few minutes."

The nurse nodded. "Doctor, what about the luggage?"

He looked at the two enormous suitcases, the wig box, the plastic bags…"And call an orderly, and tell him to put all this in my office."

"Thank you. You're a nice Jewish doctor. Tell your mother I said so. A *broocha* on your *kepeleh*."

"Come in later if you want to talk." He nodded, trying to look serious. He was going to tell his mother. The first chance he got.

She got up heavily, tucking the young nurse's arm beneath her own. Slowly, she walked through the crowded hospital corridors, glancing in wonder at the mass of electronic equipment in the lobby, as the media kept its vigil, like vultures, she thought, hoping the hostility pouring out of her veins at the newsmen would act like the valve on a pressure cooker, and by the time she reached Elise she'd be calm and smiling and encouraging. As she neared the room, she felt her legs drag reluctantly, making her pace even slower.

Walking through the snow in bandaged, swollen feet, the guards with cocked pistols waiting for you to falter. You couldn't falter, your life depended on it. And so you walked, day after day, hour after hour, when you wanted to lie down and close your eyes, because you wanted to live, to accomplish something for the people you loved.

"*At rotza lanuach, Savta?*" the nurse asked.

Leah patted her arm, not understanding a word, but grateful for the concern in her tone. She was already in love with her, this Israeli nurse, who helped sick Israelis get well.

"Shoshana means a rose, doesn't it?" Leah patted the nurse's cheeks. "Don't worry. I've got energy. For this, I've got energy."

The nurse spoke briefly to the guard placed outside Elise's room, who was under strict orders to let no one but authorized hospital personnel pass. He smiled at Leah, opening the door. Elise lay back, her curly hair dripping out of the cloth headscarf that modestly hid it from male eyes. Her eyes were closed, and two dark red spots made her cheeks seem jolly. Or feverish, Leah worried. She stood there looking, holding her breath.

My Elise. My religious granddaughter who went to the homeland, to live in a place where Jews didn't have to be afraid…

Elise opened her eyes, taking a moment to focus. *"Bubbee?"*

"Darling."

"Oh, *Bubbee!*" She lifted herself up off the pillow, hugging
the small, old woman who patted her back as she would a child's, in
long, gentle strokes.

They clung to each other, rocking in a silent paroxysm of grief,
love and understanding.

"When did you…?" Elise asked.

"What do you mean? As soon as I heard. You could keep me
away?"

"But your heart…"

"It's pumping. It pumps in Boro Park, it pumps in Jerusalem.
My heart knows where it pumps? My *neshama* is here, so my heart bet-
ter get used to it. Besides, Esther sent me a fancy doctor. He checked.
He gave me more pills. He says I'm fine. But tell me, how are you?"

Two big tears ran down Elise's cheeks.

Leah held her hands. "Don't, *maideleh*. Don't. I know what
it is, believe me. I know. But you can't give up hope. *'Lommir nisht
zorgen vos vet zein morgen, lommir besser farrichten dem beint un dem
nechten.'"*

"What does it mean?"

"I forget you are a *shiksa* and don't know Yiddish." She smiled.
"It means: 'Don't worry about tomorrow, better to fix today and yesterday.' You have no control over the universe, only over yourself, and
you have to keep hoping and praying to God."

"I pray all the time. I'm just not sure anyone is listening…"

"Shhh! Elise, *'Ver es git leben, vet geben tzum leben.'* 'He who
gives life, nourishes life.' He listens, this I can tell you. Whatever
happens, He's listening. He doesn't always answer right away." She
hesitated. "He doesn't always say yes. But He's listening. This much
I promise you."

Elise put her hands on her stomach, glancing at the monitor
with its steady green graphs. "No one will tell me anything. The doc-

tors are afraid to let the army talk to me. So I get a briefing once a day. It's driving me crazy, not knowing."

Leah pulled over a chair and sat down. "What *do* you know?"

Elise looked at her. "Only that Jon and Ilana are alive, and that the army is doing whatever it can to get them released. That's what I know."

"So, you know what everybody knows. But now I'll tell you something nobody knows. I've called up the Covenant."

"Your friends from Auschwitz? Oh, *Bubbee, Bubbee.*" She sighed, squeezing the old, beloved hand indulgently, shaking her head. "This is not your problem. There is nothing any of you can do."

"You don't know, you don't know. Four old ladies, you're thinking…So, you'll see. They know people…they have connections…Ariana has a nightclub in Paris. Every *drek* in Europe goes in there…and Esther has a granddaughter married to a Saudi Arabian…and Maria's grandchild makes movies, he's going to find out about the videotape with Jon and Ilana…"

Elise blinked. "Videotape? With Jon and Ilana? What videotape?"

Leah looked at her, stricken. It had been on all over the place. First on BCN, and then afterward, on every news program, again and again. How could it be she didn't know? Leah rose slowly. "Oy, you know what, I'm falling off my feet, Elise. And they made me promise I'd only stay for a few minutes…"

"*Bubbee, what tape!?*" She clutched at her grandmother's skirt, bunching the material fiercely in her hands. "I have to see it!" She pulled herself up and started getting off the bed.

"Elise, Elise," Leah said frantically. Oy, *gotteinu, gotteinu*, what have I done? "Please, Elise, get back into bed…if anything happens to you and the baby because of what I've done, I'll never forgive myself. Never." She trembled.

Elise looked at her grandmother. She took a deep breath, then climbed slowly back into bed. "No. Don't. It's not your fault, *Bubbee.* I'm fine. I'm sorry. Just, please, tell me—what does it show? Are they alive, well?"

"Alive and well, thank God!" The truth was, after a brief look at Jon and Ilana—which had made her sick—she hadn't been able to watch.

Elise slowly exhaled, trying to keep control. She would slam on desks, turn over tables, but she would see that tape. She'd deal with it as soon as her grandmother left. "I'm all right. I know I have to relax. I promised Jon. I want to put a healthy baby into his arms… when…when he comes home. But *Bubbee*, you should go now," she said impatiently. "You must be falling off your feet. Go lie down."

"Yes, *maideleh*." Leah hugged her. "I'll go. And you remember your promise to Jon. I'm going now. Elise…" She wants to get rid of me. And all she's going to think about from now on is that tape. And it's all my fault.

"Thank you for coming. Thank your friends for trying to help… but tell them not to worry. I'll see you later."

Defeated, Leah turned to go.

"*Bubbee!*"

"What?" she turned around, concerned.

Elise rested her head on her grandmother's shoulder, feeling like a child. "I love you." The old woman did what she had dreamed of doing high in the air, for thousands of miles: she put her arms around her granddaughter's fragile young shoulders and rested there.

Chapter fourteen

Madame Ariana Feyder sat enthroned in her red velvet swivel chair examining her accounts, looking like those photos of a vain and aged Helena Rubinstein. Like Rubinstein, who in her nineties had frightened a burglar in her bedroom so badly that he'd run for his life, she knew that she too made people sweat.

She thought of the tourists marching up and down the Champs Elysées, already in high gear, eagerly searching for a place where later that evening they could become part of the Parisian night for the price of a cheap whiskey or an indifferent glass of wine. None of them would even notice the small cabaret tucked away on an obscure side street, a place never mentioned in mass-produced guidebooks. Indeed, except for a pair of striking, massive oak doors, Chez Ariana gave almost no indication at all of its existence.

Those knowledgable enough to find their way to those doors would find themselves blocked from entering by burly, immense security guards unless they could produce both a membership card and a password. And even then, Madame Feyder had the discretion to decide whether or not to buzz them in. On occasion, they sometimes found their cards had been cancelled or the password changed. And those members who brought guests understood that they would all find themselves waiting out on the street while the guards urgently consulted with her in the back office. None of them could guess in advance what she would decide, her criteria being entirely personal and idiosyncratic.

On the whole, she allowed in rich and famous people who were—or could be—useful to her. But she also let in struggling artists or musicians whose talent she respected; people she felt sorry for, like the balding tourists who had read about her club in *People* magazine; and young college students because she liked the color of their hair, or the way they said a certain word. The criteria for female guests was undeniably their beauty.

Thus, on any given evening one could find starving writers and unemployed saxophone players, high-level cabinet ministers, an insurance salesman from Milwaukee, shadowy underworld kingpins, billionaire arms brokers, and the dictators of small Third World countries all intermingling in strange harmony in the charming restaurant and dance hall. Famous actresses, exquisite runway models and up-and-coming young call girls crowded the small dance floor, an important part of the cabaret's attraction.

Ariana made it a point to make a nightly round of her customers, greeting each one personally, making them feel like guests in her home. As a result, over the years the direct, personal phone numbers of some of the most powerful and dangerous people in the world had poured into her Filofax. On occasion, she contacted them. Most were only too happy to hear from her and to be of help.

As for those who were not, they soon found that they had made a very serious mistake. To make an enemy of Madame Feyder was no small thing. To be banished and permanently exiled from Chez Ariana was extremely inconvenient at best, and at worst, absolutely crippling to certain types of business activities. Her reputation for discretion, the guarded privacy of Chez Ariana, the cachet of membership—along with the unbelievable roster of members and their acquaintances—had made the club a unique and indispensable watering hole in the jungle for a wide variety of clandestine dealings. Ariana did not like the word "commission." She did not see herself engaged in anything as crass as commerce when she introduced people in her club to one another. She was a hostess, and these were her friends. If she helped one friend by introducing him to another who shared his business interests over a pleasant glass of the best *pastis*, well, that was her pleasure. And if she knew how to contact a certain modeling agency to arrange a discreet rendezvous between a smitten and most generous billionaire and a young Victoria's Secret catalogue model, she did them both a favor. If they then expressed their appreciation with a token of their esteem…well, that was a different story.

The jewelry, the apartment on the Ile St. Louis, the lovely chateau in St. Jean Cap Ferrat, the silver Jaguar, the jaunts on private jets to private Caribbean resorts, were all part of the tribute that regularly flowed in her direction, the way far-off colonies had once sent tribute to their emperor in Rome.

It was a system Thierry had worked out when he'd helped her open the club, and for many years, it had worked perfectly. But given present circumstances, these days she really preferred cash over lavish jewels to adorn her wrinkled flesh and tropical vacations in far-off places. These days she hardly went anywhere. Recently, she'd even set up a bed in her office and had a private bathroom installed.

She didn't like being in her apartment by herself. Without Thierry beside her in the huge canopied bed, its vastness and luxury had taken on a Louvre-like coldness, every nook and cranny shadowed by imminent dangers. She'd lie awake, chills crawling up her spine, reacting to every creak of the furniture or settling of the walls like the intrusion of a dangerous stranger. Not that sleeping anywhere else was that much easier.

She was haunted by memories, wracked by regret. She regretted never getting married. Four years ago, when Thierry's wife had finally passed away, he'd asked her. But after thirty-four years as his mistress and his love, she'd thought: Do I really need a piece of paper? Will it stop him from dying and leaving me? But now that it was too late, she wondered if it hadn't been a mistake. As his widow, people would have respected and understood the great hole in her heart.

She regretted too never adopting a child. She had wanted so much to be a mother, to lavish kindness and generosity and protection on some small, helpless creature. She wasn't the type that could get a dog and treat it like a baby. She was also haunted by the idea that no one would say prayers or light candles for her when she died, except for her Covenant friends. They were the only family she had. Perhaps, aside from Thierry, the only ones she'd ever had.

She took out a cigarette and lit up, then took a sip of her vodka and orange juice, both habits that a succession of young, dedicated doctors had assured would kill her. She liked young doctors. She enjoyed watching their hair turn gray, their flat stomachs inflate, their chins sag. At that point, she always replaced them. It would soon be time for a new one, she thought, draining the glass. It gave her immediate heartburn. Everything gave her heartburn.

She hated being old. Her legendary beauty was all but gone now. To compensate, she'd taken to dressing with theatrical overstatement. Today she wore a turban and a caftan of flowing green silk that matched her still exquisite eyes. Her long, slim fingers sparkled with rings, drawing attention from the faded blue numbers and the numerous needle marks that climbed up her arms. From her ears hung two chandeliers (the best description she had ever heard, and one she loved), handmade by her private jeweler on the Ponte Vecchio: a cascade of yellow and brown diamonds that dangled down to her shoulders, a gift for playing matchmaker between a Russian exporter of enriched uranium and an oil-rich dictatorship.

But what she hated most of all was butting up against her dreams, feeling how empty and flat they were. It was like opening a beautifully wrapped present and finding it was a sweater in the wrong color that made you look fat. Surrounded by all those riches Thierry's tutelage had brought her, she wondered often now if it hadn't been his dreams she'd been living out, her own having gotten lost somehow along the way. It was ironic, even tragic. All through the camps, she'd struggled against the downward pull of death and misery, allowing her dreams to float above her like a warming sun, something to look up to, bask in, follow. But as soon as the war was over, their light had turned to cheap glitter, almost tawdry. What did fame matter? Hitler had been famous. Millions had adored him. As for riches…she'd learned there was only so much you could buy.

Only so much…. The best part of being rich was being free. But what good was that freedom if you were free and childless? Free and unmarried? Free and wretched?

Thierry had never really understood that. Or her. And perhaps she'd never really understood him. Few did. In his obituary, they'd called him "a key figure in politics and industry whose image had been tarnished by persistent rumors of connections to underworld figures, bribes, and payoffs."

He'd been a man the most ruthless criminals had feared. Yet for her, he'd always been the most indulgent father, the most protective big brother, and the tenderest of lovers. She'd met him in some ugly Left Bank cabaret where they were letting her sell cigarettes and sing through the smoke and noise. He'd nursed a few drinks, watching her as she sang, applauding, making the others shut up. And afterward, he'd bought some cigarettes. That was how he'd seen the blue numbers on her arm.

His mother had also been a Jew, he'd told her. She had died before the war, of TB. She too had sung in a nightclub. He never spoke of the people who'd raised him, except to say that he'd made them pay for everything they'd ever done to him. She'd never wanted details.

He'd hated so many things, her Thierry, and loved so few. And she was one of them. He'd come along at a point in her life when she'd never been more vulnerable. After the brutal rape, the botched abortion, he'd taken her under his wing, taught her how to protect herself by making others need and fear her.

She looked down at her rings. He'd taught her so well how to get everything that money could buy. Yet the ability to turn wealth into happiness had been something that eluded them both.

I have missed out on all the important things in life, she sometimes thought. Baby carriages pushed in the park, a man's shirt on the ironing board, his coffee mug steaming next to mine on a cold, weekday morning…. A life of ordinary joys.

She stared at herself in the little mirror she carried in her purse, reading the story of her life in the wrinkles that crossed her face like hieroglyphics only she could interpret. The one near her temple, for example, was from the time she'd stood on the platform with Maria, Esther, and Leah waiting for that train to the front. The one in the corner of her right eye was from lying in the snow unable to move, waiting for the bullet to her head. The ones on either side of her mouth were from hearing the doctors say that the brutal, backstreet abortion had cost her her womb.

She sighed, writing out her monthly checks to the myriad orphanages, women's shelters, and child-care organizations she supported in France and in Israel. She placed them into the white envelopes and licked the stamps. I should have adopted a child, when it was still possible. But I never thought it was fair, with things being as they were.... Thierry, the nightclub, all those gangsters and low-lifes.... I should have done more good in the world....

But it was too late, too late. All too late...she thought, taking out her mother-of-pearl box. All she wanted out of life now was some peace. A life of massages and spas and witty companionship. Some release from the horror of memories and regret, the horror of constant pain, of Thierry's loss, of phantom children that haunted her in the darkness, her unborn babies that cried like kittens mewing in a box, shut out of her life by force. Release.... She opened the box, sniffing the white powder and rubbing it along her teeth.

She heard a knock on her door. "Madame."

"What is it?" she growled. "Didn't I tell you never to bother me when my door is locked?!"

"You have a phone call, Madame. It came through to the front bar."

"Can't you deal with it!?"

"She says she's your friend. Esther from California. She says it's urgent. A matter of life or death..." The bartender improvised, prudently rephrasing "Tell Madame Feyder if she doesn't get on the phone, I'm taking the next plane to Paris and will pull her out by her trademark earrings."

She stared at the desk, fingering the little box. "*Alors.* Put her through immediately, Maurice."

"Of course, Madame."

"Esther? Is this about the tape again? The tape, the tape. And Mr.

Spielberg. I will do the tape! I don't want to, but *Mon Dieu*! you will never leave me alone, so I do it. Will you call me now every day?"

There was silence on the other end.

"Esther? Don't be angry. I'm just tired. I don't sleep…"

"Didn't you see the tape that BCN aired?"

"I never watch the news. They lie and report only horrors."

"That's my Ariana. Dreams are always preferable to reality," Esther said in a strangled tone. "The tape about the kidnapping in Israel. The doctor and the child taken by the terrorists…"

She remembered something on the radio. "Yes, now I recall. Terrible story."

"Ariana…it's Leah's granddaughter. Elise…"

"*La petite* in Israel? The one who is *enceinte*…?"

"Yes. It's her husband, Jonathan, her child, Ilana…"

"*Mon Dieu*! And you say there was a tape? They ask for the ransom money? Because if it is money…"

"It's not money they want. They say in forty-eight hours they will kill them both…"

"*Mon Dieu!*"

"I already have men looking for the kidnappers' hideout in Israel. But they need time. We have to somehow get Hamas to extend the deadline…"

Ariana played with the empty glass of vodka. "If we can find out who the head of Hamas operations in Europe is, the one who gives the orders, I can make sure he gets a special invitation to my club. And once he is here, my friends and I will give him such special 'treatment,' he will do whatever we tell him."

"Can you ask around?"

"Of course. But it will take time. Call your granddaughter! The Saudis, they give money to Hamas. They will know exactly how to find him."

"I've thought of Elizabeth…" Esther said hesitantly. "But we haven't spoken in years, Ariana. Do you think she'll even…speak to me?"

"*Mais oui*! Are you not her *grandmère*?"

"It's not what you think, Ariana. Children, grandchildren…

They are not your good friends. Sometimes you give and get nothing back…"

"Call her! It is time. She will get her husband to help."

"Will she? Can she?"

"She is a good girl, your Elizabeth, *n'est-ce pas?* She will do the right thing. And this man, if he loves her…"

"But what…" she lowered her voice, "if it's dangerous? If I involve them and something happens…"

There was a long silence at the other end of the line.

Escaping the death march. Running through the woods, the gunshots ringing over our heads. Hiding in the straw, the sharp knives, the deadly pitchforks rammed in viciously just above our heads. "We choose our steps, make our choices. Elizabeth and her husband will choose theirs."

"It could be dangerous for you too, Ariana. All those *drek*s wandering around in your club. If you start up with Hamas…"

Ariana Feyder closed the box with a determined click, then slipped it into her pocket. "*Alors.* How do the *Américains* say: Make my day! Besides, *chérie*, what does any of this matter…? We made a Covenant. They are threatening to kill Leah's family…her child. We made our choices long ago."

There was silence on the other end of the line. There was nothing left to say.

"*Bonne chance, chérie!*"

"To all of us, *chérie.*"

Chapter fifteen

Kala el-Bireh, Samaria (West Bank)
Wednesday, May 8, 2002 · 1:00 P.M.

The tan Honda Accord rolled swiftly down the unpaved roads, slowing only when the army checkpoint appeared in the distance. The driver eyed the soldiers. Three were standing at attention, alert, their automatic weapons clutched in their hands, positioned for immediate use; another two were lounging in chairs, eating. Ismael took his foot off the accelerator. Flagged down, he braked, rolling down his window. "Papers," the soldier said, sticking his head through the window. He handed them over: a card identifying him as an employee of BCN, along with a British passport and a valid work permit. The soldier scrutinized his face, comparing it to the passport photo. Satisfied, he motioned for him to open the trunk. For a fraction of a second, Ismael hesitated. The soldier's eyes narrowed, his hand tightening around his weapon.

"Of course," Ismael said quickly, releasing the trunk latch. The soldier shifted his weight to a more relaxed position and motioned to his comrade to check the trunk.

"*Yesh mashehu?*" the soldier asked.

His comrade peered into the trunk, then shrugged. "*Kufsaot.*"

"What in those boxes, many boxes, in back?" the soldier demanded, attempting his high school English.

"Newspapers, magazines. Journals."

"What for?"

"Our archives. We are a news station," the driver said levelly. "Can I go now?"

"You wait here," the soldier answered firmly, walking around to the back, tearing open the boxes. He sifted through the contents listlessly. Just papers he saw, relieved. English- and Arabic-language newspapers and magazines. The soldier slammed the trunk shut and waved the car through.

This was the last Israeli checkpoint, Ismael breathed in relief. A few kilometers down the road and he was already, for all intents and purposes, in the State of Palestine. Aside from a few widely spaced Jewish communities, he was surrounded by Arab villages and townships ruled over by Arafat's gun-toting goons and wandering gangs of terrorist thugs who called themselves a variety of interchangeable Jihadic names. Tubas was just behind him, and Jenin was just ahead. He turned onto a small side road, taking a left down a gravel path almost hidden from view by thick-leafed fig trees. The car lumbered slowly, crunching on the gravel as it headed toward a large stone villa set back almost invisibly inside a large grove of olive trees. Finally, inside a small clearing, he parked the car.

He got out slowly, listening carefully for footsteps and looking cautiously in all directions. Satisfied that he wasn't being followed, he walked around to the trunk and took out two large boxes, which he carried up the front steps to the door.

He knocked seven times.

"*Ahalan.*"

"*Ahalayn.*"

"*Es salaam aleikum.*"

"*Wa aleikum es salaam.*"

"I have the papers."

The door opened, and the house swallowed him. Inside, two armed men, dressed in army fatigues, nodded and smiled, while a third caught him in a warm embrace. A fourth nodded to him briefly, then got up to shake his hand before returning to the flickering images of a European soccer game being narrated in Arabic and broadcast from a television station in Dubai.

"Where are they?" Ismael asked.

"Downstairs. Come."

"Should I bring the papers?"

The other man scratched his three-day-old stubble thoughtfully. "Yes. Bring them."

They walked down the steps. An iron door, three inches of reinforced steel, barred their way. Ismael waited as his companion knocked three times, paused, then knocked four times. A small iron window moved aside.

"It's Ismael. He's brought the papers."

The harsh, grating sound of heavy iron bolts being slipped back mingled with the sound of locks turning. Finally, the door opened to admit them. Five armed men, and a cache of deadly weapons—c4 plastic explosives, grenades, dynamite—all in open boxes—gave the small hallway the look of a deadly arsenal in an old wwii movie about the Germans in Dunkirk. Not an inch of wall space was free. If anyone were to force the door open, Ismael thought, they would be met head-on with enough explosives to incinerate not only the whole house but the entire area into black ash. Nothing would survive.

In the dimly lit corridor, Ismael made out a small desk with a phone, a computer, and a fax machine. As his eyes focused, they widened in surprise and fear. Behind the desk sat Marwan Bahama.

Known by friends and enemies alike as "The Executioner," Bahama was legendary for the ingenuity and passion of his cruelties. Details of Bahama's treatment of his own men suspected of supplying information even to rival terror groups was widely known. It wasn't enough for him to just kill them. He was a connoisseur of pain, having spent years perfecting methods to prolong the depth and span of human agony.

An admirer of the Nazis, Bahama was well read in the practices of ss officers and concentration camp functionaries. He would slice off fingers and extremities one by one, pour battery acid down throats, scorch skin with blowtorches, cover backsides with industrial glue and then set them alight…. There was no end. But his favorite torture was to abuse small children in front of their parents. This he learned from Saddam Hussein's security forces.

Bahama, who came from a middle-class farming family in southern Hebron, had not only finished high school, but had been studying for a degree in biology from Bir Zeit University. In his junior year, his unmarried sister began a series of clandestine romantic meetings with a boy from the neighboring village. When she was discovered, Marwan was given the task of redeeming the family honor. He did so without reluctance, slitting her throat as she lay asleep in her bedroom. Hamas recruited him soon after.

Bahama looked at him through half-closed lids, reminding Ismael of the cold, watchful eyes of resting crocodiles measuring prey.

"*Salaam aleikum*. Allah be praised." Ismael nodded with a brief, nervous smile.

Bahama acknowledged the greeting with a slight nod: "*Allah U Achbar*. There is no god but Allah the merciful. What have you brought, brother?"

"I have brought the newspapers and magazines with the story of the Zionists. And the e-mail addresses with instructions."

"Good."

"Are they well?"

Bahama eyed him quizzically. "Who?"

"The Jews."

"The Jews are still alive."

"Can I see them?"

Bahama stared at him: "Why?"

Ismael swallowed. "These are my orders."

Bahama shrugged, then got up, leading the way through a narrow dark hallway toward a thick red door bolted and locked from the outside. Bahama lifted his shirt, revealing a long, thick metal chain at whose end rested a key. He unlocked one bolt. Then reaching into his underwear, he produced two more keys.

"Still warm," he laughed. Ismael forced a smile, watching as two other locks came undone.

"Are they the only keys?" Ismael asked.

"Yes."

"And what if the door is forced open?"

Bahama smiled. "Look."

Ismael followed Bahama's finger as it punched a six-digit code into a small white keyboard, memorizing the numbers. "It's a motion detector. If someone fires into this door, or bangs into it without typing in the code, fifty kilos of explosives will detonate inside the room."

Fifty kilos, Ismael shuddered. The bus bombings and hotel bombings that had littered kilometers with human flesh had been accomplished with only ten kilos. Bahama finally pushed the door open.

The smell of human excrement hit Ismael like a slap in the face. The cell was too dark to see anything at first, but as his eyes adjusted, he made out the thick concrete walls, the filthy floors littered with old bottles, cigarette butts, and empty candy wrappers. A tiny bead of light from the hallway revealed dust motes as thick as carpeting in the fetid air.

"Where...?" Ismael shrugged.

Bahama pointed to a far corner. There, beneath a filthy blanket, he made out the eyes of a man who stared at him in stony silence. There was a sound, a child's voice. "*Aba!*" It took Ismael a while to make out the other pair of eyes, a child's pretty dark eyes, so like his own child's; eyes that looked up at him in terror. Bahama switched on the electricity, flooding the room in light.

"Please," the man said with parched lips. "The child's skin is burning with rashes from not being cleaned. She needs a bath, clean underwear. She needs food."

Bahama walked over to him. He reached out and smoothed down Ilana's hair. The child cringed, clinging to her father, whimpering in fear. "Do you know what the Nazis would do with squalling Jewish brats?" he asked Ismael. "They would hold them upside down by the legs and tear them in two, like chickens." With stunning swiftness, he kicked Jon in the face. "Get her to shut up, or I will," he screamed. Jon gathered Ilana into his arms, his hands now covered with his own dark blood, which streamed from his nose.

The child screamed, terrified.

Ismael looked down on the ground and spit. "I've seen enough. We need to talk."

Bahama shut off the light, and the two men went out.

"These are not the orders," Ismael told him with quiet fury, disgusted at the brutality. "Look at these newspapers and magazines. All over the world, they are writing about the doctor and his little girl…"

"…little Jewish whore," Bahama swore.

"That may be so," Ismael cut him off firmly. "But we need them for more videos to play on the western news networks. They can't look as if they've been harmed. We need them to say that they are settlers, occupiers of sacred Palestinian lands, and have been kindly treated by Izzedine al-Qassam according to the tenets of Muslim hospitality and compassion. This is going to be very bad publicity. Very bad. These are your orders."

Bahama's chin shot up belligerently. "From who?"

"From Musa himself."

"Musa, eh?" Bahama looked up, surprised and pleased. It was actually, to his mind, quite an accomplishment that the director of all Hamas political activities was directly involved on such a personal level in a local operation under his command, one he had personally planned and executed to perfection.

Like all the others, he had met Musa el Khalil in the training camps in Sudan and had tremendous admiration for him, and unbridled envy. Like all low-level Hamas operatives in Palestine, Bahama aspired to rise to the head of the general organization in Europe, to be the one who sent out the thousands of e-mails with instructions to terror cells all over the world. But he knew he had to be cautious. Hamas operatives who stepped on too many toes found information about their whereabouts leaked to the Mossad or to rival PLO factions, who were only too happy to make sure they were blown up in their cars or beds. Just like in a real army, one had to follow orders, however distasteful, and then bide one's time. "Let me see the orders," he barked, annoyed at having his rank thrown in his face.

Ismael opened up a copy of *Time* magazine, pulling out the

fax containing the coded message from between its pages. Bahama scanned the page, looking for the Web addresses he needed to find his latest orders. He sat down in front of the computer. As a security precaution, identical coded orders were posted on two separate Web sites. Only when both e-mails were posted, and matched perfectly, were the orders to be executed. Forgeries were impossible. The secret numerical codes that marked each communication had to match exactly, as did the spaces between the letters. And there was also a secret code to indicate that the e-mail was false, or being sent out under duress.

Bahama printed out the two e-mail messages, then held them together against the light to ensure their letters overlapped perfectly. They did.

"All right. We will clean them up and make the next video tonight. We will follow the instructions."

"Get a woman in here. A mother. To clean up the child. We need to show the child isn't frightened. That we are good people fighting a just war, you understand?"

"Games, games, games," Bahama shouted, slamming his fist on the table.

"Always these games they play. Arafat and his trips to hotels, signing his papers, smiling and getting his picture taken. The sodomizing bastard who fills his Swiss bank accounts and leads our people to Hell! Enough games. When will they unleash the Jihad against the Jews? Let us round them up and slit their throats? That is how you get rid of Jews. You are all soft. You sleep in soft beds with soft women..."

"Are you saying you won't do it?"

Bahama looked at him with half-closed lids. "Please tell Musa. Tell him it will all be done. We will make another tape, release the message as written. But tell him I need an answer. How long do they need the Jews to live?"

"Why?"

"Because we need to move on. Our next safe house doesn't have room for a well-guarded prison. We can't move them with us. We need to get rid of them. Tell Musa, as soon as possible. I give him another twenty-four hours. That's all. Then we will finish them off and go."

"Not without orders, brother."

"Tell Musa what I said," Bahama said quietly. "Tell Musa while he is in Paris taking baths in his fancy hotels, I am stinking like a camel in hellholes surrounded by Jews. Tell him that. We need orders soon."

"I will tell him."

Ismael walked up the stairs and out to the car. The cool night air chilled the layer of fine sweat that covered his body. He shivered, hugging himself. Then he got into the car and drove quickly down the darkened driveway.

Chapter sixteen

Leah opened the hospital door. Elise had a room full of people surrounding her bed.

"I'm going to see that tape," Elise told them.

Leah took Elise's hand and kissed it. "Don't get excited, darling. Remember, you promised."

"I am going to see that tape. NOW!" she shouted, near hysteria.

The white-coated doctors exchanged meaningful glances. Dr. Gabbay sat down beside her, putting a fatherly hand on her shoulder. "Elise, I promise you. We've all seen the tape. There is nothing on it, except a fuzzy picture of Jon and Ilana. They are both alive and look well. The rest is just propaganda. It's just going to upset you."

Elise pulled her hand away and sat up, facing them all. "My husband and child have been kidnapped by terrorists. Do you think there is anything on that tape that could upset me any more than I already am? Do you think for one second that I am thinking about anything else?" She took a deep breath, struggling for control. "Please, I have to. I have to read their faces." She began to weep.

Leah embraced her. "Please, Doctor. Show it to her already. There's no choice."

Dr. Gabbay turned to the others and shrugged, pointing to the exit. "Elise, calm down. I'll be back in a minute."

Outside in the hallway, the doctors conferred. The psychiatrist was in favor. The obstetrician undecided. And the social worker against. Dr. Gabbay found himself wavering. Perhaps the unknown is always worse than the known. There really wasn't anything particularly frightening about the tape, all things considered. The hostages were obviously surrounded by armed men, obviously frightened. But since Elise's imagination was no doubt forming images that were as bad or worse, fighting her over this was simply adding to her stress. He reentered the room with the others.

"Elise, we are bringing you the tape. But I want you to promise me that if it gets to be too much at any point, you'll turn it off. Promise me?"

"Let me see the tape, Doctor, and I'll stand on my head and whistle 'Dixie'…"

Dr. Gabbay stared at her.

"It's an expression. It means…" She tried and failed to think of a Hebrew equivalent. "I'll do anything you ask of me."

"So I have your word? You can be trusted?" He turned to Leah: "She can be trusted?"

"What do I know, Doctor?" Leah shrugged, patting her granddaughter's cheek.

They set up the video and the television by the foot of her bed. Dr. Gabbay handed her the remote control. "Remember, you promised."

Elise nodded. Then she pressed play.

She watched the blank screen impatiently, finally pressing fast-forward until the first image appeared: a man dressed in khaki, his body wrapped in bullets, a machine gun strapped to his shoulder, a black ski mask stretched over his features. Around his neck was a red and white *kaffiyeh*.

What your well-dressed, generic terrorist scum will wear, Elise thought, searching the screen. In the upper right corner someone sat on the floor, his feet tied with masking tape, his face bloodied, the eyes puffy. On his lap was an object that seemed to be a doll, until it looked up and faced the camera, its eyes wide with fright.

"My God! Ilana!" Ilana, Ilana. Elise sat motionless, her eyes glued to the screen, her heart beating, her bowels like ice water. But she couldn't show it. She willed her face to remain impassive.

The camera wobbled, then shifted back to the terrorist, who held up a white piece of paper and began to read. His voice was strident, without inflection, like some robot's. On the lower part of the screen was an English translation of the Arabic, helpfully provided by BCN.

"Elise, don't bother reading the translation. It's just propaganda," Dr. Gabbay advised.

Of course, she ignored him. She wanted to understand every single word.

"In the name of the revolutionary forces of the military arm of Hamas, Izzedine al-Qassam, and in the name of the holy martyrs who have died fighting the Zionist enemy and occupiers of our holy land in Palestine, the murderers and rapists of our women and children, the stealers of our land, in the name of Allah and His holy prophet Mohammed, this is our decree," she read.

"We have captured Israeli military soldiers, and illegal settlers, and they are now in our custody. The Zionist government is warned that they will both be executed if our demands are not met…"

A small moan escaped Elise's lips. Leah squeezed her grand-daughter's hand.

"We ask the Zionist occupying forces to heed our words well, as Allah is our witness, we mean them and will not negotiate. We ask that all Hamas prisoners being held in Israeli jails be released in no more than forty-eight hours. We ask that all occupying forces be withdrawn from the West Bank and Gaza and Jerusalem. We ask that weapons illegally confiscated from the Palestinian security forces, Hamas, and Islamic Jihad be turned over to our representative in a place that we shall name.

"If these demands are not met within forty-eight hours, we will return to you two corpses."

"Oh my God…" Elise wept.

Leah touched her shoulder. "Look. There's Jon."

Elise wiped her eyes, staring at the screen. There he was. Two gunmen stood on either side of him, forcing him to stand. Ilana was in his arms. Gently, he set her down. They pushed a paper into his hand. He lifted his head and looked into the camera.

Everything was written on his face, Elise thought: terror, pain, anger, defiance, and something else—a deep resignation that was almost otherworldly. Still, there was no mistaking his will to live.

"I am reading this of my own free will. I am a Jew and a Zionist…" Here he paused, a flicker of defiance transforming his features for a moment. It was unmistakable that he had said the words with pride. "I am a member of the Israeli army and an illegal occupier of Palestinian land. I understand that myself and my daughter, also a settler who has occupied Palestinian land, have been sentenced to death. The only way for the Israeli government to save us is to listen to the demands of these men and to do what they say. Our lives are in your hands." He turned to the child and lifted her in his arms. She grabbed him around the neck, burying her face in his shoulder. "*Aba!*" she said. Elise felt her heart give a great, strange thump, like a person falling down and banging his head. She put the video on pause, then climbed out of bed.

"Elise, you can't! No!" everyone shouted out in unison, alarmed.

She moved forward deliberately, ignoring the chorus of frightened demands until someone put a restraining hand on her arm. "Leave me alone!" she snarled, almost like a wounded animal, and the hand dropped away. She touched the screen, staring at her husband. His body looked stiff and his hands curved around Ilana with inflexible determination, as if they were made of iron, or carved from stone. His hair was matted, there was stubble on his chin, and his full lips had been stretched into thin blue lines of determination. She studied his eyes. He had come to terms with what had happened. He would pray. He would also maneuver in any way possible to save their lives. She knew she could depend on that, as her finger traced Ilana's head leaning back against his chest.

It could have been worse, she thought suddenly. Jon's alive and Ilana's in his arms. They had each other. They were both still alive. Thank God, thank God. Both alive. She looked into Ilana's eyes. Her baby was frightened.

"I yelled at her," she whispered.

"What?" Leah looked at her, shocked.

"Ilana. In the morning. She jumped on the bed, and I yelled at her." Elise hugged herself, rocking in grief. "Why did I do that to my baby, why? Why did I?" She wept. "If anything happens to her, that will be the last thing she remembers about me."

"This is just what I was afraid of," Dr. Gabbay murmured, distressed. "Elise, you've got to calm down. It's going to hurt your baby."

The words had an electric effect on her. She took a deep, calming breath, fingering her heavy stomach. She wiped her eyes. Whatever he was facing, he would take care of Ilana. And whatever she had to face, she must take care of this baby. They were parents first, and they were in this together. Together, we will take care of our family, Jon, I promise you. I promise you. "Shut it off now," she said, handing Dr. Gabbay the remote. And then more gently, when the flickering images melted into blackness: "Thank you all. I'm all right. I'll rest now. I'm sorry to have worried everyone."

Leah helped to tuck her back in.

"*Bubbee*, tell me how I'm going to live through this. How?"

"A person is as strong as iron, and as weak as a fly…"

Elise looked up at her grandmother's face: it was drained of all color. All through the video, Elise realized, she had never once considered how seeing these images of torture and imprisonment was affecting her grandmother. Throughout, she had not uttered a single sound. "*Bubbee*, are you all right?"

Leah patted her hand. "I just need to walk a little. I sit so much. I'll be back. In a minute."

She lumbered heavily to the door, closing it gently behind her.

Chapter seventeen

She lumbered down the hospital corridors.
As strong as iron, as weak as a fly…

Raus, raus.

Stripped naked. A religious young girl. The well-fed, leering men. The braided whips snapping hard above. The rows of striped skeletons holding razors. The long, dark braid, the red ribbon tied by Mama's hands, falling into dust. The hair below, shorn, like a sheep, an animal.

Still a woman? Still Leah?

Then burning needles, tattooed numbers. No underwear. Clothes— children's summer dresses, men's pants. Shoes, wooden clogs, torn cloth. Only the boots are left. A mistake. They let me keep my good, leather boots, my only connection to home.

Bottles: hollowed, emptied, labeled, laid on tiered shelves of wood, five across. That's what we are. No place to breathe, except in someone's face. Filthy feet in your face; sweat on your body. The smell. Unbearable. The noise. A thousand women. Talking, weeping. The noise. Unbearable.

Bear it. Learn to bear it.

The imploring hand of the fevered sick.

Ignore it. Think only about yourself.

Never admit you're sick. The others will kill you in the night to save themselves or else the Nazis will burn the barracks.

Put yourself first, second, and third. Then nothing. Then yourself. Then everybody else. No friendship. No love. Nothing shared.

Don't drink the water. Hold on to your bowl. Without a bowl, you'll die. Sleep with it underneath your head. Eat anything they give you, the grass and nettle tea. Drink urine. Eat sawdust. Eat the smell of meat.

Everyone has diarrhea. Twenty toilets. For one thousand women. Always clogged. Rivers of excrement to wade through. But you must keep clean.

A thousand women, and one place to wash, meant for twenty. You must wash yourself, your clothes. Get up earlier than the others. Get to the faucet. No soap. No towels. Forget the freezing cold, the wet cling of undried clothing.

Jump over the ditch, or you'll be selected. Stand on tiptoes, or you'll be selected. Pinch color into your cheeks, or you'll be selected. Cover baldness with a scarf, or you'll be selected.... Wait and wait and wait as they count and count and count. Survive the bite of the fleas. The bloody torment. The sleepless nights. The freezing cold, the boiling heat.

"Get up, you filthy bitches."

Morning, already?

"I'll send you out of here through the chimney."

When you die, guards get rations, cigarettes, home leaves. Each day, half must die.

Auschwitz is in the death business.

Be bad for business.

Live.

The hunger...it grabs you, punches you, squeezes out your breath. An enemy.

The cold. Warm yourself by the crematoria. The thirst. Drink the water in the swamps by the crematoria.

Can't mourn the dead. Envy them.

"You see that smoke?" The blockova *laughs. Mama, Fraydil, baby Shmilu...his blue hat all that is left in my hand.*

Lie on the shelf. Wait for them to smash the bottle, to load the pieces. Wait to become smoke.

Leave me alone. Let me die.

In the killing fields, carry sacks, bricks, dig up tree trunks. In no barbarous jungle, no island or rain forest, have women lived and worked as we do on cultured, European soil.

German soldiers on a passing train jeering: "Are you men or women?"

A knife in our young women's breasts.

May you lie rotting on the Russian front and may someone ask: Man or woman?

Laugh, or cry. Go mad. Scream. Guess. What will they do?

Send us home. Kill us all. The Russians will invade. The British will invade. Hitler will drop dead. Hitler will win, kill every Jew in the world. Try to think like the monsters. But there is no logic to hatred.

When will we get out? When will Ariana's parents—the film stars—Jaques and Francoise Feyder, rescue us? What will they feed us in their apartment in the sixteenth arrondissement? Their summer villa in Cannes?

Try to pray. To find God's hiding place. Give us a sign, dear God. Are you with us, here in Auschwitz? Will I ever understand how You rule Your world? How You rule Your beloved and Chosen people?

You are my dear God…

Can't see Him. Can He see me?

Away, in the fields, piles of burnt prayer books, phylacteries, photos, letters, handkerchiefs, cigarettes. Forbidden to touch. Down my blouse, the pages with prayers.

The blockova *finds it. Leaves me out in the snow, to die. All night long, pray…"From the depths, I cry to you, my Lord, and He answered…"*

The gray light of morning. Can't move.

Can't work in the fields.

Ariana and Esther weep. I'm finished, frozen, already dead.

Hear the number called. Your number. March out, barely alive.

A miracle. A transfer! To the effectkummer—*inside, warm, to sort clothes, food! To Heaven. A chance to survive!*

Maria did it. Her kuzyn, *the German prisoner. Because she saw me praying.*

Do anything for each other. To help each other.

Get through each day's inspection. Don't be too pale, too thin, too sick. Or the tenth woman, gassed to make room for a new transport. Don't be unlucky...because there are no rules. No laws.

Don't think.

Live, for your family who might still be alive.

Live, for the children you still might have. And their children.

For Elise. For Ilana.

She groped her way into the bathroom, steadying herself against white-tiled walls. She washed her face, staring at herself in the mirror, staring at her tired, old eyes, which had seen so much.

She splashed cold water on her face, then dabbed it dry.

Slowly, she walked down the hospital corridor, opening the door to her granddaughter's room.

Chapter eighteen

To Leah's surprise, Elise wasn't alone.

A young woman, a stranger, was sitting in a chair across from the bed. She turned to look at Leah, giving her a smile of bright white teeth. "Hi. You must be Elise's grandmother." She got up from her chair and walked quickly toward her.

"What are you doing here? Who are you? Who let you in…?"

"It's all right, *Bubbee*," Elise interrupted her. "I invited her. She sent me a note. She wants to help us, *Bubbee*. She's going to set up a television interview. They want to let me broadcast a message to the whole world. I can say anything I want, appeal to the kidnappers not to hurt Ilana and Jon…"

"Elise, darling." Leah walked over to her granddaughter, taking her hand. "But who is she?"

"I'm a journalist." Julia smiled warmly. "An on-air correspondent…"

Leah looked at the long, blond hair, the sparkling white teeth. A reporter. A television reporter. All the alarms in her system went off.

"Who do you work for?"

Julia hesitated. "BCN."

"Those anti-Semites…?"

"*Bubbee*…"

"Really, Mrs….?"

"You want I should give you my name? For what reason? You want to do something good for an old Jew? Was I born yesterday?"

"*Bubbee*, don't!"

"Elise, you don't watch TV the way I do. They blow up Jewish children, and BCN shows the crying mothers of the Muslim homicide bombers. They blow up Israeli buses, and BCN shows old Arab women standing at Israeli checkpoints, suffering, because the line is so long. We should let the murderers in faster…"

"Her name is Mrs. Helfgott," Elise told the reporter, embarrassed by her grandmother's cynicism, of which she had no part.

"Mrs. Helfgott," Julia Greenberg said gently. "I know that there have been some problems in the past. Believe me, our network has gotten tons and tons of mail, mostly from Jewish viewers, complaining about the lack of balance. That's why my predecessor…"

"Who?"

"The last BCN Israel correspondent…John Piggot."

"That piece of…"

"*Bubbee*!"

"Pig, I used to call him. Once, he shows Hezbollah terrorists captured trying to get over the border. He tells people they are family men, away from home, fighting for their country…. Doesn't show the weapons they were trying to smuggle in—that I saw on Fox. Doesn't remind people how they bomb Israeli towns—apartment houses, shopping centers, kindergartens, for no reason, after Israel took out every last soldier from Lebanon. Doesn't remind anybody how Hezbollah put on UN uniforms, kidnapped three Israeli boys, soldiers, and won't tell their mothers if they're alive or dead; won't let even the Red Cross see them…"

Julia got up and walked over to her. She looked into Leah's eyes and placed a hand over hers. "I know. It was terrible. That's why they finally took John out and sent me over instead…"

"*Bubbee*, she's a woman. I showed her pictures of Jon, of Ilana…

she understands. She thinks maybe someone will hear. Even terrorists have mothers, girlfriends, children. They go to doctors. Jon has so many Arab patients.... Someone needs to explain this to them...They also have hearts..."

"Elise, I know these kinds of people. These murderers. I met them in the camps. The kind that throw babies into bonfires, then go eat lunch.... Elise...please...you don't have to put yourself through this!"

"Not all Palestinians are terrorists! Maybe one of their religious leaders, or their politicians...." She persisted stubbornly. "After all, the more publicity there is that they are holding a doctor and a five-year-old.... Maybe world opinion..."

"The world and its opinion.... When we sat in Auschwitz, the world had an opinion? They put headlines in newspapers?" She took out a tissue and spat in it.

"But I have to do something...I feel so helpless!" Elise covered her face with both hands.

"Darling...don't...don't." Leah's head swam. She staggered back.

"*Bubbee*!" Elise reached out for her.

"Oh, my, here, let me help you...." Julia said, alarmed. She grabbed the old woman's soft arm, helping her into a chair.

Julia took a deep breath. "Look, Mrs. Helfgott, I understand why you are suspicious. I would be too in your circumstances. Reporters from this region tend to be pretty one-sided. But I'm not like that. That's why I made such an effort to get your daughter interviewed. The only people on the air are Palestinians. They are only too happy to describe their suffering. I believe that journalism has to get to the truth. The world needs to see your granddaughter. To hear her pain. Please, help me do that?"

Leah looked carefully into the young woman's eyes. But as hard as she searched, she couldn't read anything in them.

"Look, Mrs. Helfgott, my name is Julia Greenberg. I'm also a Jew. I even had a Bar Mitzvah."

Leah stared at her. "No." She shook her head emphatically. "You didn't."

Julia lowered her eyes in confusion. How could she possibly know that she'd never finished Hebrew School...?

"Well, I started Hebrew School..." She stammered, flustered.

So, maybe I'm wrong, Leah thought. Maybe my eyes are not so sharp anymore, to see into people's hearts. A Jewish girl. I would never have guessed it. She looked at Elise and her heart ached. She wanted so much to be doing something, anything.... And who was to say she wouldn't convince someone that harming Jon and Ilana would be bad publicity that, at the very least, might gum up their funding?

"You had a Bat Mitzvah," Leah sighed. "For a girl, it's called a Bat Mitzvah."

"Isn't that what I said?"

"No, you said Bar Mitzvah. Only boys have a Bar Mitzvah."

"Right. Of course." Julia nodded, smiling sympathetically into the face of the babbling old nuisance.

Leah squeezed Elise's hand, "If you feel you have to do this, then do this. I'll stay with you."

"Great!" Julia exulted, then reined in her glee, seeing the startled looks on the faces of the two distressed women. "You are making absolutely the right decision. The world is so small, and our network goes to every Arab country, all of Europe and the Far East, as well as America," she told them sincerely. "We have great credibility in the Arab world. Believe me, you couldn't have made a better choice on how to bring your message to them. And I promise, what you say will be heard. We won't touch a word of it."

"Maybe someone will hear me, *Bubbee*. Someone who just wants to help. They say their Allah is merciful."

"Yes," Leah murmured, "yes, darling, that's what they say." And Hitler kept saying all he wanted was peace.

"There's just one little problem..." Julia hesitated.

"What?" Elise demanded.

"Well, Dr. Gabbay is going to be furious at me for sneaking in here. And he isn't going to want the TV cameras barging into Elise's room..."

"Don't worry. I'll take care of Gabbay," Leah said. "You get your cameras. Do it fast and let my granddaughter rest."

"Deal," Julia said, hurrying out the door. "Be right back."

She took long strides down the hall. Downstairs, she high-fived the camera crew. "We're on, guys. Let's get moving." She got on her cell phone. "Jack, don't faint," she said exultantly. "I've got an exclusive interview set up with the mother! Yes, the one they are keeping behind barbed wire at Hadassah! How?" She chuckled. "Charm. The grandmother is a tough old bird, though. And she hates reporters.... Yeah, I'm setting up right now. I'll get you the tape in time for the evening news." She was suddenly silent, listening in disbelief, her eyes growing wide. "What!? You want to repeat that? Balance? But what does Elise Margulies have to do with the Sineh suicide bomber footage? Sean's footage!? You've got to be kidding! You know how he got that? He threw coins into the garbage and got those Palestinian kids to dive for them! You said yourself we should throw it out.... Pictures of Palestinian kids in the hospital? But how would you know if they were hurt by Israeli soldiers? What do you mean it doesn't matter? Time saver? I don't think so.... What, is that an ultimatum? Yeah, I understand, Jack. I understand perfectly..." She slammed the phone down.

She sat down, weary, feeling sick to her stomach.

"So, what's happening? Don't you want to put on some makeup? Because if you want the footage in time for the evening news, Julia, we have to get cracking," the cameraman urged her.

She looked up at him. If you want the footage. It was her decision. Slowly, she opened her compact. Her eyes stared out at her. She didn't look into them. Instead, she concentrated on her mouth, slowly putting on her lipstick.

"Okay," she said.

If it went smoothly, she wouldn't even be late for her date with Milos.

Chapter nineteen

Move out of the way, darling, will you? Your bum is blocking my view of the telly."

She had a nice body, he thought, in spite of himself, even if her thighs were a little on the heavy side, and her calves had a sturdiness that reminded him of Eastern European Olympic skiers. And the long blond hair was pretty, and her face lively, with even features that altogether would make someone look up and say of the overall woman: attractive. Only...there was something missing in her eyes, a warmth. They were like two little bluish ice floes. He turned over, sitting up in bed and lighting a cigarette.

Although a jury of his peers would have found it difficult to believe, the truth was it had not been Milos' intention to go to bed with Julia Greenberg. From the moment he'd glimpsed the supercilious lift of her jaw, heard her plummy British enunciation, he'd had only one thought: to enlist her as guide through the media labyrinth.

But the realization that he'd stumbled serendipitously into an incredible source of vital information, and that it could be his only if he reciprocated her obvious sexual interest, had put him into a bit of a moral bind. For the first time he thought he understood what his grandmother had gone through during the war. It was kiss Julia Greenberg or kiss good-bye to any hope of proving useful in the search for Dr. Margulies and Ilana. What he found most strange, though, was that acting like a lover made you start feeling like one. At least, he wanted to believe that. His conscience demanded it. He blew a cloud of smoke toward the ceiling.

She wrinkled her nose distastefully. "Only Eastern Europeans and the French still smoke. What is it about you people? Are you pollution junkies?"

He grinned. "Do you know they used to have commercials for cigarettes that said: 'Four out of five doctors smoke Camels.' One day it's bad for you—like butter. And the next it's good. Golda Meir was still smoking three packs a day when she was eighty. She said: 'One thing is for sure; smoking isn't going to be the death of me.'"

"Yeah, but how many of her friends were still alive?" she said, waving the smoke away irritably. She saw his eyes smile. She smiled back.

He was a wonderful lover. Not overeager, mind you. But what he lacked in passion, he more than made up for in skill and considerable charm. That was fine with her. She didn't like grasping adolescent sex. And British men were so predictable. He fit her vision of someone stylishly Third World. There was something a bit thrilling, she thought, about taking on a refugee from the gray slush of the thawing communist regime. Almost like a project. And his accent was so charming…

"Has anyone ever told you that you are a difficult woman? Why do you have to be so difficult?" he said, putting out the cigarette and snuggling back beneath the covers. He put his arms around her.

She smiled, kissing his ear, then reached behind his back and grabbed the remote. "I've got a surprise for you."

"Beautiful and full of surprises. Just the way I like my women…" He rubbed his hand over her bare stomach.

"Be serious for a minute." She took a deep breath. "I got an exclusive interview with Elise Margulies! You know, the mother…"

He sat up. "Of course I know who she is. How did you do it? They weren't letting anybody inside…"

"I bribed one of the orderlies to give her this note from me. It wasn't easy. He made me swear I was going to help the doctor and the little girl."

"Congratulations," he forced himself to say, pitying the orderly.

"Thank you very much!" she exulted. "This has got to earn me some kind of prize. Maybe the same one Suzanne Goldenberg got."

"Ah, the famous Ms. Goldenberg and her heartstopping pieces on museums honoring suicide bombers…. I don't know. It's asking a lot," he murmured drily.

But the sarcasm was lost on her as she focused intently on her own flickering television image. "Shh. Watch."

"And now we bring you a special report from BCN's Jerusalem correspondent, Julia Greenberg, who has arranged an exclusive interview with Elise Margulies, wife of Dr. Jonathan Margulies, and mother of five-year-old Ilana Margulies, kidnapped and being held hostage by Palestinian activists."

"Activists? Aren't those people who save whales?" Milos asked incredulously.

His protests were background noise to her as she studied the screen.

"Shh. I look good. That white blouse was a bit too predictable maybe, but I had no time to change. Still, damn good. Don't you think?"

"Damn good," he repeated tonelessly, watching her performance with growing dismay.

"I'm here with an Israeli settler who has paid the highest price of all for choosing to live in the Occupied Territories: the kidnapping of her husband and child. On the other side of this door, she is waiting to give her statement. This is a BCN exclusive, the first time that Israeli authorities have permitted her to speak during this news blackout."

The camera focused on Elise's soft, pale face, keeping her body hidden, Milos noted. The result was all the viewer would see was a tired but healthy young woman only moderately distressed. "Why did you have to call her a settler? Why not mention she's a pregnant woman hospitalized in intensive care? Why not tell them that keeping reporters away was a health precaution, not a 'news blackout'?" he protested.

"I think my hair could have used a washing. And maybe a trim. Is it noticeable?" She was speaking more to herself than to him. She hardly noticed him. She ran her fingers through the long strands.

"Mrs. Margulies, what would you like to say to the kidnappers?" Right look of concern in the eyes, yet the right firmness of tone, she noted, congratulating herself.

Milos got up and crouched down by the set.

"I would like to appeal to the kidnappers. My husband is a doctor. A good man, who saves lives. Many of his patients are Muslims. And my child is just an innocent baby. Whatever your grievances, please don't hurt innocent people. To kill unarmed prisoners is a sin according to Islam. Allah is merciful. I ask you too to be merciful." Her voice became choked. She cleared it with a deep breath: *"I appeal to Chairman Arafat, please. The Oslo Accords—which you signed—forbid the use of violence; I appeal to the United Nations: the* UN *Convention on Human Rights calls the deliberate killing of noncombatants a crime against humanity."* She was openly weeping now. With great effort, she composed herself. *"I would like to ask good people everywhere to light a candle and pray for the safe return of my husband and child. Jon, if you're watching this: I love you. And Ilana, baby,* Ima *is waiting for you, waiting to take you home. I beg you, please help send my family home to me safely."*

He got up, wiping his eyes. It was gut-wrenching. It couldn't help but win the sympathy of viewers. He reached out to touch Julia's hair. Beneath her callousness and ambition, did there beat a womanly heart after all? "People will need a heart of stone to ignore such words."

She nodded vaguely, the touch of his hand, his praise making her shift uncomfortably.

"There's more."

"More what?"

"Shhh. You'll see."

The tape went to herself, with the hills of Jerusalem in the background, and the wind blowing through her hair: *"A moving appeal from an Israeli settler. But on the other side of the Green Line, the wives and mothers of Palestinians, who have lived in these hills for centuries, are equally in pain. Mrs. Sineh sits and keens at the newly dug grave of her twenty-three-year-old son, Mohammed, who died as a suicide bomber on an Israeli bus last week."*

"I am also a mother," the heavy Arab woman gestured heatedly, speaking in her native Arabic as someone translated into heavily accented English, which somehow managed to retain the flavor of the native inflections. *"This kidnapped man, they say he is a doctor. But he is also a soldier. The Zionist occupation brings the Israeli soldiers into our villages. What we see every day—massacres, destruction, bombing of our homes—strengthened in the soul of my son the love of Jihad and martyrdom. Our land is occupied by the Israelis. The women and children my son killed, they are also Jews and settlers. And I want to tell Jewish mothers—take your children and run from here because they will never be safe. We believe our sons go to Heaven when they are martyred. When your sons die, they go to Hell. I am proud of my son. I hope my other sons will be martyrs also."*

The camera switched to a young woman: *"My brother was a victim. He was murdered by the Zionist occupiers, who forced him to give his life to free his homeland."*

His chest tightened at the savage words of the Arab women. It was sickening and primitive. Yet the visual image of the modern, educated, western Elise speaking perfect English pitted against the native women in their native dress speaking the native language couldn't help but weight the piece against her. It was cowboys versus Indians. Natives versus interlopers. White woman gets what's coming to her. Also, the repetition of the terms "occupied land," "occupation," "soldiers," "martyr" worked almost like a mantra, making one forget the historical facts of the Jewish history in the area, the successive defensive wars fought against five Arab armies, the displaced people from all sides who had suffered as a result of decades of conflict. Most of all, it helped to gloss over the fact that a man and child had been kidnapped and were being tortured. That unsuspecting bus riders had been blown to bits on their morning commute. It made you forget that real crimes that had no justification in the moral universe of the civilized world had been committed in the name of imagined grievances for political ends.

The screen switched to the children's ward of a Palestinian hospital.

"Some have said that the kidnapping of a five-year-old child by Palestinian activists is a new low. However, here in the Middle East, the pain and suffering of children is not limited to any one side." The camera focused on the bandaged head of a toddler.

"Palestinian children have often been the victims of Israeli Defense Force raids into Palestinian cities. Two days ago, a bomb blast ripped through a building in downtown Jenin, killing four and injuring dozens. While an Israeli Defense Force spokesman was quick to label the tragedy a 'work accident,' caused by Palestinian militants who callously housed a bomb factory inside a residential building, Palestinian sources claimed that the only factory in the area makes chocolate-covered biscuits, the kind children love to eat. But these children won't be eating any. Not today. This is Julia Greenberg reporting from Jerusalem."

There had been no picture of Jon and Ilana held hostage. So what the viewer was left with was wounded Palestinian children in hospitals, and others searching for food in garbage dumps. It was a masterpiece of propaganda. My God! Elise mustn't watch it! His heart sank. It was already too late.

She switched it off.

"So, what do you think?" She smiled.

"Oh, this is so slick..." He got up, walking around the room, furious.

"Why thanks..." she said doubtfully.

"Goebbels did that kind of thing all the time..."

"What did you say?!" she asked him, shocked.

"Julia, how could you do this?!" A flicker of pure hatred licked his heart. He was angry at her, and disgusted with himself.

"Do what?" she said, avoiding his eyes, feeling strangely vulnerable to the words of this man, her lover. She wanted him to understand, to condone, to see her in the kind, rosy light in which she saw herself.

"Skew the facts like this? You're a journalist!"

"And I did my job bloody well," she shouted at him. "How dare you!?"

"Mohammed Sineh, beloved son and brother, butchered eighteen people and wounded forty-nine, including a six-year-old schoolgirl and her seventy-five-year-old grandmother. But you neglected to mention that because that would make him look like a monster; it would ruin his image, make him and his darling, ethnic mother less sympathetic, right? And that would ruin the 'balance.'"

"I don't know what you are talking about..." She looked away.

"And those children you showed in the Palestinian hospital. The fact is, they weren't hurt by Israeli soldiers, were they? You just photographed a pediatric ward in some hospital..."

"Plenty of Palestinian kids have gotten injured by Israeli soldiers...the specific pictures aren't so important..." she cried passionately, feeling almost like crying at his attack. She had opened herself up to him, given him entry, and he was clumping around in muddy boots, slamming doors. He had no right!

"But to put that footage and the clip on kids scavenging for food together with a piece on the kidnapping of Ilana Margulies makes it look like tit for tat...and that's a lie."

She colored, remembering how Sean had gotten the garbage-dump footage. "It's complicated. It's not enough to show the victims of terrorist attacks. You have to show where the hatred is coming from. The other side. The occupation, the settlements..." She almost pleaded with him, trying to turn up the temperature of the cold stare that was chilling her.

"You know how much land changed hands after World War Two? How many people were thrown out of their countries, resettled? Millions. Russia took huge chunks of Poland. Losing land doesn't explain what these people are doing, or excuse it. What you did is unforgivable," he said, finally flinging off the mantle of lover and confronting her.

She was shocked, and a little frightened at his bluntness, not wanting to believe what her eyes were seeing in his; not wanting to recognize how badly she'd misjudged the situation. "And I suppose you think the brutal way the Israelis behaved toward these people in the West Bank and Gaza also has nothing to do with it…"

"Ah, the 'brutal occupation'…Right." His tone was full of contempt. "Isn't journalism supposed to be about facts, not slogans? My grandmother lived under a brutal occupation. She used to tell me how the German soldiers rounded up the teachers, professors, writers, and artists and shot them because Nazis were trying to turn the Poles into a slave class. There were big red posters on all the streets with the names of those executed every day. Any Pole who opposed them was executed, or sent to a concentration camp or slave labor in Germany. And the Russians? They robbed our coal, our produce, our reparations from Germany and shipped it all off to Russia while our economy collapsed. Compared to that, the Israelis were angels. They raised the per capita income. Improved health care. They never transferred anyone. In fact, thousands of Arabs have immigrated into the West Bank since 'sixty-seven…"

"Why are you so angry?" she pleaded with him, eager to recast the situation in a way more flattering to her ego and her vanity. She could now allow herself to believe she'd been had.

"I'll tell you why," he said, all pretense gone, savagely snuffing out his cigarette. "For years we in Eastern Europe envied you in the Free World because you had a free press. The kind that told the truth, told the facts. We gave our lives to have that! My father, my grandfather…we went to prison…. Don't you understand? It's one of the most important freedoms in the world, and you're letting people whore around with it…."

She felt her knees shake, and a certain strange, sharp pain in her heart. After all the things she'd marched for and protested for; all the Third World causes she'd identified with and admired. Freedom. Truth. Helping the oppressed. And he was casting her on the other side! The wrong side! Lumping her with the enemy. The corporate, moneymaking liars…. A flash of recognition tore through her defenses. Nothing he said could have hurt her more. She pulled the covers close to her chest.

"Thanks so much for the lecture," she told him in clipped, bitter tones. "But I know what side I'm on. And it's the right side. Even if I don't agree with their tactics, you can't ignore how Palestinians are suffering…"

"Oh, so it's their terrible suffering, is it? That's what gives them the right to walk onto a bus and decapitate babies and eviscerate pregnant women…?"

"I never said that! It's not an excuse. It's an explanation."

"Well then, I'm a bit confused. The Israelis have the highest concentration of Holocaust survivors in the world. They have been through five wars. They've had an average of one terrorist attack every hour every day for the past two years. They've had hundreds of women and children murdered, thousands injured…. But still, they aren't walking into Palestinian buses and blowing them up. So I suppose that means they can't possibly have suffered as much as the Palestinians. Or maybe the Palestinians have a lower pain threshold. After all, they never went through Auschwitz…."

"Don't feed me that Holocaust crap…. Plenty of Palestinians have suffered in prison camps too," she said angrily.

"I don't think my grandmother would agree that being in a concentration camp was the same as being in a prison camp. And she should know: she was in Auschwitz…"

"Your grandmother was in Auschwitz?" Her eyes widened incredulously. "But I thought…you said…." Her eyes narrowed. "You're not Jewish, are you?"

"No. I'm not Jewish. And neither is my grandmother. But she taught me that sometimes, there is only one side a decent person can be on."

"Then how did she wind up there?"

"She was in the Polish underground. She hid Jews in the basement of a house where she worked as housekeeper to a German commandant."

"That's unbelievable."

"It took tremendous courage. When the commandant discovered them, he gave her the following option: he would turn in the Jews, and she could leave. Or, he would smuggle the Jews to safety while she stayed behind and became his mistress. She was eighteen years old, a devout Catholic, a virgin, but she agreed. Long after the

Jews had been saved, the Gestapo somehow got wind of it. The commandant got transferred to the front, and she got sent to Auschwitz. It wasn't a prison camp. It was something indescribable. But even after all she suffered, she didn't bring her family up to hate. She didn't fill us with dreams of revenge, or send us out to blow up Germans. Sineh was a hate-filled fanatic, brought up by ignorant racists who taught him to value death instead of life. Blame his parents, his culture, not his victims."

"Look, the Sineh interview wasn't my idea!" she blurted out. "The network insisted. Try to understand! I had a world-class exclusive and the network refused to run it if it wasn't balanced…"

He turned to look at her with a sudden realization. "But you didn't tell Elise Margulies that, did you? You didn't mention that you were planning to add material to her statement…to give it 'balance'?"

"It wasn't relevant…" she said defensively, her sense of triumph washing away in increasingly powerful waves of discomfort.

"So, how do you think she's going to feel when you provide justification for everything they are doing to her family? When she sees the case you've made for the justice of kidnapping and murdering people like her?"

She straightened her back. "Whatever you think, I'm sympathetic to Elise Margulies. I'd have to be a monster not to be. But I'm also a journalist. I work for a news organization. She knew that. I'm just trying to do my job."

He looked at her incredulously. "You were just following orders…"

"Get out of here!"

This was his cue. He could make an exit that would salvage his conscience and take him far from the moral ambiguity of his actions. But he knew that once that door closed behind him, it could not be reopened. Some strange emotion he couldn't explain even to himself prompted him to take her in his arms. He felt her resistance. "Julia, you are better than this! Why did you do it? They're your own people, for God's sake!"

"And I hate that!" She struggled to free herself from his embrace.

"What?"

"That assumption of sympathy. I don't have a people. I belong to myself. And I don't owe anybody anything."

"But then why all this sympathy for these murderers?"

"Don't be ridiculous! I don't have any sympathy for these Palestinian thugs…. Get real. You're in this business. I didn't want to do it this way. But the network insisted, and they were right. If BCN would have broadcast Elise Margulies without something from the Palestinian side, do you think they'd ever consider talking to us again? Let alone giving us the second videotape…"

He looked at her, stunned. "There's a second tape!?"

"Please, don't ask me…"

"Are Ilana and Jon on it? Are they all right? And they're giving it to you? When…where are you going to pick it up…?"

"I can't answer that. I haven't seen it. I don't even know if they've made it yet. No one does. I'm waiting for my contact person to call me…."

"Then how do you know it's true?"

"We have our sources…."

He pulled on his pants and buttoned his shirt, his fingers trembling with anger. His *babcia* had always spoken with surprising sympathy about her Nazi commandant. He wasn't a bad man, she often said. Just the kind that wanted to get ahead, a bland rule follower without the strength of character required to sacrifice his ambitions to his conscience.

Despite everything he knew, he still somehow wanted to believe that underneath her vanity, her ambition, was a real woman, someone worthy of love. "You can't live just for yourself, Julia. This isn't just a news story; it's a terrible crime, a crime against humanity."

"Please don't preach. All of us in this business have done things we're not too happy about. It's sink or swim. If you want to get ahead in this business, then you better figure that out, Milos…." She shrugged petulantly.

He felt his body stiffen. If that was what she really thought, there was nothing left to say. He let his arms drop.

"Please…." she begged. "Please try to understand. It's not that I'm a bad person, or that I don't care about Elise Margulies. I do. But I also care about my Palestinian driver, the one who helped me get the first tape. He is such a decent person. He's also suffered such injustice…."

He forced himself to put his arm around her. "He was the one who helped you get the tape?" he asked quietly.

She nodded.

"Then maybe I *should* talk to him. Maybe it would give me some insights I don't have. A new perspective."

She looked up hopefully. "Do you really want to? He knows so much about history, about everything that's happened in this area…."

"Where's he from? What's his history?"

"I don't know really. I suppose the usual: thrown out of his home in 'forty-eight…"

"Then he's an older man?"

"Why do you say that?"

"Because that would make him at least fifty-five…"

She colored a little. "You're right. He's around forty, I think. Maybe even younger."

"So, where was he born?"

She shrugged, surprised that she'd never even thought to ask. "I just assumed…here. Anyway, what difference would that make?"

"Well, a lot of so-called Palestinians longing for a homeland were actually born in Egypt—like Arafat—or Jordan or Iraq. But I'd like to meet him."

"Would you?" Her lips brushed his ear.

He nodded. "I'm sorry for getting angry," he said stiffly.

"Well, all right then, but you have to promise to behave yourself and not go off ranting like some crazed settler…." She smiled.

He laid his hand over his heart and clicked his heels. "You have my promise as a Polish gentleman." He kissed her hand gallantly, suddenly charming again.

"Milos?"

"Hmm?"

Her long hair brushed his arms. She reached up to him, resting her wrists on his shoulders. "Can we just kiss and make up?"

He hesitated, cringing inside as he slid his arms promisingly down her back.

To his relief, her cell phone broke the momentary reverie. She mouthed the word "sorry" as she moved away, taking the call. "What? Now? Okay. What about the tape? Well, what did Ismael say?" She looked up at Milos anxiously. "No, I'll be waiting downstairs in ten minutes. Five."

She jumped out of bed. "Change of plan."

"What's up?" he asked, averting his eyes as she pulled on her underthings, and then her suit, not trusting himself to be impervious to desire.

"Emergency press conference at the prime minister's office. I'm surprised your office hasn't phoned you too."

He took out his cell phone and slapped it. "I think my battery is dead."

"You let your cell phone battery go dead!? Can't that get you fired, even in Poland?"

"Different standards." He grinned. "Polish battery. Come, I'll walk you down to your car." He hoisted his camera up to his shoulder.

The Honda Accord pulled up to the circular driveway.

"Is that Ismael?" Milos asked, pointing his camera toward the driver, unobtrusively pressing the on switch.

She knocked on the tinted glass. It rolled down. "Ismael, this is Milos. He works for Polish television. You've really got to sit down with him and straighten him out."

"Hi," Milos said, leaning in closer.

Ismael stared at him. "Why is he filming me?"

"What?" she said.

"His camera is on. Look at the red light," Ismael said, his jaw flexing.

"Oh, is it? My finger must have slipped. Thanks. Wouldn't

want this battery to run out too, like my cell phone. You know. Polish batteries." He smiled.

Ismael didn't smile back.

"Well, we've got to go. See you later, Milos," Julia said, leaning over to kiss him lightly on the lips.

"I'll be right behind you."

Chapter twenty

Bubbee, come quick. I think they are starting."

Leah sat down on the bed. It had been so hard for Elise, that interview. All those people barging into the room. All the strange men holding cameras, half of them Palestinians. The big lights. All the noise. Her effort to save her family had been heart-wrenching, taking her to the limits of her strength. But afterward, she seemed happy and relieved to have done it. It seemed to have given her some peace, some hope.

She held her granddaughter's pale hand, patting it.

The two women watched the flickering images on the little screen, images that were being brought into homes, desert palaces, international airports all over the world—images and words that had the power to influence the ideas and actions of millions of unknown human beings.

They were surprised at the use of the word "activists" to describe the kidnappers, but not unduly alarmed.

"Sha. What does it matter?" Leah comforted Elise. "They all do this. The word terrorist is only when they attack Americans in New York...Or the English in their bars..."

"I'm here with an Israeli settler…"

"She called me a settler. She didn't even use my name…"

"…who has paid the highest price of all for choosing to live in the Occupied Territories…"

"Elise, maybe we should shut it off?" Leah urged her.

"NO!"

"Mrs. Margulies, what would you like to say to the kidnappers?"

Her beautiful face. My granddaughter's beautiful face, so full of pain, facing the world, who are being coached not to care about her, the way they were coached not to care about us. We were Jews. Vermin. We deserved the camps. Deserved to die. And they are "settlers." They too deserve to be shot in their cars. Have their children kidnapped and slaughtered. Were people so unfair, so cruel, so stupid that they would fall for this again? Leah thought, her stomach knotting.

There was Elise, begging for mercy, for her husband, her child. Why, why?! Why do Jews have to beg the whole world to let them live in peace every single generation? To stop the senseless slaughter of innocents? To ask it, like it was a favor someone had the right to grant or deny? But at least they broadcast her. At least they are willing to listen. Which is more than they did for us. They didn't have news cameras in Auschwitz.

Elise heard herself pleading, straining again with the effort. She watched herself lose control and weep, feeling her eyes well anew.

It had been so hard, so hard. The effort to compose herself had been extreme.

She closed her eyes for a moment, imagining thousands of candles stretching from Maine to Abu Dhabi, churches, convents, synagogues, mosques…. Candles that would light the way home for Jon and Ilana. Candles that would banish the darkness of human souls bent on evil and destruction. Candles of mercy and kindness flickering tenderly in the dark hours ahead.

"Darling, such a good job you did. Anyone with half a heart will try to help them…." Leah comforted her.

"Do you think so?" she said, wiping her eyes.

"I do. You spoke so well, Elise. So well…Come take a rest now…"

"Wait…" Elise stared at the screen. This wasn't the end of the report, she realized, shocked.

She watched the wind in the hills blowing through the blond hair of Julia Greenberg as she introduced the mother of a suicide bomber.

"What! She never told me…!"

"Turn it off, Elise…" Leah begged her, alarmed.

Neither woman moved. Both of them sat transfixed, listening.

What powerful poison had been poured into this simple Arab woman's head that had succeeded in killing her most basic human instinct, the love of a mother for her own child? Leah wondered.

"They are saying it's justified. The kidnapping, the murder, it's justified…" Elise panted.

"Don't go overboard. Normal people are not so stupid. This woman is a monster. Everyone will see that, what monsters they are, how they devour their own children…" But then the screen switched to the children's ward of a Palestinian hospital.

"*…the pain and suffering of children is not limited to any one side…*"

"NO!" Elise screamed. "NO, NO! NO!" She got off the bed and went to the screen, shaking the television. "She's telling them to kill my baby, to kill Ilana! She's telling the whole world it's all right, it's justified, it's fair…" Elise wept, hysterical.

"Elise!" Leah cried, terrified, trying to stop her. Elise shrugged her off. Leah ran out into the hallway. "Please, somebody help me!" she screamed.

The television was on its side, its screen shattered. Elise lay beside it.

"Elise! My God!" Leah screamed.

"*Bubbee…!*" It was a panicked scream of wrenching, horrible pain.

It was then she saw it: the bright red that dampened Elise's nightgown, quickly widening into a puddle on the floor.

"*Bubbee,*" Elise screamed, "what's happening to me!? The baby. My baby!" She wept. The room was full of doctors.

Chapter twenty-one

T

Prime Minister's Office, Jerusalem*
Wednesday, May 8, 2002 · 9:00 P.M.

he area around the prime minister's office, a large complex full of tall, nondescript office buildings near the Israel Museum and Hebrew University, was packed. Police and army vehicles patrolled the roads, cordoning off streets and checking ID for blocks around. Milos had no choice but to park on the sidewalk and hope that the traffic tickets wouldn't catch up with him until he was safely back in Krakow.

He found Julia almost immediately. She was interviewing a woman who was part of a dozen or so people holding up hand-lettered signs that read: STOP THE OCCUPATION NOW! THE IDF ARE WAR CRIMINALS, JUSTICE FOR THE PALESTINIAN PEOPLE, and SETTLERS = OBSTACLES TO PEACE. They wore sandals and the cotton rags favored by backpackers who stock up on clothes in the street markets of Goa.

He shook his head. "Why aren't they protesting the terrorist attacks? Don't they understand that their country is at war? And why are you filming them? Twelve people is hardly international news...?"

"Even if there was only one, I'd interview him and report it.

I'm telling you, they are the only ones in this country that give me any hope."

"They aren't doves, Julia. They're ostriches."

"Excuse me, Milos, I've got work to do," she said coolly, turning her attention to her cameraman, her face suddenly closed.

He suddenly regretted ever having touched her. "See you later."

She nodded, pursing her lips, not bothering to turn around and look at him. Enough was enough, she thought, annoyed. He wasn't exactly a boyfriend, now, was he? She was the sailor, and he was just the equivalent of the proverbial girl in every port. But his criticism still rankled. It fed into the guilt she felt about callously producing the goods she knew her network wanted. One day, she comforted herself, I'll be Christiane Amanpour. I'll be the one who sets the agenda for the network. I'll have presidents on the phone apologizing to me. I'll start righteous wars against oppressors. I'll save the weak, champion the poor Third World against the fat cats of corporate America and Europe. But not if I get fired. First and foremost, I have to keep my job.

"No, don't pull back," she told the cameraman. "Get in as close as you can. We don't need to show how many of them there are. I'll give you the voice-over in a minute." She picked up her microphone and looked into the camera: "Here in the government complex that houses the prime minister's office, Israelis demonstrate against the brutal tactics of their own government. Some would call them traitors. Others, remarkable young people who are the voice of dissent that is so seldom acknowledged in a country that sees the daily destruction of Palestinian homes and hopes…"

She felt a tap on her shoulder. "Julia?"

"Sean. What is it? I'm in the middle here."

"They are starting the news conference now. You'd better head inside."

Reluctantly, she turned off her microphone. She'd finish the voice-over later.

The room was filled with expectant reporters, heavy cameras, and microphones of various sizes and shapes. A low buzz of excitement rippled through the crowd. There were hundreds of journalists, only a handful local. Security was extremely tight, with armed soldiers lining the walls, wearing headsets and carrying automatic weapons. Suddenly, the prime minister entered the room, a portly, silver-haired former general. He looked alert and serious.

"Good evening, ladies and gentlemen. We have called you together to issue an official statement: We, the government of the State of Israel, have done everything in our power to investigate the brutal kidnapping of Dr. Jonathan Margulies and his five-year-old daughter, Ilana. According to military intelligence, they are being held by terrorists, members of the military wing of the terrorist organization Hamas, who call themselves Izzedine al-Qassam. The brutality and ruthlessness of these men are well known. Our sources tell us that the doctor and his daughter are being held in Palestinian-controlled areas, which are, according to the Oslo Accords signed by President Arafat, under the full security control of the Palestinian Authority.

"Therefore, the government of Israel will hold Mr. Arafat and the Palestinian Authority entirely responsible for the fate of Dr. Margulies and his daughter. We ask that President Arafat fulfill his obligations."

He put down the paper and took off his glasses. "I will answer a few questions."

"*Ata be emet choshave sh'Arafat yanif eztbah? Kavod Rosh HaMemshala, Ata lo choshav sh'e Medinat Yisrael mafkira et baneha?*"

"What was that? What was the question?" Julia asked in a panic. They wouldn't let Ismael in, and so she was without a translator. A local reporter took pity on her: "He asked: 'Do you really think that Arafat will lift a finger? Don't you think that the State of Israel is simply abandoning its citizens?'" the reporter whispered.

"What the hell does that mean?" she muttered.

"It means the politicians are holding back the army from doing its job. You foreign reporters just don't get it, do you? If the IRA was kidnapping little British kids and doctors, and Tony Blair said that the British government wasn't responsible for them; that the head of the Sinn Fein was responsible…"

"It's not the same thing at all," Julia hissed, moving away. Her luck. Probably some right-wing fanatic from *The Jerusalem Post*.... She took her compact and looked into the mirror, running her fingers through her hair. She was up next.

The reporter from *The Guardian* cleared his throat, "Mr. Prime Minister, by your own words you admit that Mr. Arafat isn't involved in the kidnapping. Yet you are holding him responsible. Will the Israeli government use this as an excuse to invade Palestinian territory and break the Oslo Accords if you are unhappy with Mr. Arafat's response?"

Damn! That was *exactly* what she was going to ask.... She didn't listen to the answer, trying desperately to come up with something original.

She moved up to the microphone.

"Julia Greenberg, BCN News. Mr. Prime Minister, I'd like to ask you if you've considered meeting the demands of the Hamas for the release of Dr. Margulies and his daughter, and if not, isn't it really the Israeli government that is responsible for endangering their safety?"

She saw the face of the prime minister of Israel color. Gotcha! she thought, repressing a smile. She didn't bother listening to that answer either, looking around the room for Milos. But he was nowhere to be found.

Milos stood in the street, holding the cell phone to his ear. He hoped Julia hadn't seen him answer it. She'd no doubt wonder at its sudden resurrection. The simple truth was, despite the press credentials from *Zycie*, arranged by a friend who worked there, he wasn't actually working for anyone. He could have told her he was a freelancer, but they were bottom-feeders in the journalistic food chain, completely lacking in any prestige.

"Hello?"

"Milos-cha, *wnuk*!"

"*Babcia*?"

"How are you?"

"Don't ask. It isn't good, *Babcia*."

"Listen to me. I got a call from Leah. Her granddaughter, Elise…"

His heart sank. "Tell me."

"They had to deliver her baby."

"What?! When?"

"An hour ago."

"What happened?"

"Her placenta detached. There was hemorrhaging. They had to deliver by emergency cesarean."

"My God! Do they know why?"

"It happened right after she watched that story on BCN... We saw it here in Poland. It was terrible, how they twisted everything...terrible..."

"I know, I know," he whispered. "I told the reporter."

"No—! *She's* the girl? That one?"

He felt his jaw tighten, and his fingers curl into a ball. "Yes. *Babcia*, is it a boy or a girl?"

"A little boy.... They don't know if this baby...he's so tiny. She had six weeks to go. If something happens to her little girl now...For the love of God, Milos, you've got to do something! It never ends, it never ends..."

"I'm on the track of some important information about the tapes. Maybe it will have something to do with where the doctor is being held. I'll go see Elise." He stopped, listening helplessly, his breathing labored, thinking: *unforgivable*. "Don't cry, *Babcia*...! I've got to go. I'll call you later."

He felt his insides churn with a sickening feeling of having over-eaten something foul-tasting and full of harmful bacteria. He looked toward the lighted windows of the prime minister's office, where the press conference was still going on: preening, self-important western journalists who'd given up their sacred trust to become cheerleaders for trendy causes, the way communist journalists had once been cheerleaders for the government. He could not forgive them. They were depriving the free world of its most valuable weapon in condemning and exposing the worst human scourge since Nazism: the targeting and murder of civilians to achieve political and religious ends. He threw down his cigarette and crushed it under his heel in disgust.

He had not wanted to come. He was happily making educational videos on French culture for Polish television, drinking wine in little bistros along the Champs Elysées, when the phone call from his *babcia* came. It was a request from Mrs. Gold, Esther, the woman who had done so much for his family—including paying for his entire education. He could hardly say no. Besides, he had met Elise, years ago. He had come out of courtesy and obligation, without any illusion about really being able to help. He'd expected to spend a few days, politely express regrets he couldn't have been more helpful, then head back to Paris and saner pastures. Now, suddenly, he understood that by some accident of fate, he had stumbled on some really important information. It was almost frightening.

He walked along the sidewalk, weaving between the security guards, searching. There it was, across the street, the Honda Accord. Behind the tinted glass, he made out Ismael's dark head. He tapped on the window. It rolled down.

"So, stuck waiting out here, eh?" He offered him a pack of cigarettes.

Ismael smiled, accepting the package and looking it over. "Polish?"

"No. Lucky Strikes. In Poland, we are experts in blood sausage and bacon."

Ismael grimaced and laughed, removing a cigarette, then handing him back the pack.

Milos put it into his pocket, shaking his head affably. "Yes, I understand. We Poles aren't exporting much to the Middle East. Muslims and Jews aren't big blood sausage fans."

Ismael came out of the car and leaned against it, lighting the cigarette. "There are many similarities between Islam and Judaism. Both of us believe our forefather was Abraham. Except Ishmael was his firstborn, his heir, the one Abraham tried to sacrifice to God. 'The Dome of the Rock' is where the sacrifice happened…that is…did not happen. God spared Ishmael."

"So, both Islam and Judaism value human life?"

"Of course."

"So how do you explain Jihad? Suicide bombers?"

Ismael took a long drag on his cigarette and watched the smoke curl toward the lovely bright stars over Jerusalem's hills. "Such a beautiful place, Jerusalem. It's been invaded so many times. Claimed by everyone: Greeks, Romans, Crusaders, Arabs, Jews. People do what they want and find religious justification after. Every religion preaches goodness. But what they wind up doing is another story altogether."

"Weren't the Jews here first?"

"That all depends on if you see Abraham as the father of Ishmael or Isaac. We think it was Ishmael."

"The Bible says different."

"We have our own bible. It's called the Koran."

"Why can't Abraham be father of them both, Ishmael and Isaac?"

Ismael shrugged. "People believe what they believe."

"Where are you from, Ismael?"

"I was born in Syria. My father was an engineer. He moved to Saudi Arabia to work on the great construction boom from the petrol dollars. He died in a work accident when I was eight years old. My mother remarried, and we moved to Tul Karem to be with her husband's family. I enrolled at Hebrew University. I got a degree in languages. I went to work in England for a few years, translating articles from Arabic into English. And then about ten years ago, I came back."

"Any reason?"

He took a deep drag on his cigarette. "What did Dorothy say in *The Wizard of Oz*? There's no place like home."

"That makes you, what? Forty?"

"Forty-one."

"Married?"

He smiled. "Yes."

"Kids?"

"Three boys and two girls."

"Is your wife English?"

"No. Lebanese. My family arranged the match. They didn't want an English daughter-in-law."

"And are you still there, in Tul Karem?"

"Right next door to my parents."

"You are a lucky man. And how did you get into the news business?"

"You sound like you're interviewing me."

"Well, maybe I am. Our news bureau—"

"Which is?"

"*Zycie, Gazeta Wyborcza*—Polish dailies—anyhow, they need a 'fixer' in Palestinian Authority land. I've been shot at a few times, even with press plastered in masking tape all over my car. It's the Wild West out there. Would you be able to help us?"

"It depends."

"On what?"

"On what, exactly, you need me to do for you, and how much you are willing to pay."

"Well, let's say this. I understand from Julia that you were very helpful in getting the tape…"

Ismael stubbed out the last embers of the cigarette under his heel with more force than was absolutely necessary. "She's new. She misunderstood. I had nothing to do with it. I'm just a driver. I go where they send me."

"Julia said you were absolutely essential."

"Did she?" he said softly, almost to himself.

"Julia keeps saying that I don't know anything about the history of this area. That you are a great teacher."

"Ah. Yes." He opened the car door. "Some other time, perhaps? I'm afraid I'll have to be going. I will think about your offer, Milos. How can I contact you?"

"Oh, I'm going to be around Julia. She can always find me. And how can I contact you, Ismael?"

"The same way," he smiled. "Say, could I ask you for another smoke?"

"Sure," Milos said, handing him back the pack.

"You're running out," Ismael noted, returning it. Then he slammed the car door shut and sped off.

Milos jumped, his heart racing. The car had brushed uncomfortably close to his toes, which suddenly ached. He sat down on a low stone wall and took off his shoe. His sock was soaked with blood. God! he thought as he took it off, wiping the deep scratch on his toe with a lint-filled tissue. What have I gotten myself into?

But before he had a chance to explore that idea, his phone rang again. This time, it was his benefactor, Esther Gold herself.

Chapter twenty-two

His plan, of course, had always been to become the next Roman Polanski. But until then, filming the Louvre and the Cathedral of Notre Dame for Polish high school students was not the worst thing in the world, he thought, reaching down to massage his sore toe. As he stood in Israel's international airport holding a cardboard sign with the name of a man he didn't know and wouldn't recognize, Milos wondered—not for the first time in the last few days—if gratitude, family loyalty, and even idealism had reached their limits. His present casting in *Mission: Impossible* was not only dangerous, he told himself, but also faintly ludicrous. He just wasn't the type. He was sincerely looking forward to the day when he could fly out of this nightmare and back to his scintillating epic: *Piotr Visits Paris.*

But as the son of Witold Jankowski and the grandson of Maria and Jozef, it was, perhaps, too much to hope that he'd be allowed to live a quiet, boring life filled with ordinary pleasures.

He had been brought up with the idea that human rights were worth any sacrifice. His grandmother's tales of her exploits during the war, his grandfather's heroic death, his father's imprisonment, had shaped his childhood. One didn't live for one's own comfort; one lived to make a better world, to right wrongs, to rescue the weak and the suffering. This is what it meant to believe in Christ. All of his people were larger than life, cast in a heroic mold that he had been trying to avoid as long as he could remember.

For years his goal had been to approximate one of those characters on American television shows: long-haired boys who played in rock bands, danced with pretty girls, and rode in fast cars. He'd studied film because it gave him the chance to dream about living in places like Hollywood, New York, and the South of France. But then, somewhere in his freshman year, he'd found a box in the closet with all those yellowing leaflets his grandfather and father had written and passed around during the Communist era.

They'd been an eye-opener. He'd spent a weekend holed up in his room, just reading. The call for human rights and human dignity, for justice, and freedom to write and think and act, had done something to him. As much as he'd tried to fight it, it had stirred his blood.

This was not his first trip to Israel. When he was eighteen, his grandmother had been awarded the "Righteous Gentiles Award" by Yad Vashem for risking her life to save Jews during the war. A moving ceremony had been held, and a tree planted in Jerusalem in her honor. Esther had flown them in, along with all of her friends and many of the Jews his grandmother had saved. It was then he'd met Elise.

Such a pretty, lively girl! He would have fallen in love with her immediately if she hadn't already been married by then. Besides, as his *babcia* had admonished him, a Jewish girl needed a Jewish husband. Especially an Orthodox Jewish girl. And what Milos needed was to work hard and to find a nice Polish Catholic girl. (Since then, there had been much hard work, and many, many Catholic girls, although not of the kind his grandmother had had in mind...)

After the festivities, he'd been given the option of staying on to work at a kibbutz, and he'd taken it. It hadn't lasted long. Like most Eastern Europeans, he was not amenable to the socialist ethic so many Israeli leftists still romanticized, despite the proven failure of Communism to solve any of the world's problems and its unenviable success in inventing many new ones. He'd tried to convert the kibbutzniks, but had found them closed minded as well as utterly convinced of their liberalism.

So instead, he'd gone to work as a volunteer in a hospital storeroom, packing, unpacking, and delivering medical supplies. And on the weekends, he'd roamed around, hitchhiking up to the luxuriantly verdant land around the Sea of Galilee, and down to the almost frighteningly bare desert of the Dead Sea. Such a tiny country, but such a jewel. Every imaginable landscape was located within its borders.

Its human landscape was equally diverse, embracing more cultures, races, languages, and religious customs than almost any place else in the world. They called themselves Jews, but they had never really decided what that meant. It was certainly not a race, because the beautiful black Ethiopian immigrants with their dark skins and European facial features bore no resemblance to the Georgian Jews of the former USSR, with their squat foreheads, light skin, and almost Mongolian eyes. Was it a religion? Except for the ultra-Orthodox in their black outfits, practitioners of the faith seemed to make up the rules as they went along. Some ate pig and shellfish, while others wouldn't. Some wouldn't eat pork in the house, but somehow didn't mind eating it at a restaurant. On Yom Kippur, some prayed and fasted, while others went to the beach and stuffed themselves with pita and humous. True, the men were all circumcised. But what of the women? Girls in Tel Aviv looked like Britney Spears whore-chic-wannabes while Orthodox girls in Jerusalem were covered up from neck to ankle, with long dark skirts and under-the-chin blouses, not unlike Muslim women.

The native-born were pushy and brash, kind and warm, full of love for life and human beings. Everything they did became personal, whether they took you in their cab or sold you a package of gum. The driver, the grocer would often butt into your business, asking nosy questions, and giving kind and unsolicited advice that often turned out to be extremely helpful. It was an easy place to get lost, go broke, and not speak a word of the local language. Everyone knew directions, even if they were wrong; everyone would shove his hand into his pocket to give you a few shekels for the bus or a phone call; and everyone spoke a zillion languages and seemed open to strangers.

Only once did he encounter open hostility because of who he was. It was a woman he'd been sitting next to on a bus in downtown Jerusalem. She'd seen him reading a Polish newspaper.

"How are you enjoying your visit?" she'd begun in Polish, pleasantly enough.

He'd answered, "Very much."

"Unfortunately, I was also in your country. But I didn't enjoy my visit."

Only then had he seen the blue numbers on her arm.

"This country was built by broken-hearted people like me. Take my tears home with you along with your other souvenirs," she'd told him.

He'd sat there, speechless, for the rest of the trip. "I'm very sorry," he finally said, hanging his head. What did it matter that his grandmother had not been part of it? So many others had, their hatred making the horrors possible.

"I'm also sorry. You are a young person. It's not your fault. Here, take a cookie." She offered him one. "I made them for my grandchildren."

"I heard that," the man behind him said, tapping him on the shoulder. "Don't feel bad. We Israelis aren't vengeful."

"That's what's wrong with us," the woman on the other side of the aisle piped up. "We don't know how to hate. We forgive too fast, take chances with our security for so-called peace…"

"You don't know what you're talking about. That's what's right with us!" the man answered her.

By the time he'd reached his stop, the discussion involved half the bus and was still going strong. He'd held the cookie in his hand and waved good-bye. Almost everyone had waved back.

There was no unity. Everyone thought the rest of the country were dopes, and wrong-headed, and delusional. Yet, if there was a war, or a terrorist attack, they would lay down their lives for each other unhesitatingly, whether as soldiers and policemen or simply as passengers on a bus with a suicide bomber whose hands needed to be kept away from the detonator.

Often, in the last few days, he'd asked himself what he was

doing here, getting mixed up in a story that had nothing to do with him. But the more he understood the scale of the human tragedy that was unfolding in this part of the world, where ordinary, good people were on the front lines fighting big, well-funded terrorist machines, the more he realized that no decent person could stay uninvolved. Terrorism had to be stopped, before it destroyed civilization altogether, and no man, woman, or child anywhere in the world was safe from its terrible reach.

He looked up at the flickering lights on the board showing incoming flights. Flight 774 from Zurich had landed a half hour ago. That was the flight number Esther had given him on the phone when she called with her urgent message to get down to the airport and give John Mellon a ride and all the information he could. That it was a matter of life or death.

Who was John Mellon? And could he be trusted? And what did she mean by "life and death"? And most of all, what was taking him so long, he thought irritably, his toe throbbing, his body heavy with fatigue. Just as he began thinking about sneaking out, he noticed a large, muscular man elbowing his way past the other passengers, staring fixedly in his direction.

Russell Crowe on steroids, he thought, a little alarmed. Whatever conflict there was, you'd want him beside you, not facing you (armed) from the other side. The stranger approached rapidly, a sudden grin making him seem less lethal.

"Hello!" Milos began.

But the fellow put a warning finger to his lips and shook his head. He took out a pad and wrote: "Don't speak to me," showing it to Milos, who then gestured an offer of help with the luggage, an enormous duffel bag.

But the man just shrugged as he took in Milos' slight build, as if to say: Who are you kidding? And with no more effort than it would have taken to fling back a scarf, he hoisted it over his shoulder.

Milos walked ahead silently toward the exit and the car park, fascinated and concerned about this sudden descent into cloak and dagger.

The man threw his bag into the backseat, then climbed in

beside it. Milos sat behind the wheel. No one spoke. Finally, Milos took out a pad and wrote: "Where to?"

"Jerusalem," the man wrote back in a clear, military script. "But first let me check over your car."

He crouched down, running his fingers over the dashboard, tearing off the seat covers, opening the glove compartment. "Oh, very nice, Milos. Do you know any Israeli girls?"

Milos shook his head, wondering if it was some kind of code, or if the guy was just plain nuts.

"Do you think you could stop at the next gas station? I need to take a leak," he said.

Milos nodded.

When they pulled into the station, the man got out first, retrieving his bag, and asked the attendant for a key to the washroom. He motioned Milos to follow.

Inside the tiny stall, he took out a paper and wrote: "Take off all your clothes and leave them outside the door, then lock it."

Babcia, what have you gotten me into...? Milos thought, panicking as he undressed, thankful it was after midnight and practically deserted. Naked, he opened the door, throwing his clothes outside, then locked the door behind him. God. If there was a police raid, how, exactly, was he going to explain this when they locked him up on some sleazy vice charge...?

The man handed him a towel from his duffel bag. "Here. Sorry. Okay. Your clothes are probably bugged too."

"Too?"

"Well, it's that or your car. Or both. I haven't yet decided."

"My car? Impossible."

"Possible. One wrong word and we could both be in deep trouble, not to mention certain others not with us right now." He arched his brows cryptically. "I understand from Esther Gold you have some important information? That's the reason I asked to have you pick me up. Because we are working on a very tight deadline, and I didn't want you to risk transferring it by phone."

"Yes. But, first, who, exactly, are you?"

"Oh. Sorry. I thought you'd been briefed. I work for Esther Gold—I understand she and your grandmother are friends?"

Milos shook the extended hand. He felt his fingers crushing in the firm grip. His extremities, he thought, were not having a good day. "When you say work, what do you mean? In what capacity?"

"Okay. Let me tell you what you need to know now. I mean, just in case they threaten to pull out your fingernails, or cut off your dick, you wouldn't want to know anything you might feel compelled to hide, now would you?"

Milos swallowed hard, pulling the towel around him more tightly.

John grinned. "It won't come to that, I'm sure. I work for an organization called IKARM, International Kidnapping Rescue Mission."

"Is it private? Public? Government? Army…?"

"Totally private. We are hired by the families and companies of kidnap victims. And we do whatever is humanly possible to free them. Right now, as I said, we are working for Mrs. Esther Gold to free Jonathan and Ilana Margulies."

"You're mercenaries?"

A slight frown moved over the giant's face. "Do you get paid for what you do?"

Milos swallowed. "I didn't mean to be insulting…"

"Sure we get paid for what we do. But what we do is rescue victims of kidnappers, terrorists, and other scum. Not like police and secret service—government employees—who get paid good tax dollars to safeguard the lives of their citizens, but don't think that's a high-priority item. When we take the money, we actually do the job."

"You don't think the Israelis are going to rescue Margulies?"

His jaw flexed. "That depends."

"On what?"

"If their politicians will let them. If this country really cared about its people, they'd have gone into Gaza and blown it up the first time one of their buses blew up. Instead, they pussyfoot around, kill a terrorist here, another one there, talk, sign papers. You've got thousands parading in the streets for every scum funeral. Just bring in some planes and bomb the bastards." He shrugged. "I guess the suits got their reasons. But we're not like that. We're different. We have one consideration only: how to get the victims out alive and kill the terrorists."

"There's an 'A' in IKARM. What does the 'A' stand for?"

"Are you being funny?" he said belligerently.

"No. I'm a writer. Words interest me," he said nervously.

He calmed down. "A writer, huh? Because this is no laughing matter. Those terrorist scums are taking over the world, with the help of all those fucking reporters.... Idiots. We are going to crush them, desiccate them, annihilate them..." His face grew red.

"Ahh, John?"

"What!"

"You meant 'decimate,' didn't you? And you were talking about terrorists, right, not reporters?"

He rubbed his chin sheepishly. "I guess I tend to get carried away.... Now, that information you spoke about?"

"Oh. I believe that a BCN driver, a Palestinian, has some connection to the kidnappers. He's the one that delivered the tape from them."

"His name?"

"Ismael Abadi. He's forty-one. His family lives in Tul Karem. Wife. Five kids."

"This is what he told you?"

"Yes."

"Thanks. This saves time. We'll check it out."

"Ahh. John?"

"Hmmm?"

"My clothes?"

"Oh, sure. But when you get home, burn, or dispose, of anything you had on tonight, and check your pockets carefully."

"Why are you so sure I'm bugged?"

"Well, I have this little thingamajig that vibrates when it locates a bug. It's been shaking its maracas off since I met you. But hey, that's not a bad thing. It means there's a pretty good chance your information is worth something. But it also means you gotta watch yourself, cause Big Brother is watchin' you. Know what I mean?"

Milos felt dizzy.

"You can get dressed now, but remember, don't say anything personal to me at all. It's all right to talk nonsense, that will throw them off. That's why I asked you about the girls, you know. Write down your cell phone number. And if you need to contact me, here is my e-mail address. Best to do it through a blind cc."

"Whatever you say. Just wave your hand when you want to be dropped off."

The rest of the trip to Jerusalem was spent in silence, the radio blaring Arabic music—John's idea. At the entrance to Jerusalem by Sakharov Gardens, right before the turnoff to the residential Jerusalem suburb of Ramot, he signaled for Milos to pull over. In one swift movement, he got out, grabbed his bag and disappeared into the night.

Milos felt his body slump as a slow chill crawled up his spine. He was too exhausted to visit Elise now. And anyhow, he needed a change of clothing, disliking the *eau de public bathroom* scent of his current outfit. He decided to go home—a fleabag hotel with an unobstructed view of the site of several suicide bombings on Ben Yehuda Street. Inside his hotel room, he turned his clothes inside out, shaking out his pockets.

There was nothing.

Boy, he thought, exhaling in relief, a foolish grin spreading over his face. That guy really had me going. He leaned back on his pillow, taking out his nearly empty pack of Lucky Strikes, determined to dig out the last cigarette. As he did so, his finger suddenly and unexpectedly met a small metal object. He tore open the pack and stared. A single cigarette stared back, along with a tiny black transmitter.

Chapter twenty-three

Maria, for the first time in my life, I don't know. I can't pray. How can God do this to me, after everything I've gone through? How?"

Not like her at all, Maria thought with alarm, listening to her friend Leah's almost incoherent voice. Leah, who even in the camps hardly ever cried, who held on to her faith. Leah, who always said: "Better pray than cry!" holding on to that precious half-burnt prayer book she'd found in the forest that had almost cost her her life. "Leah, you were always the one who told us not to confuse the works of God with the works of men. This isn't an earthquake, or a flood, or fire. This is the work of evil men."

"What if she loses the baby, and then something happens to Ilana, Jon...?"

Maria was silent. What was there to say? Anything was possible in this world. But somehow, her heart told her it wouldn't come to that. It was just too cruel.

Or was it just wishful thinking?

She had a sudden idea. "Leah, why not do that ceremony?"

"What ceremony?"

"The one from the *kabbalah*…"

"The *Pulse de Noura*…" Leah's voice wavered, full of a strange discomfort. "I don't even think I'd remember how…"

"Don't worry. I will never forget it. None of us will. It saved us once. It can do it again. We will all come to Jerusalem and do it together."

"But your health! The traveling…!"

"I'm healthy Polish stock…"

"But the cancer…"

"That was five years ago. It went away along with my breast. It wouldn't dare come back after all that money Esther spent on it, getting the best doctors, flying me to Los Angeles…. Besides, what's the point of living if you are afraid to do anything? I will go to Confession, and then take Communion and get a blessing. And then I will come."

"Maria?"

"Yes?"

"When is it going to be over?"

"They didn't win then, and they won't win now. You'll see, Leah. You'll see."

"God bless you, Maria."

"And God bless you, my little sister."

She hung up the phone, then crossed herself.

The young, bald girl standing naked beside her in the showers who'd reached out to hold her hand as they waited for water or poison gas to pour from the ceiling, not knowing which. The girl ready to die for a prayer book, who'd given her back her faith. The girl who she'd convinced her German camp boyfriend to get a job in the sorting room where she would be warm, where she could steal food and clothes. The girl whose friends had become her friends. Ariana and Esther. The four of them together sharing bread, dreams, clothes, warmth…life.

She paced her small apartment, looking at the phone, hoping Milos would call with some good news. She couldn't help feeling frightened and guilty that she had involved him in all of this. But there was no choice. Not really. She'd made a Covenant. And she only knew one way to keep it. She only knew one way to live.

She looked out the window at the dark, deserted streets. What is wrong with life is human memory, she thought. What is the point of life and history—all that human beings sacrifice and endure, overcome and rejoice over—if we do not remember? What point are the centuries, years, months, hours, minutes, if they slip through our fingers, if we learn nothing?

After the war, she had had such hopes. The enemy had lost. She was determined to go home and retake all that had been stolen from her. But again and again she had been bludgeoned by new calamities. Her father's death. The poverty and devastation of the country she loved. Still, she'd managed to make a life for herself.

She'd met Jozef on a bread line. He was standing behind her when she fainted from hunger and cold. He'd wrapped her in his coat and brought her a warm loaf. Jozef, she thought, quick tears coming to her eyes. Like a mountain with a laugh that made the dishes clatter…. Jozef, Jozef.

He had been a student of literature when the war broke out. Like her, he had joined the Polish underground. He had survived the war in the forests, until the Russians picked him up and sent him to a prison camp. With no paper or pens, he began to write his experiences on pieces of wood, circulating them among the other prisoners, organizing them to demand better food and more humane treatment.

Eventually, they'd let him go.

Despite the secret police who controlled the press, Jozef wrote uncensored pieces that he circulated fearlessly. She was afraid. After all she'd suffered…but when he asked her to marry him, to join her life with his, she knew she could not say no.

They were married in church. Leah and Esther and Ariana had sent telegrams and gifts. They'd rented a small flat in Krakow.

Jozef continued to work: he published social criticism, masking it in fairy tales and allegories. Soon, the secret police began to hound their steps. So they took their firstborn, Janusz, and moved away from the city, to the Sudety Mountains in a place called Gorzanow. It was a place emptied of deported Germans and filled with Poles uprooted and transferred from their homes in areas that the Soviets meant to annex to the Ukraine.

With generous help from Esther, who was doing better than

ever, they bought a little piece of farmland on a hill right near a lovely river. Jozef, the journalist, the intellectual, was going to be a farmer. Planting potatoes, he said, was better than planting lies in people's heads.

She remembered those days—milking and plowing, pulling fresh vegetables from the earth. And the long, starlit nights, plotting their escape back to civilization. Often now her mind went back to those sunsets, watching her husband and son horseback riding through the darkening fields as they made their way home to the warm, lamplit house, filled with the scents of baking raisin bread, fresh *pierogy*, and beef and barley soup. It had taken her decades to realize that they had been the happiest years of her life.

But Jozef had to return to Krakow. He couldn't sit back idly, he said, in a Poland where the only places one could speak the truth were church, cemetery, and courtroom.

Those years back in Krakow…writing the secret monthly periodicals, setting up the secret libraries. And then the knocks on the door in the middle of the night, the secret police, the fake trials, the years in prison. The lonely nights, bringing up Janusz on her own.

When they finally let Jozef go, his huge body was gaunt, and his hair had turned ash gray. It didn't stop him. In 1965, he became one of the authors of the "letter of 34" in which writers and scientists protested censorship to Prime Minister Cyrankiewicz. And five years later, the police took Janusz, then a freshman at the University of Warsaw, accusing him of meeting with fellow students, discussing political and social problems, and distributing texts. She had no doubt it was true.

The handwriting was on the wall. In 1970, two weeks before Christmas, when price increases finally sent thousands of workers of the Gdansk shipyard out into the streets shouting: "Bread!" and "The press is lying!" the army opened fire. One of the first to fall was Jozef.

She and Janusz buried him in the mountains overlooking their fields.

When Esther called with the terrible news about Elise's family, suggesting that Milos go to Israel, she had hesitated. It was enough, she told herself. Enough sacrifice. Enough risk. She wanted him to enjoy life, all the new freedoms. To study and travel and go to parties...All the things she and Jozef and Janusz had struggled so hard to give him. She wanted him to be part of a new world, a shining new millennium in which personal sacrifice for basic human freedoms were no longer demanded; where a man had life, liberty, and the pursuit of happiness handed to him simply by virtue of being born. Besides, she had serious doubts whether or not he'd agree. He'd always seemed so lighthearted, playing his English rock music, riding his motorcycle, going to movies and concerts.

But Leah was right: the battle had begun all over again. One could not sit on the sidelines.

"Seek justice and pursue it," the Bible said. You might not find it in your lifetime, but you had to live your life chasing it down. You could never make your peace with anything less.

She was glad Milos understood this. But as she studied the silent phone, willing it to ring, she couldn't help but wish that the pursuit of justice didn't always have to be so dangerous.

Chapter twenty-four

A sudden sense of thirst woke her. Elise wet her parched lips with her tongue. "Jon?" she whispered, reaching out for his body at the other end of the bed.

"Darling," she heard. But it wasn't Jon. It was an old woman.

"*Bubbee?*" Her voice came out hoarse, cracked.

Dry, she thought. My tongue, my throat, my brain, my body. Scorched and dry. Like the pages of a newspaper used to start a fire blazing in the fireplace: black leaves that only gave the appearance of solidity, the illusion of wholeness. The minute you touched them, they fell apart, disintegrating into a million pieces.

"Thirsty," she managed.

"Come, lift your head. Take a drink. Of course you are, now, drink my love, my lovely Elise." She tried to lift her head to grasp the straw that seemed suddenly so very desirable. Her whole body ached to wrap her lips around it, to drain the cup. But the moment she moved, her body sent a shock wave of pain so powerful she felt her legs tremble. She held her stomach, gasping.

It was then that she remembered.

"My baby!" she wept.

"Elise, it's a boy! A beautiful little boy. He's alive, Elise, Elise. Come have a little drink. You have to be strong for him, for your baby. Soon you'll go to see him. Elise, Elise," Leah crooned, her heart fuller than anyone's had a right to be, she thought.

Elise felt her grandmother's hand slip behind her neck, raising her head up. She drank in huge, almost pauseless gulps, draining the cup. It tasted like plastic, like hospitals. She pulled her body up in small increments, resting after each tiny, pain-filled motion. When she finally reached a sitting position, she took a deep breath, looking around the room.

It was filled with flowers: White and yellow daisies, red and pink and yellow roses, bunches of chrysanthemums of every hue, waving orange plumes of the birds-of-paradise, anemones, tulips, baby's breath. "How? Who?"

"They haven't stopped arriving. The hall is full of them. The hospital is full. Everyone in the country. Strangers, politicians. Your grocer, all your friends. And from Esther, Maria, and Ariana. And that's not all: they are getting on a plane. Coming to see you."

"Really? All your *bloc shvesters*? The whole Covenant?" It had been years. And then, as her eyes wandered from vase to vase, again she remembered. The baby. Her little boy. And Ilana. Ilana! And Jon! "Tell me."

Leah hesitated. "The doctor will come. I'll get the doctor." She started to get up. Elise squeezed her hand almost painfully.

"Tell me, *Bubbee*. For God's sake, please!"

She took her granddaughter's pale hand into hers, careful not to disturb the white surgical tape that kept all the intravenous tubes attached to her veins. "Where do you want me to start?"

"Tell me about the baby."

"Elise, he was six weeks early. He weighs one kilo three hundred grams."

"God!"

"He's alive. He's a fighter. The doctors say he has a good chance."

"You saw him?"

Leah nodded. "A *broocha* on his *kepeleh.* Little *shefelah.* Little lamb…. May God watch over him…."

"I want to see him."

"Of course you do. Of course you do." Leah patted her arm helplessly.

"And Jon and Ilana…?"

Leah shook her head and shrugged. "Nothing new."

Elise tried to move her legs. The pain was excruciating.

"It's the cesarean. The stitches. Everything is still raw. It's only been a few hours. It will get better. You are all right. Nothing terrible. It will heal."

Elise felt her eyes well. "Why is God punishing me? What have I done to deserve this?"

She looked at her granddaughter, startled. How many times had her husband Yossi, God rest his soul, asked this question?

He, too, had been a survivor. A very religious cousin had fixed her up the same year she came to America. The truth was, she'd felt lonely among the Americans and Yossi had understood her. Too late she realized that unlike her, something inside him had died in the camps. Optimism? Joy? She didn't know exactly. His vision of God had changed. It was a vision that frightened her.

Such a didactic, uncompromising, unfeeling tyrant was Yossi's God. He was constantly criticizing, keeping track if you ate something with the wrong rabbinical supervision; if you carried a tissue in your pocket when you went to *shul*; if you washed the floors thoroughly enough before Passover. The God who created sunsets and roses cared about a crumb left in the corner of the kitchen?! He'd never forget it, that crumb, never forgive you? she'd argue in vain.

She couldn't believe in Yossi's God.

Maybe Mendel, her son, had felt the same, it suddenly occurred to her. And he'd dealt with it by throwing away the skullcap, the fringed garments…escaping as fast as he could, making his home, "home on the range…where never is heard a discouraging word." In the home he'd grown up in, all Mendel had ever heard from his father were discouraging words. He was always a good kid. Not rebellious.

But at a certain point, it was enough. He didn't want the dark suit, the narrow streets, the constant serving of an implacable deity that was impossible to please. He wanted something else. Yossi had never forgiven himself for Mendel's desertion, or for Miriam's death, viewing both as a personal punishment from God for his sins. He'd tried all the harder to please Him. That hadn't made him an easy man to live with. So many stringencies he'd insisted on! Every week he and the rabbis figured out something else you weren't allowed to enjoy. It gave them such pleasure.

"I don't believe in punishments coming down from Heaven, Elise. Sometimes people suffer because they make mistakes.... *They go shopping for a coat in a bad neighborhood.* And sometimes, they suffer for no reason at all. Wasn't that the whole point of the Book of Job?"

"You're right. I've failed Jon. Failed our baby. I didn't keep him in long enough. It's my fault." She wept.

Leah put her arms around her granddaughter's young shoulders. "Don't you dare blame yourself! There is a long list of people whose fault this is, but your name is not on it. Believe me."

"That reporter!!"

"Don't waste your time and strength on hating her. Let God deal with it. He always does, in His own time, and in His own way. The time we waste on hating, we could be using for loving. So, dry your tears. You have more important things to do. You have a baby that needs you."

"Yes, the baby..."

"But first, you have to take care of yourself..."

"I don't care what happens to me anymore! I wish I was dead."

Leah's face lost color. She put both hands on either side of Elise's shoulders, looking into her face fiercely. "That's for our enemies to wish for. For themselves and their children that they send out to murder and die. It's not for us. Pray for life, Elise, for yourself, your husband, your two children. Pray to our God. Wish for life!"

"Without Jon and my children, I don't have a life."

"Yes," Leah whispered. "Even then."

Elise looked up, in shock. "It isn't human."

"Yes, it is the most human thing in the world," she said quietly. "I know it's hard to believe, but that's what your God asks of you."

"How did you do it? How did all the people who went through the camps, who lost everyone—father, mother, sister, brother, husband, children—how did they manage to go on living? To remarry, have more children...? How?"

"By loving life. And—in spite of everything—by loving God. By having enough faith to start over again and again; enough faith to risk having our hearts break all over again. That's the true meaning of faith. It's the deepest kind of heroism."

The two women sat there looking into each other's eyes, listening to the silence.

"*Bubbee*, I don't know if my faith is strong enough. I'm no hero."

"Then depend on your love."

"What do you mean?"

Leah sat down beside her on the bed, slipping her hand around Elise's narrow, girlish shoulders. So young! she thought. So young. "Do you love your baby?"

Elise's eyes swam with tears as she nodded.

"Then don't torture yourself over things that are too big for you. Things you can't change. Do the small things. Rest and eat so that your milk supply will be good. The baby needs his mother's milk. It will make him stronger. He'll grow faster..."

Elise suddenly looked up, startled. "Yes," she said. "I can do that."

"And visit him and touch him. A mother's touch on the skin. It will help him grow and heal."

"Yes, yes. I can do that as well," she thought, surprised she had not thought of it herself.

"And then you must plan the *bris*."

Elise looked off into the distance. "Jon and I talked about it so many times. The circumcision ceremony in the Jerusalem hotel with the garden. The different kinds of fish and eggs, and pancakes, and waffles. Who we'd pick for the *mohel*. What kind of dress we'd buy

Ilana…. Who would be the *sandak*, how many guests we'd invite…"
She held her body and rocked.

Leah touched her trembling shoulder. "Come, try to sleep. Let
the stitches heal." She pulled the blanket over her, tucking her in,
watching her eyes close and her breathing grow restful.

Suffering did different things to different people, she thought,
taking out her well-worn prayer book, thumbing its familiar pages.
Some souls became tempered, unshakable in their faith, while others
became twisted and misshapen, throwing off all connection to God.
She looked at the pages wrinkled from the moisture of fallen tears,
the touch of countless turnings, the vicissitudes of different climates
and different continents and different joys and sorrows.

She had no doubt Jon would endure the pain inflicted on him
with courage. But the pain of witnessing his child suffer? He was
young, an American, a doctor. All his life he had lived among kind
people. Even in the army, he had been a medic, saving lives. Unlike
her, he had had no months in a ghetto, no time to prepare. He had
been thrust into a terrible reality with no warning.

She looked down at the ancient Hebrew words. Enemies
changed, horrors changed, misfortunes changed. Only the words,
she thought, stayed the same, a boulder in the raging stream: "From
the depths, I cry to you, my Lord, and He answered…"

All through that bitter-cold night, they had coursed through
her, keeping her alive. Wherever Jon was, she hoped their power
would be great enough to sustain him too.

Chapter twenty-five

A*ba*, tell me the story—"

He held her close, and began once again.

"Once upon a time, there was a little girl who was walking through the forest with her daddy to dance by the lake. All the way there, she danced and danced, picking up flowers and singing..."

"What did she sing?"

"Oh, you tell it, Ilana—"

"I don't know—" (This was part of the story, where she said she didn't know, and then he said he didn't know, and then finally she came up with a song, each time the same song.)

"*Eretz Yisrael sheli yaffa ve gam porachat...*" she sang.

"*My Israel is beautiful and blooming. Who built? Who planted? All of us together! I built a house in the land of Israel, so now we have a house, in the land of Israel...*" The song went on and on, each time adding something else that was planted or created, each addition followed by the chorus.

And as he told her the story of how the man and child reached the lake and got into the boat, which took them to the child's mother waiting across the shore, Ilana's eyes began to grow drowsy, until she fell asleep in his arms.

Jon sat, trying not to move, not to wake her. He had lost his sense of time. He didn't know if it was morning or evening, the beginning of a new day or the ragged edge of the terrible old one.

In the last few days, he had gone through many stages. First, there had been the shock, the idea of being detached from the ordinary life men lead. The shock that all the rules of life had changed, been broken. The shock of powerlessness, the almost unbearable longing for Elise and home, the sickening disgust at the ugliness around him. The insult and the rank injustice of the beatings that rained on him for no reason, except to amuse his torturers. And the most powerful feeling of all, that which overrode all the others, the horrendous fear that they would harm his child.

He was almost grateful for the beatings, grateful that they used up their energy on him, leaving Ilana alone. He looked at his own life objectively, almost apathetically. Not that he didn't want to live. He did. Every nerve ending, every breath, cried out for sustenance, for survival, for rescue. But he could somehow envision his death almost clinically, the ceasing to exist that would come when his heart stopped beating, his lungs ceased to fill with air, and his skin grew inflexible and cold.

But Ilana—he felt the warmth of her breath on his fingertips as he wrapped his arms around her shoulders. He could not, would not, envision this for her, his child. And each time he prayed, he offered God his life for hers.

She was tired, afraid, wet, hungry, thirsty, dirty. The last time he had begged them for help for her…He touched his nose gingerly. The blood had terrified her, and he had not asked again.

In the midst of the dark, shifting shadows whose every revelation was suspect, a cause for a new rush of blood, a greater beating of the heart, a tightening of the grip around the small, vulnerable flesh of the precious child nestled in his arms, Jon tried to pray.

Snippets of prayers would come to him, like large flakes of snow drifting down soundlessly from the branches of his memory that jutted out in all directions: his time in the army, his days in yeshiva, his childhood rituals: *He sustains the living with loving kindness, revives the dead with great compassion, supports the falling, heals the sick, unchains the bound.*

He touched the filthy floor. His fingers rubbed together, feeling the gritty white film. *He keeps His faith with those who sleep in the dust.*

Am I worthy, he wondered. Worthy of God's intervention on my behalf? Or must the course of events, the freedom God gave each man to choose between good and evil, be allowed to unfold unhampered? Was it right, fair, to ask for a miracle?

I don't know, he thought. These are decisions for God. All I can do is pray. All I can do is ask.

I trust in no man, nor do I rely on any angel but only in the God of Heaven who is the true God, he found himself repeating again and again. *May the Father of compassion have compassion upon the heavily burdened. May He deliver our souls from evil hours. He who avenges blood has remembered them, He has not forgotten the cry of the humble. Those who were innocently slaughtered will not have died in vain.*

Old words—hundreds, thousands of years old—whispered in defiance and defeat in Masada; cried out on torture racks of Inquisitorial prisons; murmured by cracked, trembling lips in Majdanek... Had it helped any of them, he wondered for the first time. Brought any comfort? Or had they all died in agony anyway, burned in Auto de Fe's, slashed by Cossacks' swords, pierced by Ukrainian gunshots, suffocated by Nazi gas, torn to pieces by Islamic bombs...? He did not know. Only one thing was clear to him: he had no control over what would be done to him. The only thing he could choose was how he felt and how he behaved.

When there was nothing left to gain, nothing more to lose, when one was face-to-face with the moment of greatest despair, to speak to God in love and thanks, rather than to curse Him and one's fate, was the ultimate choice of any human creature, and perhaps the ultimate expression of one's humanity. He drew comfort from the idea that millions of his people—facing a fate like his—had chosen to love God and believe; and that through the ages, enough prayers had been answered not only to ensure survival, but also to build an entire country on, a country that had blossomed like the most beautiful flower from the burnt and ravaged earth.

The land of Israel is beautiful and blooming. Who built, who planted all of us together.

Who would have imagined it possible?

Apartment houses, lovely red-tiled villas by a warm sea? And factories and farms, and orchards? And so many books and plays and music and art and museums and libraries and universities! And synagogues on every square block, and study halls filled with chanting Talmud students. And an army of brave, handsome young men and women, like the young Israelites who wandered out of the desert under Joshua, ready to confront the walls of Jericho.

That, too, was from God.

He hugged Ilana gently, feeling her bones, her flesh, sensing the strong young flow of life that ran through her veins. If you can't answer all my prayers, dear God, please answer this one: Let my children live! Let them go on—as our people have always gone on, generation after generation—to create something beautiful out of the ugliness. Let their mother live, to bear more children and raise them. Even—he thought, swallowing hard—if I can't be here. Even if they have another father. Let the living go on, the building, the beauty. Let the incredible story of my people go on and on and on...

He wiped the tears from his cheeks. He felt suddenly warm with the vital, young warmth of the child who nestled against his chest. And in that warmth, he felt he'd heard God's answer.

He put his hand in his pocket, touching the place where Nouara's picture had been. One of the terrorists had found it, looked it over curiously, and then begun to laugh. What do the words mean, Jon had asked him. To his surprise, the man had answered him: "It means: 'He who has health has hope. He who has hope has everything.'"

He'd laughed, tearing it up. "You have nothing."

Thank you, Nouara, he thought, remembering. Thank you.

He heard the rattle of the chains and locks, then saw a sudden ray of light on the floor as the door opened. He stiffened as the child buried her face in his chest. The room was suddenly flooded with light. Ilana looked up, surprised, then laughed, jumping out of his arms. He looked up, startled, wondering if he was dreaming.

Chapter twenty-six

Tul Karem, Samaria (West Bank)
Thursday, May 9, 2002 · 10:00 A.M.

Ismael Abadi sat in his living room in Tul Karem rewinding the second videotape from Bahama, which he had just picked up and watched for the first time. It was all right. The best that animal Bahama could manage. He thought of the way the child was dressed: the new, frilly dress they sold in children's clothing stores in Shechem and East Jerusalem, a dress no Jewish child would wear. But at least she had been fed, bathed, her hair combed and tied back with bows. The doctor looked weary, but only a bit bruised. One would never suspect the beatings he'd been subjected to. The child, thankfully, had so far been spared.

When Ismael thought of her, of any child, in the same place with that maniac Bahama, a chill ran through his body. But at least one thing was clear: a woman had been there to care for her. Maybe one with a heart, he hoped, not some fanatic Hamas or Fatah type who had successfully erased the last spark of human intelligence, decency, and compassion from their soul. These were the new leaders of Islam. The hope of the Palestinian people.

It made him nauseous.

Sometimes he thought that he had been cursed with too much

intelligence. Too much curiosity. How had the passion for a home-land turned into a passion for killing? If the Israelis moved out of the Middle East tomorrow, all of these groups would have to find new reasons to go on, because they didn't know how to do anything else. They would start killing Jordanians next. And then Egyptians. Then they'd take over the oil fields of Saudi Arabia and Kuwait. And in the end, when they'd taken over the entire world, they'd have to start blowing themselves up, because that's all they knew how to do.

They didn't want a country. Not really. The boring matters of tax laws, health care, importing potatoes, opening sewage treatment plants didn't interest them at all, nor were any of them educated or equipped to deal with any of those matters. They never imagined beyond the waving of the flags, the shooting of the guns on the day that the last Zionist Jews were either blown up or raised their hands in defeat.

Not a single one of them had given a single thought to the day after.

He shrugged, filled with a familiar feeling of contempt.

He had just enough time to deliver the tape for the afternoon news and redeem himself with Julia for disappearing after the press conference, leaving her stranded.

"Are you going now?" his wife asked.

He looked at her pretty, dark face, the hair loose around her shoulders as she never wore it outside the house. She still looked like the sixteen-year-old he had fallen in love with at his brother's wedding. After so many births, her body had not thickened, like so many Arab women's. It was still lovely.

"Yes, I must go."

He went into the children's rooms. The empty beds of his three young sons who had already left for school were still disheveled with their nighttime tossing. The light was coming in from outside the window, filling the space with a sense of peace and warmth. In the second bedroom, Mustapha, two, and Wajin, four, were playing with their toys. His daughter was shrieking with laughter. She had long, dark curls like her mother and in the closet hung a dress very like the one the Jewish child was wearing in the latest tape. He reached down and lifted her into his arms, kissing her gently on the top of her head. A wave of indescribable warmth and sadness and fear washed over him. He set her back down.

"Will you be back early?" his wife asked, leaning against the door, looking him over curiously.

"*Inshallah.*" God willing.

"*Inshallah,*" she answered, her parting smile mixed with doubt.

Even though his car had yellow Israeli license plates, he never worried about random sniper fire from wandering gunmen. He was well known in the area, and the giant letters TV spelled out with masking tape on the rear window could be seen for miles. He rounded the bend. To his shock, he saw an IDF roadblock. The Israeli army had pulled out eight years ago when the Oslo Accords were signed. This was an autonomous Palestinian area. What were the Israelis doing here?

He slowed down. It was unusual. There had been no incidents on this road, nothing warranting this kind of blatant breach of the Oslo Accords. He felt his stomach tighten, his leg cramp from tension. He stopped the car, taking out his papers and rolling down the window. He found himself face-to-face with a submachine gun.

"Get out of the car and put your hands up!" a giant of a man swore at him in English. These were not IDF uniforms, he realized, feeling a slow roll of panic.

"I'm not going anywhere! Who are you?"

A terrifying burst of gunfire flattened all his tires.

He opened the door and jumped out, shaking, his hands up. "Don't shoot!! This is a mistake. I'm a journalist…"

He felt his windpipe crush and he gasped for air. "Shut the fuck up, Ismael. We know exactly who you are." He felt his sleeve being rolled up and the sharp prick of an injection. When he came to, he tried to lift his arms, but they were chained to the back of a chair. So were his legs, he realized. The thick material of a hood blinded him.

"Where am I?" he murmured hoarsely.

"Oh, Sleeping Beauty's up," he heard someone with a Texas

accent say, then footsteps. "We are asking the questions. And you are giving the answers. We want to know where the good doctor and his child are being held, and what your instructions are."

"Who the hell do you think you are?"

"Buzz him," someone said. A pain like nothing he had ever felt before crashed through his body. He screamed.

"Look, Isma-whatever-your-name-is, ass-in-the-air-turd, I'd be happy to buzz you straight through to your seventy-two virgins if you're not going to settle down and cooperate. We are working under deadline here..." John Mellon told him.

"First, tell me who you are," Ismael repeated stubbornly.

"We are your worst nightmare. We don't have an ideology, no conscience and the rules of the Geneva Convention don't apply. We kill people, and get paid well for it. Sound familiar, you terrorist scum? We've been paid to rescue the doc and his kid. So start talking."

Ismael said nothing, his heart beating rapidly.

"Okay. You leave me no choice. Bring her in."

"Ismael."

It was his wife's voice, he understood, stunned.

"*Abu, Abu...*" He heard his children's voices. They were crying, terrified.

Wajin, Mustapha.

His hands gripped the cold metal chain, slippery with sweat. "You don't understand. Let me explain..."

"Okay. Which one of us is going to rape this bitch first?" someone shouted.

"WAIT!" he screamed. "I'll do anything you want. Anything."

"We want names. And we want addresses. And we want them now, Ismael."

"Yes," he said, slumping forward. "But take my family home first."

"I'm afraid that's not an option. You get your family back when Elise Margulies gets hers."

"I had nothing to do with the kidnapping!" he screamed. "I'm a driver for BCN..."

"And a long-standing Hamas member.... We know all about it...so cut the crap."

He took a deep breath. "You don't understand.... It's not so simple...What is it you want?"

"Cut the crap!"

"An address? Where they are?"

"For starters."

"Even if you show up there with all your weapons, you'll never get them out alive."

"Why do you say that?"

"Because it's all booby-trapped. And you all stick out like a sore thumb—so big and blond.... And your accent. The minute they whiff you, they'll know."

"Not if you go with us."

"If I show up and they aren't expecting me, they'll kill me and then they'll blow up the house."

"What would they need to be expecting you?"

"A coded message from Hamas headquarters in Europe."

"And who sends those out?"

"The person in charge of all Hamas operations. Musa el Khalil."

There was a short silence.

"So what do you suggest?"

"If you can force Musa to send them a message telling them to extend the deadline, to transfer the prisoners to another cell...to me and my cell, for example. We'd have a small chance."

"Why small?"

"Because the person in charge is an animal. Unpredictable. He could blow at any minute. The doctor could already be dead..."

"Look, how do we get in touch with this Musa? Address, phone?"

"I can't tell you that..."

"Bring his wife back..."

Ismael writhed, screaming curses. "You idiots. I can't tell you because I don't know! Nobody does...Hamas cells are set up in such a way that you only know the four or five people in your own cell. That way, when someone is caught, he can't give away the rest of the operation..."

He heard his wife scream.

"Wait...leave her..." John Mellon shouted. "Let me think... Look, Ismael. How would you suggest somebody find this Musa?"

"Go to the money."

"Money?"

"Hamas funding. It's through Islamic charities. The biggest one is in Saudi Arabia, called the Benevolent Charity Fund. It's headed by a member of the Saudi royal family. They would know."

"I've got to make a phone call," John said suddenly. "Keep an eye on him. I'll be right back."

He returned in a few minutes. "Give us the information: the safe house address, how to get there, how it's set up..."

Ismael hesitated. "I can't do that. If you fail, which is one hundred percent certain, you have no idea what they'll do to my family."

"Buzz him. No, bring in the little girl..."

Ismael's hands gripped the cold metal chain. "You are no better than they are..." He screamed, writhing in helplessness.

Suddenly, the room exploded with noises. Ismael heard his wife and children scream. He shouted out their names. There were scattered gunshots. Furniture crashed to the floor. And then, there was silence.

"Okay. Enough," a new voice suddenly commanded. "Put your hands up. The house is surrounded."

Ismael slumped down in his chair, feeling his body break out into a cold sweat. He covered his head with his hands, terrified. "Don't shoot!" he pleaded. "I'm a prisoner!"

"Relax," a deep voice said mildly, bending down to unlock the chains around Ismael's feet and hands. He felt the heavy material lifted off his face.

Who would ever have thought the face of an Israeli colonel would fill him with so much joy?

"Amos?"

"Ismael. Long time no hear..." The tall, angular man bent down, grinning.

For four out of the past six years that he had been working together with the Shin Bet, passing over vital information about Hamas' planned terrorist activities, he had come to understand that there were three things he had in common with this Israeli Jew: both of them loved their homeland and people, both of them loved life, and both of them hated the brutality of murderous idealists. He put his hands to his throbbing temples. "Get my wife and children out of here! Please!"

"You have my word, Ismael. Nothing will happen to them. They'll be in a safe place."

"What the hell is going on here? What was this all about?" Ismael shouted in confusion, looking at the tall Americans with their hands behind their backs, the Israelis handcuffing them and confiscating their weapons.

"Is this really necessary?" John Mellon asked, his big hands pressing against the handcuffs. "You know we are on the same side."

"Not exactly. I work for the Israeli government, and this is the land of Israel..." the colonel told him curtly. "And you work for?"

"I thought your government decided it was the land of Arafat and no Israelis were allowed to even rescue your own kids..." John said contemptuously.

The colonel's jaw flinched.

"What gave us away, anyway?"

"One of your operatives in Gaza was picked up with your second weapons order.... We see you got your first one." He gestured toward the growing munitions pile in the center of the room.

The Americans glanced at each other knowingly. The local boy. Figures.

"Are you boys aware of those weapons-smuggling tunnels dug underneath the houses in Gaza to Egypt?"

"Yes," the colonel said tersely. "We know all about them."

"And are you planning to close them down at some point? Or are you waiting for Arafat to do that too?" John taunted him.

The colonel said nothing. The tunnels were an old story. They put them underneath children's bedrooms. The only way to destroy them was to bomb apartment houses.

"So why didn't you pick us up immediately?"

"Well, we were curious about what you knew that we didn't."

The big men glanced at each other. "So, now you know. You've got him. Your video delivery service and Hamas operative…"

"I have nothing to do with any of this…. I'm the victim here. They kidnapped me and my family, tortured me…. I have a British passport. I've got a press pass, credentials…."

Colonel Amos looked at him knowingly. Ismael fell silent.

"Why didn't you call us?"

"Bahama is involved," Ismael blurted out. "I have children…. I couldn't risk it. I couldn't risk my children." He raised his head, looking the colonel in the eyes: "Ever since you signed those fucking Oslo agreements, Arafat and Hamas and every other group have been killing us informers—and plenty they just imagine are informers—by firing squad, raping their wives and daughters. No trial, nothing. And you Israelis with your foolish peace fantasies—you let them! You've made it much too dangerous for people like me to help you."

"Tell you what. Why don't we get you and your family out of here? Then I'll buy you lunch and we'll talk. I'll make you an offer, Ismael. A good offer. One you'll find hard to turn down," the colonel said almost gently. "Are you ready?"

"Yes," Ismael said slowly, wearily, wondering what choice he had. "I'm ready."

Chapter twenty-seven

Riyadh, Saudi Arabia
Thursday, May 9, 2002 · 11:00 A.M.

In the royal neighborhood of Nasariya, where one palatial estate after another crowded the streets beyond the extravagant fountains of its traffic island, the home of Whalid and Amina Ibn Saud was considered almost embarrassingly modest. Finished in natural white stone and gray slate, its clean lines drew shrugs from the neighbors, whose white gingerbread moldings and pink-and-green brickwork seemed to go on forever. The odd taste of the couple was usually dismissed with the reminder that Amina was a foreigner—an American—who, while embracing Islam, had embraced little else that a Saudi wife should.

Rumors about the tall, blond wife of Whalid Ibn Saud were a hobby, almost an avocation, among their neighbors. It was said that she never left the house except to drive to King Faisal Hospital to have a baby, or to the airport to leave the country. And although she had been doing this ever since she became Whalid's bride six years before, each time she left, rumor had it that he had thankfully divorced her or that she was leaving for good and would not return. And each time she came back, rumor had it that one or the other of the couple must be dying. Or that she'd repented, and would never leave the country again. And when, six months later, like clockwork, much to the consternation of the pundits who had predicted otherwise, she picked herself and her three children up and found her way out of the country once more, the rumors began all over again, with greater fury.

And thus, although hardly any of her neighbors had actually met her, everyone had an opinion about Amina Ibn Saud and at least one story they were delighted to share, embellish, and trade for others.

These were the most popular: it was said that unlike other Saudi wives, Amina refused to wear the *abaya*—the traditional black cloak that covers Saudi women from head to ankle with only two holes for their eyes to peer out at the world—and that as a result she was forbidden by her husband to leave the house to visit shopping malls or supermarkets, and had everything delivered. It was said that inside her seemingly plain and drab home was an Olympic-sized pool, a gym, and a running track, which only she apparently used, dressed in tight outfits with the names "Nike" or "Adidas" printed on them. It was purported that the family held private screenings of forbidden films, and arranged private concerts with world-class musicians flown in for evening soirees attended by the elite of American and British inhabitants of Riyadh: its doctors, company directors, and British Council cultural employees. And at these parties, it was said that Amina Ibn Saud did not cover her hair, and thus her husband refused to allow his relatives to be invited. It was also said that she held classes for women in which she and they would encourage each other to read foreign books and shamelessly discuss un-Islamic topics, including sexual practices.

As can be imagined, these rumors caused a great deal of chagrin to the local Committee Against Vice and for the Promulgation of Virtue, or as the locals called it in fearful private whispers, CAVES, who never stopped searching for an opportunity to exert their influence against such a destructive and free-wheeling wild card among the women of Saudi royalty, who were, after all, supposed to set an example. So far, however, their efforts to ascertain the guilt or innocence of Mrs. Amina Ibn Saud had been met with an unusual degree of resistance from the royal family, to the extent that a certain particularly aggressive CAVES member had been found drunk with a prostitute at the Riyadh Intercontinental. Even when faced with long imprisonment for his twin crimes, the man had maintained that he had been drugged and framed.

Many in Riyadh believed him. But ever since, CAVES had left Amina Ibn Saud alone. This in itself had contributed to the rumors becoming full-blown myths that were turning into legends. Elizabeth knew what was being said about her. And, as she often told Whally: "Frankly, my dear, I don't give a damn."

From the beginning, she never made a pretense of enjoying life in Riyadh or wanting to fit in. The twenty-room mansion with its tropical gardens, she'd labeled "Sing-Sing." In her office, she hung a calendar on which she carefully crossed off each day that passed in between trips to the States.

With the years, she had come to terms with certain things: like cutting off Marks and Spencer labels from her underwear before going through Saudi customs, because it was a Jewish store. Or like tearing out the Rubens nudes in her art books so they'd be allowed into the country. She came to terms with being unable to bring in novels and biographies because the punishment for smuggling in a book was worse than for hashish or cocaine. (People got five years in prison for arriving with copies of the Old or New Testament, for Pete's sake! And a seventeen-year-old, Abeel Karim Nima, was tortured to death for owning a Shi'a religious text.) She got used to the fact that forty percent of Saudi television programming was sermonizing Imams with bad tempers, and movies that had no sexual content, no violence, no nuns, no priests and no mention of or reference to Israel, unfriendly countries, Communism, or venereal diseases. Having a satellite dish put one in danger of having one's television confiscated. Still, Whally had managed to smuggle in some decent movies on CD and video, and others they secretly downloaded from the Internet.

She had gotten used to the fact that there was absolutely no place to go and nothing to do: no movies, concerts, theaters, discos, nightclubs. But what she would never get used to were the public beheadings between the tall clock tower and dun-colored mosque in

Dira Square after Friday morning prayers; or the way the executioners put down six inches of sand to keep the blood from staining the white floor tiles.

She would never get used to the fact that Riyadh was a hideous and claustrophobic place, from the sprawling beige Riyadh Intercontinental Hotel of sandstone and marble, with its lush gardens facing Maazar Street, to the boxy and tasteless palace of Prince Mohammed (nicknamed "Twin Evil") abu Shirieyn, who had had his own granddaughter publicly executed for falling in love with someone other than the man chosen for her.

In the first six months of her stay, Elizabeth would often wake in the middle of the night and listen to the sounds of planes taking off and feel an almost unbearable urge to flee. What stopped her was the fact that she loved her husband, and that his mother and sisters had treated her so kindly. Showering her with gold, holding parties in her honor in which the women of the family brought her endless, expensive gifts, they truly did their best to make her feel like a member of the family. Whalid's mother tried so hard to be considerate. All Elizabeth had to do was mention she liked something and the next day it arrived. They hired a foreign chef to cook for her. They spent afternoons together, and Elizabeth tried hard to return the honest affection of these very different women, women who had accepted the limitations of their lives as a given. They never asked questions that couldn't be answered.

Whalid had warned her not to raise their consciousness. "You will just be making them unhappy. Why?"

At first, she had bristled at the restriction, but thought it best to be respectful of her husband's request, and of his culture. She had married an enigma, which was part of the reason she loved him. His whole world was strange and indecipherable. With her Berkeley respect for multiculturalism and her natural curiosity, she'd prepared herself for an adventure. What she had not been prepared for was the cruel reality: it had taken her about six months to figure out that the lives of Saudi women were enough to make any normal female need antidepressant drugs just to wake up in the morning and get through the day.

Aside from beheadings, and what Elizabeth liked to call "harem" parties—fashion shows and eating fests for women friends and relatives—women did the following: they made crank calls to strangers by randomly dialing numbers, hoping to happen upon a foreign male or another girl. They got all dressed up, piling on their gold jewelry—which they owned by the kilo—then covered themselves with an *abaya*, letting only their expensive designer shoes show, and then went shopping at the mall to buy more designer shoes and jewelry. Even the little girls—in their ludicrous sequined dresses with the puffy skirts—wore gold bracelets and earrings. The supermarkets were obscenely large and sold everything from Lebanese pastries to plane tickets to the Cayman Islands.

At all times, they had to be accompanied by a man. Sometimes, in the mall, the CAVES held adultery drills, checking the papers of couples to make sure the men and women who had arrived together were married or blood relatives. Anyone they caught out faced beheading.

You couldn't get any shopping done anyway, Elizabeth once complained to Whally, since the stores seemed to close down every two minutes so salespeople and shoppers could run off to pray every time the alarm sounded at the local mosque. Actually, it only happened five times a day.

Coming to terms with six months out of every year in this place had been an enormous leap. The fact that she got pregnant right away helped. She began to realize that the only way to survive was to build her own little world within her home until the six months were up and she could once again breathe the air of freedom back home.

She began working on a doctorate, which kept her busy. She built a greenhouse and grew orchids. She spent time learning to play the oud with a local teacher. She swam, ran, ate lovely meals cooked and served by attentive servants. She took off on weekend shopping jaunts to Paris and Milan on royal family jets for the fashion showings. She cultivated a few friendships with expats who hated Saudi Arabia as much as she did, but loved the wealth that made possible a lifestyle most women could only dream about. And of course, there was always Whally. She loved him. More than ever.

And so, like all human beings who have talked themselves into making difficult and painful compromises with their lives, Elizabeth tried to work out some kind of an arrangement that would keep her sane.

She managed. Most of the time.

What she found most difficult of all was to accept the cultural differences of the women around her without proselytizing. They were truly convinced not only that there was no other way of life possible for themselves, but that their way was actually the best way. They felt virtuous in their imprisonment, even as their husbands secretly drank, read pornography on the Internet, hired call girls, and replaced their wives with newer, younger versions every few years without bothering to divorce them. Men were allowed up to four wives at a time.

To convince these women that life could—should—be otherwise, that there was a screaming inequality and injustice in all these things, would have been difficult, if not impossible. And, given their limitations in making any change in the situation, perhaps it would also have been simply cruel. They did not know they were in jail with a life sentence. Why point it out to them? Within their jail, they were for the most part treated well, and in return were warm, kind, funny and generous, and they truly loved Whally, and her and the children. They were family.

The fact that they didn't know she was Jewish, of course, always rankled. But it was the one thing Whally had insisted upon, the one thing that made their existence together possible. Saudi anti-Semitism was so wide, so deep and so fierce, there was absolutely nothing to be done.

She put that on the top of her list of things to truly hate about the country and the people who lived there.

"Americans are prejudiced against Muslims. And some hate the Saudis," Whally had tried to convince her, without success.

"There is nothing here that is remotely parallel, Whally. Americans aren't fanatic people-haters, and we excoriate racists. Saudis feel it's a virtue. How many mosques are there in America? And how many synagogues and churches in Saudi Arabia?"

He was silent. She knew he agreed with her. She also knew that there wasn't a whole lot he could do about it.

They still had physical love; the attraction between them was never stronger. They had their children, whom they adored, and they had a genuine interest in each other which never waned. Whally never bored her, because she never really understood him, not completely. And she continued to revel in the challenge of her relationship with him.

Over the years, they had found a place for all the things they could never reconcile, or discuss or change. Her Judaism. The way women were treated in Saudi Arabia. His family. His love of Islam, country, and tradition. His loyalty to them. They acknowledged the existence of their irreconcilable differences, which like a cancerous growth they needed to cut out of their relationship. They told themselves it was like the old joke of pulling out an aching tooth and placing it in a box, where you could watch it ache. The box kept getting fuller and fuller with the years, the screaming ache louder and louder as they tried to muffle it. She was dreading the day when the sides would no longer hold and the box exploded, shattering debris all over them.

That day, she understood, was rapidly approaching.

The older the children got, the more impossible it was for her to ignore the influences of their Saudi education. The boys were learning that only Muslims were God's chosen, and every other religion was subordinate, its adherents *dhimmis*, lesser beings meant to serve Muslims; that men were meant to be lords and masters over all women. And her daughter couldn't help but see the way women were treated, the sharp contrast between their lives in America and their lives in Saudi Arabia. So far, they were still young. But the time was soon approaching when it would be impossible to fly back and forth between cultures without giving the children some serious answers, answers neither she nor Whally had.

Deep down, she'd always secretly believed that by the time the children grew up, Whally—her intelligent, kind, generous, loving Whally—would realize that the children would be tainted by the evil that surrounded them in Riyadh—the nepotism, the fanaticism, the lack of tolerance. But that wasn't happening. More and more, he threw himself into his work. He owed his loyalty to his king, who was also a great-uncle. It was an irrational, emotional dedication that she couldn't begin to fathom. After all, she'd abandoned her own culture, her own heritage, without a backward glance. She believed in the love between them, in a philosophical kind of goodness in which people didn't need religion to do the right thing, which was to treat each other as they would like to be treated and to live lives in tune with the cosmos, the environment, human values. Her loyalty was first to her personal feelings, and then to the world. She would never do anything to betray either.

The phone call from her grandmother caught her by surprise. She had come to terms with her grandmother's vociferous and unbending objections to her marriage. Of course, it hurt. But she'd always assumed that her grandmother would eventually come around. When she realized how badly she had misjudged the depth and strength of the old woman's heartbreak, it was much too late to do anything about it. She had made a few overtures in the past six years, sending pictures of the children, New Year's cards, birthday greetings. They had all been returned unopened.

"Elizabeth."

"Granny?"

"Yes, it's me."

"Well…" Elizabeth swallowed, speechless.

"I know you weren't expecting it. Believe me, I'm as surprised as you are. I never thought I'd even be able to dial Saudi Arabia…"

"Was it so hard?"

"It wasn't easy, Elizabeth."

"He's a good man, Granny. He loves me and the children."

"What's not to love, my beautiful Elizabeth? How are the children?"

"They are lovely, smart, funny, healthy."

"The boys will be *Bar Mitzvah*'ed before you know it…"

Elizabeth stiffened. "Why did you call?"

"I called because I need your help."

"Of course. If I can."

"No. Not 'if.' You must."

"What is it you want, Grandmother?" Elizabeth said coolly, beginning to feel uncomfortable.

"I never spoke to you—to anyone—about what happened in Auschwitz."

"Auschwitz…?" The evasive answers, the averted eyes, the feeling you were opening a box of horrors you had no right to open, that you had no right to ask. Elizabeth had always wondered, always wanted to know….

"Well, one of my friends from those days, a woman who saved my life a hundred times, who lives in Brooklyn, has a granddaughter in Israel named Elise. A few days ago, Elise's husband and child were kidnapped by terrorists…"

"Oh my God!" Elizabeth covered her mouth in horror. "Look, don't say anything. I will call you back." She hung up the phone and hurried into the house, picking up her cell phone, the one Whally said was safe to use. She went into her "safe room," the one swept for bugs several times a day. She closed the door. She didn't want anyone listening in on this conversation.

The religious woman with the wig from Brooklyn in the photographs on her grandmother's dresser, the one with the pretty little girl in her arms. She called back immediately. "Grandmother, how horrible! Are they all right?"

"I don't know. No one does. Look, Elizabeth, there's no time for me to make chitchat, to lead into this subtly. The kidnappers are Hamas. We need to convince the Hamas leadership to extend their ultimatum, to order a stay of execution. Otherwise, in twelve hours, both of them will be murdered."

"Is that why you called?! Six years, you send back all my letters, but now, when you need help with terrorists, of course who else would be the expert…?" Elizabeth fumed, her voice full of controlled fury.

"You have no reason to be angry! We are trying to save a life. Two lives. And don't kid yourself. The Saudis are up to their necks in connections with Hamas, Bin Laden, and every other Islamic terrorist group. And you know it."

"I think I should hang up now…"

"Don't you dare, Elizabeth! If you've got a drop of Jewish blood left in you. Don't you dare…! I never said your husband supported terrorists. The truth is, I don't know. And neither do you."

The box, she thought. All those things…"What are you asking exactly?"

"Listen. We just found out that the Hamas person who is giving the orders lives in Europe. My friend Ariana found out from her contacts that he lives in Paris. But we don't know where, and there is no time…."

"What do you want me to do?"

"There is an organization in Saudi Arabia called the Benevolent Charity Fund. It's a front for Hamas fund-raising. The person in charge is Faisal Ibn Saud."

"Do you know how many people in Saudi Arabia have that name?"

"Yes. Which is why I got a private investigator to check it out. Elizabeth, he's Whally's brother."

Elizabeth felt her heart drop. "Are you positive?"

"Elizabeth, I wouldn't have called at all if I wasn't sure," Esther said slowly. "All we need is for him to give us the address and phone number in Paris of a Musa el Khalil."

"Just the address and phone? That's it?"

"That's it."

Elizabeth hesitated. "You know, this is a delicate matter for me."

"Believe me, Elizabeth, I didn't want to call you. I'd never forgive myself if I put you or your family into any danger. But you're our only hope. And Leah…. I never liked to talk about the camps, but I'll tell you one thing, and then you decide. I'd been in Auschwitz only a few months. I weighed nothing, and we were out in the freezing cold, carrying bricks. And then one day, I stepped on glass and my shoes fell apart. I covered my feet in rags. But they were bruised, infected. I couldn't walk. I couldn't work. And in the camps, if you can't work they gas you and burn your body to ashes."

She could hear her granddaughter's breathing grow labored.

"There was a woman whose sister had died. She had her sister's boots. They were too small for her, but good for me. I tried to buy them. I offered her half my bread for a month and any extra work rations of sausage for a month…. It was an enormous price for a starving person. But the woman refused. She wanted shoes, boots. I was dead, finished without those shoes. Leah went to talk to her. 'My sister's boots for your boots,' the women said. 'That's the deal…' It was the only thing Leah had left from home, her warm, good leather boots. But she took them off and gave them to her. She put on the woman's wooden clogs…and brought me the sister's boots. She saved my life. And risked her own…."

"I never knew…" Elizabeth said in a strangled voice.

"Elizabeth, do you remember when I would take you to the synagogue all dressed up like a bride or a queen to hear the story of Purim?"

She was taken aback. "I suppose."

"Let me refresh your memory. The king of Persia gets drunk, orders his wife to strip to amuse his guests. When she refuses, he has her killed. When he sobers up, his 'advisors' tell him to hold a beauty contest to find a new wife. At the same time, his chief advisor…"

"The sound of the noisemakers drowning out the reading of the hated name. The happy sound of children shouting. 'Haman,' Elizabeth suddenly cut in.

"Very good! Haman gets the king to agree to pick a day on which to murder all the Jews and steal their property. In the meantime a Jewish girl, Esther, is chosen as the new queen. Her uncle sends her a secret message, demanding that she talk the king out of murdering the Jews. Do you remember what happened then?"

"No, I don't."

"She said: 'You're asking me to do a dangerous thing. Anyone who goes to the king uninvited risks being put to death.' Do you remember what her uncle answered?"

From some faraway place in her childhood, the words suddenly came back to her with shocking clarity: "'If you will not help your people at this time, help will come from another source, and you and yours will perish….'" She was silent.

"There was another part."

"What?"

"He told her: 'Perhaps for just this reason you have become queen.'"

"Granny, I'll do what I can."

"Believe me, I know what I'm asking of you. But I have to tell you something else: we made a sacred pact, Leah and I, and my friends from Poland and France. We called it a Covenant. If it was you or your child who was in danger, they wouldn't hesitate to risk their lives for you. Please, think it over, my child. You have a chance to do the greatest *mitzvah* in the world. To save lives."

A *mitzvah*. Tears sprang to her eyes. Such a long time since she'd heard that word. "It's good to hear your voice."

Esther hesitated, wiping a tear from her left eye, drying the phone with her palm. "And it's so good to hear yours...my Lizzy..."

"I will talk to Whally."

"I'll never forget this. As soon as you have the answer, call me immediately. You have my number? My cell phone?"

"I've had it for a long time, Granny. Granny? Are you well?"

"Yes, well, I've had better days. This is hard on all of us. But it seems as if our enemies aren't finished with us yet. We have more battles to fight before we can rest."

"And Granny?"

"Yes?"

"For what it's worth, I think these Muslim extremists are scum. Whally's not like that. I swear."

"I believe you."

"Good-bye, Granny."

"Good-bye, my Lizzy."

Elizabeth closed the phone with a tremor of fear. If anyone had overheard that conversation.... She shuddered.

The years had not been kind to Whalid Ibn Saud. His once black hair was peppered with more than its share of gray, and the lean runner's body had gone heavy and slack with too many hours spent behind a desk and dining table. What remained the same was the intellectual curiosity that still shone out of his dark, intelligent eyes.

Choosing a foreign wife who expected a monogamous marriage and insisted on keeping her own lifestyle left him the constant butt of family criticism. There was also no question that it had affected his ability to rise up the ladder of influence in Saudi life, the plum jobs in foreign relations, commerce, and trade going to his more traditional cousins. While few knew that his wife was a Jew before her conversion, those who did never let up on the pressure to divorce her, take away the children and remarry. At the very least, he was admonished to take an additional wife or two who would provide the traditional Saudi home life for him in the months his American wife chose to spend abroad.

Quietly, stubbornly, he had continued to fend them off.

He did not want another wife. He did not want a divorce. Everything that he had promised Elizabeth when he asked her to marry him, he had tried his best to keep. Some things, of course, had proved impossible.

There was no way that he could spend six months out of the country every year. There was no way for him to be part of her family. When they married, he had honestly believed that the winds of change were blowing over his homeland. It was just a matter of time, he thought, before women would be allowed to pursue an education, work, drive, and do away with the medieval black *abaya*. He hadn't expected it to happen overnight, but he had expected that his royal cousins, hundreds of them, who, like him, had been given western educations in the best Ivy League schools America and Britain had to offer, would usher in a new era in the monarchy.

To his shock, the exact opposite was happening: the entire Middle East, led by murderous illiterates like Saddam Hussein, had taken a huge step backward into the Middle Ages. All the Arab states were interested in now was a religious holy war! At this day and age! And the masses, pumped up by the sickening rhetoric of the ignorant clerics who saw themselves as the true leadership, were being harangued into becoming ever more backward and radical.

They were being taught that they should blow up discos, in

order to have their private orgy in Heaven with seventy-two virgins; that they should offer their children as sacrificial lambs to some crazed Islamic hysteria of world domination. The financial, social, and sexual frustration of the young who had no education, no prospects, no way of satisfying their minimal human needs to marry and support a family, was being directed into a murderous rage against the west in order to deflect it from their own corrupt leadership, which had put them into this situation and offered them no hope.

As part of their arsenal, the Arabs had discovered that age-old cure for disenchanted oppressed populations: anti-Semitism. Taking a page from Germany's dark history, forgetting they themselves were Semites, they were dreaming up ludicrous ways of convincing the people that the Jews were pigs and monkeys, that the Jews were the devil. So-called moderate Egypt had even turned *The Protocols of the Elders of Zion,* that classic anti-Semitic fantasy that had the Jews running the world, into a TV miniseries…?!

Morons.

Of course, the Israelis had made it all too easy for them. Instead of kicking out the troublemakers and sending Arafat to Hell, they had bent over backward to pretend they were going to solve the Palestinian problem, raising expectations that could not possibly be met, and resolving the inevitable backlash with brutality. No Arab could watch their Palestinian brothers fighting Zionists and getting beaten without fury.

Who knew how it would all end?

He sometimes looked at his wife, his children, with secret fear. How long in this crazed atmosphere would she, with her western ways, continue to be tolerated? When would the whispers behind closed doors turn into a brutal public spectacle, a tidal wave that would crash against their solid, private world, turning it into a shipwreck of debris? With each passing year, he found himself becoming more and more circumspect, more cautious, more secretive, more frightened, more uncertain.

"Whally, can I talk to you?"

He was sitting behind the desk in his study, surrounded by hundreds of books in leather-bound volumes. He was going over the budget for the equipment purchases he would need to modernize the production line in his factory. It was a small operation, a sideline really, that made generators. It had done very well, becoming a popular item in many Middle Eastern countries, and in Third World areas like Pakistan and India. Orders were up. It gave him satisfaction to think that some Third World child in a cave might be able to have light to read by because of his work.

His cousins, he knew, sneered at him. They were all wheelers and dealers, involved in brokering multibillion-dollar trade deals between the Saudi family and huge defense or construction contractors. They lived off the bribes and kickbacks.

He wanted no part of it. As a member of the Saudi family, he had received an automatic income from the time he was born. In 1984, each prince got $20,000 a month. And a prince with a large family could get up to $260,000 a month. Those who actually had a job could make as much as $100 million a year. No question, times were getting harder, and money was running out in the kingdom, but there were still over fifty princes who were billionaires.

It was, he often thought, obscene. A whole country owned by a single family who had swarmed out of a single desert tribe, taken over the land, raped its resources for themselves and relegated the rest of its inhabitants to mere serfs.

No wonder there was a Ministry of Information that had the power to license newspapers and magazines, and thus had a say on every word the Saudi people were allowed to read and hear; who had the power to destroy books, jail authors and even give the death penalty to those possessing so-called subversive literature.

He looked up at Elizabeth and smiled, reaching for her hand. A small flash went through him, the same one he had felt that first morning in the library at Berkeley, when he had seen that long, curly, California-blond hair, that perfect body, reaching up for a book. He'd thought his heart would stop. It always did, a little, even now.

"What is it?"

She hesitated. "Whally, can we take a walk in the garden? This is very private."

He nodded. In addition to the phones, they were both aware

that the house could be bugged too. Although they had brought in experts to go through it, they could never be certain one of the house-maids or porters hadn't been bribed to cooperate with CAVES.

The garden was a wonder, she thought, with its fountains of cool, spraying mist, its fragrant rows of orange, apple, and lemon trees, now all covered with delicious blossoms. They walked along the shady path beneath the row of date palms whose fronds spread out above them like angel wings. The sound of the water, the scent of the flowers, the blooming rainbow colors enveloped her like a dream. "Paradise," she breathed softly into his ear, slipping her arm through his.

He nodded, almost sadly. "An oasis, in the midst of a desert." His tone was bitter with irony.

"Whally, I just got a phone call from my grandmother, Esther."

His brow shot up. "The cosmetics queen? The one who's refused all these years to read your letters, or take your calls?"

She nodded.

"Well."

"Well." She took a deep breath. "She's asked a favor of me...of you, actually. It concerns a matter of life or death."

He stopped walking and faced her. "Go on."

"The Hamas have kidnapped a member of her family.... Actually, not a blood relative, but someone even closer in many ways...."

"Where? In California?"

"No." She paused. "In Israel."

He dropped her hands and put his fists into his pockets. "Elizabeth..."

"I know, I know. But this is.... There were four women. My grandmother was one of them. They survived Auschwitz together. The child is the great-granddaughter of one of them. And the man—her father—a cancer specialist..."

"*Ana marid!*"

"I know. It's sickening. They were abducted from their car. Terrorists just opened fire, then took them. If the terrorists' demands aren't met, in twelve hours they are going to kill them."

"What is it they are demanding?"

"Release of Hamas prisoners. Dismantling settlements. Right of return for Palestinians who ran away in 'forty-eight…"

"Idiots. Why not ask all the Jews to jump into the sea?" he murmured. "What do you expect me to do?"

"Whally, you and I both know who is funding Hamas here…."

"You want me to call them up on the phone and ask for the Israelis to be released? And they'll listen to me, because…?"

"Give me some credit!"

He sighed. "Well, what, then?"

"I have a name. Musa el Khalil. He lives in Paris. All I need is his address and phone number."

He turned around and looked up at the sky, his hands gripped behind his back. Suddenly, he turned to face her. His face was red, the veins in his temples bulging. He was as angry as she had ever seen him.

"I will get the name and address. And then, when the Mossad picks him up, my brothers and cousins will come here and give me—us—a medal. Is that the plan?"

Involuntarily, almost instinctively, her body wanted to move a step backward. Instead, she forced herself to move even closer. She gripped his shoulders with both her hands. "What about '*Adl*,' justice? Did I not learn that Allah is just, that his prophet Mohammed was just and perfect in all his ways? How can the murder of a doctor and his small child be just? I ask you to help stop this terrible thing, this crime. I ask you to be a true Muslim, to bring honor to Allah and to his Prophet…"

"You don't know what you're asking of me! We are in terrible danger, all of us. Our own children…"

She dropped her arms, looking up at him. She felt frightened. "What do you mean?"

"I mean there are forces in this country that are working against us. You refuse to wear the *abaya*. You refuse to stay in the country. You give parties for westerners. You hold classes for women…"

"I haven't done anything wrong according to Islamic law. I have been a good Muslim. I believe in one God. In His Prophet. I pray, I fast, I have gone on *Haj*. Twice. I give charity…"

"Stop it! You know exactly what I'm talking about. You are not submissive. You are not obedient to the words of the Imams, Allah's representatives on earth…."

"They are wrong in what they are doing. They misinterpret all the good, turning it into evil. You cannot justify the kidnapping and murder of an unarmed innocent and a child. This is absolutely against everything the Koran teaches, and you know it…."

"What does it matter what I know?"

"It matters to me! I'm your wife. I'm part of you…."

"I'm trying to protect you!"

She looked into his eyes. "What is your answer, Whally?"

"It would be suicide for me to make such inquiries. Suicide."

"But what if you said you wanted to make a donation?"

"A donation?"

"To the Hamas. You know that your cousins are some of the biggest contributors. And your brother, Faisal, is head of the Benevolent Charity Fund. You know where that money goes. The *Zakat* we are required to give to the poor according to the faith. He takes that money and it goes to terrorists."

"It's protection money. We Saudis are adept at keeping Palestinian thugs, Syrian terror operatives, Iraqi hit squads, and other psychopaths off our backs. It's a Mafia extortion racket called 'Arab solidarity.' We never met a problem we didn't try to solve by throwing money at it. We keep the Americans happy by buying billions of dollars' worth of weapons we don't know how to use, airliners we don't need, and goods we could live without. In exchange, the Americans and other western countries understand they'll have to protect us to keep the oil and dollars flowing," he said tonelessly. "It's the way we live. Everyone is proud of it."

"What if you called your brother and said as part of your *Khums* and *Zakat*, you wanted to give your obligatory charity money to this person directly? That you didn't want it to be traced because of the Americans and their war on terror and our frequent travel to America? That you wanted to hand it to him in cash at his house in Paris…?"

"Don't be stupid. My brother knows how I feel about these low-lifes. He'd never be fooled. If anything happened, he'd know it was me. Do you want to have Hamas target us? They are all over Europe and America. If they ever found out…"

"But Faisal is your brother! Surely, he wouldn't tell. Look, Whally, every day, just being married, we are risking our lives here! You know I love you. I converted to Islam for you. Brought my children up in your faith. But that faith has changed…."

"I don't understand you."

"Yes. You do."

He turned away. "Don't push me, Elizabeth. I can't…."

"The Wahabis have been at the root of all that's evil in Islam. They've made the adoption of anti-Semitism part of the religion, which it never was. They've made it a respectable religious obligation of Jihad to join terror cells. Wife-beating, the murder of daughters, is not the exception, it's the rule, and you know it, all over the Muslim world. And now, they are insisting on spreading this backwardness to the west…."

He sat down and held his head in his hands. "I'm only one man."

"You can make this one phone call. Get this one address. Save these two people. For your own soul. For us. For me. Because if we sit back and they die, I couldn't go on living with myself." She paused, taking a deep breath. "I couldn't go on living with you."

His face went pale as he stared up at her. "Elizabeth…. "

She reached down and kissed his lips, pressing her body against his. And then she turned. Slowly, alone, she walked back into the house, closing the door behind her.

He sat in the garden for a long time, gazing at the flowers planted through the years that now thrived in tropical abundance. He looked beyond to the running track and the blue tiles of the pool.

Their own little world, a comfortable, delightful place with every luxury. What Elizabeth never realized—because he had protected her from this knowledge—was just how fine a line it was they walked. Like trapeze artists balancing on a thin wire over the shouting crowds, they and their children tipped this way and that, the hard, punishing ground always looming down below, ready to smash them should they lean too far to any side and stumble. And now she was asking him to jump off the line with both feet, to fill it with uncontrollable vibrations that might send them all tumbling down.

He tried to imagine life without her. His family would simply tell him to behave according to the accepted norm regarding failed east-west matches: divorce her and take the children. Have her exiled to America and deny her a visa to visit them. It was actually very simple, and could be accomplished before Elizabeth understood what was happening. There would be nothing she could do. He would find another wife, one suitable to his station. And the black line over his name would be erased, and all opportunities would suddenly open for him.

And he would never see her again, his Elizabeth. Never. And she would mourn for her children, and she would hate him.

He walked back into the house. He picked up the phone and called his brother Faisal.

That afternoon he handed Elizabeth a piece of paper. On it was the name Musa el Khalil and an address and a phone number in Paris.

"Thank you."

"Memorize it, then destroy it. The car is outside waiting to take you to the children's school and then on to the airport. Here is the letter of permission from me for you to travel. Tickets are waiting for you at the counter. You have a stopover in Amsterdam. Wait until you get to Europe before you pass on this information. And then go directly to California. Promise me. Make the call from a public phone."

"Aren't you coming with us?"

He shook his head. "That would only cause suspicion. Go."

"Then, when are you coming?" she begged him.

He held her close, kissing her long and hard, with a touch of desperation.

"*Inshallah*, soon." And then he took her to the door and watched her go.

Chapter twenty-eight

After the long confinement in her room, the hospital corridors felt almost like a change of season, Elise thought as she walked slowly and painfully down the airy halls. How strange that feeling of lightness, the absence of all those burdens that her body had grown used to: the swelling abdomen, the soft pressure of the tiny head against her bladder, the rolling elbows and knees that punched out her flesh like a cat in a sack. She brushed her fingers lightly over her stomach, and a sense of loss so sharp, so palpable, brought an ache to the back of her throat. Now his fate was out of her control. She leaned against her grandmother's shoulder.

"Maybe you should get a wheelchair, like the doctor said?" Leah suggested, worried.

"No. I need to walk. After all these months, it's a pleasure."

"Our NICU—Neonatal Intensive Care Unit—is the best in the Middle East," Dr. Gabbay declared, meaning to be comforting. To Elise, he sounded very much like the guest of honor at a fund-raising luncheon. She wanted to hear something personal, something about her own baby and his personal fate as she walked into the unit where he lay fighting for his fragile life.

"From all over the country, hospitals regularly send their most urgent and complicated cases to Hadassah. A special ambulance is equipped with incubators and portable surgery units to transport them. Your baby is in the best hands, Elise," he continued.

She hardly heard a word, focusing on the blinking green and red lights of sophisticated and no doubt expensive monitoring equipment, the heavy wump of breathing machines that forced air in and out of tiny lungs. "Hadassah ladies," people sometimes called them, rolling their eyes, never realizing how all those smart, savvy, generous women had—in their spare time—created the finest medical facility in the Middle East in this tiny country, saving the lives of their babies. *Thank you….*

And in the midst of all this *Star Wars* technology, she suddenly noticed the tiny bundles of human flesh. Stuck full of needles, bandaged, with eye patches and foot patches, and dressings and tubes coming in and out of every orifice, tiny human beings fighting against relinquishing that gift they had so recently been given: life. Elise felt her chest constrict. They looked like a community of miniature car-crash victims on their last legs. My God! How could any of them survive all this?

"Don't look so worried! We have a ninety-five percent survival rate among those babies born one kilo or more!" Dr. Gabbay assured her.

"Kilo? How much is that in pounds?" Leah asked.

"About two-point-two pounds."

"Imagine." She shook her head in wonder. "Less than a decent *Shabbes* chicken."

"And even the ones born half that weight still have a fifty-fifty chance of survival. Believe me, most of these infants are going to be perfectly fine. Don't look at the equipment. Look at the babies."

Elise examined them. Little faces, tiny hands and legs waving furiously. Alive, surrounded by little stuffed animals, tiny mobiles, and bright pictures placed around them by loving hands. No one had given up hope on any one of them, she suddenly realized, deeply comforted.

"Here he is, Elise, Mrs. Helfgott."

They looked down at the tiny head, the dark hair peeking out of the fishnet bandage. A whole gamut of emotional extremes washed over Elise: fear verging on terror, thrilling love, tremendous hope, undaunted faith. She felt almost faint. "Can I touch him?"

"Of course."

She put her hand into the sterile plastic glove that was attached to the clear plastic crib's side, reaching into the incubator. Gently, she laid her hand on top of the dark hair, trying to imagine its softness. His skin, she told herself, would feel like warm, slightly gritty soap. She brushed his tiny cheek with the tip of her forefinger. From head to toe, he would reach from the tips of her fingers to the middle of her arm. She felt a sense of slow panic, born of wonderment that the functions of human life could exist in all their complexity in the ridiculously confined space of this tiny, human package. She nudged his palm. With a shock that moved her to tears, he suddenly wrapped his tiny hand around one of her fingers.

It was almost too much to bear.

"Will he be all right?" she demanded hoarsely, almost rudely, not allowing herself to examine him too closely until she got the answer. She couldn't stand it, to add this uncertainty, this life-or-death watch, to all the other uncertainties, all the other watches. "Please, just be honest. Just let me know what I'm up against."

"Why don't you come into the office and sit down, Elise?" Dr. Gabbay said kindly, "and we'll explain everything." Slowly, with a sense of heartbreak, she removed her finger from the baby's grip.

"This is Dr. Levy, the head neonatologist. He's taking care of your baby," Dr. Gabbay said, introducing a tall, red-haired giant of a man. For no reason, Elise wondered if his wife was one of those petite little women big men sometimes married, the kind who could fit into their pockets; if that was how he had learned to use his big hands so gently. "Hello, Mrs. Margulies, Mrs. Helfgott. Let me give you a little background," Dr. Levy began in unaccented American English.

An American-trained doctor, Leah thought. Good. Not that Israeli doctors weren't…but someone who knew English…someone she could understand.

"A baby that's born at thirty-two weeks still has some growing to do. It doesn't have enough body fat to keep it warm, so we keep it in a warm place, an incubator. It doesn't have the reflexes to suck on the breast or bottle yet, so we feed it through a tube in its nose. But if you can pump breast milk, that would really be very helpful. We'd feed your baby that."

It had not been just talk. There was something she could do, something she had control over. "Of course!" Elise said, feeling her spirits rise.

"Believe it or not, preemies grow faster than regular babies, so it will need lots of nourishment. And all those big machines with the blinking lights…they are just a way of keeping abreast of how things are going. We check the glucose levels, the salt, the calcium…"

"But tell me…is there anything really wrong? Anything dangerous?"

"Well, his most serious problem is the immaturity of his lungs. A baby that young doesn't produce surfactant…"

"Sur…what?"

"Surfactant. It's a substance that keeps the lung tissue flexible so that it expands and contracts. Years ago, preemies often died because of this. But we've made enormous advances. We gave you some artificial surfactant before you gave birth, and have been giving him doses ever since. So far, so good. He has a little jaundice, and he's slightly anemic. Both of these things are common problems in preemies. We'll keep him under ultraviolet light for the jaundice, and if the anemia gets worse, we'll transfuse some red blood cells until he starts manufacturing his own—"

"He's in good shape, Elise. Really," Dr. Gabbay reassured her.

"Well—" Dr. Levy hedged.

"What?" she asked.

"Elise, this is going to sound terrible, but believe me, it's not," Dr. Gabbay said, with a long glance at his colleague, who shrugged.

"WHAT?" she demanded, pushing away from the desk. "TELL ME!"

"This morning, your baby had an incident of intraventricular hemorrhage."

She blanched. "What does that mean?"

"What it means," Dr. Levy said calmly, "is that bleeding took place into the normal fluid spaces of the brain. A baby this size is very fragile, and there is a whole network of tiny blood vessels around the brain. All this means is that one of these tiny vessels burst. It wasn't serious. He didn't lose much blood. These incidents are commonplace in preemies and most of the time don't cause any damage at all."

No. No. No, she thought. God, don't do this to me. I can't take this, no. It's not fair, God. "Are you telling me the truth, about it not being dangerous, about it being commonplace?" she demanded.

"Absolutely. I don't believe in sugarcoating the truth. I want parents to be team players, and there is no point in stringing them along with false hopes. I'm telling you that it wasn't serious. And we don't expect any damage at all from it." He was calm, assured, and matter-of-fact.

Elise searched his face, the kind brown eyes, the young, healthy cheeks, the genuine smile. She decided to believe in him, in God. In mercy, and small miracles. "Thank you, Doctors. Dr. Gabbay, Dr. Levy. For everything." She got up. "I'm going to spend a few minutes with my baby now."

He was a person, she thought, startled. Her son. Jon's son. Ilana's brother. A person with a place in the world. He had his own face: widely set eyes, like Jon's. His nose too had Jon's tiny little downturn. She could almost see Jon's face wrinkled in laughter and pleasure as he saw his big features miniaturized in his tiny son's. He was his father's son, and like his father he would hold on, he would fight for his life, she told herself. God willing, father and son would both win.

With that thought, something lit up inside her, a moment of bright certainty. This will be your story, baby. The story of when you were born. How your parents were in all the newspapers. And how your father didn't get to see you for a day or two, until the army brought him and your sister home.

They would tell this story on green lawns festooned with red and blue balloons, as children laughed and ran around, and a portable radio played over the hissing of an outdoor grill. And Jon would hold out his arms, *my Jon*, and the baby would take his first steps into them, like a little drunk, waddling on the soft grass, smiling into his father's happy, satisfied eyes. And his big sister would hold his hand, and teach him ballet steps on the green lawn, and they would twirl until both collapsed on the soft grass, the summer grass, next year... "Everything is going to be all right, little fellow," she whispered, her forefinger stroking his tiny forehead. "I just know it."

"Elise..." Dr. Gabbay was touching her shoulder. "I've just gotten a call. General Nagar is downstairs waiting in your room."

Her heart had the strange sensation of hiccuping: a sharp draining, an emptiness and then a sudden filling. She felt faint, grabbing the back of the chair. General Nagar was the Israeli army's chief of staff.

"Oh, Elise!" Leah called out, alarmed, rushing forward.

"Get a wheelchair!" Dr. Gabbay ordered.

"No..."

"Don't be stubborn," Leah begged her.

She had no struggle left, she thought, sitting down gratefully when the chair arrived. They wheeled her out of the unit.

"Mrs. Doctor Jon...?"

She looked up at the pale young woman who stood in her path outside the NICU. She was dressed in a hospital bathrobe and modest head covering. At first, because of the head covering, Elise thought she might be an Orthodox Jewish woman, one of her neighbors. But as she drew closer, she realized the woman was a Muslim. A Palestinian.

"What do you want?" Elise asked her cautiously.

"I don't know...My name is Nouara. Your husband is my doctor."

Elise felt a complicated range of emotions, everything from primitive hatred for a faceless enemy to true affection and concern for a fellow suffering human being.

"Nouara. Jon talked about you so much. How are you?"

"Your husband is not here to tell me how I am..."

"I have the feeling it will all be over soon," Elise said wearily.

"*Inshallah*. Mrs. Doctor Jon?"

"Yes?"

"I am so ashamed, so ashamed. I want to kill the people who did this. They did it to me too. And to my husband and my children. They are not Muslims. May Allah punish them. I don't know what to do."

"Just keep yourself well. Make sure when Jon comes back, he finds you well."

The young woman shook her head in doubt and despair. *"Inshallah, inshallah.* I will try. I will pray for him. May Allah keep him and Ilana safe and return them to you. And to me." She leaned forward and kissed Elise on both cheeks.

Elise took the young woman's fragile hand in hers and held it. Understanding passed between them, and a strange kind of solidarity. They were, in a way, in this together, both their lives dependent on the outcome.

Elise watched her as she shuffled down the long corridor, her shoulder brushing the wall for support. A young Palestinian woman. A young mother. A neighbor. She too was a victim of the coarse and hateful people who seemed to be in control of all their lives, people who had created a world without intelligence, or fairness or compassion or justice. A world that made no sense at all.

"Ready, *Bubbee.*"

Leah wheeled her down the corridor.

Chapter twenty-nine

Hadassah Hospital, Jerusalem
Thursday, May 9, 2002 · 2:00 P.M.

General Moshe Nagar was not at all the image one would have expected of the toughest man in the Israeli army. A short, intense, wiry man, with a sharp face and balding scalp, he was barely an inch taller than herself. But his posture reminded Elise of one of those aggressive breed of pit bulls who made up for their small stature with the ferocity of their natures. He was a man, she thought, whom no one should underestimate, particularly not the enemies of the State of Israel.

Born on the eve of Israel's independence to Jewish refugees who had been thrown out of their home in Egypt, along with 650,000 other Jewish refugees from Arab lands, he'd been brought up to understand the meaning of sacrifice and the worth of Jewish self-rule and self-defense.

"Mrs. Margulies," he said warmly, extending his hand. He was surrounded by tall, taciturn army men.

She remembered watching him on television on Memorial Day, as he addressed the friends and families of fallen soldiers. Instead of speaking of glory, pride, and duty, he had spoken about little boys in Purim costumes and mothers kissing new recruits on their way to the induction center. He had spoken about beloved sons and daughters, each one an incalculable loss to their boyfriend or girlfriend, brother, sister, father, or mother—each one an unbearable rip in the fabric of the country's life. If your son had to be in the army, you'd want him under the command of such a man, she'd thought.

She got up and held out her hand. He took it, warmly.

"Please, both of you. Sit down."

Leah took his advice gratefully. She was as weary as she had ever been in her life.

"First of all, we think we have located where your husband and child are being held."

She felt her body tense. "Thank God!"

"Yes. But now comes the hard part. To get them out alive and well."

"When?" Elise pleaded, her eyes boring into his.

He didn't look away. "I don't know yet. I don't want to lie to you. They are in a safe house in one of the villages in Samaria. But we believe the house is booby-trapped. We need time to organize."

"But the deadline…!"

"We have every reason to believe that they will extend it."

She looked up at him. "Do you believe that?"

He shifted uncomfortably. As former commander of forces in Judea and Samaria, he'd had extensive contact with terrorist groups and had observed firsthand how they cynically exploited all agreements to build up their infrastructure, train terrorists, and smuggle arms. How they hid behind small children when they fired. How they placed their explosives in ambulances to ferry them around. No. He did not trust a terrorist to be a gentleman.

"It's not a question of trust. We are working on another angle. I can't say much right now…"

Elise studied her hands, then hugged herself tightly. "You know who I keep thinking about, General?"

He didn't move, studying her silently.

"Danny Haran."

The effect of the name on the army men was immediate and devastating.

On April 22, 1979, the Abu Abbas faction of Yassir Arafat's Palestinian Liberation Front (PLF) landed four terrorists on the seashore in Nehariya. Armed to the teeth, they walked into an apartment building and broke into the home of Danny Haran. They kidnapped the young father and his four-year-old daughter, while the mother hid in the storage space beneath the ceiling with the baby, covering its mouth in a desperate attempt to keep it from crying and revealing their hiding place.

Danny Haran and his daughter were taken to the beach. As the young father was forced to look on, terrorists smashed in the head of the little girl with rocks just before shooting him. Back home, in a tragic accident, the baby suffocated. Only the mother survived.

"I have a question for the general," Leah said suddenly. "Elise, translate for me?"

"*Bubbee*, please..."

"No, no, it's all right. What is it?" General Nagar said in Israeli-accented English, kindly. "My English is not wonderful, but also not so terrible."

"I heard on the news that the prime minister of Israel called on Yassir Arafat to free my Jon and Ilana. Is your prime minister joking? Is this a joke?"

The general didn't meet her eyes.

"Maybe Elise, you should translate?"

General Nagar exchanged glances with his entourage. "No, it's not a language problem. For the IDF to go into these territories is a political problem.... We aren't supposed to go into Palestinian-held territory. That was the Oslo Accords we signed. We pulled our troops out so that they could police themselves...."

"Are you telling me that you are going to keep an agreement that the other side has broken? They aren't fighting terror. They are the terrorists!" Leah said incredulously.

Elise saw the muscle in Nagar's cheek flex. "This may all be true. But we are not a military dictatorship. We are a democracy and the IDF is not the one who makes the final decisions. The prime minister does. And the defense minister. We simply carry out the government's policy."

"And what, exactly, is 'government policy' concerning the kidnapping of Israeli citizens from their cars and holding them in Palestinian-controlled territory? What do the prime minister and defense minister say about getting my husband and child released...?" Elise's voice rose.

He stared at the floor. "Official policy is to give Arafat more time—twenty-four hours—to allow his security forces to free them."

Leah rose up off the chair. "I was in Auschwitz. I know how a murderer of Jews thinks. He thinks how to kill, not how to save. A whole day, your government needs, to figure out who's the murderer, and who's the saver? How many thousands of attacks you had already? Twelve thousand, fourteen thousand? And how many dead Jews? How many crippled children? From Arafat's own police! He didn't try to bring in a ship full of arms? Your government should have its head examined. If they let my family perish, then there is no Jewish State, and no Jew should be foolish enough to live here!"

"*Bubbee*, please."

"Bunch of idiots!" She got off the chair and stalked out of the room, leaving the unsmiling men with looks of astonishment and shame on their faces.

"I'm sorry..." Elise muttered.

"No, don't apologize..."

"She's upset. The prime minister said this yesterday. Does that mean that Arafat's time is up...? And if yes, when will you be moving in our troops?" Elise asked.

The general seemed taken aback.

"May I?" A tall young colonel stepped forward.

"Go ahead, Amos." General Nagar nodded.

"Please, Mrs. Margulies, not a word of what I tell you must leave this room. It's a matter of life and death."

"I understand. You can trust me...us," Elise promised.

"Whatever the politicians say publicly, they haven't held us back. We in the army haven't acted until now because we didn't have the information we needed. But now we do." He saw the information sink into her eyes. "I can't give you any more details. Please." He reached out and took her hand. "Trust us."

She looked up at him, at the clean-cut face, the dark, intelligent eyes. He was some mother's son, some young woman's husband. Someplace else, in another country, he would be a young executive, or an engineer. He would be building a new home for himself, expanding his business, planning a vacation. But he wasn't someplace else and he would be risking his life and the lives of other young men to free her family. She squeezed his hand back, nodding. "I do trust you. Believe me."

"And please tell this to your grandmother, from me, personally," General Nagar added warmly. "Whatever the official policy, there was not one minute of the day when the IDF sat back and waited. Not a second. Do you understand?"

Elise blinked, her chin trembling, as their eyes met in perfect understanding.

"There's another reason we came. We've brought you something. A second video from the terrorists. We picked it up before the networks got it. I thought you'd want to see it first."

Elise was stunned. Another video! Can I stand it? "Yes! Please, put it in. And call my grandmother back, will you?"

The images flickered across the screen. Again the brutally dressed Islamic killers with their gunbelts and submachine guns, their headbands with Arabic lettering across their foreheads, looking like some monstrous parody of themselves, she thought.

"What do you think they have written there?" Elise mused.

"I'm an idiot, kick me?" Leah suggested.

"I seriously doubt that, Mrs. Helfgott," General Nagar said solemnly, just a flicker of a smile crossing his somber face.

There was the usual rambling, hyperventilating words of wisdom from the little monster of the hour, Elise thought, probably more threats, more demands. Unlike last time, she didn't even want them translated. What difference did it make what they wanted? What difference did it make what they threatened to do? She was helpless to meet their demands, and helpless to prevent them from carrying out their threats. She wondered for the first time if the men standing around her felt the same way.

"Please, just fast-forward it, to Jon, Ilana!"

There they were.

"Oh, my God! Something's the matter with Jon!" Elise shot up.

The soldiers, even Leah, searched the wan image of the young man in vain to see what had so alarmed Elise. They looked at each other, puzzled. He seemed tired, but otherwise...He was still in control, and there didn't seem to be any new physical signs of abuse since the last tape.

"Don't you see? His hands!" Elise shouted. "Look! Look how he's holding them!"

Only then did they notice that the thumbs seemed off-kilter. "They've broken his thumbs. And his head. He can hardly hold it up! You've got to do something. He's being tortured!" Jon, my Jon.

Leah's head swam. This was not supposed to happen. Those days were over. They'd cried a tear, laid a wreath, made a speech. Jews were not supposed to be taken out of their homes and tortured anymore.

"Look at Ilana!" Elise burst out.

She was dressed in what seemed almost like a Queen Esther Purim costume: the frilly white dress with its bows and ruffles and puffy sleeves. She had a big, strange bow in her hair, hair that had been carefully washed and brushed. She was leaning back into Jon's arms when suddenly, unexpectedly, she began to hold out her arms to the camera and smile.

They watched, stunned.

Elise pressed rewind and watched it again, flabbergasted. What in heaven's name? Who could she be looking at that would make her smile and hold out her arms? Who? A sliver of light, tiny and as sharp as glass, suddenly pierced the thick darkness of Elise's despair: someone had made their way inside, past the booby traps, to where Jon and Ilana were. Someone her daughter smiled at and held out her arms to. A friend. Even the soldiers seemed amazed.

"What could your daughter be looking at, Mrs. Margulies?"

Elise shook her head helplessly, rewinding the tape, pressing pause and touching the screen. Was it a trick? A cruel stranger holding out a doll, or candy to make the child smile for the cameras, to demonstrate for BCN, CNN, and BBC reporters and their village-idiot viewers, how happy and content the kidnapped little Jewish child was, and how well they were treating her just before they murdered her and her father...?

No. She knew that smile. It was real. Ilana didn't smile like that at people she didn't know, no matter what bribes they were holding out. More than that, her willingness to leave her father's arms was also uncanny and impossible to stage.

"Maybe they are holding out candy?"

Elise shook her head. "Ilana can't be bribed. She doesn't even like sweets!"

"Under normal circumstances," the young colonel said softly. "But if she were very hungry?"

Elise looked at him. She hadn't thought of that; hadn't thought of Ilana being very hungry, so hungry she'd be willing to leave her father and run smiling toward a stranger holding out food...She couldn't imagine it. Any of it. She knew what her child would do under normal circumstances. But under these conditions? Was the colonel right?

Yet some instinct told her otherwise: Ilana would want the food. But she wouldn't go about it that way. She'd reach out for it, but she wouldn't give them a smile, not her Ilana.

But maybe she was drugged, or—she thought with alarm—in a state of shock. Who knew what scenes she'd been subject to in the last few days? If they'd harmed Jon, and she'd been in the room, a witness.... Oh, I can't even think, can't even imagine how something like that would have frightened her. But shock wouldn't get that kind of smile out of her, that real, bonafide, from the heart, honest-to-goodness, true-to-the-bone Ilana smile. You only got that if she loved you.

She studied the child's face, her body. Her whole being was stretching toward a familiar, welcome sight.

"It has to be someone she knows! Someone she trusts!"

The army men looked at each other in confusion.

But how was that possible?! For someone Ilana knew—they knew—to be inside a house surrounded by Hamas terrorists? She wracked her brain helplessly, pondering the impossible riddle.

Leah put her arm around Elise's shoulder. "There's an angel in the room, and Ilana's seen it. Only an angel could make her smile like that."

It was, Elise thought, as reasonable an explanation as any other.

The last and final deadline, the tape said, was in twenty-four hours. She looked at her watch. It was 2:25 P.M. How much time was left? And when, exactly, had the clock started ticking?

Chapter thirty

Musa el Khalil was the perfect product of his culture. Born in the Jebalya refugee camp northwest of Beit Lahiya in the notorious Gaza Strip, a camp set up more than fifty-five years ago for Arabs who had heeded the call of their own leaders to get out of the way of advancing Arab armies, he'd had the word "refugee" baked into his soul for as long as he could remember.

A runty child with a badly formed leg who had been constantly teased by his older brothers, Musa had learned early how to defend himself by virtue of a viciousness and stealth that left those who teased him forever wary. His schooling minimal, he joined youth organizations funded and run by Al-Mujam'a, or "The Assemblage," an organization founded in 1978 by Sheik Yassin. There the angry, needy child found nourishment for his body, and sustenance for his bitter soul. Along with the free helpings of soft drinks, humous, and pita bread, he was fed such teachings as that of Abu Hurayra: "The Day of Judgment will not come until the Muslims fight the Jews and kill them…" and the Hadith that declared: "It is Allah's wisdom that the struggle between Muslims and Jews shall continue until the Day of Judgment and the ultimate victory."

Musa, like many other children, took the message to heart, desiring nothing more than to make the cut for membership and to receive the training and weapons that would raise him into the highly honored *mujahid* fellowship.

Recognizing something in the teenager's dark, pitiless eyes, Hamas recruiters gave Musa el Khalil his heart's desire when he turned fifteen. He soon proved their instincts correct. Sent to dispatch a storekeeper in East Jerusalem accused of collaborating with the Israelis (actually, a Hamas member's cousin had a less successful store next door), Musa got a job carrying the heavy sacks of spices for the elderly, portly Arab merchant. And then, early one morning, he used the knife meant to open the canvas sacks of cumin and *kamoun* to slit the unsuspecting old man's throat. By the time he'd walked out into the bustling Arab street, and taken a crowded blue Arab bus back home, he was ready for his next assignment.

It was not long in coming. Indeed, numerous assignments followed, allowing him to establish a reputation for ruthlessness and cruelty that flagged him as a rising star among the new recruits. In reward, he was sent to a terrorist training camp in Syria, one of many that operated in Egypt, the Soviet Union, Poland, North Korea, and Cuba.

There he was taught that dying while killing the enemies of Islam was a privilege. A blessing. All who joined Hamas, it was drummed into him, had to be ready to die in a religious war. It was Islam against the corrupt west. Islam against the infidels who believed in Hinduism, Judaism, and Christianity...

Musa el Khalil, however, was not interested in dying. He was interested in climbing up the ladder of success in an organization in which his natural abilities had made him supremely qualified to serve. Secretly, he laughed at the sermons of the crippled sheik, delivered in a high-pitched girlish monotone from a wheelchair. If a man with no legs, and no strength, could command respect by virtue of his viciousness and cunning, he had no doubt his own physical disabilities, lowly birth, and lack of schooling would do nothing to impede his progress.

He couldn't have been more correct.

In 1983, he was secretly delighted when the Israelis put the sheik behind bars, seeing in it a power vacuum that would allow him more freedom to develop his own ideas. Two years later when the Israelis traded Sheik Mansour and fifteen hundred other terrorists for three Israeli soldiers kidnapped from Lebanon, he had already begun implementing those ideas with great success.

Under Khalil's direction, operatives began spreading rumors amongst Palestinians of nonexistent Israeli atrocities. Making up stories of soldiers raping Palestinian mothers, slicing up small children and using their blood in bread, they fanned hatred to a fever pitch. Soon, young people began throwing rocks at soldiers. The rocks then turned into Hamas-supplied Molotov cocktails, and eventually into the Intifada.

Inevitably, Yamam—the counterterrorist unit of the Israeli Police Force—picked him up. He was sentenced to six years in Israeli prisons. Musa found the experience most instructive—even better than the training camps. Watching how his cellmates often traded information for cigarettes and other trifling privileges, leading to Israeli raids on ammunition caches and terror cells, Khalil devised the idea that Hamas members be set up in such a way that no cell member would know more than four or five other people.

Through coded messages taken out of prison under visitors' tongues, he communicated with the Hamas bigwigs abroad, and together they worked out the internal organization of the Hamas in Israel: it was terrorism with a corporate structure. There were departments for recruitment, funding and job placement; departments in charge of communication, propaganda and internal security.

Released from prison, Khalil was put in charge of his pet project: The al-Mujahidoun al-Felastiniyoun cells, that vied with each other in the bloodthirstiness of their planned attacks against civilian targets. To hone their skills, they practiced on their own people. With encouragement from the Saudis, they killed drug dealers, prostitutes, and liquor salesmen who defied Islamic law. In consequence, Hamas suddenly found itself awash in Saudi cash.

Musa el Khalil was paid handsomely for his work. For the first time in his life, he had wealth beyond the imaginings of any who had come from his tribe. He built a red-tiled villa in Bir Naballah, bought a black Mercedes and married the prettiest and most voluptuous daughter of another Hamas operative. She was fifteen.

The problems began when the Israelis began to understand who they were dealing with and began deporting Hamas operatives. To his surprise and delight, the election of Yitzhak Rabin in 1992, and secret negotiations with Yassir Arafat in Oslo, led the Israeli prime minister to rescind deportation orders. What followed was a banner year for Musa, with over 192 acts of terror in Israel that spread death and mayhem all over the country. When the Israeli government finally deported him and 415 other Hamas terrorists over the border to Lebanon, Musa used it as the ultimate photo opportunity.

It became a media circus. During the day, amid corps of cooperative reporters, he shivered on camera over makeshift pots of soup. And at dusk, when reporters conveniently disappeared, he partied with members of Hezbollah and Iranian intelligence, attending workshops in advanced terror techniques.

Facing worldwide condemnation to repatriate the "cold and starving men," Israeli leaders caved in once again. One hundred well-trained terrorists were led back into the country, and the others, including Musa, had their banishment period reduced to only two years.

Musa el Khalil made good use of that time. Sent to southern Sudan to the elite Pasdaran camp run by Iranian intelligence, he was schooled in how to make inexpensive pipe bombs from acetone and detergent. How to connect less than a hundred grams of explosives to gas cylinders, grenades and hundreds of carpenter's nails in order to kill dozens and destroy everything within a ten-foot radius. How to plant trip-wire land mines to explode cars.

But Khalil wasn't satisfied. One of the problems with planting bombs was the alertness of the well-practiced Israeli civilian, who nine times out of ten discovered these devices in time. But what if, he thought, there were no suspicious packages? What if the bomb was a person, a person who looked like everybody else?

Facing the skepticism of his colleagues that anyone would be willing to come to such a gruesome end, Khalil set out to prove them wrong. He went searching for men and women who had no expectations from life at all. Amid the squalor of Gaza and the West Bank, he had no trouble finding them. Befriending mosque loners, young men from poor families who were terminally ill, the unemployed, the unmarriageable, he began to work. Brainwashing them with videotapes that promised them part in "a unique operation that only you can carry out" and the reward of a ruby palace set in a "place near Allah and his prophets" and a heavenly harem of seventy-two virgins who would help him "drink from rivers of honey," he found to everyone's shock—including his own—that there was no end to the waists willing to strap on ten or fifteen kilograms of explosives; enough to blow up an entire hotel, a whole school, or an entire busload of unsuspecting people on their way home from work and school; enough to fill anyone who survived with enough nails in their lungs, brains, livers, and eyes to make them wish they hadn't.

Aided by Oslo—which took the responsibility of fighting terror out of the hands of Israelis and put it into the hands of the PLO—Musa enjoyed eight years of unmatched successes, helping to ensure that Israelis would find themselves the target of one terror attack every hour, every day. It was an unprecedented triumph.

It was just then, at the height of his career, that Musa el Khalil began to get nervous. He saw the Oslo agreements collapsing and realized that he had enemies—relatives of those he'd killed, Hamas members who envied his rapid rise—who would be more than happy to see him pick up a cell phone and have it explode in his ear. He worried that in that explosion, something might also happen to his family. Worse, he worried that it wouldn't, and that his beautiful young wife would be available to another man.

The idea tortured him.

In the ten years of their marriage, she had grown even more beautiful. She had given him six children, four sons and two daughters. He wanted himself and his family out of harm's way. The opportunity arrived when the head of operations in the U.S. wanted to replace the head of operations in Amman with his cousin, and needed information leaked to the Mossad that would get the present head murdered by secret agents. Musa, who felt each man had his time on earth decided by Allah, had no problem arranging for destiny to take its course. He was rewarded with a plum job: coordinator of operations in Western Europe.

He took his family to Malta and set them up there. In a short time, he received a forged Libyan passport from Khadaffi's cooperative regime, allowing him to travel alone by ferry from Tripoli to Valleta, and from there to Paris.

His job in Europe was diversified. He collected cash from Muslim and European supporters and made deposits. He also continued to be involved in all stages of planning terror operations in Israel. Officially, he was the final authority on confirming how and when such operations would be undertaken. And how they would end. Most of the time, though, he let local operatives run their own show.

With the help of the fax machine and computer set up in his elegant Avenue Foch hotel room, he received information from operatives in Israel and sent back coded instructions. When he wanted to communicate, he sent out two identical messages with coded instructions to two separate locations.

Sometimes he looked at the little portable machine on the elegant Louis XVI desk by a bed canopied in blue watered silk and smiled. He had come a long way from filthy huts packed with greasy explosives.

Gradually, something happened to Musa el Khalil. Far away from his wife and children, from the arid landscape of refugee camps and terrorist training grounds, he suddenly opened his eyes to the wonders of being free and alive with money in his pocket in a city like Paris. He strolled along the Seine. Paid a visit to the Eiffel Tower, riding to the top with childish delight. He had his suits custom-made, developed a taste for forbidden brandy and fine cigars, and sank deeper and deeper into the indolence of a career that left him plenty of time for nightclubs and brothels.

On May 9, it was past midnight when he finally returned to his hotel room after a wild night with one of his favorite call girls. He felt elated, and a bit dirty, as he turned the key in the door, looking forward to undressing and washing himself in a long, hot bath of soapy water. To his surprise, he heard the phone ringing insistently when he opened the door.

He wasn't expecting a call.

He picked it up, frowning, but as he listened, his face gradually relaxed, finally broadening into a large grin. It was the famous Russian arms dealer, known only as V.C. Khalil had been trying, unsuccessfully, to contact him for months. He wanted to talk, and also, apparently, to deliver personally a large donation in cash.

Khalil loved cash, especially cash handed to him personally that no one else could count. It would help him to cover gambling debts, and increase the action and variety of his nightlife. He was also flattered at the sudden invitation to the famous nightclub where one needed a private pass or membership to enter and mingle with the likes of V.C.—not to mention heads of rich Arab sheikdoms, supermodels, French politicians, and famous hairdressers. V.C. said he would be waiting outside to usher him through its famous oak doors and its forbidding security.

Khalil didn't think twice. He smelled his underarms and shrugged. A bath would have to wait. He straightened the diamond pin on his tie and walked jubilantly back out into the lively Parisian night. He hailed a taxi, giving the driver the address of Chez Ariana.

Chapter thirty-one

Kala el-Bireh, Samaria (West Bank)
Friday, May 10 · 5:00 A.M.

Marwan Bahama downloaded his e-mail. There it was. The coded message from Musa he'd been waiting for. He went to the Web site indicated. As he read the carefully worded document, his face grew red and his fist tightened. He got up, slamming his fist into the wall. The startled men around him backed away, exchanging glances that were both furtive and alarmed; when Marwan Bahama was angry, no one was safe.

He took in the alarm of his men and tried to calm himself. Maybe there was some mistake. Some misunderstanding. The message couldn't possibly mean what he thought it meant. He went to the second Web site, then he printed out both messages. He held the two up to the light. The letters overlapped perfectly.

"*Ibn-al-Mutanaka,*" he cursed under his breath. "*Boos teezi!*" he screamed. The men around him, used to foul language, blushed. He sat down and went through the letter once again, looking for the special code words that would indicate it had been sent under duress, or was fake. But no matter how much he pored over it, he could find no indication that it didn't mean exactly what it said: he was being relieved of his command of the operation. The two settlers were to be handed over to Ismael. The e-mail said Ismael would pick up the prisoners in the late afternoon and that until then, they were to be well treated.

Under his breath, he wished his knife a speedy entry into the heart of that *gawwaad* Ismael, and that ibn-al-Mutanaka Musa el Khalil, grown soft from whores, forbidden wine and pig-tainted food in the decadent capitals of the degraded western world. None of his demands had been met. Not one! Why should he let the Jews go? This was his operation. His! His successful planning and execution. Their blood belonged to him. Why should Ismael have the honor and glory of the kill?

"*Khara beek!*" he screamed at the missing man who had upstaged him. He had never liked Ismael, with his ironed, British shirts and superior attitude.

He glanced at the men who stood around him sweating, their eyes wary, their hands behind their backs, fingering prayer beads. The thermometer had risen to almost thirty centigrade, and except for the lazy rotation of a single ceiling fan, the fetid air, reeking of stale cooking oil and cigarettes, lay over them as thick as a fog, and as unbreathable.

"Look, look at what orders we have been given, brothers! We have been betrayed!" he screamed. His men picked up the papers as Bahama threw them to the floor, reading. Bahama kicked the wall, and plaster snowed down on the floor. "Before I turn them over, I will have a little talk with them, the Zionists, no? Is that not owed to me, at least?"

He went swiftly to the door and began unlocking the cell.

"Marwan, please. Be careful. The orders are from Musa himself. There must be a reason," his second in command said mildly.

Bahama turned to him. With stunning swiftness, Bahama grasped the man's beard and kneed his groin with such forcefulness that blood began to darken the light cotton material around his crotch. Then, using his own head as a battering ram, Bahama butted him full in the stomach, until the man lay stretched and gasping on the plaster-covered floor.

The other men hung back. No one moved.

Panting, Bahama moved again toward the holding cell.

It took a while for his eyes to adjust to the darkness. Like a predatory night animal, he sought his helpless prey. There, in the corner, he saw the blanket move, the whites of eyes. The man. But where, he thought, was the child? The little Jewish whore? The video was over now. She didn't need to be a movie star anymore.

He walked toward Jon, then pulled off the blanket.

But the child wasn't there.

"Get up, Jew dog!" he screamed.

Jon stumbled to his feet.

Bahama switched on the light, his eyes darting swiftly around the filthy room. He searched the piles of garbage, scattering them to the floor. He kicked the papers and pieces of cloth, but his feet did not meet the resistance of young flesh.

"Where is she?!" he shouted, shaking Jon.

Jon said nothing. He felt the vicious kick to his face and heard his teeth crack.

"Where? Where is she? Talk or die!"

With effort, Jon allowed a small smile to curl his bleeding lips.

Bahama went wild. "Where is she, where is she, where is she?!" He panted, each exclamation punctuated by another vicious blow.

In a good place, Jon prayed. In a good place, he repeated to himself until, mercifully, he lost consciousness.

Chapter thirty-two

Hotel Intercontinental, East Jerusalem, Israel
Friday, May 10, 2002 · 7:00 A.M.

Julia awoke with a feeling of heaviness behind her forehead, and the drumming of small hammers at her temples that were, she knew, her body's familiar disciplinary actions against itself for three or four gin-and-tonics too many. Still, she had no regrets. There had been an excellent reason for every single one of them.

The first was for being left standing outside the prime minister's office after the press conference, searching in vain for her driver, not to mention her erstwhile boyfriend, the Polish charmer, who had disappeared like a genie in a bottle. The second was for having to listen to Jack Duggan's threats all day Thursday if she failed to get hold of the second video in time for the evening news. Drinks three and—maybe—four had to do with the fact that Ismael Abadi was not answering his cell phone, and had disappeared with the staff car and presumably the videotape as well. He was nowhere; beamed up whole by aliens, she thought irritably. Without him, she reluctantly admitted to herself, she was just one more clueless blond Brit with a microphone in a foreign country where she didn't speak the language. And to top it all off, the bureau was holding her responsible for all of it. As if!

She groped her way into the bathroom, surveying the evening's damage in the mirror. God.

She splashed cold water on her mascara-streaked cheeks and wiped off the lipstick mustache. With unsteady hands, she tore a brush through her hair. At least that was all right. That and her eyes, those blue eyes (although contact lenses to deepen the color would be a worthy investment, she often thought).

Lovely eyes, she contradicted herself defiantly. Golden hair. Screw Milos.

She tossed her head and went back to find her cell phone, once again dialing his number. The fact that he had been filming Ismael, and the fact that both of them had very conveniently disappeared at the same time, left her with questions she wanted answered.... No one picked up. Then she tried Ismael's number. It rang and rang and rang.

Listless, she flicked on the television, flipping through the channels. She stopped, stunned. There it was, on a two-bit local station, the Hebrew-language Channel Two news: her video! BCN's exclusive! Dr. Margulies and the child, and the gun-toting Hamas militant spouting belligerent Islamic rhetoric, all accompanied by a voice-over in Hebrew!

Her video! Her network exclusive!

No wonder Ismael was nowhere to be found. That little rat...!

She flipped to the other stations. CNN was broadcasting. Sky was broadcasting. BBC was broadcasting. Only BCN had nothing.

She stood there in her underwear, livid, confused, and worst of all, helpless. All day yesterday, she had been expecting Ismael to deliver the tape to her at any moment. That, at least, had been the agreement between them as they discussed it in the car on the way to the press conference. She'd allowed herself to be persuaded by him that to go back personally to the sheik's would be a waste of time and an unnecessary danger. He was better off, he'd told her, handling it alone. At the time, she'd been secretly delighted. Who needed another bumpy ride into the wilds of the terrorist-infested country-side? Besides, she'd calculated it would give her extra time, time she'd planned to spend with Milos…. She watched the video, furious. That smooth-talking Islamic rat had stabbed her in the back—and after she'd gone out of her way to be so understanding, so sympathetic! Her phone, she saw, had sixteen messages. She flipped through them. All of them were from Jack Duggan, with the exception of one or two from Sean Morrison. She'd be back on the next plane to Heathrow. No one would help her with her bags. And this would be her last foreign assignment, if they didn't fire her altogether.

What had she done wrong? What? she asked herself despondently, when suddenly the answer dawned on her, a bright neon light flashing in her consciousness with a one-word revelation: Milos. Outside of Duggan and Morrison, he was the only other person besides herself who knew about Ismael's involvement in acquiring the first tape, and the coming delivery of the second. And now the tape—*her* tape—was being whored around, common property of practically everyone except her own network.

Could Milos have tipped someone off, even unwittingly? And what could have gone wrong with Ismael? Had he been bribed? Threatened? And why would these men she liked and trusted do this? To her?! When she'd been so professional, so kind, so…stupid, she thought, her hands shaking with fury as she dialed Milos' bureau number. Someone answered in Polish. "Can I speak to Milos Jankowski, please? No. I can't understand you. Oh bloody hell, just put him on, will you?" she screamed. "What did you call me, you piece of Eastern Eurotrash!" she said hotly, before slamming down the phone. They said he didn't work there. Had they misunderstood? Or had she?

There was no point in trying to call. She'd have to physically track Milos down, then find Ismael. Worse came to worse, she thought with a touch of desperation, she could always get Jack to find another fixer and make her way back out to the sheik's house alone. What if she got an exclusive interview with the sheik? Or maybe…. Her heart began to pound…or maybe an exclusive interview with the Jewish doctor…

The brilliance of the ideas, the possibilities for a triumphant comeback, took her breath away. She considered the risks. Well, BCN was known to be an advocate for Palestinians…. But some of these

Palestinian types, however just their cause and however much they'd suffered, hadn't actually seemed all that sympathetic. But there was no time to think about it, or go wobbly, she scolded herself, putting on her makeup, giving particular care to her eyeliner and shadow. You've gotten yourself into this mess, dearie, and you'll just have to do whatever you can to climb back out, however far up and however slippery-steep the slope. She pulled on the white suit that had just come back from the cleaners and the dark, sensual emerald blouse. She put on her sunglasses and a green velvet hairband. It looked lush against her light hair, she thought with satisfaction. There was no point in even attempting to get men to behave and cooperate if you looked like hell.

She caught a taxi and slammed the car door shut with urgency, telling the driver: "Center of town," while she considered where, exactly, she was planning to go. What was the name of Milos' fleabag hotel? "Hotel Judah, on King George Street," she told the driver.

The best scenario was to get her fixer back. She had a hunch that if she found Milos, she'd find Ismael. Anyway, it was worth a try.

Hotel Judah was more like a hotel where you rented rooms by the hour, not the day, she noted, glancing distastefully at the grimy windows, the half-torn curtains, the broken venetian blinds hanging at a forty-five-degree angle. And there was such a nice little hotel right nearby.... Why did he have to pick this one? She took out her press card and showed it to the security guard. Unimpressed, he motioned for her to open her purse, then passed a metal detector over her body with more thoroughness, she thought, than was strictly necessary.

"Moron," she said under her breath as she took the elevator up to Milos' room. Arabs, Jews. Palestinians, Israelis. No wonder the Middle East was a sewer. They were all brain-dead, she thought. Thank God for London!

Not surprisingly, there was no answer to her insistent knock. Livid, she returned to the lobby. "Pardon me, but can you tell me where I might find one of your guests, a Milos Jankowski?" she asked the reception clerk, a heavy Russian bleached-blonde with a bad attitude.

"Not detective agency. Hotel. You leave message." The woman

shrugged, concentrating on holding a glass of hot tea by her finger-tips. She placed a cube of sugar on her pink tongue.

"Well, thanks so much. I don't think I could have managed to come up with that brilliant idea all by myself," she retorted in clipped, icy syllables, followed by a poisonous smile. "If I'd wanted to leave a message, I'd have called," she said.

The woman looked up from her tea unsympathetically and shrugged. "English, not good."

"Well then, can you at least tell me if he's still registered? Or if anyone saw him come back last night? Or if he ate breakfast here this morning?"

The clerk sucked the tea through the sugar cube, then licked her forefinger and turned the page of a local Russian-language paper, ignoring her.

"Well, thanks for nothing!" Julia shouted, slamming her hand on the counter. She pushed the revolving door into the startled faces of two Nigerian Christian tourists, who had no choice but to hurry through.

Out in the morning heat, she felt the Middle Eastern sun bake the top of her head like the worst setting on a two-thousand-watt hair dryer. Her temples pounded, and her cell phone rang and rang. Finally, she picked it up. "Look, Jack, I'm doing my best. No, I haven't heard from Ismael. I was about to ask you the same thing. After all, you know him better than I do. But there must be another Palestinian fixer to take his place. There is? When and where is he picking me up?"

She took out a pen and wrote it down. "David's Harp, King David Street? At one? That's four hours from now! All right, all right. Jack?" She took a deep breath. "I'm sorry about the tape. I honestly don't know what went wrong." Her face turned a bright red as she listened to the voice of the bureau chief. "I'm sorry you feel that way, Jack. I didn't tell Milos anything." She paused, her face flaming. "And I don't agree that I think with my vagina." She hung up the phone.

Everyone knew, of course.

She walked slowly down the street. They'd all be sorry! She was going back into the lion's den, and they could all eat her dust.

Maybe she'd even get Duggan fired? Or get a better-paying job at CNN.... And maybe—why not?—she'd even wrangle another exclusive with that settler woman! See her reaction to the second tape. After all, the baby was fine, wasn't it? No harm had really been done. She shifted uncomfortably. No, better not, she thought, remembering the old woman. That bridge was burned. Well then, maybe she'd find the mother of the Palestinian in the headband with the gun, find out something about his upbringing, his hardships.... Kind of woman-to-woman...

She had four hours to kill. She turned, heading aimlessly along King George Street. Just ahead she saw Jerusalem's Great Synagogue with its pillars and stained glass. There was a bus stop crowded with people. A woman with a baby carriage, an old man wearing a light gray fedora, two teenagers giggling on cell phones, a female soldier with a heavy backpack. Maybe she'd just interview them, random Israelis in the center of a city where people blew themselves up. It suddenly occurred to her that their simple act of waiting for a bus might be considered by some an act of courage and defiance.

She turned away, surprised at the thought. At herself. How must it be to live in a city where your steps were dogged by armed terrorists whose only job in life was to find unarmed civilians and cause maximum slaughter? The question made her queasy and she looked for a distraction.

She spied a little bookstore called Stein's with boxes of dusty used books on the pavement in all languages. That would be interesting, she thought. To see what kinds of books people were reading. She knelt, rifling through them. A few novels by Steinbeck. A graying book of 1950s etiquette. A wrinkled text of German grammar. The journals of Anaïs Nin. Now, this was interesting, she thought, picking up a book called *Perfumes and Cosmetics in the Ancient World*. It looked fairly new too. She stood up and began flipping through the pages. They fanned her face, which suddenly felt strangely cold in the morning sun.

For no reason, she suddenly looked up and into the glass of the storefront. A dark shadow passed behind her, filling her with inexplicable fear. She thought: I should turn around and see who it is, that dark figure, so dark in the morning sun.

The force of the explosion was a noise she had never heard before, a sound that was a personal attack, a statement of purpose both obscene and emphatic, whose meaning was unmistakable. And then there was a strange and eerie silence. Time was suspended, removed from the context of measurable units, each second an eternity. She watched, mesmerized, as the glass of the storefront shattered and flew out toward her, like something in a cartoon. She watched, fascinated, never even attempting to cover her face with her hands. Everything was suddenly silent, slow motion, dreamlike. One of those old, voiceless films.

She didn't feel afraid, not for those first few moments, as she slowly pivoted. The baby carriage wheels and a bottle, she thought, staring at the littered pavement. Someone's arm. Half a head. And blood, blood everywhere, and the choking smell of something so foul and dense she tried not to breathe for as long as she could. Mouths were opened as if screaming, but she heard nothing. She tried to take a step, but the ground was suddenly slippery, like ice. Ice in the Middle Eastern morning sun, she thought, looking at her arm, or what was left of it. She opened her mouth to scream. Only then was she fully aware she wasn't going to be reporting this from the sidelines. That she was going to be part of the story.

She could hear no sound as she slipped down to the pavement. My hair, she thought, feeling the glass needles in her scalp. My ears, my head, my blue eyes, my body. For the first time, she was terrified.

Terrorism. To instill terror. Yes. That word. The perfect word for who they are and what they do. Terrorists.

Am I going to live, she wondered. Or have I been killed? Is this the way you feel when you are killed? Or am I alive? She held on to that idea, until she thought of something else. Maybe it wasn't over. Maybe someone was going to come after her now with a machine gun, someone who doesn't know I have been on their side all along, who didn't understand her being here at this moment was just an accident, an accident. This is all a huge mistake! A mistake! I'm not part of this conflict! It has nothing to do with me, something inside of her screamed.

It was then she saw it. The baby bottle that had rolled on its side and lay near her on the ground. She felt herself suddenly sob.

A spasm of pain went through her that she found unbelievable in its intensity, and then the pain in her body was strangely dulled. She felt oddly calm as she lay there in the dark, silent, slippery ground. As she lay there, waiting. My white suit, my favorite emerald blouse, she remembered. And then she felt nothing, nothing at all.

Chapter thirty-three

I t was a little strange having such a handsome young man accompany her, Leah thought, holding on to Milos' arm as he ushered her carefully into the arrivals lounge of Ben Gurion Airport to await the arrival of Esther's private plane carrying her three dear friends. It had been some time since a man, any man, had been good enough to open a car door, chauffeur her, help her across a street....

Not that she was feeling sorry for herself. Thank God. Feet she had, to walk; hands she had, to open her own car doors.... But as she gripped his strong, young arm (Leave me alone! I'm an old lady, she told the disapproving little voice shouting in her ear that it was forbidden for a man and woman not married to each other to touch) she couldn't help but think of Mendel, her son, so far away. She'd called him, told him all about what was going on. He'd been very nice. Really. He and his wife. He wanted to come, to help. Maybe he would. She gripped a little harder.

"Come, *Babcia*...Come sit down," Milos said, leading her over to the seats with a good view of the giant projection screen that flashed the images of incoming passengers to those waiting for them in the arrivals lounge, making them look, Leah thought, like movie stars.

"'Bo-Chuh?'.... This is what you call your own grandmother?"

"Yes," he smiled, helping her carefully into the seat.

"You're a good boy, Milos. A good grandson."

She thought of her own grandson, the skateboarding cowboy...God bless him. Maybe he too was a good boy...

She settled back, seeking a comfortable position on the modernistic metallic-mesh seating. Who designed such a thing for the backsides of human beings, she wondered. A robot? And did you need to be a genius to buy them for a whole airport, to make old ladies suffer? But this new arrivals lounge at Ben Gurion was still a big improvement on the old one with that glass partition separating the passengers from the welcomers—all those people smoking and the babies crying and everyone pushing to get a little look at who had gotten off the plane.

The Israelis had rebuilt the thing after that Japanese murderer—that Kozo, Bozo, something Aki-*meshugana*-Moto—took out a machine gun from his suitcase and began to shoot.... What did a Jew ever do to him? He didn't have enemies in Tokyo? He had to invent them halfway around the world? She shrugged. Should have hanged him. But go convince the Israeli government that the death penalty was good for somebody less than an Eichmann. He was probably still sitting in some Israeli jail eating gefilte fish and humous with chopsticks....

So, this was a nicer terminal, even if the seats were like putting your behind in a blender.

She looked up at the flickering red lights on the arrivals board, even though she knew the flight she was waiting for wouldn't be listed. "A private plane. Imagine! Your own plane to fly around the world in! What a girl, that Esther! What a girl. And beautiful, blond, blue-eyed Maria, who could get any man to do anything, even bald in Auschwitz. And tall, slim, lovely Ariana, with her stories of summer homes in Cannes, and banquet feasts prepared by her famous parents' chef...stories that had wound around them like magic, banishing the freezing cold, the starvation.... They had only made it through because of each other. Because of the Covenant. They had all lived to see children and grandchildren; to see their hair turn gray, their stomachs grow fat.

She wondered if they'd changed much, and if they'd be shocked when they saw her.

She looked around at people, all of them in various stages of decay. Because that's what it amounted to: from the moment you stopped growing in your twenties, you started deteriorating. You could, of course, with vigorous exercise, expensive creams, good food and plenty of rest, slow down the sag, shrink the bulge, lighten the creases. You could cajole the organs to keep up their pumping and emptying, without too many strikes or slow-downs. But sooner or later, it caught up with you. One day, you could be the kind of old lady who jogged to the supermarket and whipped up gourmet dinners, and the next you could slip on a sidewalk over nothing and find yourself in a wheelchair in front of *The Bold and the Beautiful*, wolfing down Meals On Wheels. Or you could get a bad grade on a medical test, the only kind of test where when you flunked, you died. Hearts, lungs, bones, blood—the raw materials that kept one alive—were so vulnerable. They wore out, wore down. But the spirit, that was another story. The soul of good people got stronger and more beautiful as time went by, experiencing life with more wisdom and gratitude. Her friends were all such good people.

How she longed to see them!

She saw Milos come toward her across the terminal.

"Milos! You look as white as the moon! What's wrong?" she asked, shocked at the change in his appearance.

"I'm sorry to bring you bad news. But there's been a terrorist attack in the center of Jerusalem. A suicide bomber detonated himself."

"*Oy. Gotteinu!*" Leah's fingers gripped her dress. "How bad?"

"Six dead. Forty-five wounded."

"*Gotteinu.*" She placed her hand over her heart.

"One of the victims was Julia Greenberg."

Leah looked up sharply, incredulous, then resigned. "*Baruch Dayan Emes.*"

"What does that mean?" Milos asked.

"'Blessed be the true judge....'"

"Look, *Babcia*, I know what she did to you was terrible. But she didn't deserve this. No one does."

She put her hand gently on his arm. "It's what we always say when we hear bad news."

"Oh, I see. Look. I feel somehow.... I don't know.... I've got to go to her. I feel...I owe...." He stuttered.

"You have a good heart, Milos," Leah said kindly, shaking her head. "Not like mine. Like your own *babcia's*. Go, child."

"You'll be all right here by yourself? You'll explain to my grandmother what happened?"

"Yes. Of course. Go, go. Anyway, do you think Esther Gold would travel to Jerusalem in your beat-up Skoda? Go," she said, pinching his cheek.

He kissed each wrinkled hand, then walked away.

She sat back on the metal mesh, staring at the screen, thinking with horror of the young, pretty reporter. And then she closed her eyes, remembering another roomful of pretty young women, so long ago....

"You, you, you, you, raus, raus!" the SS guard shouted, pointing his whip at all four of them. Snarling dogs bared vicious teeth, straining at their leashes. "To the side, all of you! And you, you, you, you, you, you, you!" He pointed his whip at other girls: "Raus, raus."

It took a few moments until the realization sunk in. After all the mornings the selektion *had passed them by, letting them live another day; this time, they'd been chosen.*

"It's because of me! It's my fault, because I am sick," Esther sobbed. "I told you to leave me behind!"

"Jesus have mercy," Maria whispered, holding on to Esther. "Wait a minute. Look around!"

But they were not among the old, the sick. They were surrounded by dozens of the youngest, prettiest girls in the camp!

They were herded into a truck and taken to an empty barracks.

"Take off your clothes!" the SS guards barked at them. They slipped

off the pitiful rags, shivering. With agonizing modesty, they spread out their fingers, trying to make their hands cover their bodies as they huddled together for warmth and protection from the terrible unknown.

SS doctors in warm clothes and shiny leather boots passed through their ranks, shining flashlights over their bodies, and into their mouths.

"Hold out your hands! We are taking you to a factory in which delicate work must be performed. We want to see if you have the hands for it!"

They looked at each other, not daring to hope.

"If they touch my hands, they'll feel I am sick…" Esther whispered, sobbing.

"You have cooled off from being out in the cold. You have no sores. Your eyes are lovely. They will not find anything. Just don't cry…" Leah begged her. "Don't cry, my Esther." She held her waist in a strong grip.

They could see the doctors' male eyes focus on their bodies, their young women's bodies, making them all merge together. They would not notice something as human as a face. They would not notice Esther's limbs were only upright because of the women's hands that grasped her firmly on either side.

"RAUS!"

But no whips were used, no clubs. No dogs. They didn't want to damage the bodies, Maria realized. Their women's bodies. They were taken to another barracks and allowed to take a shower.

Pandemonium broke out. Clean water! And real soap! They laughed and wept and held each other, shampooing each other's hair for the first time since they'd arrived, scrubbing their bodies, evaporating the accumulated layers of filth.

They were in a state of shock, almost giddy with delight, almost ready to die from the joy of it! A shower with soap! A new light came into Esther's eyes at the feel of the water streaming over her body, as if her downward spiral had suddenly halted, found some solid ground, some base. She suddenly felt human again, connected as a human being back to the world of human beings she had been ripped out of with such brutality.

They dried each other off. Towels? Were they dreaming? Were they already dead and in heaven?

They were taken to the storerooms and given clean women's under-

wear: bras, panties, camisoles, and scarves to cover their heads…And then they were given dresses and shoes, and asked to try them on, to see if they fit.

Imagine! Fitted clothes!

It was like a dream, a dream.

"In a minute, we'll wake up, and it will all vanish." Leah shook her head.

"No, my parents have finally come for me. We are being dressed to go home," Ariana said dreamily.

"All of us?" Esther smiled, glancing at the hundred other girls whose excited chatter filled the room with almost a normal sound, after the desperate noises of the lager.

"My parents can arrange everything." Ariana laughed, pulling on a pair of stylish high heels, and a red wool dress. "My father is the director Jaques Feyder, my mother the actress Francoise Rosay!" she told them, as if she hadn't said it a thousand times a day every day since she'd arrived.

They stared at each other, at the wondrous transformation. They were human again. Girls again. It was unbelievable.

"Look at Esther!" Leah giggled.

Esther adjusted the rose-colored collar on her dress.

"Like a fashion model." Maria smiled, adjusting the buttons of a white blouse.

"I feel like the Sabbath is coming." Leah laughed, adjusting a gray woolen jacket over a blue blouse and zipping up a matching gray wool skirt. "Ariana, that dress doesn't fit you. It's much too short. Take it back and ask for another."

The pleated skirt stopped halfway down her thighs.

"I need something longer," she told the kapo. "This doesn't fit."

He looked at her strangely. "For where you are going, it is long enough…"

The women stopped dressing and turned to look at him.

"Where is that?" Maria asked, her smile suddenly gone.

He beckoned for her to come closer, then leaned over, staring down at her breasts. He whispered something in her ear. Her face went white.

She crossed herself and stumbled to a corner, collapsing to the floor. She grasped her knees and wept, rocking back and forth.

"*Maria?*"

"*Maria, what is it?*"

"*Tell us!*"

She averted their eyes: "*We are being sent to the front.*"

"*But…. For what? We are not soldiers!*"

Maria looked up at them, her eyes full of pity and love. "*To be the whores of German soldiers.*"

Ariana jumped up: "*No!*" *She bolted toward the door.*

It was locked from both sides. The guards watched her lazily, grinning as she ran along the walls, banging her head against the boards. "I am not a fille de joie! *Never!*" *Ariana wept.* "*When Lissette bought the brothel from Madame Heupert, she sold me to a man for the night. I was thirteen. A virgin. She got a lot of money. That was why I ran away…. That is how the Nazis caught me…No one will force me to be a whore…never!*" *She wept, hysterical.*

"*Brothel?*" *Esther repeated, in shock.* "*But your parents, the director and the film star? Your house, and the chef and the chauffeur? The summers in the South of France—*"

"*I never had anyone! I was left in an orphanage with a Jewish star around my neck, and a birth certificate that said my mother was a young Polish Jewish immigrant. She left the space for my father blank. I picked my parents out of an old movie magazine, and my name out of a book. In the orphanage, they called me Albertine. One day, when I was ten years old, the director took me into his office and laid me down on his desk. He took off my clothes. I…I…picked up—this sharp thing—how do you call this thing?—a letter opener! It was lying on his desk. I held it in my hand like a dagger and stabbed him there, down there. When I saw all the blood, I ran. I lived on the back streets of Paris, all alone, until a whore took pity on me and took me back to her brothel on Rue Peirot. The Madame was very kind to me. But when I turned thirteen, Madame died, and the brothel was sold to Lissette. When the other girls told me what she had planned for me, I ran away to Toulouse. I always wore that Jewish star around my neck. Lissette must have told the SS. They picked me up as soon as I got off the train…. No one is going to make me into a whore…. Never! Never!*"

Maria and Leah struggled to gather her into their arms.

"We might survive it. Who knows?" Esther said.

"No. They will use us up, then shoot us," Maria said. "That is why they aren't bothering to sterilize us first, the way they do the other girls they put into Nazi brothels. We will be dead in a few weeks!"

Ariana tore at her flesh. "I'll kill myself first."

Maria grabbed her hands and held them. "Suicide is a mortal sin."

"Yes! Why should we do the Germans' work for them?" Esther said, trembling. "Anything is better than dying."

Leah shook her head. "No, Esther. Death is not the worst thing that can happen to a human being. My father was a Kohen, a member of the priestly class. And I am his daughter. Maria is right. They will use us up and throw us away. I will not defile myself before I die. If that is the only choice left me, I will make it."

"Maria, you are the oldest, what do you say?" Esther begged.

"I once met a German doctor in the infirmary," Maria said thoughtfully. "She was a prisoner too. They'd sent her to Auschwitz because she'd hidden some Jews in her apartment in Berlin. One day, the SS sent word to her that they wanted one of her patients. If she didn't turn the patient over, she'd endanger herself, and the SS would simply choose another patient, maybe even a healthier one with a better chance of survival. She had to make a moral choice. And this is what she told me: 'Sometimes one must do something for its own sake, without regard for its actual results.' She chose to hide the patient. When I asked her if by endangering herself, she was not doing something wrong for her own child, she answered: 'Perhaps he will have to wait longer for his mother, but he won't have to be ashamed to look her in the face.'

"If we decide not to be whores for the Germans, then that's the right decision, whatever the consequences."

The women sat together silently, staring at the bolted doors, the guards with machine guns.

"Whatever we do, let's make a pact to do it together," Esther said, trembling.

"Yes, a sacred pact that can never be broken...." Ariana agreed.

"Like the one God made with Abraham in the Bible, when He said: 'To your seed have I given this land, from the river of Egypt unto

the great river, the river Perath. To your offspring, who will be like the
stars in the sky....' God called it a Covenant," Leah told them. "An
agreement for all eternity."

"Let's agree that if they try to load us on those trains to the front,
we will all bolt for the fence, and die together."

"And if we survive, let us swear to join our lives together forever,"
Maria said.

"As if we were all limbs attached to the same body..." Leah added,
with tears in her eyes. "We will do anything to help each other survive
and live good lives. Make any sacrifice. Agreed?"

They all nodded.

"Then let's join hands," Maria said.

They touched each other, feeling warmth flow between them like
an electric current, connecting them.

"God of Abraham, Isaac and Jacob, look down on us four women,
and save us...." Leah began.

"I don't know this God, I never met Him," Ariana interrupted,
dropping their hands. "And if He did exist, there would not be an Auschwitz or Nazis. Hitler would have died at birth. On a planet ruled and
created by a good God—we would not be here! Let's make a Covenant
with each other. Let's leave Him out."

"But if there is no God, if everything is simply random, an accident, then why, Ariana, do you want to live? Why do any of us want to
live?" Leah asked.

"Because life can be so beautiful," Ariana whispered. "The world
can be such a beautiful place. I have always seen this in my dreams."

"But when an artist paints a beautiful picture, is it an accident?
Did the paints simply fall on the page, with no directing hand? Life is
not an accident. Auschwitz is not an accident. There is a God who created us, and fruit trees, and sunsets, and new babies, and oceans and
stars...who gave us the ability to make human choices. Human beings
created Auschwitz, not God! It was a human choice. And we can also
choose. If we choose to include Him in our Covenant, then whatever
happens, it will not be meaningless. Not our lives, and not our deaths."
Leah reached out, bringing Ariana back into the circle.

"Finish your prayer, Leah," Maria urged.

"God of Sara, Rivka, Rachel and Leah, our Covenant is this: If
we have no choice but to give up our lives to sanctify them, we will do it
together. But if we survive, we will survive together, becoming one person,
risking everything, giving everything, to help each other live in happiness
all the days of our lives."

"Amen," Maria said, crossing herself.

"Amen," said Esther.

"If only we could do something," Ariana mourned. "Even if it's
only just to curse them before we die."

"Would that make you feel better?" Leah asked, a strange look on
her face.

"It would make all of us feel better," Esther said.

"My father's rabbi was a mystic who studied the kabbalah. There
was a ceremony they did—no one would speak of it, it was so frighteningly powerful—called the Pulse de Noura. It was meant for the most
severe cases, against the most terrible evildoers." She hesitated. "But it is
also very dangerous."

"Why?"

"Because if God doesn't accept your curse, it can backfire on those
who made it."

The women felt a chill creep up their spines.

They debated the issue long into the night.

"Surely the SS are the most evil of evildoers. Surely the curse would
not turn on us," Ariana argued.

"They are drunk with power. The Ten Commandments mean nothing to them. They don't even have the most primitive moral code. They
can kill millions of people, and be happy because they got a leather purse
out of it. That makes them happy, that purse. It makes it all worth it.
The SS think they are so smart, but they are all infinitely stupid, rushing
toward Hell." Maria nodded.

"Do your Pulse de Noura, Leah!"

"Yes. Let's not leave this world without at least trying to fight back,"
Ariana begged her.

"Are we all agreed?" Leah asked, trembling. They nodded. "All right.
But once we start, there is no turning back."

"Tell us what to do," Maria said firmly.

"First, make a circle. Give me your bowl, Ariana." Leah squatted, holding the metal bowl upside down in her lap as she used the spoon to scratch four letters into the metal.

"Is this what the rabbi did?" Maria asked skeptically.

"Exactly," Leah assured her.

"What does it mean?" Esther asked.

"It's the secret name of God."

A sudden silence enveloped them.

She placed the bowl upside down on the floor. "We need earth."

"Wait!" Maria went to the corner of the room and reached her hand through a crack, bringing in the cold, wet mud. She slipped it into Leah's hands. Leah worked it like clay into the figure of a man and placed it carefully over the bowl. "Now bring me some string…"

"String?"

"Take it from the hem of your dresses," Leah scolded impatiently, getting caught up. She gathered the strings, winding each one separately around another finger. Then she spit on the ground and closed her eyes:

Ana Bekoach, Kal Sha-day

Et Oyevanu Le hashmeed

She rose, circling the women and the bowl seven times, all the while tying the strings into knots: "Destroy the destroyer," she chanted. "Make knots, impediments, to all he does, revoke his rule." She stepped into the circle: "In the name of the Holy One, His secret name I invoke." She turned the bowl over, smashing the mud figure into the floor.

"Now, step on it: the German army. The SS. Hitler. The whole Nazi regime. Step on it."

The women got up and ground the mud into the floor, crushing it beneath their heels until nothing remained but dust.

Then they sat side by side, waiting for the morning.

Leah opened her eyes, looking up at the screen. It couldn't be mistaken! There they were: Esther! Maria! Ariana! It couldn't be mistaken. Three old ladies, she smiled.

Esther led the way, of course, with the puffed-up hair, the stylish dress, the red fingernails and red lipstick. What a dame, she chuckled, getting up out of her seat, walking toward the screen. And there, half-hidden by the head of some tall, pushy businessman, was Maria. The long, blond hair was silvery white now, cut short and plain above her ears. Maria, the glamorous, someone's bo-chuh! And Ariana! She stared, shocked. Not tall anymore! Stooped, and underneath that caftan no longer slender. The looks were almost completely gone, the face a mask of too much useless camouflage that hid nothing. But that headdress! It was a turban, with a great jewel in the middle, like some Indian Raja. Oh, my Ariana. My dreamer.

Her eyes blurred as she walked toward them.

"Leah!" they called out to her.

She reached out, and all four stood for a moment holding hands like they had once before, so very long ago. Once again, the magic circle was complete.

Chapter thirty-four

Hadassah Hospital, Jerusalem
Friday, May 10, 2002 · 12:00 P.M.

Elise looked at the four women who stood around her bed. Ariana, with her flamboyant makeup and glamorous flowing dress, covered in jewels, her long gray hair pinned back into a French knot, her green eyes mesmerizing; Esther, the famous businesswoman, chic in her black suit and long string of pearls, her silver hair expertly done, framing her still amazingly youthful face; Maria, straight-backed and proud in the unstylish white blouse and black skirt, the gray curls cut short around her tan and weathered face, her eyes still sparkling with life. And last of all, her *Bubbee*, simple and matronly in her flowered Sabbath dress, the gray wig pulled down low on her forehead, her smile as comforting and full of goodness as a warm glass of milk on a cold, dark night.

"You all came!" she finally managed to whisper, the knot in her throat almost painful. This is what had become of them, those four teenaged girls who had walked into the worst blizzard of evil in modern history and had emerged to tell the tale. This is what survival looked like. You got to grow old. To smile.

It was the most beautiful sight in the world. She reached out to them.

They all reached back, knocking into each other and crowd-
ing the bed. They laughed at their clumsy eagerness, pulling back
a little sheepishly, allowing Ariana—the only childless one among
them—to bend down first. She took Elise gently in her arms. "*Ma
chère fille.*" She kissed her on both cheeks. "Courage! We pray for
you, for your family. This terrorist, the one in Paris, we take care of
him. *Bien sûr!*"

"What did you say?" Elise gasped.

Esther put a restraining hand on Ariana's back. "Maybe, Ariana, we should wait with the details, *non?*"

Ariana considered this. "Perhaps you are right."

Before Elise could pursue it, Maria came forward. "*Jak sie
masz?*" she said, hugging her. She smelled of wildflowers, clothes
hung in the sun, ironed carefully with starch, Elise thought, hugging
her. Maria of the thousand stories. Maria who had gotten her *Bubbee* the job in the sorting room that saved her life. Who had given
her bread when she was starving, a scarf when she was bald, a warm
drink when she was freezing.

"She doesn't understand Polish, Maria," Esther reminded her,
turning to Elise. "It means: 'How are you?'"

"*Przepraszam!* Excuse me! My English, not good very. *Modlmy
sie!* We pray!" She kissed both Elise's hands, taking them into her
own. Elise studied the swollen fingers: these were the hands my *Bubbee* held, she thought, comforting her in her darkest hours, and now
they hold mine. Dear hands! she thought. The kindest, most beautiful hands in the world.

Esther sat on the edge of the bed, smoothing back Elise's hair
into her head scarf, studying her face. "This is the face your grandmother had when I first met her. Of course," she glanced at Leah,
"she had less hair."

A titter went through the women.

"This is true! We were bald!"

"But we had our heads, and so the hair grew back. This you
told me, Maria, remember?"

"*Tak, tak,* my Leah. And now you cover your hair with a
wig!"

Leah made a dismissive motion with her hand. "These days, the wig is nicer, believe me, Maria."

I have only been suffering days; they suffered years. I have not yet lost anyone I love, and they lost almost everyone. Yet, they had not only survived; they had triumphed. Nothing could have brought her more comfort. "I...can't...even...say how much this means to me," Elise choked, motioning for each of them to come closer. One by one, she kissed them. "Thank you for saving her, for saving my *Bubbee*."

"Elise, you have a lot more than that to thank them for..." Leah told her granddaughter.

Elise turned to her grandmother, surprised.

"Tell her. All of you," Leah urged them.

"The head of Hamas in Europe sent a message from Paris to the kidnappers to treat Jon and Ilana well. I saw him send it. He did it from my club," Ariana said.

Elise was flabbergasted. "Really?"

"A friend of mine—an arms dealer—invited him to dinner and a show at our club. But once he got there, he found a different kind of show.... That he himself is the star." She chuckled. "The Israelis, they were waiting for him. They give him—how do you say?—the 'treatment.' In the end, he did exactly what we told him."

"But how did you know who he was, where to find him?"

Esther stepped closer. "I hired a private kidnap service to free Jonathan and Ilana. They were able to pick up the Hamas person who delivered the videotapes, to threaten him until he talked and admitted who was giving him orders. My granddaughter, Elizabeth, and her husband were also very helpful. They gave us this man's address and phone number in Paris. Otherwise, it would have taken weeks to track him down."

"Esther didn't even mention it, but she spent a fortune on that kidnap service...." Leah pointed out.

Esther waved her hand dismissively. "They didn't do much, believe me. Got themselves arrested and deported by the Israelis. All they wanted to do was help! But you know Israelis...they never think they need any help. But at least they got that BCN driver arrested and interrogated. Turns out he wasn't only picking up those tapes, he was a member of Hamas.... Who knows how long it would have taken the Israeli politicians to decide to let their army go into Arafat land to pick him up otherwise? And it was your grandson, Maria, who found this out. Milos put himself into real danger. Hamas were recording his calls, tracking him...."

Maria shuddered. "But he's safe now, right?"

"Yes."

"How did Milos find out?" Elise asked.

"He made friends with that BCN reporter...that Julia...."

"Julia Greenberg.... The one I gave the interview to? It was her driver who worked for Hamas?" Elise said in shock.

Leah nodded. "But I don't think she knew that. You know she was badly injured in today's bombing on King George Street?"

Elise leaned back, stunned. "I heard there was a bombing...I can't believe it. How terrible!"

Slowly, she leaned back, looking at the four elderly women who milled around her room, letting it all sink in. They'd found the person who knew where Jon and Ilana were being held and had gotten him into Israeli custody. They'd gotten to the head Hamas operative in Europe, forcing him to move the deadline..."You were able to do all this...?" She hadn't taken anything her grandmother said seriously. She felt numb. "I never believed.... How can I thank you all? Where do I begin?"

Maria kissed Elise on her forehead. "You are our child. Ilana and Jon, the baby. They are our family."

"Yes, as if we gave birth to you, *compris*?"

"When your family is home safely, you may thank us. Until then, we haven't done anything," Esther said somberly.

"How is the little one?" Ariana asked, wanting to change the subject.

"Getting a little stronger every day, thank God. He hasn't had any more problems. And he's drinking plenty of my milk. He's going to be fine, God willing. I just know it."

"Of course he is!

Nie przejmuj sie!"

"When can we see him, *le petit?*"

"I think you could probably go now. I'll just call the nurses and tell them you're coming."

"Yes, we will go to see the baby. And then we all want to go to the Kotel. To pray."

"I guess I'll only see you all after the Sabbath, then…"

"After? Don't be silly! Where would we spend the Sabbath if not with you and the baby…?"

"But…."

The women looked at her, smiling.

"It's all taken care of."

"They'll set up a table for us to eat in the lounge outside. We'll feast on a Sabbath meal of hospital food. All five of us. Dr. Gabbay, God bless him, also got us a room with four beds here in the hospital, so we can spend the night nearby," Leah explained. "Did you even dream we would leave you here alone, tonight, of all nights?"

"*Bubbee*…" The words wouldn't come.

"My pride and joy, my Elise"—she stroked the fine young back— "my darling child." It was all for you, everything I did. For you and for your mother, and uncle and cousins…You made it all worth it.

"Is that him?"

"*Le petit!*"

"A *broocha* on his *kepeleh*, little *shefeleh*, little lamb…"

"*Jeste retak piekna!* So beautiful!"

Ariana stumbled. Maria and Esther caught her. "Come…"

"I'll get her a glass of cold water! Fan her, she's hot…" Leah said frantically.

"It's all right. It's nothing. *Rien!*" Ariana protested.

Esther held her hand. "Seeing babies…is that it?"

Ariana squeezed her back. "*Très difficile*…"

"You heard what Elise said. He is yours too. Without you, he wouldn't be here."

"Look at all the tubes, the bandages…Will he really be all right? I don't think I could stand it if anything happened…not to this baby…." Ariana shook her head.

Leah put her arm around Ariana's waist. "Come, get up. Look at him again."

"I don't know…"

"Come on…"

They stood there, staring at the tiny face. He was putting on weight, Leah thought, amazed. "Look, already he has two cheeks and little pads on his tiny shoulders, and that *tuchas*…what a little *tuchas*! Someone should take a picture of that *tuchas*, to embarrass him when he becomes Chief Rabbi of Israel…!"

"This we leave up to you. This is your specialty!" Esther laughed.

"Would I take a *tuchas* picture? Never. This is *your* idea of a picture. Elizabeth and Morrie in the bathtub…A *shandah*."

"Look at the eyes, how they look around already!"

His eyes did seem to be focussing, looking at the bright colors of the tiny bear mobile that swam above him.

"Come, Ariana, put your hand in. Touch him."

"I couldn't!"

"Come on."

She took off her big rings and handed them to Esther, then slipped her hand inside the bassinet, her long, wrinkled finger tenderly stroking the child's tiny, smooth hand. Immediately, his fingers opened, grasping hers.

"*Mon Dieu!*" she gasped, falling instantly in love. "He is very strong, this little one. Very brave."

"Like his father," Leah whispered.

Esther held Leah's hand. "Like his dear father. May God watch over them both."

"Amen." Maria crossed herself.

Leah opened her purse and unwrapped a package.

"What is that?"

"It's a doll. I bought it in Meah Shearim. See the sidecurls? And the yarmulke? And wait, listen to this." She pressed his red nose. A small boy's sweet young voice began reciting the morning prayer in Hebrew: "*Modeh Ani…*" (I am grateful before You, living and everlasting King, for returning my soul to me in Your infinite mercy and faithfulness.)

The women laughed.

"But why is it wearing a dress if it's wearing a yarmulke? Isn't it supposed to be a boy?"

"Well…" Leah said doubtfully, noticing this for the first time. She examined the label. It said MADE IN CHINA.

"I guess that would explain it." She placed the doll in the corner of the crib.

"It shouldn't give him nightmares, such a giant!"

"Or gender confusion," Esther pointed out.

"*Vus?*" Leah asked her.

"Never mind…"

"Sleep well, little beauty," Maria whispered. "And may you wake to find yourself in your father's arms."

Chapter thirty-five

They sat in the taxi silently as it drove toward the Wailing Wall.

Suddenly, Leah turned around from her seat beside the driver, looking at them. "Do you ever think about it?"

There was a gentle rustle in the backseat as the women changed positions.

"I have never, ever stopped," Ariana whispered. Maria and Esther reached out to her, each enfolding a hand in theirs. "Remember how we all dreamed about the day of liberation? We expected so much joy!"

"Instead, it was like a ton of bricks, *tak*—" Maria agreed.

"It was that way for everyone. All the pain of all the years, all the losses, all coming back to us at once...." Esther shrugged.

"Because we finally allowed ourselves to feel...*Compris?*"

"I thought: Why me?" Leah said softly. "Why was I spared? Was it *mazal?* Or a reward? But then, if God rewarded me, why did He punish the others, such good people, my mother and father?...I thought: I'm alive because someone else died. Because I took the easier work; because I didn't give them my bread...."

"That's what we all thought." Esther nodded.

"The guilt." Ariana nodded.

"The anger." Maria squeezed her hand. "It was the first time we let ourselves mourn...."

They were silent.

"And then we fell over that crate...." Esther said, looking around at the others. Maria began to giggle.

Ariana clapped her hands. "*Oui! La* crate that fell off the German truck!"

Maria howled, covering her mouth with her hand. "And how we pried it open and took out the bottles!"

"What a sight we were, the four of us, standing on that road, skeletons in filthy striped uniforms..." Esther laughed, the tears flowing down her cheeks.

"Four hairless skeletons, drinking the most expensive French champagne, toasting each other." Leah sobbed, tears of laughter sweeping down her cheeks as Maria leaned forward to hug her. Ariana and Esther embraced each other, shaking, their stomachs weak with laughter, as they seached for tissues in their pockets, wiping their eyes on their sleeves.

The cab driver looked at them through the rearview mirror, wide-eyed and open-mouthed at the sight of four old ladies in hysterics in his taxi.

"When we get back to the hotel, I'm going to order a bottle of the best champagne in the house," Esther promised. "And don't any of you dare complain about your diabetes or your cholesterol, or your diet..." she warned, blowing her nose. "To life!" she toasted them, raising an imaginary glass. The others joined in, laughing.

"*L'chaim.*"

"*Santé!*"

"*Jestem pijany!*"

Leah's hand suddenly trembled.

Esther leaned forward, putting both hands on her friend's shoulders. "We will take one drink and save the rest of the bottle for when Jon and Ilana come home," she promised.

Leah patted her hands, nodding, her eyes wet. "God willing. Let's pray."

The ride only took a few minutes, but as they entered the gateway in the stone wall that separated modern Jerusalem from the ancient city of David and Solomon, they felt they had crossed over in time and were seeing with a different set of eyes.

The driver opened the car door with gentlemanly aplomb. "*Kol Hakavod,* four *savtas* who have guts to come. Even Israelis in Tel Aviv are scared," he said, viewing the old women with genuine admiration.

"Is that true?" Ariana said, looking around nervously.

But the streets belied any sense of danger. They were bustling with life. A group of religious Jewish girls crossed paths with a bevy of their Arab counterparts. How similar they both looked with their long-sleeved, high-necked blouses and midcalf skirts, clutching books and schoolbags, the only visible difference being that the Arab girls covered their hair with scarves, Esther thought. And none of them wore makeup! They watched a bearded Hasidic man stop to buy fragrant, warm pita bread fresh from the oven of an old Arab baker, whose store was tucked inside the stone walls of an ancient building.

It was all totally unexpected, the reality of Jews and Arabs living side by side, a place where peaceful daily intercourse was not the exception—a subject for TV documentaries or news flashes—but the rule. It was simply a way of life. It was a neighborhood, and these were neighbors. With good will, the solution seemed so clear, so simple.

"Jerusalem was King David's capital, but he never built the Temple. That he left to his son Solomon. It lasted until Nebuchadnezzer of Babylon destroyed the country. That was twenty-five hundred years ago. Saddam Hussein thinks he can do it again!" Leah shook her head. "People don't understand this about the Jews: we lose and die, yes. But we are also very stubborn. We never give up. We keep coming back here, again and again."

"Why didn't they start over someplace else?" Ariana said irritably. "Is it worth all these problems...all this fuss?"

"That's where the French in you comes out!" Maria scolded.

"You let the Germans roll into Paris. You don't fire a shot. If the Americans hadn't rescued you, you'd all be speaking German."

"Never!" Ariana protested, shocked.

"Some things you can't give in to, no matter what. This is the only place in the world that's ours."

The women looked at each other with a flash of recognition.

Survive, and rebuild. Because there is no other choice. No place else to go.

"You see this?" Leah pointed to a sign that said: BURNT HOUSE. "The archaeologists found it after 'sixty-seven. A temple priest once lived there. It was full of ashes—the same ashes from the fires the Romans set when they burned down our temple two thousand years ago. Imagine! They also found the skeleton of a young woman. Maybe his daughter."

Ashes. Piles of ashes. The burning fires, the fetid smoke. Thousands of young, strong, handsome Jewish boys and girls deported in boxcars, starved, murdered, burnt. Because they had no weapons, no country to flee to, no one to protect them.

They watched groups of handsome young men and women in khaki IDF uniforms amble through the square, along with pregnant young Jewish women wheeling baby carriages. Groups of three- and four-year-olds in side curls and knee socks held hands as they walked in twos behind their teacher. Little girls speaking Hebrew rushed across the square, their ponytails bobbing in the sun.

A place that bubbled with life, a place that grew up over the ashes, the white bones growing young new flesh, like the fulfillment of some Biblical prophecy.

"Come, the Wall is just down here." Leah guided them.

As they began the long descent down the steps that would lead them to Judaism's most sacred site, they walked slowly, clutching the handrails. There were hundreds of steps. It was tiring, but fitting, they thought, to reach the Wall only after much effort. A security check, including an airport x-ray machine, screened their bags, and metal-detector wands passed over their bodies before they were allowed to pass through. Then, there it was.

The Wall.

At this level, they realized, the golden Dome of the Rock had all but disappeared from view. They were confronted by the huge ancient stones.

A blank wall. It meant whatever you brought to it. Whatever was in your own soul, Leah thought, wondering what it would mean to these, her dearest friends. Would it be possible for them to connect with this experience at all?

Maria heard the church bells ringing, and then the sound of the muezzin calling the Muslims to prayer. From over the partition separating the men from the women's section before the Wall came the chanting sounds of a Jewish prayer service.

Mosques and synagogues and churches.... And all of them started with Abraham. The Jews were the big brother of all the other religions. Jesus was his descendant, Isaac and Ishmael his sons. Judaism and Islam and Christianity all had the same father. The same Father.

As they approached the Wall, a band of lady beggars descended upon them from all corners, their eyes glittering with avarice. "Leave us alone. Let us pray in peace," Leah complained.

"Isn't that a bit harsh?" Esther whispered, shocked.

"They turn this place into a business. It's not a business," she repeated stubbornly. "Let them *schnorr* someplace else."

A religious female guard checked them over to see if they were modestly dressed. She offered Esther a scarf to cover her hair.

"No thanks, darling. I come equipped," Esther said, taking out a large, silk Gucci scarf and tying it around her head.

They took a prayer book out of the pile and made their way one by one to the row of women positioned in touching distance before the gleaming white stones, each searching for and finding a small break in which to squeeze through.

"Out of the depths I cry to you!" Once more, the same cry to heaven, Leah thought. Once more, He is my dear God, whom I cannot see. Can He see me? Here, in this frightful world, still so full of evil, hatred, danger, she thought. And we and our loved ones had no choice but to walk through it every hour we lived. And it made no

difference if you were very rich or very poor; if you moved to the Jews' ancient homeland in the Middle East or stayed put in Brooklyn.

Miriam, my sweet Miriam!

She wept.

Where was the strength to come from that let us risk rebuilding and loving? She wiped her eyes, looking up. The blue-and-white flag of Israel, with its ancient symbol of the six-cornered Star of David, waved above her. A teenager wore a T-shirt that said: DON'T WORRY, BE JEWISH, above a Hasidic-style smiling face with side curls. A beautiful blue-eyed baby sat in a carriage.

"Have mercy on my family, dear God, as You have kept me alive in Your compassion. And whatever happens, give us who live the strength to go on...." She caressed the stones tenderly, like a beloved face.

Ariana walked up close, eyeing the tiny prayers crammed into every nook and cranny, left behind by the hands of yearning strangers. I don't know how to pray, she thought, laying her forehead against the smooth, cool surface. I never even decided if there was a God.... But if You are up there, I'd like to say this to You: You never gave me a childhood. You never gave me a child. And now I am old. Too old. I am asking You to be fair. Give me the lives of these children: Ilana and her tiny brother who fights so hard to live. Let them live. Save them from all pain, all harm, if You are as compassionate as they say. She paused, then exhaled. If someone has to suffer and die, then let it be me. My life is over anyway.

She kissed the stone, now moist with tears, glad that no one could hear her sacrilegious prayer. If there was a God, this was as close as she would ever come to touching Him. Only much later would she remember, with horror, that she had forgotten to include Jonathan in her prayer.

Maria held her cross in the palm of one hand and laid the other flat against the surface. Here I am again, she thought, surrounded by Jewish women, weeping, praying...in their own land, the land God promised them, once again being slaughtered by sickening evil. Oh, people called it politics—as Hitler spoke of German pride and German suffering to excuse his crimes. Jewish politicians fought amongst themselves, blaming each other for the causeless hatred that had come their way. They couldn't see the grinning dark skull, the devil's own face, behind it all.

Sparrows rested in the strange, dry shrubs that grew impossibly between the stones. And up above, pigeons marched along the parapets like sentinels, flying easily between mosque and synagogue. The men were loud, but the women's lips moved silently, their bodies swaying. The mosque gleamed with its painted-on gold; the ancient white stones glistened with the rays of the golden sun. Maria's lips moved in silent prayer, beseeching salvation.

Esther reached out and touched the weathered surface. Its rough-hewn appearance did not prepare her for its almost silky texture, polished to porcelain smoothness by a million entreating hands. She touched the expensive silk that covered her hair. All she had earned, and stored. Her fortune. But a shroud had no pockets. She would go as she had come, naked, to a God she hardly knew. God, she said voicelessly. Forgive us for all our sins. For raising children who don't know You; grandchildren that got lost because we didn't show them the way, because we didn't know the way ourselves. Have mercy. Bring us back our granddaughters, Ilana, Elizabeth, she wept. Save Jonathan! And help me use all I have been blessed with for the right things before I die.

They backed away slowly, taking small steps as they had seen other women do, out of respect. One did not turn one's back on the Wall. As they withdrew, they had a sense of leaving behind a presence—call it God, or something else—a spirit of holiness, that hovered around them, almost palpable.

"Buy a string against the evil eye?" one of the beggar women pleaded aggressively, accosting them.

Esther stared at the long red strands that dangled from her hand. "Here, give me all of them," she said impulsively, handing the woman a wad of bills.

The beggar handed them over gleefully, taking the money and hurrying away before Esther could come to her senses.

"What's gotten into you? This is all silly stuff...idolatry." Leah pursed her lips in disapproval, scandalized. It was almost pagan, this *kabbalah* nonsense, and they were at the holy Wall.

"Here, take these! Tie them into knots. Remember, Leah, like that night?…"

"She's right. Say the words, Leah!" Ariana demanded.

"Do it, darling." Maria embraced her. "Come. Sit down here. I'll be right back."

There was a low stone wall that faced the Wall. Maria returned with a handful of earth taken from the base of a tree. She dampened it with bottled water.

"What do you think you're doing?" Leah asked them.

"The *Pulse de Noura,* of course. This time, against the terrorists."

"But it was never real! I made the whole thing up."

"What!?"

"But you said…the rabbi, the mystic…the *kabbalah!*" Ariana protested.

"Do you think they ever made one in my village? And if they had, do you think they would have let me, a young girl, watch a *Kabalistic* ceremony?! I made it all up, I tell you. Every word. I did it to make you feel better. To give you hope!"

Ariana gasped, then chuckled. "It worked. Something came over me. *Un sentiment* that I had nothing to lose. The idea that once they opened the doors and began to herd us inside *les trains,* it would be *la mort, l'électricité* for all of us. And besides, I always imagined myself a great *actrice.*"

"You were magnificent!"

"Amazing!"

Ariana blushed. "It was not so bad."

"I still remember how I felt when I saw you suddenly barking orders like a *kapo,* telling people to move this way and that way, pushing people out of the way, waving those pages you tore out of my old prayer book over your head, saying that you had orders to take us out because we had a communicable disease and weren't fit to serve the Reich…" Leah laughed.

"And the way everyone suddenly fell into step, moving out of the way, clearing the doors, letting us go." Maria held her face in her hands. "To this day, I still see that train loading up, all those women getting on. And then the doors pulling closed and the next train whistling in the distance, pulling in…"

"By then, the SS had arrived with another group of girls… Remember how the officer in charge couldn't explain why we hadn't gone with the first group?"

"When I saw the next train pull up, and how they started to force us on, I remember looking ahead at the fence. I was fifteen steps away from it…. I could almost feel the *choque*, the burning heat rip through my body."

"I had already said my '*Shma*.'"

"I also gave myself Last Rites…"

"I was shaking all over, thinking I would soon see my mother again…."

"Did you understand what was happening right away, Ariana?"

"No, not exactly. I saw the planes, but I didn't understand they were Allied and they were deliberately bombing the tracks, the train. Only when I saw all the SS run away and leave us, I understood: it was *les Americains*."

"It was a miracle." Leah nodded. "A miracle. But just as the miracles of Egypt didn't happen without God's messenger, we needed you, Ariana. You were our Moses. If you hadn't convinced them to let us out of that barracks, our miracle would have come too late; we would have already been on a train on our way to the front…." She shivered, suddenly cold in the Middle Eastern sun. "Or blackened corpses, clinging to the fence…"

"But it was Maria who actually pushed us through. I didn't have *la force*," Ariana insisted.

"And it was Leah who was the first one to march out through the soldiers. If she hadn't, I don't know if I would have had the courage," Maria admitted.

"Or I." Ariana nodded.

"We did it together. Destroyed the German army. The Third Reich. And we survived. We outlived them all."

They suddenly moved toward each other, pressing their old

bodies together, barely noticing the shocking changes that the years had brought: the soft, heavy flesh where once there had been hard, young bones; the ridged skin that once lay flat and smooth.

Their bodies meshed again into one flesh, the lifeblood sharing its warmth, coursing through them strong and undefeated, giving them life.

"And we can do it again. Destroy these terrorists…these monsters…." Esther whispered.

"But I feel so foolish," Leah protested weakly. "Besides, I don't remember a word of it. These days, I'm happy I remember what street I live on…."

"But I do remember." Maria comforted her, pulling away. "You said: 'Destroy the destroyer. Make impediments to all he does, revoke his rule and destroy his tools.' You think I didn't use this on the Communists in Poland…?" She chuckled. "It worked there too!"

"And there was a circle. Remember?" Ariana said, getting up and pulling the others with her. "Now you must step inside the circle."

Leah felt suddenly light, filled with a strange sense of momentum, of things moving quickly out of control. They knotted the red strings. Made the clay figure. She stepped into the circle, the words suddenly coming back to her: "In the name of the Holy One, His secret name I invoke. Destroy the evil that seeks our deaths. Bring a vast destruction to all that is theirs." And as she said it, she smashed the earth figure beneath her feet. They pressed it beneath their heels, grinding it into dust.

God forgive me, Leah thought, wondering what furies she had unleashed.

Chapter thirty-six

Kala el-Bireh, Samaria
Friday, May 10, 2002 · 5:50 P.M.

It was just after sunset when the three cars pulled into the clearing behind the house in Kala el-Bireh. The twelve tires made a soft crunching sound on the unpaved road as their engines turned off. Two of the cars kept their headlights on and their doors closed. The third flung open its doors and four men jumped out. With one exception, each wore a ski mask and fatigues that were the official uniform of Hamas terrorists; they carried hand grenades, an automatic weapon and a sophisticated array of listening devices. "*Muchanim?*" the tallest one asked in Hebrew. His two colleagues, highly trained members of the counterterrorist unit of the Israeli army, and a Shin Bet informer called Ismael Abadi, nodded their assent. The police checked their assault rifles. Ismael went first. He knocked on the door.

"It's Ismael."

The door opened, and all four men walked through.

"*Kayf Halak?*" Ismael asked politely.

"*Al-hamdulilah,*" the men answered with a sullenness Ismael had not expected.

"Marwan says for you to come down, alone."

"*Ana mish araf....*" Ismael said doubtfully. "I'm in a hurry...."

"*Waj ab zibik!*" A shout came from the chambers below. "You will come down here now!" Bahama screamed up at him.

Ismael exchanged glances with his masked companions, then nodded.

"*Ma feesh mushkilla.*" Ismael walked slowly down the stairs. "Relax."

The heavy metal door was already flung open for him, he noted, but no one seemed to be down there waiting. As he reached the bottom of the stairs, Bahama came out of nowhere, with all the venom and swiftness of a cobra. "You have come to collect my prisoners?" he screamed.

"I got these orders, just as you did, my brother. They are from headquarters, from Musa." He held up the computer printout. "Check it against your own."

Bahama grabbed the paper. "These are not from Musa."

Ismael wiped his brow. "What makes you say that? I checked it. It did not have the alarm code." (The word "Jihad," followed by an exclamation point, indicated that the e-mail contents were being sent under duress. Ismael had warned Shin Bet agents in France to watch out Musa didn't slip it in. Could there have been a screw-up?) "Did yours have the code?" Ismael felt the sweat on the back of his neck drip into his collar.

Bahama slammed the paper down. "No. No code! But whoever gave these orders is a traitor! Hamas never gives in!"

"No one gives in, Marwan Bahama. The operation goes on. Just not with you. You are too involved. The Zionist pilot Ron Arad has been a prisoner over twenty years, and each year it is another knife in the heart of the Zionists. The doctor and the child are a sword over their heads. You will be rewarded, Marwan. Everybody says you are the next in line for promotion..."

"Yes?" Bahama said, slightly mollified.

"But you want them dead too fast. Hamas has plans."

"What plans?"

Ismael shrugged. "I only know my orders. Get them ready."

Bahama did not look him in the eye. Instead, he sat down and put his feet up on a desk, scattering the papers to the floor. He took out a hunting knife and began to clean his fingernails. He seemed unsure of his next step. He looked up at Ismael. "And what if I tell you one or both of them might not be here anymore?"

Ismael put his hands into his pockets, jingling his change. "Is that what you are telling me, brother?"

"Maybe."

Ismael's heart sank. Something unexpected had gone wrong. But what?

"And that you did it without orders? And that you now defy the direct orders of Musa el Khalil to hand them over to me? Is that what you are saying?"

"I want to speak to Musa. To explain."

"I don't know how to contact Musa. Do you?"

Bahama scowled. "You sweat like a pig, my brother," Bahama told him, circling him slowly, running the knife blade lightly around the circumference of Ismael's chest.

"*Hamsin.*" Ismael shrugged. "You need an air conditioner."

"Yes, and a villa in Jaffa with fruit trees.... What did you tell them that they take the operation out of my hands and put it into yours?"

"What do I know?" he suddenly shouted, pushing the blade aside roughly. "What are you hiding? What have you done with the Jews?!" he screamed.

Bahama took a startled step backward and blinked. He was thrown off balance, his arrogance fading. He was hiding something, something that was not in his control, Ismael realized.

"I just need to speak to Musa, that's all. To explain...."

"And waste time!" Ismael screamed. He took the safety lock off his weapon. Marwan's second in command immediately raised his weapon, aiming right between Ismael's eyes. Ismael lowered his gun. "Do you know what happens to brothers who question Musa el Khalil?"

"It is my operation! Mine!" Bahama screamed back. "Before I let the Zionists out, I have to see who is in charge."

"Then the two are still here?"

"I didn't say yes, and I didn't say no," he said, with strange playfulness, in singsong mockery. "And what is not here now can be brought back here soon. But right now, I am still giving the orders. I want to see who is waiting in the car outside."

Ismael shrugged. He took his *sibha*, prayer beads, from his pocket and began to fondle them rhythmically. "You have nothing to worry about. The Zionists will not escape. There are three cars. Twelve of us."

"I will check." Bahama put his knife into his pocket and swung an AK-47 assault rifle over his shoulder, a weapon designed by the Soviets to kill from up to a range of one thousand meters. In his pocket, he shoved a high-capacity magazine holding one hundred rounds of bullets, each one capable of piercing a bulletproof vest of titanium.

Ismael began to follow him up the steps.

Bahama turned: "No! You wait here." He turned to his second in command. "If something happens…." The other man nodded.

Ismael watched Bahama's feet resume their climb. He looked toward the red iron door locked and bolted at the end of the corridor, wired with enough explosives to turn him and everyone else in the building into ash. Clutching his *sibha*, he slowly began to count: How many until Bahama reached the cars parked outside? How many until they rolled down the windows and spoke to him? As he counted, the years of his life rolled before him: His childhood. His father's death. His mother's remarriage. How he had joined the Hamas. The smell of the explosives, the dead bodies, the torn limbs. The decision to be a soldier, not a baby-killer. The secret meetings with the Shin Bet….

What would happen, he thought, when the men in the cars saw Bahama approach them? He counted off the beads: one for his wife, one for each child, one for his own life…

Marwan Bahama had no fear as he approached the headlights of the waiting cars. He was filled with anger, hurt pride, and guilt. Soon these people would know his secret shame. There was no way to stop it. That's why it was so important for him to find out who they were, to see their faces, or, at the very least, to have the name of their cell. If they decided to use the information against him, he'd have no choice but to take care of each and every one of them. He walked quickly, his gun over his shoulder.

About ten steps away, he paused. He took his weapon into his hand and loaded the magazine, all the while aware that the men in the cars had him in their headlights. He pointed the gun skyward as he slowly approached the first car. He tapped on the side window. When nothing happened, he started to curse, spitting at the glass and lowering his weapon.

Slowly, the window began to move downward. He pointed the gun upward again, sticking his head belligerently inside the window.

"*Es salaam aleikum.*"

"*Wa aleikum es salaam,*" the driver responded.

Bahama relaxed. "Where do you take the Jews?"

"We cannot say, our brother."

"Who is the leader of your cell?"

"I am." A voice came from the back of the car. Bahama peered into the darkness.

"Give me the code name for your cell, my brother."

There was silence.

"The code name!" Bahama screamed, lifting his weapon, cocking the firing pin and putting his finger inside the trigger guard as he closed the breech.

"*Jihad fi sabili-Llah.*"

He took his finger off the trigger. "And where are you located?"

"This, as you know my brother, we cannot say."

He knew this was true. "Where do you take the Zionists?" he repeated insistently.

"To a safe house in the Jordan Valley, then by boat from Aquaba to Cyprus. A plane waits to take them to our brothers in Iran."

"Why so far? You will never get through the roadblocks.... And the Jordanians are unreliable!" He spit contemptuously. Then reconsidered. What did it matter if the operation was taken out of his hands and then met with catastrophic failure?

"Will you bring them now? We must hurry, brother."

"Take off your masks. Let me see your faces," he demanded.

There was a deadly calm.

"This we cannot do, my brother," a voice he had not heard before said calmly in perfect Palestinian Arabic.

Bahama seemed to hesitate. He took out a flashlight and slowly shined it into the eyes of the masked men, lighting up their faces one by one, pausing more than once. No one moved. Finally, apparently satisfied, he shut it off. "Wait," he said, turning his back and walking briskly toward the second car. Halfway there, they saw him suddenly crouch, lowering his gun and pointing it in their direction in what seemed to be firing position.

Had he seen something that tipped him off? Was he going to create an incident in order to cover his tracks and hide his secrets? Or was there simply a pebble in his sandal, which he was bending down to remove?

The decision was split-second: the Israelis opened fire. Bullets ripped through the head and groin and stomach of Marwan Bahama, turning him from an instrument of torture into the kind of corpse he had delighted in leaving behind.

Hearing the gunfire, the soldiers inside the house opened fire, killing the guards upstairs. They ran down the stairs.

"Don't shoot—the door!" Ismael screamed, standing in front of the red door, his hands outspread.

"Allah is great," Bahama's second in command answered him, getting off a single shot before the Israelis took him out.

Ismael never even felt the wound that pierced his shoulder, ricocheting off the door. The explosion threw up a fireball that made the Israelis outside drop to the ground. Sitting in the second car, Colonel Amos covered his head as the earth shook beneath them. Black ashes fell like falling snow.

Around the Sabbath table, Elise and Leah sang:

Peace be upon you, angels of peace,
Angels of the most high
Who come from the King, King of all Kings,

The Holy One, blessed be He.

Come in peace, angels of peace,
Angels of the most high
Who come from the King, King of all Kings,
The Holy One, blessed be He.

Bless me in peace, angels of peace,
Angels of the most high
Who come from the King, King of all Kings,
The Holy One, blessed be He.

Go in peace, angels of peace,
Angels of the most high
Who come from the King, King of all Kings,
The Holy One, blessed be He.

Esther and Ariana and Maria looked on.

Chapter thirty-seven

The sound of birds woke Dr. Jonathan Margulies. For a brief moment, he forgot where he was, a smile stretching his dry, swollen lips. "Elise?" he whispered, stretching out his hand. The cold, stone floor sent a chill through his fingertips that made his body shudder. *The nightmare...he thought. The nightmare.* "Ilana!" he called out in panic, but then he remembered: he'd been transferred to a new hiding place. And Ilana?

Where was she?

A better place, he prayed, his eyes filling with tears.

When Bahama realized she was missing, he'd gone wild. But as the beating went on, and the tortures began, Jon realized that Bahama was being very careful not to cross the line that would result in his sure death. Bahama didn't want him dead. At least, Jon thought, not yet.

And when it was over, he remembered how he'd been almost grateful for the blindfold tied over his bleeding eyes that had acted like a bandage, and for the cool, pine-scented air that had washed over his aching body like a compress as they smuggled him outside and stuffed his half-conscious body into the confines of a small space, probably the trunk of a car.

He must have, thankfully, lost consciousness, he realized, otherwise the rough ride that jostled his sore, broken body would have been unbearable. He lifted his head, examining his surroundings in the light for the first time.

It was a bedroom with a normal bed, a window—barred, but not covered in any way. He heard the shouts of young children playing, the voices of women talking to each other over the clatter of pans and the clicking of spoons and knives. His blindfold had been removed, and his mouth untaped. He touched his damp face. It had been washed, and beside him sat a plate of pita bread and a glass of water. His hands had been tied in front of him to allow him to eat and drink.

Yes, orders had been given to keep him alive, he thought. At least for now.

The blood from the wounds on his face and hands had congealed. The place where his fingernails had been torn out, festered with pus. The pain from his broken thumbs was constant, and the wounds in his stomach and back continued to throb. With professional detachment, he tried to analyze if his injuries were life-threatening. He thought about it in the way he would have considered the prospects of any patient under his care, trying not to let his personal feelings cloud his judgment.

It wasn't easy. As a matter of fact, he finally admitted to himself, it was downright impossible. One's own life was always a very special story, and he couldn't help but consider himself a very special patient, one he cared very much about. It pained him that he had nothing with which to treat himself. And so he tried, as best he could, to do the things that under the circumstances were possible to do.

He tried not to move unnecessarily. If something was broken, movement could be fatal. He drained the cup and called out for more water. It was important to keep hydrated.

A boy of no more than ten or eleven came in.

"Water, please," he begged, holding out the pitcher.

The child looked at him curiously, taking the empty pitcher from his hands and returning with a full one.

"*Shukran,*" he said hoarsely, trying a faint smile.

The boy smiled back, surprised and pleased, the way a child would view a rare animal in a zoo doing tricks. His face lit up with curiosity and interest.

"Mohammad!" a woman's voice called urgently. Still, the child lingered, testing Jon's knowledge of Arabic, delighted when Jon answered him.

A young man burst into the room. "What are you doing in here?" He cuffed the boy. He was about sixteen, Jon estimated, with an AK-47 flung over his shoulder. It was shocking to see the child's features hardened and set into an implacable expression of unrelenting hatred in the older boy's face. It was only then Jon understood where he was.

These were Bahama's brothers.

The terrorist had taken him home.

He looked at the young man's closed face and the words of another doctor came to him: "All the evils that men cause to each other because of certain desires, or opinions or religious principles, are rooted in ignorance," wrote Moses Maimonides. All hatred would come to an end "when the earth was flooded with the knowledge of God." He was glad then that Ilana was somewhere else. He tried to comfort himself that although he had no idea what had happened to his daughter, she was at least no longer in Bahama's hands. What these beastly men were capable of doing to a small child, a Jewish child, a little girl.... He shuddered, praying to God to send His angels to watch over her. He was totally dependent on the goodness of his fellow man, or—to be more exact—woman.

He listened to the birds, remembering those lovely mornings a thousand years ago when it seemed as if he was covered with an abundance of blessings. For the first time he thought: I might never wake up again.

I don't want to die! I don't! Something inside of him panicked. It's too soon.... I'm so young, the father of a young child—children!

The husband of a young wife! I have my patients…. Who will care for my patients…? His heart raged.

But slowly the anger left him, the panic. He breathed deeply, feeling a strange, inexplicable calm. He thought about his life, as he would a story in a book, something that had happened to someone else.

It had been such a wonderful life. So few people in the world were free to make their own choices the way he had, to follow their hearts. And he'd been one of them. He'd lived out his dreams, and instead of the hardships he'd expected—been reconciled to—in moving to a new country far from his birthplace, he'd had a life filled with so many blessings. In many ways, it had been such an easy life. His heart, body and soul had been at peace, nourished, satisfied. If he was afraid of anything, it was meeting God and being found unworthy of all the good that had been his portion, the abundance that he had enjoyed. I have no complaints, he realized with surprise. None.

He thought about Elise—that first walk they'd taken along the Promenade, the wind at their backs, the beauty of the city of Jerusalem spread out at their feet. He thought of how her hair had blown in the wind, curls dipping over her eyes, and how she had smoothed it back, tucking it behind her small, tender ears; and then how she'd reached out and smoothed his hair out of his eyes, her small hand warm on his forehead, despite the cold. How kind her eyes had been as she looked into his; how they'd sparkled and danced with humor.

"You are going to make a good girlfriend," he'd whispered boldly, shocking himself, as he reached out to hold her hand, the touch of her fingertips still making his forehead tingle. She'd made no move to pull away, a slow, reciprocal smile spreading across her face.

That was the moment, he thought, that I stopped being alone in the world. The moment his "I" had become a "we." Even now, he thought. Even now.

He remembered the words of Viktor Frankel, a psychiatrist who had been sent to Auschwitz, survived and written a remarkable little book. In one of the most memorable passages, Dr. Frankel recounted being asked by the senior block warden to encourage his despairing fellow inmates. The hopelessness of their situation, he told the dying men, did not detract from its dignity and its meaning. Someone is looking down on you, he'd told them. Someone living or dead, a wife, a child, a friend, or God. "We do not wish to disappoint them. They must find us suffering proudly, and knowing how to die."

He rolled this thought over in his head.

No one knew the day of his death. Men had lived through much worse than this, he thought, looking around. They'd suffered the death of those close to them—parents, wives, children, relatives; they'd been starved and tortured mentally and physically for years—not days—and yet they had still managed to survive, marry, raise a whole new family, enjoy a whole lifetime and die peacefully in their beds. And young men had left soft beds and Cheerios in bowls on the counters of suburban kitchens on Long Island to work in Manhattan only to find themselves leaping to their deaths from the hundredth story of burning skyscrapers.

Who was to say he wouldn't live through this? That he wouldn't return to his family whole? That he wouldn't get his life back and continue to do deeds and think thoughts, and live the precious life, the one life, that God had granted him on this earth? He also knew there were no guarantees that he, or Ilana, would live through it either. It was all in the hands of God. And in the freely-made choices of his fellow men.

Don't give up hope, he told himself. You have a glass of water. A pita bread. Which is more than they gave the Jews of Auschwitz. And you've managed to put your daughter into good, kind hands. He had to believe that. He drank and ate and tried to sleep, trying to keep as still as possible.

Closing his eyes, he tried to imagine what had turned a ten-year-old's childish openness into a sixteen-year-old's fossilized hardness. What had intervened to destroy a child's natural sympathy toward his fellow man, his instincts toward generosity and goodness? What terrible machine had succeeded in deadening the expression of those eyes, draining them of inquiry, replacing them with the unseeing, blinded eyes of the fanatic?

He remembered a talk he had once had with Nouara about the education of her children. The schoolbooks rewrote the maps, wiping Israel off the earth, she told him. The incitement was constant and unrelenting.

What could one do to help good parents like Nouara and Shawan to raise their families with love and tolerance and open-mindedness? What? he thought in despair.

A child did not become a hate-filled fanatic, a terrorist, without entire, elaborate structures of educational institutions, training camps, expensive weapons, and the backing of legitimate national support. It was a gargantuan beast, and it had spread its tentacles throughout the world. Like the ancient Caananite cult of Molech, which sacrificed children to a Satanic god in beastly rituals, this new beast demanded the lives of its children, forcing them to kill and convincing them it was a good thing to die.

He thought of the young boy, and then he thought of Ilana. Their lives were inextricably intertwined. What chance would either have to embrace life to its fullest? What chance?

He thought of his own tiny country, his own small and scattered people. A land so small no map could fit its name in its land mass. A people so small they represented one-tenth of one percent of the world's population, a few million. A tiny creature, the Jewish people in the land of Israel. And right now, it was facing the beast alone. Just like me, he thought.

Chapter thirty-eight

Excuse me, nurse, but I've been waiting since yesterday. Can you tell me if Julia Greenberg is out of the recovery room yet?"

"Are you family?"

"No." Milos shook his head, hesitating before he chose the word that would describe his relationship to Julia Greenberg. "I'm a colleague. A reporter."

"The BCN people were here a half hour ago. I told them I'd call them if there was any change."

"I'm not with BCN."

"No reporters are allowed in, I'm sorry."

"No, no…. You don't understand. She is my friend…. My girlfriend."

The nurse looked him over curiously. "She's very badly injured. I don't know if she's up to having visitors…."

"Please! I won't stay long. But I have to see her. Please. She's got no one." He touched her arm. "And can you please tell me what happened to her?"

The nurse hesitated. "She lost her right arm, from the elbow down. Her hearing is impaired. Her corneas are scratched. And she had some of the nails removed from her kidney and liver…"

"Some?" he said, reeling in shock from the recitation of injuries. "Why not all?"

She shook her head. "Some are too dangerous to touch. It was a six-hour operation. She's just regained consciousness. She's in terrible pain…but she's on a morphine drip…."

"Oh God!"

The nurse eyed him sympathetically. "You say you are her boyfriend?" Unlike the other victims, who had been surrounded by family and friends, Julia Greenberg had had no one, aside from a few middle-aged men from her office, who, frankly, seemed anxious to go. "You say you've been waiting for hours?"

He nodded. "Since I heard."

"Room three-twenty-four," she finally relented, "but you can only stay ten minutes."

He stood at the threshold, looking through to the bed beyond. Steeling himself, he walked inside. Bandages covered her right arm. Her skull was also bandaged, and several deep gashes trailed across her face. Her eyes were black and blue, her lips cracked and her yellow hair—of which she was so fond, he thought—singed black. It was horrible.

The most terrible thing about terrorism, the thing that people fond of saying "one man's freedom fighter is another man's terrorist" didn't get, was that even siding with the terrorists gave you no immunity. The terrorist never knew his victims, and didn't give a damn. When you sided with them, you were taking sides against yourself.

What am I doing here? he asked himself. He had no idea what he had hoped to accomplish. All he knew for certain was that he had no choice. He was a human being, and she was a human being. And she was a victim of the most antihuman act that existed. However briefly they had known each other, their lives were now connected, the way the lives of all good people who hate the shedding of innocent blood are connected to all whose blood is shed without reason. By this act of horror, the terrorist had made their connection permanent.

"Julia?" he whispered, standing over her. He could see her eyes move back and forth rapidly. "It's me, Milos."

He heard what sounded like a groan rise from her lips, and she tried to lift herself up.

"No. Don't." He touched her shoulder gently.

She whispered something he couldn't make out. He brought his ear to her lips.

"Where…"

He leaned closer. "Where…? Where…are you? Is that it? You're in Hadassah Hospital. You've just had an operation…."

She shook her head. He listened again.

"Where were you?" she whispered.

He knew exactly what she was talking about. It was time to tell the truth. "I was picking up my grandmother from the airport. She and Elise Margulies' grandmother Leah are friends. They met in Auschwitz."

He saw two large tears roll down her scarred cheeks.

"Oh Julia, my poor Julia." He took her left hand in his, caressing the fingers. "I'm sorry. I'm so sorry. I'm so sorry…"

She didn't try to move her hand away.

Chapter thirty-nine

El Khadav, Southern Hebron Hills
Saturday, May 11, 2002 · 11:00 A.M.

The children of El Khadav moved quickly out of the way as the familiar black Mercedes, known to all as the vehicle of Marwan Bahama, entered the village, followed by an entourage of other Hamas vehicles. The children would never have suspected that the men inside, who now drew their *kaffiyehs* more closely around their faces, were members of the most elite commando unit in the Israeli Defense Forces: the General Staff Reconnaisance Unit, better known as *Sayeret Matkal*, meaning "the chief of staff's boys."

Nearby, Israeli air force choppers equipped with sophisticated listening devices hovered in the sky, tracking all telephone conversations and keeping in direct contact with the men of the *Sayeret* at all times. In one of them sat Colonel Amos. He had had four hours' sleep after receiving information from a Shin Bet informer in El Khadav about the whereabouts of Dr. Jonathan Margulies.

Lieutenant Yigael Glickson, the commander, had already been supplied with a complete map of the interior of the Bahama home by Shin Bet informers who included Hamas members, PLO rivals, Bahama's neighbors and many others who had good reason to hate him.

The fifteen men jumped out quickly from their cars. Two took positions on the roof of the house, and another four secured all possible exits. It was Glickson himself that broke down the door and entered, his machine gun already cocked, his finger on the trigger.

He looked around and saw a room full of frightened children and old women. For a split second, he hesitated.

That was all Bahama's brother needed.

The volley of gunfire in the ensuing battle shook the house, echoing deep in the olive orchards that covered the nearby hills and valleys.

Jon threw himself on the floor, trying to cover his head. The door to his room burst open and the young boy ran in.

"Lie down behind me, Mohammad. They won't hurt you!" Jon beckoned the child. It was only when the boy raised his hand and pointed it at him that Jon noticed the gun. "Allah is great!" the boy screamed, pulling the trigger, as the soldiers' gunfire tore into his young flesh, piercing his heart.

Jon felt the bullet slam into his body, and the ooze of blood as the soldiers lifted him onto a stretcher. He turned his head to the side, looking down on the young body of the boy, which lay stretched out, faceup, his eyes staring into space, all curiosity and intelligence forever extinguished. Jon felt the darkness envelop him, spreading over his eyes even before he closed them. And then he saw it, coming toward him, a hurtling beam of light that gathered the darkness into its embrace, catching and holding it, keeping it penned.

"Don't..." he tried to say.

The soldiers were shouting in all directions. The helicopter engine and propellers roared in his ears, swallowing his words. Suddenly, he felt human breath on his face, a mouth close to his ears. Someone was leaning over him. "What?"

"Don't..." he begged.

"Don't what?" the medic asked.

"Don't let it out."

And then, he was silent.

Sitting at his desk waiting for word, General Nagar heard the ringing of his private line. He hesitated for a moment before picking it up, listened, then slammed his fist down on his desk.

When Elise saw him and Colonel Amos standing there at the entrance to her hospital room together with Dr. Gabbay and a nurse who was holding an injection, she already knew.

"NO!" Her screams resounded throughout the floor, where new mothers sat eating their second Sabbath meal of the day; they echoed in the nursery, where the babies lay dozing in their cribs.

The general bent over her bed, quietly telling her the details.

"We did everything we could, Elise. Everything," General Nagar said wearily. "Colonel Amos was in both operations. He can give you details."

She looked at the tall, young colonel. His uniform was wrinkled and dusted with black ash. His eyes had aged. She put her arms around him, sobbing quietly, her tears wetting his shirt. She felt the young, strong bones, breathed in the scents of battle...

How many times had she leaned on Jon like this, she thought, as he came walking up the path, home on leave after days of reserve duty, unwashed, sleep-deprived, his only thought to hurry home to her and Ilana the moment they let him out? How many times had she breathed in that gritty scent of gunpowder mixed with a young man's sweat? She listened to his strong heartbeat, felt the warmth that rose from his skin. Soon his mother would hug him, his sister, his girlfriend or wife. They would have him back this time, alive...this tall, handsome young man they loved. She was glad for them.

She pulled back, gaining control. "I'm sorry. I didn't mean... Who else did you lose?"

"We lost two in the safe house when it exploded, three if you count our informer Ismael...and in the second house the commander, Yigael Glickson, was badly wounded. He's being operated on now."

"God watch over him," Elise murmured, thinking of the other mothers, other wives in mourning. "And Ilana?" Elise suddenly remembered with a rising hysteria. "What happened to Ilana?"

The general shrugged. He hated to say this, hated it. "We don't know. She wasn't there with your husband in the second house. And the safe house…." He hesitated, seeking courage, this general, to tell this to a mother: "The safe house was totally destroyed. It will take us days to sift through the rubble…"

"NO!"

"Please, Mrs. Margulies. Elise," Colonel Amos said soothingly. "Ilana wasn't with your husband. But chances are she wasn't in the safe house either. We just don't know. She's vanished. One of Bahama's brothers and his sister are still alive, also badly wounded. As soon as we can, we will interrogate them to find out what they know."

"So, there is still a chance that my baby…?"

The colonel looked down at the floor, while the general lifted his hands, spreading his palms upward in a gesture he remembered from his pious mother when she said blessings over the Sabbath candles.

There was a knock on the door.

"General…"

"What is it? I didn't want to be disturbed…"

"General. There is a woman outside. An Arab woman who calls herself Fatima…." The soldier whispered into the general's ear.

"Let her in!" Elise cried. "I know her…."

"By all means, let her in." Nagar nodded, a strange look passing over his features as Fatima walked into the room, a large basket of grapes on her head. "I brought you something, for you and for the doctor," she said, lowering the basket and lifting off the cover. Two legs emerged, and then the rest of the body slipped out, almost like a breech birth, Elise would tell people later. Elise watched the small back, the loose, flexible limbs as the child turned around and ran into her arms. "*Ima!*"

"Ilana, Ilana, Ilana," Elise wept, holding the child in her arms, and then looking beyond into the old Arab woman's stern, wrinkled face, which was filled with pain, and love, and pride of accomplishment.

God did not work alone, Elise suddenly understood. He needed human goodness, human compassion to answer yes to prayers. Sometimes He found it, and sometimes He didn't.

"It was you! In the room with her! You who she was smiling at, when she lifted her arms to be held."

Fatima nodded. "I am ashamed to say this, Mrs. Doctor Jon. But Marwan Bahama is my nephew, child of my sister. When they needed a woman to care for the child, she called me. I could not say anything, because the Hamas would kill me and my children. But when I was there, Dr. Jon begged me to take the child away, to hide her. I was very afraid. He was my nephew, but he was evil, a beast. Even his own mother was afraid of him. But as a true Muslim, I could not see the death of an innocent child, or a man who has done only good. It was very late. The men were tired, they slept. They didn't think to check my basket as I left. In the morning, I knew they would come for me. So I hid with her in a cave in the hills. I took care of her like my own. Here, look. You will see, no harm has come to her. Please, Mrs. Doctor Jon. Forgive me. Forgive my people." Her proud, straight back and beautiful posture seemed suddenly to bend, as if under a great weight. "Have your soldiers freed Dr. Jon?"

Elise gathered the child in her arms and carried her over to Fatima. "Dr. Jon is dead," she whispered. She felt the child's arms tighten around her neck, heard the great intake of breath and then the sob. She hugged her. "Your nephews have also been killed, and your sister. I'm so sorry, Fatima. So sorry."

The two women, their souls seared and dissolved by shock waves of grief and loss, rocked together in a desperate embrace. The Arab woman's ululation of mourning mingled with the Jewish woman's heartrending cries of grief.

Arab and Jew, the tears were the same tears. The broken heart, the grief, the mourning, both the same, General Nagar suddenly thought. He wondered, for the first time, if the world would not be a better place if it was in the hands of women like these instead of men.

"We will need to talk to her, Elise," General Nagar said gently, motioning for his men to take Fatima into custody.

"Don't harm her! She saved my baby's life!" Elise begged.

"I swear to you. No harm will come to her. She might even get a medal…. But for her own good, she needs to be protected now. I'll leave you alone with your daughter…."

"General? Could you tell my grandmother and her friends what has happened?"

"I will take care of it. I promise," he said kindly, saluting her.

She reached up and kissed him. "This is for the entire Israel Defense Forces. Thank you. I will pray for Lieutenant Glickson. Perhaps this time, God will say yes."

The general nodded and walked quickly down the corridor, his hand touching his cheek. Beside him, the young colonel kept pace, his steps measured and slow. They had lost this battle, because their humanity had gotten in their way. In fighting terrorists who hid behind women and children, it always would.

She had no real understanding of all she had been through, she thought. The story would unfold slowly, understanding entering her soul drop by drop, over all the years of her life, she realized. She would think about Jon's last days, his last hours, imagining what he had thought and felt. She would scrounge for every detail, from every source—the soldiers who had been with him, Fatima, Bahama's young sisters. She would go over each passing moment of these short days again and again, searching them for some shape, some meaning. And she would never really know.

The doctors wanted to examine Ilana. And Elise agreed to let them. In ten minutes, she told them, as she took the child into her bed and wrapped her arms around her, rocking her, telling her the story of her tiny brother, and how soon they would all go home and pick the figs from the trees to give to Fatima. How they would listen to music, and celebrate the coming holidays. How they would be a happy family again, one day, Elise promised Ilana. The kind of family your father wanted us to be. The kind of family we planned to be, your father and I, when we came to live in this land, the land that God promised to the Jewish people in His Covenant with Abraham.

Epilogue

On Saturday night, May 11, 2002, Dr. Jonathan Margulies was buried in the Har Hamenuchot cemetery in Jerusalem. Thousands surrounded the place where his body lay on a stretcher, wrapped only in a prayer shawl, as is the custom in Jerusalem. Elise spoke movingly of her beloved husband, and of the son he would never know, who would be brought up to believe in all the same values: to love life and mankind, to do good deeds, and to love and protect his tiny country. Friends from the army described a loyal comrade. Fellow doctors described an irreplaceable colleague. And a young Arab woman, a patient, wept and said that the evil that had killed her doctor had destroyed her life as well.

As she spoke, four elderly women surrounded a small girl, placing a hand on her tiny shoulders. They were not sure she should be there, but they acquiesced to her mother's insistence that this would bring Ilana closure, and eventually comfort.

In time, the child would bless her mother for her foresight and wisdom.

And when the funeral was over, Elise asked the women to take care of Ilana, because there was something she needed to do alone.

The taxi let her off at the Promenade. She walked along, looking out at the bright lights of Jerusalem. Of her many losses, time had been another. For how could you gauge what had happened to her in measurable units? Hours, days? Like the six days of creation, when worlds came into being, and worlds were lost.... All that had happened had taken less than a week. Lives had been lost and a life created. Irreparable loss had been followed by a miraculous redemption.... It was impossible to take it all in. Her mind had shut down, responding only to that which was most pressing, most urgent; only enough to play the part assigned her. She had put on the brave face, been the loving mother, the patriotic Israeli; everything they wanted she had given them, she thought. But now, now, I want to be left alone. Now, she thought, I want to talk to Jon.

She took out a picture from her purse. Leaning against a lamppost, she examined it. It was her favorite wedding photo. She stared at Jon's smiling face. He looked like such a kid, she thought. The acne on his forehead. The unruly hair, and those widely spaced teeth that gave his grin such mischief. This is what she would have, she thought, through the years. This face, this silent, smiling face that would stare back at her through time, never growing any older. A face that would listen, but never answer.

She hugged herself and began to walk along, alone, in the darkness, the world a mystery, the future indecipherable. She looked up at the stars in the overarching sky and thought of all the human beings since the beginning of time who had looked up at that blank space, crying out to understand its meaning, never getting any answers. Herself, Jon, Nouara, Fatima's young nephew, everyone shaped by the answers of other men who had stared, equally confused, some of them incredibly wise, some unspeakably evil. And all around her she sensed a planet teeming with fragile life, struggling to go forward.

If only, if only.... I could talk to you one more time, Jon. If only I could tell you how much I loved you. If I could thank you for the years we spent together—such good years!—for the children you helped me bring into the world. The stars blinked back in silence.

Her feet were reluctant against the hard pavement as they took her forward. She was so tired. So tired. So alone. But she had a life ahead of her, she knew, children to care for. She needed to wake up every morning. Up ahead, she saw a young couple. The man wore a skullcap on his dark hair, and the girl's long hair fell down her back. They were holding hands.

A soft wind touched her face, drying her tears, smoothing back her hair like gentle fingers. She would never have to look for him in yellowing photos, or a faceless sky, she realized. Whenever she saw a tall, young man, she would see him. Whenever she heard a joke, she would hear his laughter. And when she held the children, she would feel his joy. His silent footfalls would accompany hers as she walked through life. "My hand is still in yours, Jon," she whispered. "I will never let go."

On Sunday, May 12, the body of Musa el Khalil was found floating face down in the Seine.

On Monday, May 13, Whalid Ibn Saud was found in his car on the highway outside Riyadh. Saudi newspapers reported that he had had a heart attack. His body was never autopsied, and his wife was refused entry to attend his funeral. She and her children live in California, not far from her grandmother's home. They no longer attend Islamic services.

On May 20, Noura lost her battle with leukemia.

On May 21, the wife and children of Ismael Abadi began to receive payments from the Israeli government, in thanks for the services of their husband and father to Israel's Secret Service.

On May 29, Julia Greenberg was airlifted to a British hospital specializing in burn victims. She continues to undergo numerous operations for skin grafts to restore her face and scalp, and has made progress in using the prosthesis for her right arm, which needed to be amputated at the elbow. Her body continues to suffer from imbedded nails that cannot be removed without injuring vital organs. She left political reporting and became a reporter on science and medicine. She has become an expert in typing with one hand. Whenever Milos' work takes him to London, he takes her out to dinner.

On June 15, Elise Margulies was finally able to give her son his circumcision ceremony, a ritual marking the entrance of a Jewish male into the Covenant of Abraham. Esther brought in her private plane carrying Ariana, Maria, Elizabeth, and Elizabeth's children. The baby boy was named Jonathan Hayim (meaning "life"), and the following week, Elise was able to bring him home from the hospital permanently. He is a healthy, happy child, who brings much joy into his family's life.

Leah Helfgott moved to Maaleh Sara. Last summer, her grandson Liam came to stay with her.

On August 15, 2002, Ariana Feyder died peacefully in her sleep. In her recently changed will, she left everything to Ilana and Jonathan Hayim, whom she calls "my children," a phrase her lawyers puzzled over. The will also allowed for a generous monthly stipend for Elise.

Fatima still works at Hadassah Hospital's oncology unit.

The United Nations International Covenant on Civil and Political Rights states: "Every human being has the inherent right to life. No one shall be arbitrarily deprived of his life." The Geneva Convention on Human Rights calls the deliberate killing of noncombatants (including off-duty soldiers) a war crime, and a crime against humanity.

According to an IDF spokesperson, between September 29, 2000, and January 11, 2003, Palestinian terrorists carried out 15,992 terrorist attacks against Israeli civilians (not including firebombs or rock throwing), killing 717 Israelis and injuring 5,041. The great majority of those killed and injured were noncombatants.

About the Author

Naomi Ragen

Naomi Ragen is the author of several international best-sellers, among them *Jephte's Daughter, Sotah, The Sacrifice of Tamar,* and *The Ghost of Hannah Mendes*. Born in New York, she earned a BA from Brooklyn College and an MA in English from the Hebrew University of Jerusalem. For the past thirty years, she has made her home in Jerusalem. The translation of her books into Hebrew in 1995 has made her one of Israel's best-beloved authors. An outspoken advocate for gender equality and human rights, she is a columnist for *The Jerusalem Post*. Ragen's hit play, *Women's Minyan* commissioned by Israel's National Theater, Habimah, has been running for two years, and her weekly e-mail columns on life in the Middle East are read and distributed by thousands of subscribers worldwide.

The author welcomes reader comments and can be contacted at POB 23004, Jerusalem 91230, Israel, or through email: Naomi@ NaomiRagen.com

The fonts used in this book are from the Garamond family

Other works by Naomi Ragen
published by *The* Toby Press

NOVELS

The Sacrifice of Tamar

Jephte's Daughter

Sotah

Chains Around the Grass

PLAY

Women's Minyan

The Toby Press publishes fine writing,
available at leading bookstores everywhere. For more
information, please visit www.tobypress.com